# An Unlikely Agent

Jane Menczer lives in Cambridge and teaches drama at a local comprehensive school. She won an Escalator Literature Award and a Grant for the Arts to help fund the completion of *An Unlikely Agent*, which is her first novel.

# An Unlikely Agent

Jane Menczer

Polygon

First published in Great Britain in 2017 by Polygon,
an imprint of Birlinn Ltd.

West Newington House
10 Newington Road
Edinburgh
EH9 1QS

www.polygonbooks.co.uk

1

ISBN 978 1 83697 380 2
eBook ISBN 978 0 85790 925 1

*British Library Cataloguing in Publication Data*
A catalogue record for this book is available on request
from the British Library.

Typeset by 3btype.com

*for Oliver*
*for Daisy and Jack*
*and for my parents*

# An Unlikely Agent

*The mist covers everything; all around him there is an endless white hush, broken only by the dreary slap of the waves. He waits, feeling the chill sink into his bones. The emptiness and the waiting are so familiar that it has started to seem as if he has always been here, suspended in this nothingness, drifting on the slow tides of his body.*

*Then, in the very instant that someone whistles to give the signal, he sees MacIntyre moving through the blankness. Startled by the sound, MacIntyre stops and listens. The faint blur of his head turns this way and that with a deliberation that is almost theatrical, but he detects nothing. Quiet settles over them again and for a few moments they both stand completely motionless; even the vapour seems stilled. From somewhere high above a gull keens faintly. MacIntyre takes a tentative step across the shingle, hesitates, and strides on towards him.*

*Wary of being seen, he crouches down behind a rock, leaning against it to relieve the stiffness in his knees. His fingertips meet the barnacled dome of a limpet and he turns it speculatively, countering its tightened grip until, seized by impatience, he wrenches it away from its anchorage. He presses his hands hard against the rock; beneath its cold, slick surface there is a weight and solidity that is somehow gratifying. When MacIntyre passes by a few feet away, the feeling intensifies; he is rooted, secure in his purpose, his whole being channelled to a point of will.*

*MacIntyre is stooping, his neck and shoulders dragged down by a bulky satchel slung crosswise against his chest, but he steps along quite jauntily, singing under his breath. The song seems tantalisingly familiar, and as his mind begins to scan and puzzle his gaze eddies away through the swirling whiteness. Then, abruptly, he snaps back and his eyes lock on to MacIntyre, vanishing into the dark mouth of the cave. He heaves a long sigh and folds his hands in front of him. It has all proceeded to plan. Now he must wait. There is no other way out; sooner or later one of them will reappear and, really, it does not matter which.*

It is very cold standing here; the dead are cold like this. And all this will end in death, like a neat line ruled across a page, with nothing to follow.

His head turns. He hears a sound like a gull mewing; it is a woman's voice, dampened by the fog. She is calling and then waiting and then calling again. He cannot see her yet, but of course she is moving this way. She ought not to have come here; he is tired of complications, tired of these people and their silly, pointless gestures.

A gunshot rings out inside the cave. He readies himself. There is a clamour of footsteps and then a man emerges at breakneck speed, running straight at him. He grabs the man's coat by the collar, looks him in the eye and pushes the knife into his throat. The man's pupils flare in shock and his eyes film over as he drops forward, choking and gurgling, his blood spattering the sand. He draws a few last rasping breaths, shudders violently and then lies still.

For a short time the assassin stands with his head bowed. Then, bending down to rest one palm on the shingle, he eases himself into a squatting position and cleans his knife on the dead man's jacket, gentling the blade to a silver sheen before straightening up and setting it snugly in his belt.

Another cry: a seabird's shriek. He knows she's watching him. When he turns round he will see her there, bewildered and afraid; he will be obliged to give her an explanation. The prospect exhausts him and so he closes his eyes and stands perfectly still, feeling the mist on his eyelids.

And his mind moves away from him again, and he is thinking of what comes next, now that all of this is done: the scurrying forward, the keeping on while the clocks keep ticking and the politicians jabber away. For he is part of the machinery that mustn't be stopped, the wheels within wheels that drive the march onward.

He opens his eyes, he sets his lips into a smile, and then he turns towards her.

# One

## 1905

Since it has fallen to me to relate MacIntyre's story, it is necessary to begin by telling my own, or at least that portion of it that is relevant to the matter in hand. My first encounter with MacIntyre was brought about by a chain of circumstances that commenced, inauspiciously enough, on a bright May morning, nearly six months before the day on which we lost him; though if one were to look further into the past, as I have been compelled to do very frequently of late, one might trace the first tiny ripples in the current that drew me towards him right back to the days of my girlhood.

I was at that time employed as a secretary in a small firm, a position that I had held for nearly ten years, and would have been astounded had I known that this period of my life was shortly to come to an end. Yet how much more it would have astonished me to learn that I had become an object of interest to people whose existence I should scarcely have credited; that my future was no longer subject to the workings of chance; and that an intricate and insidious mechanism had been set in motion by invisible hands, a mechanism that was shortly to propel me into a sequence of remarkable adventures of the sort that I had hitherto encountered only in books.

On my way to work I had lingered a little, enjoying the early sunshine and the scent of lilacs coming into bloom. I alighted from the tram at five minutes to nine, somewhat later than was my custom, and darted across the Holloway Road to the familiar, grimy-looking building with advertisements for New Pin soap and Pinnace cigarettes blazoned across its exterior. Without pausing for breath I sped up three flights of stairs to a poky landing on the topmost storey and turned the handle of the single, plate-glass door, which bore the legend *Plimpson and Co.* in bold white letters. To my surprise, however, it remained firmly shut. Relieved that I was not to be caught out in my poor timekeeping after all, I took the key from my reticule, turned it in the lock and passed through the door, wriggling out of my coat as I went. However, as I reached to hang it up, I saw that Mr Plimpson's hat was already on its hook and realised to my dismay that he must be in the office after all. I opened the blinds, reflecting how peculiar it was that my employer had locked himself inside his own business premises and allowing myself a brief moment of speculation as to whether this had been done unintentionally, or whether in fact he might be trying to evade an irate customer. Such a necessity would not have been unprecedented, though on two of the three previous occasions on which it had arisen he had simply avoided the office for a few days, leaving me to soothe the clients' injured feelings as best I could. The third, more memorable episode I shall come to in its proper place.

I tore off my gloves, seized my pen and notebook from the top drawer of my desk and knocked briskly on the door to the inner room, just as the clock on the mantelpiece chimed nine. Inwardly, I berated myself for my lack of discipline; I took great pride in being punctual and always made sure that I was in the office at least ten minutes before the hour struck. In the usual course of things Mr Plimpson took little notice of my comings and goings, but during the past few days he had become uncharacteristically short-tempered, scolding me for committing all manner of bureaucratic misdemeanours, every one of which was either imaginary or caused by his own absent-mindedness. Indeed, I could not recall his ever having been quite so on edge; only the previous day, I had brushed against a stack of ledgers which, to my considerable annoyance, he had piled up on my desk, and sent them crashing to the floor. Immediately, he had burst into the room wearing such a look of terror that my own heart had begun to race. He had attempted to make light of his agitation by scolding me for my clumsiness, but his voice had been thin with relief, and when he had reached into his breast pocket for his cigarette case his hand had trembled.

I knocked again, and, hearing nothing, turned the door handle and peered into the room. Mr Plimpson was pacing up and down on the faded Turkey rug as though intent on mapping out its pattern with his feet. He looked as if he had been in the office all night; his cheeks and nose were flushed an unhealthy red, a sheen of perspiration glistened on his forehead and there were wet marks beneath the arms of his shirt. The blinds were still drawn and I hurried across to open them, for the air in the room smelled strongly of tobacco smoke intermingled with a fug of other stale and unpleasant odours.

"Stop!" cried Mr Plimpson, rushing to intercept me. "Don't touch the blinds, Miss Trant . . ." As if recollecting himself, he stopped short. "Ahem! That is, as you may have noticed, I have not been at all well of late, and the doctor has advised me to avoid getting too much sun. It tends to bring on my headaches, you know."

His voice trailed off and he dropped onto the chair behind his desk with a groan. I watched with some anxiety as he sat staring into space and stroking his moustache, for I was perturbed by the wildness of his appearance, and more particularly by the fact that I could detect whisky on his breath at such an early hour. He took out his handkerchief and mopped his brow.

"Miss Trant, I have some news . . . 'Tisn't good news, I'm sorry to say. I am at present experiencing some business troubles . . . nothing too serious, you understand." He loosened his tie and licked his lips, his eyes darting about the room as if he were weighing up what he would say next. "As a result of various ill-judged invest-ments made, I freely admit, on the advice of a once loved and trusted . . ." he paused, appearing to grope for the word before continuing, "friend, the firm has incurred some bothersome debts. Unfortunately, that donkey of a landlord has chosen this moment to raise the rent on these premises. Ergo, the books do not balance. Ergo, we shall have to move elsewhere. To Deptford, in fact."

I found myself suddenly short of breath and was obliged to sit down; it seemed clear that the situation must be far worse than I had originally suspected. Mr Plimpson, though small in stature, was rather portly. He manoeuvred his bulk with some difficulty round the side of the desk and patted me awkwardly on the arm. I shrank from his touch, but he seemed unaware of my discomfort, for his damp fingers continued to linger on my shoulder.

"You have no cause for concern, Miss Trant, no cause at all. Your job is perfectly safe; I would never dispense with your invaluable services so lightly. Fear not, the fortunes of Plimpson and Co. will rally in due course! There has been a temporary reversal in the markets, nothing more."

Sighing, I bowed my head. "As you can imagine sir, this news is rather a shock to me. Much as I value my situation here, such a move would present me with a number of practical difficulties. I do hope that you will not consider me guilty of ingratitude if I ask for a few days in which to consider my position."

He snatched his hand away from my shoulder as if he had been burnt.

"But Miss Trant, it never occurred to me that you might leave! After all, you are not a married woman. You have no domestic responsibilities, no children. Surely it would present no great diffi-culty to take new lodgings? I dare say you could find rather a nice little place in Deptford; the rents are very reasonable."

I stood up. It was on the tip of my tongue to tell him the reason for my hesitation, but when I looked into his eyes, which were regarding me with the beady intensity of a bird determined to catch a worm, I held my peace.

"I'm terribly sorry, Mr Plimpson, but I will need some time to think the matter over. I'll let you know as soon as I have come to a decision."

He exhaled mournfully. "Very well, Miss Trant, you must do as you think best. But it would make me very happy if you chose to stay."

He took my hand in his clammy grasp, leaning over it earnestly as though he were about to kiss it. I drew my arm away and hurried out of the room, murmuring an excuse about a letter that needed to be typed in order to catch the morning post.

I crossed behind my desk to the window and pulled up the sash with trembling fingers. The clip-clop of traffic on the road below was broken through abruptly by the roar of an approaching motor bus, which sped past a grocer's van moving in the opposite direction, causing the horse to rear up between the shafts. The driver of the van got to his feet and shook his fist at the receding bus, yelling a string of curses that were drowned by the rumble of its engine. I drew several deep breaths of the sooty air, then sat down at my desk and laid my head on my arms.

Though he had been a friend of my father, Mr Plimpson knew nothing of my domestic circumstances. It struck me that he might attribute my hesitation about moving to Deptford to a lack of enthusiasm for my work, whereas in fact the prospect of losing my job filled me with despair, for I feared that a woman of my age and limitations would be unable to find a suitable position elsewhere. Yet I was not free to act as I wished, for in contemplating such a significant change in my life I was obliged to consider someone besides myself.

I did not reside alone, as my employer seemed to suppose, but shared lodgings with my mother. Ten years earlier, my father's untimely death had left us in a state of near penury and in order to pay off his debts we had been compelled to sell our house in St John's Wood, together with most of the furniture. My aunt Sophie, my mother's elder sister, whose husband had died some years before, had attempted to rescue us from our plight by inviting us to live with her and her daughter in Hertfordshire. I was at that time still at school and she had pledged that she would support us until I had completed my education and been trained as a teacher. However, it was not to be. My mother had long held a grudge against Sophie who, she asserted, held her in contempt for marrying beneath her. Claiming to act out of loyalty to my father, she objected with such violence to the notion of leaving the district in which she had dwelled since her wedding day that all my aunt's plans had to be abandoned. Instead, much to my dismay, we took up residence in a seedy boarding house just a few streets away from our old home.

Aunt Sophie, it seemed, had also inherited the family tendency towards stubbornness. She wrote me a letter in which she explained in a sorrowful tone that until my mother had come to her senses, acknowledged the foolishness of her behaviour and apologised, "family pride" would permit her to have nothing further to do with either of us. She kept her word; though I wrote several times pleading with her to relent, we did not hear from her again.

Mother had never been strong; her health deteriorated under the strain imposed by the misfortune that had befallen us and she lay confined to her bed for days at a time. I was obliged to leave the small private school that I attended on a scholarship and was sent to work in a department store. Then, a few months after my father's death, Mr Plimpson had offered to train me to become his secretary.

Ever since, we had struggled to preserve the veneer of shabby gentility that Mother insisted was of the utmost importance. She clung to her memories of the old days with pathetic determination, and the fact that our lodgings were located in the familiar surroundings of St John's Wood did much to reconcile her to the shabbiness of our rooms and all the other daily ignominies that boarding house life compelled her to endure. I was aware that to force her to abandon all this, to leave behind the ghost of my father's memory for an unknown district on the other side of London, might well be too much for a woman of her delicate sensibilities to bear, and the prospect of broaching the subject filled me with dread.

I looked up at the framed photograph of my father and Mr Plimpson that hung on the opposite wall. It was an object to which

I had grown so accustomed that I scarcely saw it any more, though when I had first come to work at Plimpson and Co. I used to pretend that if only I stared at it with sufficient intensity, my gaze might have the power to bring my father back to life. But time is a great healer; gradually I had stopped indulging in this ritual, and familiarity – and my increasing short-sightedness – had conspired to cause my perception of the two figures in the photograph to blur.

Impulsively, I took down the picture, exposing an oblong of much whiter paint on the grubby stretch of wall. The two men, wearing evening dress, stood side by side, beaming at the camera. Mr Plimpson was slimmer than of late and had a great deal more hair, and my father looked carefree and boyish; very different from the way I remembered him. Peering more closely, I was struck by a detail that I had missed entirely; what I had taken for so long to be handkerchiefs in the gentlemen's breast pockets were in fact white lilies. I responded instinctively to the realisation by humming a few bars of my father's favourite song.

*Oh! Lilly, sweet Lilly,*
*Dear Lilly Dale,*
*Now the wild rose blossoms*
*O'er her little green grave*
*'Neath the trees in the flow'ry vale.*

The clock struck the half hour and I stood up, guiltily aware that I had sat dreaming at my desk for at least twenty minutes. I was loath to disturb Mr Plimpson, lest in his excited state he should begin a second, more agitated discussion about the matter of my staying on, so I resumed the ongoing task of devising a new filing system for the firm's correspondence, a conundrum with which I had been wrestling ever since I had started the job. To begin with I had been sufficiently innocent to believe that I would be able to invent a method of organising my employer's affairs within a day or two, yet I soon found that his business dealings were so confused and obscure (sometimes, I allowed myself to suspect, deliberately so) and of such a mixed character that it was well-nigh impossible to resolve

7

them into any kind of order. Nevertheless, I had persisted in trying to do so, and I still drew a perverse satisfaction from the performance of this Sisyphean labour. I removed several deed boxes from the cupboard and began to sort through their contents, and was soon thoroughly bogged down in a mental quagmire of conjecture and classification. The minutes plodded by, but despite my best efforts I made little progress.

At twelve o'clock the office door opened and Mr Plimpson emerged, stumbling on an uneven floorboard. I observed that he had made some effort to smarten himself up; his jacket was buttoned snugly over the bulge of his stomach and he had plastered his fringe of greying hair over his scalp with scented oil.

As soon as he saw the open window he dropped down onto his knees. "Miss Trant! Pull down the blinds!" he hissed.

I did as he asked and, puffing and blowing, he heaved himself back into a standing position. He walked unsteadily up to my desk and leant across it, regarding me sternly through bloodshot eyes. At such close quarters the reek of alcohol and cheap scent was almost more than I could bear and my fingers itched to whisk my handkerchief out of my pocket so that I could cover my nose.

"Miss Trant, I am sorry to say that I was not quite straight with you before – about the headaches, I mean. I didn't want to frighten you, but I have been wrestling with my conscience and for your own safety I feel obliged to tell you that most unfortunately Plimpson and Co. has become embroiled in some dealings with what I have lately discovered to be a highly disreputable and unscrupulous . . . er, firm. I truly believe that the individuals concerned will stoop to nothing to get what they want. Ergo, it would not be sensible for us to draw attention to our presence here; ergo, we must keep the blinds closed and the door locked at all times. And whatever cunning pleas or unpleasant threats may be addressed to you, you must admit nobody onto these premises!" He thumped on the desk for emphasis. "*Nobody*, under any foreseeable or conceivable circumstances whatsoever, is to come into this office. Do I make myself clear?"

"Yes, sir," I replied, considerably taken aback by this tirade.

Apparently satisfied that he had impressed on me the necessity for caution, Mr Plimpson tottered towards the door, remarking rather thickly and with forced brightness, "Such lovely weather we're having, Miss Trant. I'm off to meet a client now – a little light luncheon – always does the trick. Be sure to lock the door behind me. I shall be gone for the rest of the day and therefore entrust the running of this great enterprise to your capable little hands. Remember, my dear, we must tread with caution, but with our heads held high."

As he went out onto the landing he tripped and narrowly avoided plunging down the stairs. I sat listening to his precarious descent until he was safely on the ground floor, then got up and locked the door.

I was not sure how seriously to take Mr Plimpson's fears; after all, he had been drinking, and even when completely sober he was the sort of man who tended to exaggerate in order to instil in his auditors a sense of his own importance. Moreover, I was aware from bitter experience that he was capable of working himself up into a dreadful state if things were not going his way. Feeling thoroughly oppressed by the dinginess of the room, I crossed to the window and opened the blinds again, reflecting that it was surely more conspicuous to leave them closed and that, furthermore, it was unlikely that anyone would go to the trouble of spying on us, situated as we were on the third floor of the building.

I passed a dispiriting afternoon straining my eyes over a collection of yellowing import receipts from Germany, which had mysteriously appeared in a box of correspondence from a factory manager in Birmingham. My thoughts were awhirl with visions of the approaching conversation with my mother, and several times I was obliged to stage a painstaking reconstruction of a train of thought in order to retrieve a sheaf of letters or receipts that I had wrongly categorised. At twenty minutes to five, still surrounded by drifts of paper, I suddenly lost patience, bundled the unsorted documents back into the deed boxes and put them away in the cupboard. Dejectedly shrugging off the conviction that my efforts had only served to worsen the chaotic state of Mr Plimpson's affairs, I pulled down the blinds, locked up the office and caught the tram back to St John's Wood.

# Two

*I* disembarked at an earlier stop than usual and walked slowly along the tree-lined streets, nodding every now and then to a person of my acquaintance, but moving on before I could be engaged in conversation. I racked my brains for the words with which to persuade my mother that we must move to Deptford, yet every sentence I rehearsed seemed weak and unconvincing. By the time I arrived at the door of our lodgings I still had not found a satisfactory way of breaking the news.

As I entered the hallway, I was engulfed by the familiar mingled scents of furniture polish and boiled greens. It always took my eyes several moments to adjust to the murky gloom, for the walls were papered dark brown, the same shade as the scuffed floor tiles, the doors to the adjoining rooms were kept closed, and there was no window save for a pane of coloured glass in the front door. I hung up my coat and glanced at the hall table to see whether there were any letters. There was nothing for either Mother or me, only a picture postcard with a view of Weymouth for Mr Smith, who lodged in the garret. I am curious by nature and I am ashamed to say that I turned the card over and furtively examined the message on the other side. As I had suspected, I could make nothing of it: Smith, a taciturn fellow who kept himself to himself, had received three other postcards from coastal resorts since he had moved into the house nearly three months before and each of them, like this one, had been written in a foreign alphabet. Naturally, my interest was aroused by the mysterious nature of these communications; I had rather a passion for detective stories at that time and imagined that I had stumbled upon a mystery like those in the magazines.

I took care to replace the card in the same position as I had found it and then, aware that I could put off the evil hour no longer, I ran up the two flights of stairs to our rooms.

Whenever I try to remember my mother's appearance in detail, the image of her face as it was on the last occasion I saw her, stricken and distorted, steals unbidden into my thoughts and blots out any other recollection. Therefore, I keep as an *aide memoire* a portrait painted some weeks after the day with which we are presently concerned, in circumstances that were to prove instrumental to the course of this narrative. The painting shows a shrunken, sharp-featured woman with a sallow complexion, high cheekbones and startling blue eyes, like stones of pale turquoise. Her hair, formerly dark brown, is liberally touched with grey and there is disappointment etched in the lines of her mouth, which turns down discontentedly at the corners. She looks towards the artist with a seductive tilt of the chin, which hints at the consciousness of former beauty, long since shrivelled and faded through prolonged illness and ardent grief.

Mother was lying on the sofa by the sitting room window, with curl papers in her hair and wearing a bedjacket. I perceived at a glance that she was in one of her difficult humours and my heart sank. I helped her to sit up and plumped up several cushions to support her back before saying, "Shall I open a window? It's very close in here and it's such a lovely evening outside."

She frowned in irritation. "Don't be foolish, Margaret; you know my constitution can't tolerate the evening air. Go and fetch my blue shirtwaist. Quick-sharp now, or we'll keep everyone waiting."

"Mrs Hodgkins wouldn't wait for us in any case," I muttered, adding with a twinge of compunction, "Perhaps you ought to stay upstairs, if you're not feeling well. I could bring your dinner up on a tray . . ."

"Just do as I ask; I have no strength to argue," she sighed, turning her face away.

My mother was very hard to dress. She was physically capable of putting on her clothes herself, but lacked the will to do so. Her spine was stiff and unyielding, and her limbs seemed so brittle that I touched her somewhat apprehensively and with painstaking care, earning many rebukes for my slowness. Today my fingers were trembling with nervousness, which made matters worse, and I fumbled terribly with the buttons and fasteners until at last, as I was stooping to do up her boots, she snapped, "Good gracious, whatever is the matter with you? You've been behaving like a moonstruck ninny ever since you got home!"

I straightened my back and laid the buttonhook on the table. "Mother, I have some news." I stopped, suddenly overcome by a breathless, fluttering sensation in my chest.

"Well, what is it?" she demanded. "I knew there was something you were keeping from me."

I flailed desperately for the right words with which to continue, but they refused to come. She raised her eyes to the ceiling, as if seeking heavenly solace.

"I see. Well, if you won't tell me now it must wait until after dinner – no doubt whatever it is will keep for a little while longer."

I eased her legs over the edge of the sofa, smoothed her skirts and took her arm to help her up; she never used a stick unless through absolute necessity, though she was incapable of walking unaided. I was fleetingly conscious of the bird-like fragility of her bones as she leant against me and felt a surge of disquiet just as I found myself saying in a matter-of-fact tone, "Mr Plimpson has told me that he intends to move the office to Deptford. Of course, it means that you and I will have to find new lodgings nearby. I don't believe that Father would have wanted us to stay here and starve."

She stopped stock-still in the middle of the floor. My heart was pounding and for a moment I was too fearful even to breathe; then I forced myself to glance at her and saw that she was weeping noiselessly, as if her heart would break. I led her back to the sofa and went over to stand at the window, at a loss as to what to do next.

Since my father's death, it had become a habit with us never to refer to him. To begin with Mother had been so overcome by grief and shock that she had found it unbearable to hear him mentioned, and gradually our silence had grown to be the great unspoken taboo on which our lives together were founded. I dug my nails into my palms with frustration, desperately wishing that I had never allowed his name to pass my lips.

At length Mother spoke, in a voice quavering with distress. "I should have thought you would have more consideration, Margaret. I only hope you haven't allowed yourself to turn into one of those dreadful New Women, thinking only of your own career . . ." Her face crumpled and she burst into tears. She started to cough wretchedly and I hastened across to pour her some water. Her hands were shaking so hard that she was unable to hold the glass and I was obliged to lift it to her lips.

Suddenly, she grabbed me by the wrist. "Put me to bed. My appetite is gone."

"Mother, you really ought not to miss dinner. The doctor said . . ."

"I am perfectly aware of what he said! But if I were to attempt to eat now, the food would choke me. Besides, it might be preferable, given the circumstances, if my strength did fail and I was no longer here to trouble you."

She was as pale as a ghost and her red-rimmed eyes seemed to have sunk deep into their sockets. Somewhat alarmed, I helped her into her bedroom and onto the bed. It was a terrible struggle to remove her clothes and put on her nightdress, for she made herself as rigid as a post, staring unblinkingly ahead as if I didn't exist. I did not attempt to speak to her, for I knew that to do so would only provoke further tears, and so we continued in silence until I left the room.

I had missed dinner, which was something of a relief, for I could never have brought myself to sit and make conversation with our landlady, Mrs Hodgkins, and the other lodgers. I heated some water on the gas burner to make tea and cut two slices of bread, for I had been too overwrought to eat luncheon and I had begun to feel weak and unsteady after the excitements of the day. Having forced down this scanty supper, I decided I would attempt to blot out my troubles for a time by reading one of the detective magazines that I kept hidden beneath a loose floorboard in my room. I had inherited my taste for detective stories from my father, who had possessed a great fondness for puzzles of all kinds. Mother knew nothing about the magazines but would undoubtedly have regarded them as a selfish extravagance, and despite all my scrimping and saving, despite the fact that without my salary we would be destitute, I always found myself unable to suppress a pang of guilt when I thought of them.

I prised up the floorboard with the butter knife, selected an edition that contained several of my favourite stories and lay down on the sofa to read it. The prospect of two hours' undisturbed leisure was rare for me, for Mother seldom went to sleep early, yet I now found myself distracted from the heroine's adventures by my own nagging anxieties. At last I lost patience, closed the magazine and returned it to its hiding place, picked up my shoes, and crept out of the apartment.

I tiptoed down the stairs in my stockinged feet and sat on the hallstand to put on my shoes. Just as I was about to get up, the front door opened to admit Mr Smith. He did not seem to see me, but snatched up the postcard from the hall table and began to pore over it eagerly. I studied him with some interest, for he looked very much like the villain in the story I had just been reading. His hair was cut very close to his scalp and he had a large, hooked nose and hooded eyes that creased downwards at the corners in symmetry with his sullen mouth. I moved towards the front door, poised to greet him in case he should look up and acknowledge me. The strange message on the postcard appeared to absorb the whole of his attention, however, for though I passed right in front of him he seemed unaware of my presence.

I slipped out, closing the door softly behind me. The air was balmy, though the pale glimmer of the street lamps already shone out through the gathering dusk. As I strolled along, half listening to the snatches of domestics' conversations drifting up through the area railings, my thoughts turned once again to Mr Plimpson's shocking tidings. I tried to picture the lives Mother and I might lead if we were to uproot ourselves from these familiar streets; I knew little about Deptford, but I possessed a shadowy notion that it was rather a grim and gloomy place, inhabited by sailors, dock-workers and other rough people. However, I was under the impression that the neighbouring district of Greenwich was comparatively respectable, and after all it ought to be perfectly possible for us to find a decent place to lodge there . . . I brought myself up short and heaved a deep sigh. It was no use; all this speculation was a foolish waste of time. Mother's nerves were so delicate and her attachment to St John's Wood so strong that it was absurd to suppose that she could ever be reconciled to leaving it.

I drifted on, lost in vague dreams, until I realised with a shock that it was almost dark and, moreover, I had strayed further from home than I had intended. I turned round at once and started walking quickly back. What if Mother had awoken in a panic and called out for me, only to find that I was gone? I strode along faster and faster, picturing her livid, tear-stained face, and in a sudden flash of understanding I knew that though I wanted very much to stay on at Plimpson's there was no point in deceiving myself any longer. Mother's fussy ways could be very trying – indeed, when she was at her most cantankerous I felt sometimes almost as if I hated her – but my conscience would not allow me to pursue a course of action that would make her utterly wretched.

I crossed the Finchley Road and passed onto one of the quiet streets adjacent to our lodgings. I found that I was crying and breathed deeply into my handkerchief. How would I ever get another job that paid as well as my current position? My experience was very narrow; I had been with the same firm for effectively the whole of my working life and Mr Plimpson and I had grown accustomed to one another's peculiarities. Worse still, I was twenty-five years old; undoubtedly most employers would prefer to take on a secretary who was younger and more malleable. But I had no choice; I must start looking for a new post at once, for our savings would support us for no more than a month or two once I stopped working.

From the corner of my eye, I glimpsed a man walking a little way behind me on the other side of the street. I turned into another road and looking round saw that he was still there, moving stealthily through the pools of gaslight. I began to feel somewhat ill at ease, for there was no one else in sight, and I quickened my pace. With a thudding heart, I saw that the shadowy figure at my back had also started to walk faster and, hoping to shake him off, I made an abrupt turn into a side street and hastened across the road, glancing over my shoulder as I did so.

As I stepped onto the pavement I bumped into someone coming from the opposite direction with a jarring shock that sent me stumbling onto my knees.

"Miss Trant! Are you hurt?"

I looked up in bewilderment to see the massive form of Mr Smith towering over me. He extended his immense hand and I took it and allowed him to pull me to my feet.

"Thank you! I'm quite all right. I'm terribly sorry – I wasn't looking where I was going." I dusted down my skirts and glanced about, but there was no sign of the man I had thought was pursuing me. To my dismay, I realised that Mr Smith was regarding me with curious intentness.

"You ought to be careful, Miss Trant. I should say it wasn't safe for a lady to go out walking on her own so late at night." He made a courteous inclination of his head. "I'd be glad to accompany you the rest of the way home."

"That's very kind of you, but I shouldn't like to put you to any trouble."

"Not at all – it's not very far in any case."

I should have liked to turn him down, for there was something about the way he was looking at me that made me feel decidedly uncomfortable, but I felt that to do so would be rude, so I nodded without meeting his gaze and murmured once again, "You're very kind."

I could think of nothing else to say to him and we walked back in silence. At the garden gate he lifted his hat and his lips curved in a smile that did not reach his eyes. "Good evening, Miss Trant."

"Good evening, Mr Smith – and thank you."

He turned abruptly and strode off in the direction from which we had come. With the toe of my boot, I pushed aside a newspaper that someone had dropped in front of the gate and walked despondently towards the house.

# Three

The following day, as I alighted from the tram, I noticed a man in a checked jacket gazing up at the windows of Plimpson and Co. To my surprise, the blinds were all open, but the morning sun shone in at such an angle that it was impossible to see inside. I hurried across the street, glancing over my shoulder at the stranger, whose eyes remained fixed on the upper storeys of the building. Filled with anxiety, I ran up the three flights of stairs and turned the handle of the plate-glass door, which was unlocked.

I removed my hat and coat, then approached the door to Mr Plimpson's office, clutching my letter of resignation.

"Come in!" My employer was writing at his desk and scarcely looked up to acknowledge my entrance. To my great relief, he was clean-shaven and dressed in a freshly laundered shirt and a neatly knotted tie, and looked in every respect utterly transformed from the unhappy wretch I had seen leaving the office on the previous day.

"Good morning, Mr Plimpson. There is something I should like . . ."

"Wait a few moments, would you, Miss Trant? I don't want to lose my flow."

He continued to write with painstaking concentration for several minutes, mouthing the words to himself as he formed them with his pen. I watched impatiently as he signed his name with a

19

flourish, folded the paper in half and inserted it into an envelope. At last he looked up, and his eyes fell on the letter that I held clasped against my chest. "Is that for me?" he asked. "I'm glad to see the postman's decided to come at a decent hour for once. Or was it delivered by hand?"

"Mr Plimpson, before I give you this I think I ought to mention that on my way in I saw a man on the other side of the street staring up at the windows of this office."

He narrowed his eyes at me, looking smug. "Oh, I shouldn't concern yourself about that, Miss Trant. Just nerves on your part, I expect – quite understandable after what passed between us yesterday. However, I don't think we'll have any more trouble from the parties I alluded to – I have resolved the situation most satisfactorily. I imagine he was just some innocent fellow looking up at the advertisements on the building while he was waiting for his tram. The girl with the soap bubbles is remarkably pretty, you know – why, sometimes I even stop to glance at her myself." He flashed me a smile and gestured towards the window. "Go on – I'll wager you a day's pay that he'll be gone already." He held out his hand to seal the bet, but I pretended not to see and went across to look outside.

Mr Plimpson was quite right; though the opposite pavement was thronged with passers-by, there was no sign of the man in the checked jacket. Feeling rather foolish, I turned back into the room and laid the envelope on his desk. As I did so tears sprang unexpectedly into my eyes and I hurried out, determined that my employer would not see me crying. However, I scarcely had time to blow my nose before he bellowed out my name. With a palpitating heart, I stood up and scurried back into his office.

He brandished the letter at me and demanded, "And what, Miss Trant, is the meaning of this?"

"With the greatest respect sir, I explained . . ."

"I suppose you've found another job and are too frightened to tell me. Well, whatever it is they're paying you, I can match it . . . within reason, of course."

"Mr Plimpson, as I explained in my letter, I am obliged to hand in my notice due to personal circumstances. I am unable to move house and Deptford is simply . . ."

"Not getting married, are you?" He eyed me in disbelief.

"No, Mr Plimpson."

His face went ashen and he hesitated for a moment before saying with a quiver in his voice, "I say, that fellow Peters hasn't been writing to you has he?"

"No sir, of course not," I said stiffly. "I haven't seen Mr Peters since . . . I haven't seen or heard from him for many years, as you know."

Mr Plimpson blew out his cheeks and expelled a breath of relief. His bright little eyes scrutinised my face and, although I had done nothing wrong, I felt myself blush. "I should warn you, Miss Trant, there are some unpleasant people in the world – people who would besmirch the good name of Plimpson and Co. for the sake of a personal grudge. I do hope you haven't been listening to any rumours."

"I really have no idea what you mean."

My employer turned puce and thumped his desk. "Well, what is it then? Have you no sense of loyalty to the company? Don't you realise that you will struggle to find another position even half as good as this?"

"I am only too aware of that, sir. I am more sorry than I can say to be obliged to leave and I regret very much any inconvenience that my departure will cause you. I will, however, work as hard as I can to ensure that your affairs are left in the best possible order before I go."

"I see. Like that, is it, eh?" He stood for a moment as if deep in thought, his paunch resting on the edge of the desk, his forefingers pressed together to form a triangle across the bridge of his nose. But then, all at once, he appeared to make a resolution: his face brightened and he took up his pen with such vigour that it sent a spasm of plum-coloured ink flying across the surface of his blotter.

"Very well, you may go," he said, as if suddenly in a great hurry to get rid of me.

"Mr Plimpson," I protested, finding myself once again on the verge of tears, "my mother is ill . . ."

He took out another sheet of writing paper from a drawer in his desk. "Miss Trant, I have no more time for your excuses," he snapped, wiping his pen on the blotter. "Go now and get on with your work."

For the rest of that day, a Friday, Mr Plimpson treated me with cold politeness, but by the following Monday he seemed to have forgotten about my leaving altogether. Nor did I see any evidence that he was looking for a new secretary. He made no further reference to the business troubles that had driven him to near despair only the week before. However, during the days that followed I regularly observed the man in the checked coat or, at other times, a tall fellow with a black beard looking up at the windows of Plimpson and Co. When I mentioned the matter to Mr Plimpson, he chuckled and told me not to "begrudge them their one bit of pleasure" and to "let the poor chaps alone" and so I did not bring up the subject again, though I saw them loitering outside on numerous occasions and sometimes passed one or other of them on my way to or from the office.

There followed an unhappy month, during which I scanned the newspapers daily in pursuit of the fading hope that I might find a situation before my notice had been worked out. But, though I posted several letters of application, I was not called for a single interview, and the prospect of imminent penury began to keep me awake at night.

It was with a heavy heart that I walked through the door of Plimpson and Co. for the last time. The rooms by now were cluttered with half-filled packing cases and a sack containing old correspondence had been hooked onto the peg where I usually hung my coat, obliging me to lay it instead on top of some cardboard boxes. I went in to say good morning to Mr Plimpson, who was writing at his desk. Without looking up, he told me to continue packing and to come back at eleven o'clock. I returned to the outer office and began to remove bundles of papers from the cupboard.

Since the day of my resignation I had lost heart with my projects for categorisation and so I piled the documents straight into boxes without troubling to sort them out. The painful task of preparing for the firm's removal had done much to contribute to my misery during the past few weeks, for I was continually wrenched by the thought that I was helping to undo almost ten years of hard work and that soon all evidence of my labours during that period would disappear without trace.

Just as the clock on the mantelpiece was striking eleven, I knocked on Mr Plimpson's door and entered his office. Immediately, he got to his feet and without looking at me began to speak in an oratorical tone as if addressing himself to an imaginary audience in the far corner of the room.

"Miss Trant, you have been with the company now for almost ten years. During that time your services have been invaluable, and they will be sorely missed. We should like to commemorate the sad occasion of your departure by presenting you with this small token of our esteem, engraved in recognition of your dedicated service."

He wiped his forehead with his handkerchief and handed me an open jeweller's box containing a silver pocket watch. He gestured impatiently and I turned it over to look at the inscription on the back, which read *To Miss M. Trant, devoted servant of Plimpson and Co. 1896–1905*, then he sat down and gave a blustery sigh through his moustache.

"I believe your father would have wanted you to have this too." He opened his desk drawer and took out a flat parcel wrapped in brown paper tied with a grubby piece of string, and watched with a faraway expression as I picked at the knot.

"It marks an occasion when Fortune was smiling upon me more fondly than she appears to be at present. Your father had a marvellous head for figures, Miss Trant – better than any man I've ever known. It could have been the making of us, if things had turned out differently."

I continued to work away at the knot, reflecting how strange it was to hear him refer to my father in such a matter-of-fact tone, after the passage of so many years during which he had made no mention of him at all. At last I succeeded in untying the string, and unfolded the paper to reveal the framed photograph of the two of them in evening dress which had hung in the room next door.

"Thank you, sir – it's very generous of you to give me such thoughtful presents. Do you know, I have only recently noticed the lilies . . ."

Immediately, he glanced at his watch as if the time for reminiscences had run its course and declared, "Take a half holiday, Miss Trant, as a reward for your hard work." I opened my mouth to protest, but he anticipated my objections. "No, I have an extremely pressing appointment this afternoon and I intend to close the office early." He ducked his head below the level of the desktop and began rifling through the drawers.

This was by no means the first of Mr Plimpson's "pressing appointments", and I gathered at once that the "holiday" was merely a convenient excuse to get rid of me. Therefore I did not pursue the subject, but muttered, "Thank you, sir," and left the room.

Ever since I had started working for him, Mr Plimpson had been in the habit, once a month, of closing the office at midday, giving me a paid half holiday. For nearly nine years I had unquestioningly accepted his explanation that he was meeting a client who "liked to keep things private", and it was only by chance that I had ever discovered the truth. On one such afternoon, having waited for some time at the tram stop, I recalled that I had left my purse on my desk. I hurried back to the office, where I discovered my employer locked in a feverish embrace with a brassy-looking woman in a bright blue dress. Mortified, I stammered an apology, snatched up my purse and ran out. The incident was never mentioned by either of us, but after that he sometimes sent me out to buy flowers, scent or cheap trinkets shortly before one of these assignations was to occur.

I began to empty my desk drawer, but was interrupted by the sound of the outer door closing. I looked up in surprise, for we rarely had visitors at Plimpson and Co. Standing before me was the very woman with whom my thoughts had been occupied a few moments before. Today she wore a low-cut dress of a viridian hue, and a little feathered hat was perched jauntily on top of her red curls. It was difficult to make a judgement as to her age, for her face was heavily rouged and powdered, but I should have said that she was nearing forty.

"May I help you?" I enquired, endeavouring to conceal my surprise.

The woman scrutinised me closely, gave a grim little nod as if she found me to be no better than she had expected, and said in a tone of shrill and unconvincing gentility, "Indeed you can, Miss Trant. I should like to see Horace at once, if you please."

"I'm sorry, but Mr Plimpson is busy this morning. If you like I could give him a message."

She gave a toss of her curls. "Oh, Horace will certainly see me. I'm Miss Hagger."

"I'm afraid I don't recall his mentioning that name."

"So he hasn't told you?"

I shook my head. "I'm afraid not. Would you care to make an appointment for later in the week?"

She broke into a peal of artificial laughter. "Appointment, indeed! That's a good one! We're to be married this afternoon."

"Married?" I repeated weakly.

At that moment the door to Mr Plimpson's office opened and we both looked round.

"Aggie, my dearest! I didn't expect to see you so early."

"That's clear," she said, directing a smile of triumphant self-satisfaction towards me. "Your secretary has been very short with me – looking down her nose as if I wasn't fit to set foot in the office, when it was only yesterday you said to me, 'what's mine is yours'."

"Indeed I did, my dove, indeed I did."

Miss Hagger glared at me, then turned away with a great swishing of skirts and minced across the room, leaving behind a lingering aroma of cheap violet scent. She took her fiancé's arm and propelled him back into his office, slamming the door behind them. There was a murmur of voices and then the door opened again to emit Mr Plimpson. He cleared his throat several times and ran his hand nervously across the top of his head.

"So, Miss Trant, it's goodbye at last," he said, without meeting my eye. "I expect you'll want to be off. Plenty to do now you're a free agent, what?" He gave a nervous laugh, rocking back and forth on his tiny feet, oblivious of the fact that one of his trouser legs had rolled itself up to reveal his garter.

"Horace!" Miss Hagger called piercingly from the other side of the door. "Horace – have you remembered to write down her address?"

"Would you mind, Miss Trant?" he said, looking more ill at ease than ever. "I might have questions to ask you about the filing and so forth."

I wrote down the address and gave it to him, then held out my hand. "Goodbye, Mr Plimpson – and might I offer my best wishes to you and the future Mrs Plimpson?"

"Thank you . . ."

"Horace!" Miss Hagger shrieked once again. Mr Plimpson gave a violent start, jerked away his hand and retreated hastily into his office.

Shaking my head over the astonishing tidings that Mr Plimpson was getting married – and to such a woman! – I wiped away the traces of hair oil from my fingers with my handkerchief and continued the task in which I had been interrupted by Miss Hagger's entrance. I had brought a carpet bag to carry home my possessions, and into this receptacle went an embroidered handkerchief case given to me by my cousin Anna long before the estrangement from my aunt, a fountain pen with a broken nib presented to me by my father on the occasion of my winning the scholarship to St Margaret's, an old detective magazine, a bottle of smelling salts and sundry articles of stationery, upon which it would be tedious to elaborate. Last of all, I picked up a studio portrait of my mother and father in a silver frame, taken perhaps two or three years after their marriage and some ten years before my birth. Though the young people in the picture were scarcely recognisable as my parents, I found some obscure comfort in the sight of their youthful faces and solemn, self-conscious smiles. Tenderly, I put it inside the bag and did up the clasp.

The hands of my new watch showed that it was now a quarter

to twelve. My gaze travelled around the room, lingering in turn on each of the objects that had grown so familiar to me: the battered walnut cupboard, the hatstand, the tarnished gilt-framed mirror, the cracked Japanese vase in which we kept our umbrellas, the glass-panelled door with its back-to-front writing, and the ornamental carriage clock on the mantelpiece, which had been given to Mr Plimpson in lieu of an unpaid debt. Only a few weeks before, all these things had seemed to me as immutably fixed in their places as I was in my own. Yet now the open packing cases served as an unhappy reminder that the little world I had inhabited for so long would soon cease to exist. With a sigh, I buttoned up my jacket, glanced at my reflection in the mirror, and stood for a moment breathing in the odour of pomatum and cigars before walking out through the plate-glass door for the last time.

The tram came roaring up just as I was approaching the stop; I hurried towards it and as I took my place at the back of the queue I felt a tap on my shoulder. I went cold with dread, remembering the two men who had been lingering suspiciously in the vicinity for weeks. However, when I looked round I saw neither the man in the checked coat nor his black-bearded confederate, but a broad-shouldered fellow with the brim of his hat pulled down over his face. "You dropped this," he said, handing me a rolled up newspaper.

"You must be mistaken . . ." I began, but he had already walked off, so I got on the tram and paid my fare with the newspaper still clutched under my arm. I took a seat on the upper deck, which at that hour of the day was occupied chiefly by maidservants and housewives clutching shopping baskets full of groceries. An elderly man sat down just behind me, alternately puffing on his pipe and hacking away with a hoarse, racking cough; the stench of cheap tobacco turned my stomach and so I stood up to move elsewhere. As I brushed past him, he cursed vilely under his breath and spat on the floor. The tram moved off with a jerk and I sank down in the nearest seat, my cheeks flaming and tears pricking at my eyes. The old lady next to me peered at me with short-sighted sympathy and I blinked fiercely and swallowed hard to get rid of the lump in my throat. Loath to be drawn into conversation, I unrolled the newspaper, which I now saw was that day's edition of *The Times*. I began to read the advertisements for "Situations Vacant", for by what seemed to me then a serendipitous quirk of fortune the paper was folded in such a way that they were uppermost. Prominent amongst them was a notice edged with a thick black border, which appeared at first glance to have been accidentally transposed from the obituary pages. It read as follows:

### SEIZE THIS UNIQUE OPPORTUNITY!

### OPEN NEW HORIZONS BEYOND YOUR
### WILDEST DREAMS!

A position has arisen for a person of enterprising character to perform secretarial and administrative tasks in the offices of a small organisation located in central London. Honour, discretion and a calm temperament are essential. Substantial remuneration will be awarded to the successful applicant for the execution of his or her duties.

Intrigued by the gulf between the thrilling headline and the mundane description of the post, I looked for the name and address of the organisation concerned but could not find it; applications were to be returned to a post office in the West Central district of London. I am not by nature superstitious, but I was struck by the queer manner in which the advertisement had come to my attention at the precise moment when my association with Plimpson and Co. had ended, and the coincidence began to assume a fateful significance in my mind.

I am a person who likes to keep things in order. When obliged to make an important decision, it has always been my habit to draw up a list of the issues under consideration, each of which I mark with a tick, a cross or a question mark, as appropriate. With this purpose in view, I took out my pencil, wrote *Honour* and *Discretion* in the margin of the newspaper and ticked both words. Below that I printed the word *Calm*, underlined it and made another affirmative stroke, reflecting that there was no more effective training in maintaining one's composure in the face of the utmost provocation than to spend years tending a fretful invalid. Next, I set down the word *Enterprising*, and hesitated uneasily before marking it with a cross. For though I passed long hours reading detective stories and dreaming of adventure, I knew that as a rule I was far too timid to act upon impulse or to take an unnecessary risk.

Yet, once again, I found my eyes drawn to the tantalising headline. *Open New Horizons.* I pictured myself standing on a high peak, gazing out over endless waves of dark green wooded hills, and felt an unfamiliar surging sensation in my stomach. For an instant I feared I was going to be ill and then it dawned on me that I was in fact quite heady with excitement. I drew a deep breath. Was it really possible that my life could change? It was a question that for the moment I was unable to answer; perhaps I was fearful of doing so. Nevertheless, I made up my mind that I would apply for the job.

# Four

After an interminable week during which the inclement weather kept me penned up inside the house with my mother's petty anxieties and complaints, I was surprised and delighted to receive a cursory note inviting me to attend an interview at an address in Whitehall on the following Wednesday. Folded within it was a small card stamped with a curious device in red ink, which I was requested to show upon my arrival. Nothing so momentous had befallen me for a very long time, if ever, and the prospect of the interview threw me into a tumult of nervousness and excitement. Nevertheless, I refrained from telling Mother the news, for in my heart of hearts I believed that I was unlikely to be successful and wished to avoid raising her hopes unnecessarily.

When the critical day came round at last, I informed her that I was going into the city to make enquiries at some employment agencies and set out for Whitehall, weighed down by the awareness that the next few hours were to be of the most vital importance.

I found the building that the letter had stipulated with little difficulty and entered through a pair of gleaming glass-fronted doors, to be intercepted by a porter in dark blue livery who glanced at the card that I held out to him, then rang a little brass handbell which stood on his desk. A pair of mahogany doors shutting off the entrance hall from the rest of the interior sprang open to reveal another uniformed attendant, who stepped towards me to inspect my card and then beckoned me forward with a white-gloved finger.

I found myself in an echoing, high-ceilinged chamber with a chequered marble floor and immense, gilt-framed oil paintings on the walls. My guide led me across to the far end of the room, through a second set of doors and down a long passageway. We passed in silence through a maze of corridors, queerly shaped rooms, cramped alcoves and narrow staircases before he stopped abruptly and ushered me into a small, windowless office.

Sitting behind a desk bestrewn with papers was a lean, grey-haired man. He raised his eyes towards me for an instant, then looked down and continued writing. I waited nervously as he read through what he had written, took up the pen in his spindly fingers and rapidly signed his name. Having done so, he sat back in his chair and looked up at me once again, removing his spectacles to rub vigorously at the bridge of his nose with his thumb and index finger. Then he put the spectacles back on and gestured for me to sit down.

"Good morning, Miss Trant. I'm so sorry to have kept you waiting," he said, scrutinising my person carefully, as if noting every last detail of my appearance. "Let's move straight on to business, shall we?"

He began by asking two or three questions about the nature and extent of my secretarial skills, but the subject was touched upon only briefly and almost, it seemed to me, as a matter of form. Then, just as I was wondering whether the interview could possibly be over so soon, he clasped his hands together on the desk and said with a languid air, as if he were thoroughly bored by the question but was obliged to ask it anyway, "Could I ask you to expand a little on the nature of the business carried out by Plimpson and Co.? Mr Plimpson is an exporter of goods, if I understand correctly?"

I tried not to appear flustered at this, for I was aware that some of the more dubious aspects of Mr Plimpson's dealings might be frowned upon by this gentleman, who, after all, must be a functionary of the state. Consequently, I framed my response as vaguely as possible, murmuring something about "shipping goods from Europe" and "overseeing negotiations between different parties".

The official's eyes were watchful and as I spoke he listened so intently that he might have been a figure carved in stone. "And the 'Co.'? How many individuals does the firm employ?"

"I believe the 'Co.' is purely ornamental, sir," I said, feeling my cheeks grow hot.

"Really?" he said, raising his eyebrows. "How very interesting. And are you able to tell me with which companies your former employer regularly does business?"

I gave him the names of one or two shipping merchants, who were among the more respectable of Mr Plimpson's clients.

"Is that all? Surely you can give me a longer list than that?" he said, regarding me slyly over the top of his spectacles.

"Of course, sir, but I'm afraid that I would have to consult the paperwork in order to be able to give you the names. There are so very many of them, you see."

The expression on his face hardened from one of irony into a look of outright scepticism, and all at once it occurred to me that the two men I had seen loitering at the tram stop might have been policemen, and that the man behind the desk might be a policeman too. I remembered the peculiar way in which the job advertisement had come to my attention, at the exact moment my connection with Plimpson and Co. had come to an end. Could it be that there was in reality no job; that the interview was simply a pretext, a trap into which I had fallen all too readily, preparing the way for my interrogation? Worse still, might it be possible that not only Mr Plimpson, but I too was under suspicion?

The official glanced at a sheet of paper on his desk before saying, "Can you tell me about any of the recent negotiations that Mr Plimpson has carried out, Miss Trant? With what types of goods is the firm dealing at present?"

With these questions he seemed to confirm all my fears. I was so frightened of condemning myself through some unwitting slip of the tongue that my mind froze and I began to babble. "Goods? Oh, all kinds really – it's never the same from one week to the next. I seem to recall that there were some Bibles recently – those were being sent to a German charity, for slum children, I believe. And there was a shipload of buttons . . ." The official shook his head and tutted. Almost on the point of tears, I said, "I'm sorry, sir, but I can't tell you much more. As a matter of policy, Mr Plimpson has always been extremely discreet about such matters; I'm afraid that I have never been privy to the full range of the firm's undertakings."

The official gave a cold smile, then removed his spectacles and passed a hand across his eyes. There was a silence of sufficient length to make me wonder once again whether the interview might be over, and inwardly I began to congratulate myself on having traversed such dangerous terrain without having committed any glaring indiscretions.

My relief, however, was short-lived. The official put his spectacles back on, leant forward with his elbows on the desk and his chin resting in his cupped hands and then, choosing each word with deliberation, said, "Tell me something about your father and his connection with Mr Plimpson."

This was so unexpected that for a few seconds I was lost for words. "My father?" I said, observing that my interrogator's spectacles glinted and caught the light so that I was unable to see his eyes. "I don't quite see . . . They were friends. Mr Plimpson is an old family friend."

"And they never worked together?"

"No, sir – my father was an accountant, at Bellows and Tuttle."

The official wrote something down and then said, "Your mother is an invalid, I believe?" I nodded. "And she had a sister?"

"She *has* a sister, sir – my aunt Sophie. Sadly we haven't heard from her for quite some time."

"I see. And was your aunt ever acquainted with Mr Plimpson?"

"Not to the best of my knowledge, sir."

"And you used to reside at . . ." He gave the address of the house in St John's Wood where we had lived until my father's death. I nodded once again, feeling thoroughly unnerved by the fellow's uncanny familiarity with my family history. "Did Mr Plimpson ever visit the house?"

"No sir, I don't believe that he did. I certainly never saw him there."

The official shifted back in his seat and regarded me thoughtfully for a long moment. Then he stood up, holding out his hand.

"Thank you, Miss Trant – that will be all. Good day." He reached behind his chair and unwound a snake-like speaking tube, into which he enunciated the single word "Travers". Then he walked across to the office door, which opened to reveal another liveried attendant, who bowed and gestured for me to precede him into the corridor.

I was led out by a different, though equally circuitous, route from the one that I had entered by, and when at last I stepped through a little door that opened onto a poky courtyard and felt the fresh air on my face, I experienced an overwhelming sensation of release. Still considerably agitated by the ordeal that I had undergone, which I had found as unsettling as it was unexpected, I made my way to Green Park and sat down on a bench to eat the thin slices of bread and margarine that I had prepared before leaving that morning. The sunlight slanted down through the leafy branches of the trees, dancing in jewel-like patterns on the path in front of me and warming the back of my neck. Yet in spite of the summery weather and the knowledge that there stretched ahead of me a few precious unclaimed hours, which I might pass as I chose, I could not help feeling utterly cast down.

There was no secretarial job; I was now convinced of it. For one thing, the precise nature of the duties that I would be expected to undertake had never been revealed to me. And, more strangely still, the questions that I had been asked had almost all, albeit in some instances rather tenuously, been connected in some way with Mr Plimpson and the history of his business dealings. Undoubtedly, the whole proceeding had been concocted as a smokescreen, so that the police could find out what I knew without alerting me to the fact that an investigation was being carried out. New horizons, indeed! I had been a gullible little fool to believe that such a position might exist, or that someone like me would have had a chance of being considered for an interview, much less of being offered the job. My only consolation was that I had said nothing to incriminate either myself or my former employer, towards whom, despite everything, I still retained a lingering sense of loyalty.

The next morning I slipped out of the apartment early, before Mother was up, for I had decided that the best course of action was to purchase a newspaper so that I could resume my search for a new situation at once. As I passed through the hallway I glanced, out of habit, at the hall table. There were no postcards, but there was a solitary letter, which, I saw upon closer examination, was addressed to me. I opened the envelope with trembling hands, removed a sheet of bond paper and read, to my utter astonishment, an official confirmation of my appointment as the secretary for – – (the word was blacked out). The letter stipulated that I was not to discuss the interview or the nature of my new post with anyone, on pain of instant dismissal, after which injunction it concluded abruptly, with an official stamp instead of a signature.

I went out and walked about for a while through the surrounding streets. Once I had got over my initial surprise and confusion, my predominant emotion was one of blissful relief. In the short time since I had stopped bringing home a weekly salary, Mother and I had edged closer to outright poverty than ever before: we struggled to pay the rent, and had lately been obliged to rely on the unpalatable evening meal cooked by our landlady as our main source of sustenance. These privations had at last penetrated the shell of Mother's indifference and her doom-laden predictions of our imminent ruin had begun to tell on my nerves.

Now that I knew that our savings would not have to last us indefinitely, I felt as if a great burden of anxiety had been lifted from my shoulders. The knowledge that I had a job to go to at the beginning of September made my domestic cares seem less overwhelming, and I was able to endure Mother's fussing and her sudden changes of mood with greater composure than before.

However, this is not to say that I had had such an abrupt change of heart that I now looked forward to commencing my new role

35

with anything like complete equanimity. I was both thrilled and alarmed by the wall of secrecy surrounding the organisation that I was to work for and, of course, I was intensely curious; I wore away countless hours speculating about its scope and purpose, and about the nature of the duties that I would be required to perform. However, I was unable to move beyond the vague supposition that I would be taking up a situation in some obscure government department, perhaps one that dealt with official secrets of some kind, which would explain why the Whitehall official had been obliged to test my discretion in matters relating to my former employer.

I remember little of what I did in the following weeks. I do recall that the time passed slowly, but I did not resent the tedium of my daily life, for I sensed that after I took up my mysterious post in the autumn things would never be the same again.

# Five

On the appointed day I left the house dressed in a new tweed suit, though the portfolio I was carrying was still the one that I had used throughout my time at Plimpson and Co. The September sun shining on my face gave off a lingering echo of the summer's warmth, and I felt as if I were stepping out of a long, dark tunnel into a new world. I was so glad to have regained some independence at last and to have a legitimate object that would take me out of the house every day that for a time I forgot the churning anxiety that had kept me awake for much of the night. My mood of calm optimism lasted until I reached the tram stop, but as we began to rattle along past the grimy backs of houses, faded scraps of lawn and miserable-looking suburban trees the shadowy qualms that had plagued me ever since I had received my letter of appointment came crowding back to the surface of my mind and I sat fidgeting in my seat, half wishing that I could turn back.

I alighted at Tottenham Court Road and, stopping every now and then to consult the roughly sketched map that had been enclosed with my letter of appointment, made my way slowly along the thoroughfare and turned off into a narrow side street. I had not supposed that my new place of work would be quite as imposing as the grand Whitehall offices in which my interview had taken place; nevertheless, I had anticipated that it would be reasonably smart and substantial. Imagine my surprise, then, when in place of the respectable premises that I had expected I saw only a run-down shop, in the window of which was displayed an assortment of appliances for the hard of hearing. Surely it was impossible that this poky little place could be a headquarters of any kind! I stood gazing in perplexity at the shabby array of ear trumpets, speaking tubes and other less readily identifiable contraptions fashioned from rubber, pewter and wax, until a stooped figure in a green gabardine brushed past me and scuttled in through the door. Startled into action, I straightened my hat and went in after him, for it seemed clear that I had taken a wrong turning and I hoped that the shopkeeper would be able to give me directions.

The interior of the shop was as neglected as the state of its window display had implied. Everything was covered in a fine layer of dust; motes danced in the sunlight that flooded in through the window and cobwebs hung in fronds across the shelves filled with numbered boxes which lined the walls from floor to ceiling. To my puzzlement, the man I had followed in was nowhere to be seen. I made my way over to the counter and looked for a bell to ring for service, but there was none. So, hoping that the shopkeeper might be lurking behind the faded baize screen at the back of the shop, I called out an uncertain "Hello!"

Almost before the word was out of my mouth I heard the clanging of footsteps descending a metal staircase, and a fair young man wearing a dark suit appeared from behind the screen and proceeded to look me up and down with such acute interest that I was somewhat taken aback. I blurted out my enquiry with the discomfiting awareness that a hot flush was creeping up my neck. He peered around the shop, as if fearful that we might be being watched, before pointing to the screen and indicating with a jerk of his head that I should accompany him behind it. With the litany of dire warnings that my mother had showered upon me as I break-fasted ringing in my ears, I backed away and turned to hurry outside, but he was too quick for me and grabbed me by the sleeve.

"My dear Miss Trant!" he exclaimed, intensifying my confusion even further. "I'm so sorry to have alarmed you. I can assure you that, however unlikely it may appear, you really are in the right place. Once you are better acquainted with the nature of our operation, you will understand the necessity for concealing our headquarters in this way. Please, do allow me to show you upstairs; the other chaps are all there and are most eager to meet you."

I stood rooted to the spot, torn between my mistrust of the keen-eyed stranger and an anxious desire to avoid causing offence to my new employers. At last, with a degree of recklessness of which I had hitherto never imagined myself to be capable, I indicated with a stiff nod that I would do as he asked and preceded him behind the screen and through a low doorway that opened onto a spiral staircase of elaborately wrought iron. We ascended to a cramped upper landing with one door and the young man squeezed past me and executed a rhythmic series of knocks. Immediately, a peephole swivelled open, a key ground in the lock and the door swung back.

I received a fleeting impression of shadows, bare floorboards and a high ceiling before I was obliged to give my full attention to the welcoming party that stood just inside the doorway.

"Come in, come in! Most glad to meet you, Miss Trant! Welcome to Bureau 8. We've been awaiting your arrival with great impatience, haven't we, chaps?" The speaker, a stocky man of about fifty with greying hair and a ruddy, good-natured countenance, shook my hand and gestured in turn toward each of his associates, who were ranged behind him.

"May I introduce Max Liebowitz, the philosopher among us?"

Liebowitz was the man in the green gabardine whom I had seen going into the shop. He was thin and hunched, and wore a gold-rimmed monocle through which he peered earnestly, shaking my hand with great vigour.

"Tom Hunter – our intrepid adventurer."

A good-looking young man stepped forward and engulfed my hand in a muscular grip. I felt my cheeks grow hot and my eyes slid away from him despite my most strenuous efforts to maintain my composure.

"James Hampson-Smythe, our resident expert in poisons. Oh, forgive me – you met downstairs, of course."

Hampson-Smythe gave a small bow.

"And finally: the great MacIntyre."

A tall, auburn-haired fellow with a neatly trimmed moustache, who until now had hung reticently behind his colleagues, came forward and grasped my hand with hasty diffidence before drawing back.

"And that concludes the introductions . . ."

Tom Hunter interrupted him, grinning. "Not quite, old man." He turned to me and made an elaborate flourish. "This is Anthony Rivers, Miss Trant – universally known as the Chief. He's in charge of operations here, and a jolly good sort, though he can be rather a tyrant at times."

"Hear hear!" added Hampson-Smythe, sotto voce, though it was impossible to detect from his narrow, inscrutable face which part of Hunter's statement he so heartily endorsed.

Rivers, or the Chief as I shall henceforth refer to him, passed over these interruptions and resumed his address. "As I say, Miss Trant, we're most awfully pleased to have you here. We've been nagging the chaps at head office to appoint a secretary to deal with administrative matters at Bureau 8 for, oh, absolutely years, but they insisted that we were perfectly capable of organising ourselves – in which supposition, as you can see, they were sorely mistaken!"

It was impossible to avoid granting this statement my most fervent assent; every surface in the room was strewn with clutter, save for a lone oasis of neatness, a large ebony office table, upon which stood a battered typewriter. I cast my eye over the nearest of the desks, which was littered with test tubes, bottles and jars containing a multicoloured array of powders and potions. On one side, a stack of leather-bound volumes teetered precariously; their spines bore titles such as *Poisons – a Dictionary*, *Arsenic and Its Uses*, *Hemlock, Nightshade and Belladonna – Nature's Deadliest Plants* and, more allusively, *Deadly and Undetectable*.

Somewhat unnerved, I looked up, and noticed for the first time that despite the glorious sunshine outside all the blinds were drawn and the gas mantles lit.

"Of course we have to prevent the possibility that we might be overlooked by prying eyes," the Chief explained, as if he had read my thoughts.

"Who . . ." I began, as there flashed into my mind an image of the blinds pulled down over the windows of Plimpson and Co. on the day Mr Plimpson had informed me about the move to Deptford.

"Yours is the desk with the Remington; she's rather a monster, I'm afraid, but no doubt head office will send us another if she's not up to the job. The meeting room and the kitchen are over there." He gestured towards two doors on the other side of the office. "I do hope that you won't take it amiss if I insist that the meeting room is out of bounds – sometimes we're obliged to discuss some very sensitive information, as you can imagine. And in addition there are various highly confidential documents and so forth . . . However, I don't think we need bother you with all that for the time being, Miss Trant. Please, do take a look round."

Rigid with self-consciousness, I put my portfolio on the ebony table and made a hasty tour of the office. I walked past two desks laden with papers and ledgers and stopped at a third, my attention arrested by an open book, the pages of which displayed a table of the tides at a port on the Baltic Sea. Tide tables were a prominent feature of a story I had read only the night before and I looked down at the book with a thrill of curiosity, which was intensified when I saw the leaves of paper scrawled with strange symbols and mathematical formulae that spilled out from between its pages.

"How many times do I need to remind you to put out your cigars, Liebowitz?" The Chief extinguished the offending article, which lay smouldering on the floor beneath the desk. "This is where MacIntyre sits," he informed me, pointing at another table, which was buried beneath a bizarre assortment of objects, among which were a revolver, the remnants of a German sausage, a tin of oxblood shoe polish, a crumbling loaf of black bread, a nail file, a jar of brilliantine and a small bottle of brandy.

I turned to the Chief and ventured a bright little remark about the diversity of this collection, but my face must have betrayed me, for he patted me on the shoulder and said, "Please don't be discouraged, dear lady. We won't expect you to work miracles overnight, and of course we'll do all we can to assist you. Now then, which one of you fellows will make some tea for Miss Trant?"

There was an exchange of glances before the intense little man with the monocle stepped forward.

"Why thank you, Liebowitz! Don't forget the sugar bowl whatever you do; this poor young woman appears to have had rather a shock." The Chief turned towards me with a smile. "Now, my dear, we must allow you a few moments to gather your thoughts. You shall drink your tea in tranquillity and after that I'll explain something of the nature of our work. I don't suppose they told you anything at the interview?" I shook my head. "No, I thought that would be the case. Ah well, it's probably for the best." I stared at him in consternation and he added hastily, "No, no, please don't misunderstand me, dear lady; there is nothing improper nor untoward about our business whatsoever, I assure you."

With an air of boyish gallantry, he helped me to remove my coat and hung it on a hatstand near the door. Then he swept a pile of books and papers off the chair that stood to one side of his desk and invited me to sit down. Once I had done so, he tapped his finger mysteriously against his nose and asked, "Would you excuse me for a moment?" then turned away and began rummaging about in a large Gladstone bag.

Meanwhile, the other men had drifted off one by one, resuming the tasks that had been interrupted by my entrance. Hampson-Smythe sat down and started turning the pages of an immense tome, pausing every now and then to consult a notebook that he had removed from his pocket. Hunter unfolded a map, laid it out so that it covered the whole surface of his desk and then leaned over it with a magnifying glass held up to his eye, as if he were scrutinising some minute feature of the terrain. As for MacIntyre, he had taken out a pat of butter from the bottom drawer of his desk and appeared, with the aid of a penknife, to be immersed in the construction of a sausage sandwich.

My eye fell upon the clumsy, old-fashioned typewriter that squatted on my own desk. I pictured the gleaming Hammond that Mr Plimpson had bought for me not six months ago with a surge of nostalgia for the dingy little office in which I had worked for so many years, and all at once my doubts about taking up the post at Bureau 8 – and what a peculiar appellation that was – began to bear down upon me once more. As I sat contemplating the disorderly office and its eccentric occupants, I quite lost my nerve. I decided that I would feign illness so that I could get away before it was too late, and removed my gloves from my reticule as a precursor to departure. After all, I told myself, it ought to be perfectly possible to find work in a shop or as a domestic servant until I could get something better. I can only recall this moment of faint-heartedness with a shudder at the thought of all I should have missed had I chosen to pursue such a course.

Fortunately, however, my train of thought was interrupted by the arrival of Liebowitz, bearing a tray weighed down by a large earthenware teapot and a motley array of china. His monocle gleamed fitfully as he glanced about for a place to deposit his burden, before laying it on the floor at my feet. Then he crouched down, wincing as if his joints pained him, and began to pour the tea. A moment later the Chief, who had been scrabbling about in one of the cupboards, gave a loud whoop of triumph and held up a brown paper package which he proceeded to unwrap, revealing a large fruitcake. "Now, you fellows! Who's for cake?" he called, precipitating an eager stampede towards his desk.

I just had time to bundle away my gloves before I was handed a chipped cup of poorly strained tea and a slice of cake on a saucer, though to my consternation there was no cake fork. The gentlemen, who did not seem concerned by such niceties, munched and sipped contentedly until only a scattering of crumbs and currants remained. I found myself unable to swallow more than a few morsels, for I was not used to eating under the scrutiny of so many masculine eyes and experienced an agony of self-consciousness every time I brought my fingers to my lips. MacIntyre, whose task it was to clear away, gazed mournfully at the large piece of cake that I had left on my plate, and for a moment I thought he might snatch it up and devour it then and there. Courtesy restrained him from consuming it in my presence; however, when he returned from the kitchen I observed that he was cleaning his moustache with a crimson pocket hand-kerchief and reflected that most probably the cake had not gone to waste after all. I watched from the corner of my eye as he replaced the remnants of his sausage sandwich in the bottom drawer, opened a dashing, purple-covered notebook and started to scribble away with the inspired urgency of a poet.

"Miss Trant," said the Chief, folding his arms across his stomach and sinking back into his chair with a sigh of contentment. "First, let me say that for your ability to maintain your composure, despite what must have been a series of severe shocks, you have won my sincerest admiration."

I was on the point of acknowledging this compliment with a polite denial of the necessity of its being made at all when he chuckled and I realised abruptly that his intention had been iron-ical. I drew a deep breath, knit my fingers together as if to hold in my foolish words, and gave a tremulous smile.

"Now, we must address ourselves to the matter in hand," he continued. "It's time that you learnt something about Bureau 8's purpose, wouldn't you agree?"

I nodded and looked down at my feet. I noticed that my toes were turned inwards and adjusted my posture so that my shoe straps were lined up neatly, one against the other.

"May I ask, Miss Trant, what prompted you to apply for this job in the first place?"

I looked up hurriedly at this, but his eyes were serious and the lines of his mouth betrayed not a hint of sarcasm. I explained the circumstances under which I had been obliged to resign my previous post and then, since his patient silence seemed to indicate that he expected me to say more, I added, somewhat stiffly, that I hoped that

I possessed in some measure the personal qualities that were mentioned in the advertisement. The Chief listened to my hesitant explanations with a flattering attentiveness that was new to me, and which flooded me with a pleasant self-consciousness. So gently that I was hardly aware of it, he continued to draw me out, and at length, to my own astonishment, I found myself confiding something of the difficulties that I had faced in my domestic life and acknowledging that I had been powerfully struck by the phrase "new horizons", which had stirred my desire to lead a freer and more fulfilled existence. The Chief seemed pleased by this and I received the impression that the words had been included in the advertisement at his suggestion.

I had just mentioned my father for the first time when we were interrupted by the approach of Tom Hunter, who had put on a leather jacket and a red paisley scarf which brought out the warm tones of his complexion and the brilliance of his green eyes. He strode up to us with an apologetic grin and cleared his throat. "Sorry to break in on you like this; I'm about to go out after Henriquez. I've spoken to the other chaps, but there are one or two points I'd like to confirm with you sir, if you could spare a moment."

"Sorry, Miss Trant — rather urgent business!" the Chief said, standing up. "I'll be with you again in a jiffy."

"Delighted to have met you, Miss Trant!" said Hunter with a smile that set my heart fluttering. "*Au revoir*."

Left alone, I felt disoriented, as if I had been dragged rudely back into consciousness or awakened from a hypnotic trance. My cheeks were suffused by a flush of embarrassment as I began to reflect upon the half-acknowledged thoughts and desires that I had just confided to a virtual stranger, a man I had met scarcely an hour before. I glanced around the office and saw to my immense relief that Liebowitz, Hampson-Smythe and MacIntyre all remained absorbed in their allotted tasks, and had clearly overheard nothing of our discussion. I gravely doubt whether it would have comforted me then to know that Tony Rivers' famous charm had been exerted in like manner on countless foreign spies and other shadowy denizens of the international underworld, and that as an interrogator he had an unblemished record of success. When, later, I looked back on that conversation, it gave me an obscure satisfaction to know that I had experienced for myself the power of that mysterious ability to extract a confession from the most unlikely subject which has, for so many years, been such an asset to Bureau 8's work.

The door to the meeting room reopened and at once the other men abandoned their various pursuits and crowded around Hunter.

"Look after yourself, old man!"

"Goodbye, old chap – and good luck!"

"We'll be thinking of you."

"Do remember to be cautious – at the first sign that they suspect, get out!" advised the Chief, laying a hand on Hunter's shoulder.

"Yes sir, I will. And I'll do my best to let you know as soon as there's anything to report." Then, amid much back-slapping, Hunter shook hands with each of the men in turn and walked towards the door, giving a cheery wave as he went out.

A hand was laid on my shoulder from behind and I started in surprise as the Chief moved past me and sat down in his chair.

"Now that I have heard your story – and let me say, my dear Miss Trant, that it does you great credit – it is most certainly incumbent upon me to tell you something about our organisation, and the life and death struggle in which we are currently engaged."

For years I had been trapped in an endless round of tedious domestic and secretarial responsibilities, and the shadowy inner life that I had nurtured through daydreaming and reading had been my only refuge from Mother's nagging and complaining, the countless petty economies and the soul-destroying tedium of it all. As the Chief spoke, I understood that the new horizons opening up before me were so unexpected and so thrilling that even the dizziest heights of my most impossible dreams were flat and dull by comparison, and I felt my face break into a radiant grin.

"Have I said something amusing?" he enquired, giving me a puzzled look.

"No sir, of course not!" I hastened to assure him. "I'm simply happy to be here!"

# Six

On my second day at Bureau 8, I arrived to find the premises apparently deserted and the shutters closed. I felt a fleeting moment of panic before I remembered the bunch of keys with which the Chief had presented me just before my departure on the previous afternoon, one of which was labelled *Shop* in Liebowitz's scrawled handwriting. I took care to lock the door behind me then paused for a moment, inhaling the odours of dust and fading beeswax. Pale rays of sunlight slanted in beneath the blinds, casting pools of opalescence on the parquet floor and gleaming on the brass till. I walked up to the counter and examined the shelves that lined the walls behind it. Boxes of ear trumpets and bottles containing patent cures for deafness or lotions for removing blockages in the ear were jumbled haphazardly together; the labels on the bottles were faded and grimy and everything was covered in a thick layer of dust. Squeezing past several empty packing cases, I passed behind the baize screen and climbed the metal staircase, holding my skirts closely about my legs. I halted on the cramped landing outside the office door for a moment, smoothed down my hair and drew a deep breath, then rapped out the special sequence of knocks that acted as a password.

Almost at once, the Chief peered through the peephole, before opening the door with a beaming smile. Behind him I could see Liebowitz hunched over his desk, but otherwise the room was empty.

"Miss Trant! Good morning! Glad to see you here so bright and early!" He closed the door after me and turned the key. "Well! Hampson-Smythe should be in at any moment. As for MacIntyre, one never quite knows whether he will appear or not – if he does turn up it won't be until much later, anyway. And Hunter will be away for a while, I should imagine. You'll find that he and MacIntyre often have business that takes them out of the office. Now, I expect you'd like to get to work straight away. There are some letters to be typed on your desk – use the headed paper – and then, once Hampson-Smythe gets in, perhaps you could begin work on the new filing system by establishing the requirements for his department – the headings under which he'd like the documents to be classified and so forth. I'm sure you know the kind of thing."

I hung my jacket next to Liebowitz's gabardine, sat down at my desk and eagerly leafed through the small pile of papers that had been placed next to the typewriter. During his explanation of my duties on the previous day, the Chief had taken particular care to impress upon me the vital importance of Bureau 8's work, so I picked up the first letter with a thrill of expectation, feeling as if I were on the edge of some great adventure. To my disappointment, I found myself perusing an obscurely worded memorandum regarding German imports of an unspecified nature, which was badly punctuated and reflected an uncertain grasp of English grammar. As I laid it down in disgust, the rhythmic knock sounded on the door, and Liebowitz got up to admit Hampson-Smythe.

I turned my attention to the next item of correspondence, which listed the types of dye used at a textile factory in Vienna, and with growing resignation skimmed a third, which comprised a series of statistics connected to the output of a copper mine in southern Bohemia. Both were clumsily phrased and full of errors. Feeling rather despondent, I took out a sheet of writing paper, inserted it into the typewriter, and began typing rather gingerly, for it was some time since I had used a machine with an old-fashioned up-strike mechanism, and I had grown accustomed to seeing the words appear as I went along rather than working "blind".

At the first clatter of the keys, Liebowitz got up and approached my desk.

"Excuse me, Miss Trant, but I beg you to remember that not a single letter in these communications must be out of place – not a comma even. And please make sure to leave two spaces after each full stop. Absolute accuracy is of the most vital importance."

"I will do my best, Mr Liebowitz, but it's difficult to avoid errors with such an old style of typewriter. I'm accustomed to using a visible writing machine," I explained, rather nettled by what seemed to me unwarranted interference.

"I apologise; please do not think that I am making a criticism of your methods. It is just that it is essential that the documents are copied exactly – even the mistakes must be preserved intact – or else the recipients will be unable to break the code. I too have had great trouble with this antiquated heap – I will speak to the Chief about obtaining a new machine for you as a matter of urgency."

He continued to hover over me, tutting impatiently whenever I hesitated over the misspelt words and confused phrasing. All the while I was racking my brains to puzzle out the encoded messages, but of course I had no experience in such matters and did not realise that I would get nowhere without the secret key (a book or an article in a newspaper, for example) that had been decided upon by the correspondents. After several attempts I managed to complete the letter to Liebowitz's satisfaction and was about to begin the next one when I was startled by the ringing of a bell.

As I have already explained, Bureau 8 used the hearing appliance shop as a façade to disguise the location of its headquarters, and until the time of my arrival Liebowitz and Hampson-Smythe had taken it in turns to serve behind the counter. These duties did not encroach greatly on their time, for the specialised nature of the business, its unenticing appearance and its position in an obscure alleyway were all expressly designed to discourage customers from coming in; indeed, had it been a genuine concern, its owners must long ago have been forced to close it down. Nevertheless, they regarded the extra charge as a burden that interfered with their other more vital work, and it had been decided that henceforth I would bear sole responsibility for running the shop.

To my delight I had been instructed that when performing my duties as shop assistant I must use an alias, and accordingly I had chosen Miss Sophie Wade; Sophie after my estranged aunt whom I still sorely missed, and Wade after the heroine of my favourite detective stories. Liebowitz, whom the Chief had designated to pass on all the information I would need before I could take charge, was adamant that under no circumstances should I discuss Miss Wade's personal life with the customers. On the other hand, he advised me to use the spy's old trick of ensuring that I was thoroughly acquainted with the details of her character and background, so that when the time came I could "slip into the mantle" with the greatest possible conviction. It was vital that Miss Wade was sufficiently unexceptional to avoid arousing the customers' curiosity, so we determined that she would be a timid, taciturn woman with no living relatives and no close friends, eking out a miserable existence in a seedy lodging house close by. And if a customer asked to speak to Mr Stein or Mr Flowers, then I was to fetch Liebowitz or Hampson-Smythe immediately, for these were the aliases by which they were respectively known by Bureau 8's network of underground informers.

The bell rang again and, raising his bushy brows, Liebowitz said, "You should go down at once. Leave the letters for the time being." He removed a blue apron from the hatstand and handed it to me, saying, "Remember, Miss Wade always insists on sticking to the business at hand. Helpfulness and efficiency, yes – personal gossip, no. And send the customer to Healy's on the Strand if you can do so without arousing suspicion."

Still tying the strings of my apron, I descended the staircase with a sense of mounting excitement. I regretted the fact that I was not required to assume a more elaborate disguise in the manner of Sherlock Holmes; nevertheless, I relished the sense of intrigue that surrounded the proceedings and made ready to throw myself into my role with zest.

A short, weasel-faced man with tow-coloured hair and a pallid complexion was tapping his fingers impatiently on the counter. He was dressed in a grubby shirt and waistcoat and a ragged pair of trousers and carried a large envelope, somewhat stained and curled up at the edges. When he saw me he pulled a face and demanded, "Who are you? There's usually another feller in 'ere – I need to speak to 'im, on a urgent matter."

"The manager is busy at present, sir. Can I help?"

"No, it's 'im I want – Stein."

"I see. If you'd like to wait, I'll go and find out whether he is available. I won't be a moment."

I hurried up to the office and informed Liebowitz that someone was asking for Stein.

"What does he look like?" he enquired, glancing up reluctantly from his work.

I gave a brief description of the man, and he sighed and remarked to the Chief, "It's that blasted Towler again!"

"After another ten bob, no doubt. I wonder what nonsense he'll try to fob off on us this time. I haven't the foggiest what MacIntyre was thinking when he recruited him. Get rid of him as quickly as you can – and don't give him any money!"

I went back to typing the second letter, but I was still ebullient at having performed my first mission "under cover" and kept drifting into speculation about what the informer might have to say. Therefore, although the letter was short, it was a good twenty minutes before I finally succeeded in reproducing it accurately. Liebowitz had still not reappeared and I began to feel anxious about what might have befallen him; not, it seemed, without good reason, for the Chief suddenly said, "I say, Smythe, perhaps you'd better go down and see what's keeping Liebowitz – he should have been back long before this. But don't let Towler see you unless it's absolutely necessary."

Hampson-Smythe nodded. I watched with bated breath as he removed a revolver from a hidden cubbyhole beneath his desk, took off his shoes and crept out of the office.

A moment later there was a commotion on the stairs and he burst back in, followed by Liebowitz, who declared, "I should never have thought it possible – Towler, it seems, has finally come up with the goods! If he's telling the truth then the Scorpions have been recruiting among some of the anarchist cells in London. What's more, he claims they intend to move in on the trade unions next."

The Chief gave a low whistle. "Well, I'll be blowed! That's the first sign of activity in this country for a good ten years! Dig out everything you've got on the Scorpions, chaps. Could we have some tea in the meeting room please, Miss Trant?"

The meeting room was a cramped, windowless space, little more than a cupboard, and the air had grown stuffy even in the short interval that I had been making the tea. The men were huddled round a deal table, craning their necks to pore over the contents of a notebook. The Chief signalled that I should put the tray down on the table and muttered his thanks; Liebowitz and Hampson-Smythe were too absorbed in what they were doing even to look up. Tearing my eyes reluctantly from the haphazard assortment of maps, diagrams and ground plans that covered the walls, I went out, shutting the door behind me.

I returned to my desk feeling somewhat crestfallen and finished typing the third letter. After that I began leafing through a catalogue of ear trumpets, but my thoughts kept wandering back to the discussion that was going on in the meeting room and I found myself gazing restlessly around the office. I realised that I was in the throes of what Mother always referred to as "the fidgets", a condition for which the simple yet entirely efficacious cure is physical activity. I closed the catalogue with a bang and stood up resolutely: I would put things in order!

I began by gathering together the dirty test tubes on Hampson-Smythe's desk and placing them on a tray, ready to be washed. Liebowitz's desk was still piled with heavy leather-bound tomes; I did not like to move them, for they were interleaved with bookmarks and scraps of paper scribbled with complicated-looking formulae. Instead I contented myself with emptying his overflowing ashtray into the wastepaper basket, then swept the crumbs off MacIntyre's desk, and removed several pieces of orange peel and a shrivelled apple core. It was much less cluttered than on the previous day and there were no books, papers or other oddments to neaten up, but as I turned away I caught sight of a document lying on the floor underneath the chair and stooped to retrieve it. It was a broadsheet advertising a meeting of trade unionists, which was to take place the following evening. In light of the news that Liebowitz had passed on from Towler, I reflected that it might be significant and smoothed it out and set it in the middle of the desk. Then, feeling that it would be presumptuous to interfere with anything belonging to the Chief, I glanced round the room to see what else I might do.

My eye fell upon a silver picture frame that had toppled face down on Hunter's desk, and I picked it up and examined it with some curiosity. It was a photograph of an attractive girl of about twenty with large, thickly lashed eyes and full lips that curled in a demure smile. She wore a white ruffled dress and a picture hat, and her fair hair was tied back with a large bow. One arm rested languidly on a chair-back and in her gloved hand she held an ox-eye daisy. I speculated as to whether she was a relative of Hunter's or his sweetheart and decided that she must be the latter, for I could trace no family resemblance between the two of them. Dreamily, I wondered how it might feel to be adored by a man like Hunter (for my romantic fancy had already determined that she *was* adored), but imagination failed me and I sank down onto his chair with an aching feeling of emptiness.

I gazed across the office towards a thin rectangle of sunlight that glowed from beneath one of the blinds, and by some shadowy process of association my mind went back to a short period in my life when I had nurtured an inexplicable yearning for a man I scarcely knew.

The gentleman in question was a business associate of Mr Plimpson's, a man called Peters (I never knew his Christian name), who was a daily visitor to the office during the first months of my employment there. I thought him rather handsome; he was tall and distinguished-looking with clever brown eyes, greying hair and a youthful face. He was quietly spoken and unfailingly courteous towards me; and yet there was a disconcerting air of stillness about him, a quality of suppressed energy, which flashed out in the occasional flintiness of his gaze or a too-vigorous gesture. We never discussed personal matters; our chief topics of conversation were the weather or the state of business, yet when he spoke he fixed his eyes on my face with an attentiveness that was both thrilling and peculiarly disturbing.

Mr Peters' conferences with Mr Plimpson were generally brief; indeed, he often spent longer talking to me than to my employer. One morning, however, he arrived earlier than usual and with no more than a distant "Good morning" strode straight into the office and slammed the door, cutting off the surprised murmur of Mr Plimpson's greeting. I hovered indecisively for a few moments and then, gripped by an irresistible curiosity, got up and pressed my ear to the wood.

Mr Peters, ordinarily the most softly spoken of men, sounded furious.

". . . ruined! You have let us down very badly! You must have known the consequences! You have behaved like a common criminal! You will not be allowed to get away with this."

"Now then, Peters – it was a calculated risk. You knew the difficulties that were involved . . ."

Here Mr Plimpson lowered his voice and I could hear nothing more until, seconds later, there was a sound of footsteps moving across the creaking floorboards towards the door. I dashed over to the filing cabinet and pretended to search through the documents in the top drawer. Someone came up behind me and touched my shoulder. I spun round to see Peters gazing down at me. Stupefied, I watched as his hand moved towards my face, and when he touched my cheek I began to tremble. Then, abruptly, he drew back, and I turned round to see a red-faced Mr Plimpson waddling towards us.

"Go and sit down, Miss Trant!" he barked. "Peters, that's quite enough! You would be well advised to leave these premises before I compel you to do so. Don't forget that if I choose I have the power to land you in very deep water. Yes, very!"

Mr Peters looked him up and down, then turned on his heel and without another word, without even a glance or a pressure of the hand, stalked out of the plate glass door. Feeling faint, I did as I was told and sat down at my desk, tears springing into my eyes. I bent my head over a pile of papers and shuffled through them with shaking fingers, fighting to conceal my distress from my employer, who hovered beside my desk as if he wanted to say something.

"Don't upset yourself, Miss Trant – that scoundrel isn't worth your tears," he burst out at last. "He was up to no good, you mark my words. Did he ever ask you to find out anything about me?" I shook my head. "And you never talked to him about the contents of any papers, or anything of that sort?"

"No sir, of course not!"

"Good girl! And he never made any . . . improper suggestions?"

"No!"

Afterwards, whenever I recalled the incident, I did so with a shudder of distress and humiliation at the ease with which I seemed to have fallen under Peters' spell. The more I reflected upon Mr Plimpson's words the more convinced I became that from the very beginning Peters had been grooming me to carry out some obscure purpose of his own, and that the moment when he had stood over me in the office had been a reckless attempt to bring his plans to fruition before the appointed time. Nine years later, I still had no idea whether he had designed to seduce me as a means of humiliating Mr Plimpson, whether he had hoped to persuade me to spy on my employer – or whether his intention had been a different one altogether.

There was a sudden clamour of raised voices. I leapt up and hastened across to my desk just as Hampson-Smythe burst out of the meeting room.

"I tell you, it's absolute tosh!" he bellowed. "The man is an unreliable ass!"

"Now now, Smythe," said the Chief, following him out and placing a hand on his shoulder. "Calm down. You know that it never does any harm to play things safe in this game. Besides, dear old MacIntyre's hunches do sometimes prove correct."

Hampson-Smythe gave a loud snort. "Pah! MacIntyre! I give *that* for the man's precious hunches!" He snapped his fingers with a flourish and turned towards me, sneering. "Pray, what was your impression of our *dear* MacIntyre – a first-class agent, what?"

I felt my cheeks grow hot. "Well . . . I . . . That is to say, I don't think . . ."

"That's quite all right, Miss Trant," said the Chief. "Smythe here has merely lost his temper – it happens to the best of us. I should walk it off, dear chap – and pick up some ginger biscuits and a bottle of milk while you're out, will you? Here's a shilling."

Hampson-Smythe pocketed the money with an ill grace and put on his coat and hat before stumping out of the office, slamming the door behind him.

"Now then, did you manage . . ." The Chief broke off, distracted by a strangled cry from Liebowitz, and we both looked round to see him crouching over the wastepaper basket.

"My papers! All covered in ash!"

"What on earth is the matter?" The Chief looked at me, raising one eyebrow in mock exasperation. "Sometimes I think I'm the only sane man in this organisation, Miss Trant. One or other of them is always getting wrought up about something!"

"A ruin! The coded communications from Mannheim – an utter ruin, I tell you! A few more days and I should have solved it!"

I watched aghast as the Chief took Liebowitz by the shoulders and sat him down at his desk, where he remained, muttering to himself and running his fingers through his curly hair. Meanwhile, the Chief removed the scarlet silk handkerchief from his breast pocket, knelt down by the wastepaper basket and began taking out the crumpled leaves of paper one by one and wiping them down.

I threw him an appalled glance. "I'm awfully sorry, sir. I had no idea," I said, my breath catching in my throat.

"Now now, my dear, don't trouble yourself. Liebowitz is a fool to keep vital documents in such a ridiculous place; I've told him so a thousand times. It was inevitable that something of the sort would happen. And it might have been much worse: the papers could have been thrown away altogether. Here, Liebowitz!" He tossed him the handkerchief. "You finish the job – they seem to be brushing up nicely."

With a frown, Liebowitz began to dab fussily at the papers and the Chief turned towards me with a rueful smile.

"You can see, dear lady, why we are in such desperate need of your services. Once Liebowitz has finished I would be most grateful if you could help him to arrange his papers properly in the pigeon-holes over there." He gestured towards a set of shelves on the far wall, near the door. "You can begin, if you wouldn't mind, by emptying out the items that are already there."

I fetched some boxes from the kitchen and began filling them with the miscellaneous clutter from the pigeonholes. When I had finished, Liebowitz was still cleaning the soiled documents and I would have liked to offer to help him, but I was made shy by consciousness of his irritation and of my own clumsy stupidity, so instead I plucked up my courage and went over to the Chief, who looked up at me with a smile.

"What can I do for you, Miss Trant? Don't tell me that you need more boxes!"

"I hope you won't think I'm prying into matters that don't concern me," I faltered, my cheeks burning. "I was wondering about the Scorpions and whether, perhaps, I should know a little more about them."

"Bravo, Miss Trant!" said the Chief, gesturing for me to sit down. "It's very encouraging to see you displaying this kind of initiative at such an early stage. I'll give you a potted history, shall I?"

"Yes, please," I replied, struggling to control the smile that sprang to my lips in response to these words of praise.

The Chief folded his hands on top of his stomach and settled back into his chair. "The Society of Scorpions first came into being during the 1840s. As I'm sure you're aware, secret societies were very popular in those days. Most of them were tinpot little groups that awarded themselves grand, dangerous-sounding names, though their members never did anything more daring than to give pompous after-dinner speeches, and for many years the Scorpions were no exception. All that was changed, however, by a chap called Richard Arrowsmith, whom you might have heard of."

"Wasn't he the one who married an American heiress and then murdered her for her money? I remember the story being in the papers."

"Yes, that's right. There was a big trial ten years ago. As a matter of fact, we – that is, Bureau 8, and MacIntyre in particular – played an instrumental part in securing Arrowsmith's arrest. After he was found guilty of murder and condemned to death, most of his followers left the country and the Scorpions became inactive – at least in Great Britain. However, we'll come back to that.

"In the late seventies Arrowsmith wrote a book called *A New Dawn*, which was highly influential and led to the transformation of the Society of Scorpions into a revolutionary organisation. I wouldn't recommend reading it – it's rather a dry work on the whole, as political treatises tend to be. Really, all one needs to know about Arrowsmith's philosophy is that it was shaped primarily by greed, ruthless self-interest and disdain for what he termed the 'flabby complacency' of contemporary society. His creed was 'each man for himself' – he viewed Christian precepts such as loving one's neighbour and the fellowship of man as sentimental nonsense that ought to fall by the wayside.

"He concluded his book by setting out a chilling vision of Europe under the dictatorship of the Scorpions. This 'New Dawn' was to be achieved through a series of phases: first, the education of the masses – essentially a process of widespread indoctrination. This was to overlap with the second phase, which comprised the assassination of a number of strategically selected public figures. Then, once the key national institutions were plunged into a state of chaos, the Scorpions would move in to stage a coup. In the fourth and final phase the 'inner circle' of the society would preside over a regime of terror, where every aspect of people's lives was to be controlled and 'protected' by the government.

"You are too young to recall the eighties, but it was a time of great revolutionary zeal and there was a variety of subversive movements working to overthrow the governments of Europe and North America. Like many of these groups, the Scorpions soon found a multitude of practical difficulties standing in the way of the successful implementation of their plans. Chief among these was money – or rather the lack of it. And so Arrowsmith set out to court and then to marry the American heiress Lillian Lauderdale."

At this juncture the familiar pattern of knocks sounded on the door. The Chief looked through the peephole and admitted Hampson-Smythe, who swept in, handed him a bottle of milk and a grocer's bag without a word, and went to hang up his hat and coat. As he passed MacIntyre's desk he glanced down at the broadsheet I had found on the floor, took it up and gave a muttered exclamation.

"What is it, Smythe?" asked the Chief.

"How typical of MacIntyre – discovering something important, only to forget all about it. I'm pretty sure that this advertises a meeting at which the Scorpions intend to recruit new members. If you will give me permission, I'd like to attend – in disguise, naturally."

The Chief shook his head. "That's very good of you, Smythe, but I think we can rely on MacIntyre to have the matter in hand. We don't want to go treading on his toes, after all."

"But sir, as I said before, we can't rely . . ."

"Now, Smythe, that's quite enough! I don't want to hear any more about it. MacIntyre is an agent of great resourcefulness and many years' experience – I'm sure he has already decided on the best course of action to take. Undoubtedly he will report back to us about the meeting in due course."

Hampson-Smythe turned away. "You may end up regretting it," he muttered, and slunk scowling to his desk.

I turned back to the Chief, hoping that he would finish telling me about the Scorpions, but he had already picked up the telephone and was speaking to the operator. And so, with considerable reluctance, I went back to my desk, my mind resounding with unanswered questions.

# Seven

By the time I got back home it was after six. I hung up my coat and went straight into the dining room, where the curtains had been drawn and a table lamp decorated with beads of jet cast a meagre light, intensifying the faded and dingy atmosphere that always pervaded Mrs Hodgkins' establishment, even in the height of summer. The landlady presided over a large silver soup tureen at the head of the table; on one side of her sat Mother, straight-backed and pale in her widow's black, and on the other were the tenants from the first floor, Mr and Mrs Krackewicz. The place at the far end usually occupied by Mr Smith was empty.

Sighing, Mrs Hodgkins stood up and reached for the lid of the tureen, but Mother stopped her, saying, "Now then, Minnie, don't let your soup get cold – Margaret will help herself, won't you, dear?" She turned her gaze towards the lurid depiction of the martyrdom of St Sebastian which hung on the opposite wall and added darkly, "It's pea and ham."

I ladled out a small serving of the congealed green liquid and sat down, but it was not many minutes before I laid down my spoon and pushed away my bowl. "Had enough already?" the landlady enquired acidly. "I hope you can bring yourself to eat the mutton stew I've been slaving over all afternoon." She got stiffly to her feet and began to clear away the soup bowls, grumbling to herself over mine, which was still half full.

Becky, a whey-faced girl who had been taken on from an orphanage after the last maid of all work had eloped with the coalman a few months before, appeared in the doorway. "Where's the stew, you silly creature?" demanded her mistress. The little maid cowered as if she expected to have her ears boxed then turned as if to run straight back to the kitchen. "Wait a minute! Whatever's the matter with you, Rebecca? Take these and bring the stew back; quick-sharp, my girl, or there'll be trouble!" Mrs Hodgkins shoved the tray of crockery into Becky's arms and the girl hurried away with a clattering of porcelain. "Not so fast, you little fool – you'll chip my china!" the landlady yelled after her.

"I don't know how you put up with it," said Mother. "*I* should have given her notice weeks ago."

"Well, Mrs Trant, one has to give these unfortunates a chance. Besides, it's hard to find any kind of slavey these days; one can't be too fussy."

"No, not at the wages you pay," I muttered under my breath, too quietly for Mrs Hodgkins to catch what I said, though Mother turned and gave me a reproving look.

At this juncture, I will digress a little by giving a more detailed description of Nikolas and Irma Krackewicz, for they are destined to figure quite prominently in this account. Nikolas was a theatrical scene painter, perhaps thirty years old, and wore his black hair in a tumbling mass of curls that hung down below his collar. Instead of a tie he sported a brightly coloured cravat, knotted at the throat. His beard and moustache were neatly clipped, revealing full red lips, and when he smiled he displayed a gleaming gold tooth. His brown eyes were deep-set and hooded, and could shine with warmth or dim to a brooding intensity, according to the rapid fluctuations of his mood. Irma, a Frenchwoman, was very slender and petite and moved with a dancer's grace. The bones of her face were angular and her mouth was wide and mobile, while her large dark eyes, fringed by thick lashes, sparkled with vivacity. She dressed elegantly, with an artist's eye for cut and colour and a fearless disregard of convention; even if I had had the courage to emulate her, as I longed to do, I could never have managed it. This evening she wore a dress with a square-cut bodice in wine-coloured velvet, a heavy jade necklace and earrings, and several flowers fashioned from narrow red ribbons, which were plaited into her hair. I was so busy admiring her *ensemble* that I failed to notice when Becky returned with the next course.

"The stew is getting cold, Margaret, and other people are waiting," snapped Mrs Hodgkins, brandishing the ladle. "Or perhaps you don't want any of this either?" I leant to one side and she banged the plate down in front of me, slopping gravy onto the tablecloth.

The meal continued in uneasy silence. Mr Krackewicz gobbled down the last of his stew before the rest of us were half finished and then proceeded to gaze about the room, occasionally darting glances at his wife's plate. His eyes came to rest on my face and he remarked, "You know, I meet with an old friend of yours earlier in this week, Miss Margaret."

"Really? Who?" I asked in surprise.

"It is a most remarkable coincidence – one would never have guessed it! It is your Mr Plimpson, of who we hear so much. I know a little his wife; she has worked in the halls for years, off and on. I have not seen her for some months, and when she introduces me to her husband you can knock me down with the feather, as you English say."

"I had no idea that Mrs Plimpson worked in the theatre," I said, though in fact it came as no surprise to me that she was an actress; I could easily picture her in some seedy music hall.

"Naturally, when I tell Plimpson that we board in the same lodging house, he is most interested – also very much wanting to be remembered to you with his best wishes. His wife is most angry at this, I observe – such a look she gives him when he asks where are you working!" Krackewicz gave a dry chuckle. "I cannot recall the name of the company. Is it Healy's?"

"No, I work at Stein and Flowers," I replied, somewhat flustered. "They're a very small firm – I'm sure he wouldn't have heard of them." I attempted to direct the conversation onto a less dangerous topic. "Did Mr Plimpson say whether business had improved since the firm moved to Deptford?"

"Oh, I think there are some changes. 'Got lots of pots on the boil, Krackewicz,' is what he says to me." Krackewicz rose to his feet. "Come now, Irma, we must go. Please excuse us, Mrs Hodgkins. Ladies, good evening."

"Good evening," I said. The landlady nodded ungraciously and took another mouthful of stew, while Mother maintained a haughty silence until they had left the room. We had embarked on our marmalade pudding – which, though a trifle heavy, was undoubtedly the most palatable part of the meal – before, once more contemplating St Sebastian's beatific surrender to his gory fate, she remarked, "I wonder where Mr Smith is today. This must be the third time that he's missed dinner this week."

"Well, as I said yesterday, so long as I get his rent on time – which I always do, every week like clockwork – then he can do as he chooses so far as mealtimes are concerned," said Mrs Hodgkins. "He pays for his dinner along with his board, so I'm not the one'll be out of pocket."

"Yes, but he's a very *odd* man, don't you think? So very close. I don't believe I've exchanged more than two words with him."

"Well, he does keep himself to himself – I can't disagree with you there. But to my mind that's a good thing. He keeps his room very nice – you'd hardly know anyone was living there. Never has anyone round to visit, never makes any noise. Very different from some others, I must say!" Mrs Hodgkins' protruding eyes rolled pointedly towards the door through which the Krackewiczs had gone out.

"Yes, I suppose he must lead rather a lonely sort of life," said Mother reflectively. "One would feel sorry for him if he weren't so peculiar and unappealing. Don't you think so, Margaret?"

I felt a shiver of unease, for I sometimes suspected that Mr Smith took more interest in my comings and goings than was strictly necessary. "I suppose so," I muttered, carefully folding my napkin.

Mrs Hodgkins rang the bell for Becky and began to clear the table. "What concerns me is what those foreigners are up to," she said, banging the salt cellar down onto the sideboard. "Where do they have to rush off to without finishing their dinner, I'd like to know. I shouldn't be surprised to discover that they were socialists, the pair of them!"

I stood up, my tolerance of the landlady's malicious insinuations having reached its limit. Mother looked at me sharply. "Where are you going, Margaret?"

"Oh, I thought I might take a stroll."

"You ought not to go out walking on your own at night. It isn't safe."

"It's still light outside, Mother – I don't intend to go very far."

"I don't know where you get these odd notions, I must say. But you've grown so pig-headed of late, there's no point in trying to change your mind. However, I do beg that you will have sufficient consideration for me to make sure that you get back before dark." She heaved a deep sigh then added, "And don't go anywhere lonely."

I hastened out of the room. Glancing back through the doorway I saw the landlady whispering animatedly and my mother shaking her head with a censorious expression. I turned away in exasperation and almost collided with a dishevelled-looking Becky, who gave a shy smile as she scurried past me into the dining room.

"Where on earth have you been, Rebecca?" Mrs Hodgkins' scolding tones drifted into the hallway as I moved over to the table from which we collected our letters. There was nothing on it except for a seaside postcard with a picture of a donkey chewing a straw hat, emblazoned with the slogan *Greetings from Bournemouth*. I examined the back and saw that it was addressed to Mr Smith and that the message was written in the same strange symbols that had been used on the other cards. It had been nearly six weeks since I had last come across one of these communications; I felt gratified that the mystery had been given a new lease of life, and acting on a sudden impulse I slipped the card into my pocket.

An instant later I heard the sound of a key in the lock and the front door swung open to reveal the looming bulk of Mr Smith. Guiltily, I shoved the card further down into my pocket and stepped towards the door. Smith gave me a brusque nod and made straight for the hall table. Just as I was about to close the door behind me, his deep, toneless voice called me back. "Miss Trant! Was there any post today?"

Quivering inwardly I shook my head, and without meeting his eye answered,

"I'm really not sure, Mr Smith. I've been out of the house all day. Were you expecting a letter?"

"Oh, just a picture postcard from a friend. Never mind – I won't trouble you any further. Good evening."

I shut the door and hurried down the path and out of the gate. A fine detective you would make, Margaret Trant, I told myself. There was no doubt that he would ask Mrs Hodgkins about the postcard, and if he was indeed up to anything untoward he would immediately be set on his guard.

I took the postcard out of my pocket and examined it again. Why shouldn't Mr Smith receive cards from a foreign friend? Was I being unreasonable to imagine that the messages were written for disreputable purposes, simply because they were set down in an unfamiliar script? Yet I could not dismiss the nagging misgiving that there was something rather strange about Smith. I decided that I would keep the card for a little longer, and see what Liebowitz could make of it.

# Eight

The next morning I slipped Smith's postcard into my portfolio, pondering how I was to explain the fact that it had come into my possession. I was loath to have Liebowitz think me dishonest, and I spent much of the tram journey refining a rather elaborate tale, which could well have furnished the plot of a shilling shocker. However, during the walk from the tram stop to the office, I remembered a remark that he had made in the course of our discussion about "Miss Wade", to the effect that the most successful deceptions are generally the simplest. I decided that rather than risk giving myself away by embroidering my story with too much detail, I would tell him that the card had arrived for a tenant who had left the house some time ago, that I had found the text intriguing and had kept it; nothing more. In the event, my concern was entirely unnecessary; Liebowitz merely glanced at the picture on the front and then placed the card among the piles of papers on his desk with a vague promise that he would try to decode the message when he had a moment.

His lack of interest, though disappointing, was perhaps to be expected. Only a few hours after Towler had alleged that the Order of the Scorpions was showing signs of becoming active again after having been dormant for nearly a decade, Bureau 8 had received the news that Marcus Stone, a close associate of Richard Arrowsmith and a leading light of the Scorpions during the syndicate's most notorious phase, had escaped from prison. Stone was a ruthless man and a dangerous one, and Bureau 8 had already begun working closely with the police to effect his recapture. The Chief, Liebowitz and Hampson-Smythe were making a thorough investigation of Bureau 8's archives in order to retrieve information that might be relevant to the search. Hunter had still not returned from pursuing the individual whom he had referred to as Henriquez, and MacIntyre was absent from the office on some mysterious errand of his own. I resigned myself to the fact that Smith's postcard would remain unread, at least until we had weathered the present storm. I even began to doubt whether there was anything in it at all and to wonder whether I had been foolish to give it to Liebowitz in the first place.

Two days passed by without incident and then, on a rainy Friday morning, we were shaken by a crisis. At about a quarter to ten I was startled by a sudden loud knocking. Everyone else was in the meeting room, so I abandoned the letter I was typing and went to peer through the peephole, where I saw a bedraggled-looking MacIntyre waiting to be let in. I unlocked the door and he staggered across the room and collapsed into the nearest chair.

"Where are the others, Miss Trant?" he gasped.

"They're all in the other room, sir. Don't worry; I'll fetch the Chief at once!"

I was filled with consternation at the sight of his livid, blood-streaked countenance, but I admit that I also felt a certain excited appreciation of his spectacular entrance. Pleased to be playing a part in an unfolding drama, I hurried straight into the meeting room without knocking. The three men looked up from the documents they were reading in surprise.

"Mr MacIntyre's here and is in rather a bad state," I blurted out.

Without a word, the Chief got up and strode past me into the office, with Liebowitz and Hampson-Smythe crowding behind him. I hesitated in the doorway for a moment before hastening over to offer my assistance.

"Sir, perhaps it would be a good idea if Mr MacIntyre were to sit in front of the kitchen stove for a while? Shall I put on some more coal?"

The Chief, who was peeling the shivering MacIntyre out of his coat, shot me an approving look. "Jolly good idea, Miss Trant. Just what I was about to suggest myself, in fact. Liebowitz, perhaps you could see to the stove? Let's get you out of these wet things, old chap."

The four men disappeared into the kitchen and I sat down at my desk and began to fidget disconsolately with some papers, longing to play the heroine at this moment of crisis. I knew something about first aid from nursing Mother for so long and from what I had read in those invaluable volumes of *The Home Surgeon* that always stood on the shelf at her bedside, but before I could lose myself in a fantasy of Florence Nightingale-like self-sacrifice Liebowitz poked his head round the door and called, "Miss Trant! Could you bring the spare set of clothes from the bottom drawer of Hunter's desk, if you please?"

I hurried to fetch the clothes and handed them to him, peering round him into the kitchen as I did so. I glimpsed MacIntyre sitting swaddled in towels in front of the stove and various sodden garments steaming on the dish rack, which had been suspended above the hearth, before Liebowitz turned away and the door clicked shut. I went back to my desk with a sigh.

A few minutes later the door opened again and the Chief strode into the office, accompanied by Liebowitz and Hampson-Smythe. "Right-o! Parley in the meeting room," he announced, and the three of them disappeared at once.

Feeling rather flat, I resumed my typing. I had just put the completed letter to one side when the kitchen door was edged open for a third time and MacIntyre appeared, dressed in Hunter's clothes, and looking somewhat sheepish. Hunter was a strapping young man, about six feet tall, but nevertheless his trousers were several inches too short for MacIntyre, and hung loosely on his wiry frame. Similarly, the pullover and shirt were much too baggy in the shoulders and torso but were very short in the arms, all of which combined to give him the sartorial elegance of a lanky schoolboy, and made him appear more gangling than ever. He limped self-consciously over to the mirror and gingerly examined the wound on his forehead before smoothing down his reddish hair and flicking some stray cake crumbs from his moustache with his handkerchief.

"Filthy weather, isn't it, Miss Trant?" he remarked, turning towards me. "Aren't you coming to the meeting? I should imagine you'll be needed."

"The Chief hasn't asked for me, Mr MacIntyre; I'm not supposed to go into the meeting room while you are in conference."

"Well, we'll see about that! Good gracious, it's absurd – we've waited long enough to be allocated a secretary, after all. Just give me a few moments to talk some sense into them."

He limped away before I could protest and a moment later the meeting room door slammed shut. I strained unavailingly to hear what was being said and then, overcome with restlessness, began to pace around the office, humming quietly to myself and stopping every now and then to rearrange some papers or to pick up a stray object from the floor.

Fortunately, I had not long to wait; after a few minutes the door opened and MacIntyre poked his head out. "Miss Trant, the Chief says won't you come in and to please bring a notebook and a pencil. You do take shorthand, don't you?"

I nodded nervously, and allowed him to usher me into the meeting room and into an empty chair next to Liebowitz. The Chief cleared his throat.

"Thank you for coming in, Miss Trant. MacIntyre is quite right – there is no good reason why we shouldn't make full use of your talents as an amanuensis. Now, will you be able to write down everything we say? Do let us know if you need anything to be repeated, won't you."

"I'm sure that won't be necessary, sir."

"Splendid! But as I say, don't worry if you do need to ask. And of course, you realise that anything you hear within these four walls must go no further."

"Yes, sir."

There was a pause as the Chief glanced round at our expectant faces before saying with a smile, "Once again, dear fellows, MacIntyre appears to have been one step ahead of us all." Hampson-Smythe raised his eyebrows at this and looked as if he would have liked to pass comment, but he said nothing. "He deduced some time ago that the Scorpions were likely to make an attempt to infiltrate some of the unions – working from the ground up so to speak – and when he came across the broadsheet that Smythe noticed on his desk . . . Well, perhaps I should surrender the floor to MacIntyre and he can tell you the rest himself. Are you ready, Miss Trant?"

I had been so overwhelmed to find myself present at a conference in the meeting room at last that I had momentarily forgotten that I was supposed to be making a transcript of the proceedings. Rather flustered, I nodded and took up my pen.

# *Nine*

## MacIntyre's Story

*M*acIntyre possessed a wealth of contacts in what he called the "underworld"; shabby careworn creatures who would flock to him with bizarre stories, obscure hints and other scraps of information, most of which turned out to be dross. He was sometimes tempted to sever contact with these sordid informants altogether, yet he never did so, for occasionally a hidden gem would gleam out inadvertently from amongst the welter of lies, boasts, half-truths and irrelevances, reminding him that these distasteful transactions were, after all, worthwhile. The broadsheet that advertised the meeting at the Rose and Crown, put into his hands by a retired sailor, a drunkard whose face was a seeping mass of sores, turned out to be one of these rare treasures, as we were to hear.

MacIntyre sallied forth on the appointed evening carrying a pewter tankard and dressed in his oldest suit, a flat cap and a curly wig that had proved invaluable during several previous investigations. It had been raining all day; the gutters streamed with filthy water and the few passers-by he encountered as he approached the Rose and Crown looked miserable and bedraggled. As he entered the inn, a fug of tobacco smoke, stale beer, damp clothing and sweat broke over him. The place was already crammed to the rafters with chattering hordes of working men, interspersed with a few disreputable-looking individuals, on their own for the most part, or in little clusters of two or three, among them a few blowsy, ill-kempt women.

He took off his cap and, glancing around at the claret-coloured walls and the sawdust-covered floorboards, shuffled over to the bar, which was presided over by a bear-like man in a shirt and waistcoat and a trim little woman, whom MacIntyre took to be his wife. He waited his turn, idly examining the gleaming glass fittings and the highly polished surface of the long wooden counter and eyeing his own unfamiliar reflection in the cloudy mirrors that lined the opposite wall. Having attracted the attention of the barman, he held out his tankard to be filled, paid his twopence and pushed his way through the heaving throng to an out of the way corner, from which he could keep an eye on things without attracting any particular notice.

Before long the speeches began. A series of crimson-faced men took it in turns to climb onto an old beer barrel that had been sawn in half, gesticulating with mounting fervour as they were carried along by the flow of their own rhetoric. MacIntyre smoked a great deal and applauded with as much enthusiasm as he could muster, though as the evening wore on and, once again, it began to seem increasingly unlikely that he would uncover a lead to set him on the trail of the Scorpions, his spirits started to flag.

Fortunately, before he reached the point of giving up hope altogether and going home, his interest was aroused by a small dark man with spectacles and a gammy leg, who was moving back and forth among the crowd. He did not appear to be acquainted with any of the men he spoke to, but he seemed to have an awful lot to say for himself and MacIntyre soon came to the conclusion that he would be worthy of further investigation.

Perhaps he noticed that MacIntyre was rather out of things, for as soon as the official speeches were finished and the listeners began to drift off the man limped over to the corner where he was sitting.

He held out his hand with a smile that revealed a gleaming gold tooth, and when he spoke his voice was inflected by the suggestion of a Spanish accent.

"Good evening. My name is Saunders. Whom do I have the pleasure of addressing?"

"I'm Eddie Symes," said MacIntyre, returning his handshake.

"Might I perhaps buy you a drink?"

I will not transcribe their whole conversation here, although I am gratified to report that Sir Isaac Pitman's celebrated system of phonetic shorthand did not let me down, and I was able to present the Chief, in due course, with a word-perfect rendering of MacIntyre's account. Suffice to say that his portrayal of an embittered, down-on-his-luck working man was so convincing that the meeting ended with the Spaniard's instructing him to turn up at a certain address at eight o'clock the following evening, when he would learn more about an organisation "dedicated to the cause of the working man", and a job they wanted him to do.

MacIntyre was loath to take the risk of being followed back to either the headquarters of Bureau 8 or to his own lodgings and so he spent the night in a dreary boarding house. He rose late, and having breakfasted on greasy kidneys, overcooked eggs and a pot of strong tea he set out for Whitechapel, intending to scout out the address that Saunders had given him while it was still light.

It was a miserable day; dank and cold, with a yellow fog that grew thicker as the hours wore on. Usually, MacIntyre's sense of direction was pretty reliable, but on this occasion, perhaps because of the fog, he found himself wandering through a maze of squalid yards, courts and alleys littered with filth. The place he was seeking turned out to be an ordinary, if rather shabby-looking house at the blind end of an alleyway. Cautiously, he walked down to get a closer look at it, but all the shutters were closed and there was nothing of any interest to see. He returned to the main thoroughfare and loitered there, hoping to spot something that would be to his advantage later on. A series of shifty-looking men hastened up and down the alley with their collars turned up and their hats pulled low over their faces. However, none of them approached the house that he was interested in: their comings and goings all centred upon the building next door. MacIntyre swiftly drew his own conclusions about what type of establishment it must be that was capable of attracting such a broad range of gentlemen callers, and decided that it might prove enlightening to pay a visit there himself.

He rapped smartly on the door and was admitted by a sorry-looking creature wearing a faded kimono and a few feathers in her hair. She leered at him and then, clasping her hands together, she bobbed her head in a clumsy bow.

"I am maiden Peach Blossom, servant to your whim and pleasure," she droned mechanically, lunging towards him.

MacIntyre drew away. "Good afternoon, miss," he said somewhat primly. "As a matter of fact I'm here on business."

"What are you after?" the girl demanded, folding her arms.

"Can you tell me anything about the people who live next door?"

"They owe you money or something?"

MacIntyre responded with a non-committal shrug.

"Well, I don't know nothing about them."

"Is there someone else I might speak to?"

The girl looked him up and down, scowled, and then said defiantly, "If you're a peeler, you won't find nothing wrong. Wait here while I fetch the missus."

She went upstairs, and a few minutes later a wasted old woman appeared at the top of the staircase and descended towards him with agonising slowness. As she came closer he perceived that her face was so heavily rouged and powdered that it had the texture of ancient plaster, and that she wore a butter-yellow wig which, like the rest of her, had seen better days. She batted her lashes and smiled, showing several rotten teeth, then held out her hand to be kissed, regarding him shrewdly all the while. He bent over it, holding his breath, for her glove was blotched with stains and smelt faintly rancid.

"How might I be of service, Mr . . . ?" she enquired in a reedy, unexpectedly genteel voice.

"Mr Lyons," replied MacIntyre, giving the first name that came into his head. "I am following an official line of inquiry with regard to the occupants of the premises adjacent to yours. I'd like to know whether you or any of the . . . young ladies who live here can give us some information."

She examined MacIntyre's face and the particulars of his dress with a cool curiosity that made his hackles rise. "Well, I must say, Mr Lyons, you don't look much like a policeman to me," she observed at last. "But don't worry, I shan't ask who it is you're working for – I always allow gentlemen to preserve their little secrets. As for your question, all I can tell you is that they are despicable wretches, filth of the worst kind. And please believe that I have had sufficient experience to know about such men and to recognise them when I see them." She fell silent and drew in a long breath through her nose.

"But surely, there must be something more . . ." MacIntyre suggested.

In answer, she raised a finger to her withered lips then turned and began to hobble back up the stairs, leaning heavily on the banister. MacIntyre watched her disappear into the shadowy recesses of the upper storey before making his way through the grimy hallway to the front door.

He was relieved to be in the open air again, despite the heavy smog that hung over the streets, and it suddenly occurred to him that he ought to plan an escape route, in case such a thing should become necessary later in the evening.

The light was beginning to fade, and as he paced through the warren of dingy lanes and alleyways he couldn't shrug off the sensation that he was being watched from doorways and street corners. By the time he had satisfied himself that he would know the best path to take if he found himself in a tight corner, dusk had fallen and the damp chill had begun to work its way into his bones. He saw an inn with a listing sign which read *The Man O' War* on the opposite side of the street and walked in. There were two men drinking in the dark, smoky interior and neither of them looked up as he approached the bar. He downed two Scotches and smoked a cigarette, breathing deeply and taking time to focus his mind on what lay ahead. Then, at five minutes to eight, he went into the lavatory to load his revolver before going outside.

Everything was eerily quiet as he approached the alleyway. A red lantern had been set above the front porch of the brothel and its rays gleamed in the puddles of slack water that pitted the surface of the lane. When he reached the neighbouring house he found the front door open and walked straight in, his right hand poised to whip out the revolver in his coat pocket. In the hallway stood a smallish man holding an oil lamp which cast his face into shadow, and it was not until he turned on his heel and limped away into the house that, with a jolt, MacIntyre recognised him as Saunders. He followed him into a room with sagging walls and dirty floorboards, through a low passageway and into a poky kitchen, which smelt of mouse droppings and mildew. Then they climbed a staircase and came out onto a narrow landing. Saunders glanced back to make sure that MacIntyre was still following, hobbled over to one of several closed doors and knocked three times.

A voice instructed them to enter and they walked into a bare room with cobwebs hanging from the ceiling. A tall man in a wide-brimmed hat stood with his back to them, looking out of the window.

"Pleased to meet you, Mr Symes," he said without turning round. "My colleague, Mr Saunders, informs me that you might be willing to do some work for us."

"Yes, I might be," MacIntyre replied, glancing round for Saunders, who stood blocking the doorway, next to a wiry rat of a fellow who was holding a gun.

"The work is not without risk. And we demand the utmost loyalty. *If* you get the job, then you must guarantee that you will carry out your orders in precisely the way that you are instructed, even if some difficulty or obstruction happens to arise. And you mustn't say a word about this matter to anyone. Understand?"

MacIntyre strained to see the tall man's face, but it was thrown into impenetrable shadow by the brim of his hat. "Yes, guv, I do. And if I don't do it, whatever it is, then I don't get paid?"

The short wiry man – the rat – stepped forward and swept away MacIntyre's cap, crushing it in hands which MacIntyre now saw were monstrously outsized: the powerful, brutish hands of a giant. "If you don't do it, you'll answer to me," he said in an absurdly deep voice.

"And what will you do, pal?" MacIntyre growled.

The rat dropped the cap on the floor and ground it under his heel, staring at him impassively from under heavy brows.

"Thank you, Polti, that will do for now," said his chief and at once the little man stooped to pick up the cap, dusted it off with his huge paw and handed it back to MacIntyre, before resuming his position by the door. "Let me assure you, Mr Symes," continued the tall man, "we will keep things civilised so long as you don't cause any difficulties for our organisation. Is that clear?"

MacIntyre sighed. "How much do I get paid?"

"Twenty guineas."

MacIntyre tried not to look taken aback.

"I see you cannot quite believe your good fortune,' the tall man remarked drily. "I had better tell you what you need to do in order to earn this generous sum. I have some packages that I'd like you to deliver. There will be three of them, one larger than the others and all of them going to the same destination. I should warn you that the recipient is very particular and it is essential that the goods arrive in pristine condition. If we were to receive a complaint of any kind, you would not be paid. They must be picked up tomorrow morning at seven thirty precisely from the left luggage office at Victoria station. Further instructions, together with the delivery address, are attached to the largest parcel. Here's the ticket – put it somewhere safe, and whatever you do don't lose it."

He held out a small piece of red card with a number printed on it. MacIntyre took it and tucked it into his wallet, ducking his head in another fruitless attempt to glimpse the shadowy face.

"Another thing, Symes. Make sure that you work on your own

– don't bring anyone else in on this. We will express our displeasure very strongly if you disobey us in that regard."

"So who is this 'we', then? Who will I be working for?"

"I'm afraid that is something I am unable to divulge."

There was a brief silence, during which MacIntyre pretended to weigh up the proposal that had been laid before him. Then he shrugged and said, "All right, I suppose I'll do the job anyway. When do I get the money?"

"Half the amount will be given to you now; you'll get the rest once you've completed the task successfully. And if you do get caught, make sure you don't blab to the police, or to anyone else for that matter. You wouldn't be believed in any case, and I can assure you that you'd end up regretting it. Polti is a cruel and inventive man and he cannot bear sneaks. Here's your money." He took an envelope out of his pocket. "Now, go."

He turned back to the window. Polti seized MacIntyre's arm and shouldered him roughly out of the house. On the threshold, he set his big square hand in the small of MacIntyre's back and gave him a shove that sent him sprawling down the front steps.

"You needn't trouble coming back," he growled. "We're clearing out tonight, for good."

The door slammed behind him and MacIntyre got to his feet, brushing the filth from his trousers and thanking his lucky stars that he hadn't broken his neck.

He glanced at his watch and saw that it was nearly a quarter to nine. The day had been a tiring one and he felt ready for bed. The prospect of a long walk home in the fog was not appealing, and he had reluctantly made up his mind to spend another night at a boarding house when he recalled that he was quite close to the residence of one of Bureau 8's most reliable, respectable and long-standing informants. He thought it unlikely that Mrs A would object to putting him up for the night, and set off in the direction of the street where she lived.

The sulphurous pall of fog stung his eyes, and with every breath the damp soot of it crept deeper into his lungs. The blankness wrapped itself around him so that he seemed to be surrounded by the muffled echo of his own steps as he moved along, but he wasn't alone; he heard mutterings and coughs and bleak sighs, with no real sense of where they came from. Most of the houses he passed were dark, though here and there a light still shone faintly. He heard a door open and shut again a few feet away and waited, expecting to see a figure emerging through the darkness, but the street remained empty.

Gradually, he became aware of footfalls other than his own keeping pace with him, and he realised that he was being followed. He thought it likely to be Polti or one of his associates and, pretending not to notice anything out of the ordinary, he plodded along with his hands in his pockets, whistling through his teeth. After a minute or two, he stopped to light a cigarette. While he was searching for some matches he heard a scuffling behind him, and before he could get hold of his revolver someone grabbed him by the neck. He struggled, but found that he was held in an iron grip. A hand in a leather glove was clamped over his mouth, someone else tied his wrists together with a cord and rifled through his pockets, and then he was pushed to the ground. He fell awkwardly, banging his head on the cobbles, and before he could get a look at his attackers they had disappeared into the fog.

He lay stunned for a few minutes before he managed to drag himself into a sitting position. His head throbbed with a searing pain and he felt sick and dizzy; then, suddenly, he vomited. After that he felt better, but when he tried to stand up he found he couldn't move an inch without untying the cord around his wrists. That wasn't an easy matter, for it had been bound so tightly that it bit into his flesh. Several times, he heard the footsteps of passers-by; once he looked up and saw a hazy figure moving through the fog only a few feet away, but he didn't call out, for fear he might attract trouble that he was in no state to deal with.

At last he succeeded in freeing himself and staggered to his feet. With a sinking heart, he went through his pockets and discovered that his revolver, his second-best watch, his wallet and his ancient cigarette case were all gone. He scrabbled around on the cobbles in case his attackers had left anything behind, but the only thing he found was his cigarette case.

Mrs A, a stout woman with a worn, kindly-looking face, answered the door in her nightcap and curlers. She blinked at MacIntyre sleepily, as if she scarcely recognised him, but as soon as she saw that he was hurt her eyes widened and she took him into the kitchen. She sat him down on a wooden chair and set about cleaning his head with pursed lips, for she was a woman of admirable discretion and understood that this was not a moment for chatter or idle questions. Only after she had finished did she say, "And now, Mr Rushforth, I'll just put on a bandage and we'll be done."

"No thanks, Mrs A – that would make me far too conspicuous."

"Very well, sir, if that's what you wish. You can sleep in my son's room; it's on the left, at the top of the stairs. He's away at sea at present."

"Bless you, my dear. Might I beg one more favour of you?"

"Of course, Mr Rushforth. What is it?"

"Could you be sure to wake me up at six o'clock? It's most important that I set off in good time."

Mrs A nodded. "I will, sir – I'm always up before then. I'll be off to bed now. I'll leave you the candle to go up with. Good night."

Left alone, MacIntyre sat back for a smoke and all of a sudden his arms and legs grew as heavy as lead. He stubbed out the half-smoked cigarette and dragged himself up to the spare bedroom, where he lay down on the bed with his boots on and passed out before he could rouse himself sufficiently to undress.

He woke to the sound of rain against the window and for a few moments he lay still, wondering where he was and why his head ached so badly. Then there was a knock at the door and he heard Mrs A calling, "Mr Rushforth, are you awake?" He croaked faintly in reply and managed to sit up just as she came into the room.

"I've been trying to wake you for ever such a long time," she said. "It's nearly quarter past six."

Then she caught sight of his face and gave a gasp of consternation. "You're never planning to go out with a head like that!"

"Morning, Mrs A," MacIntyre croaked. "Don't worry. I'll be quite all right if you would be kind enough to make me a strong cup of tea, with a splash of Scotch, if you've got it, and plenty of sugar."

She regarded him doubtfully for a moment, then, heaving a sigh, hurried off to the kitchen. MacIntyre got up to wash his face. When he looked in the mirror he saw that the bruise on his forehead had deepened in hue to a florid purple and a nasty bulge had appeared above his left eye. He tried to cover the marks with his wig, but he looked ridiculous, like a prize fighter wearing an ill-fitting toupee, and he combed the locks of hair back again. Having tidied himself up as best he could, he hobbled downstairs to the kitchen.

After a few sips of the sweet tea and whisky, MacIntyre's head began to clear. With a shock, he remembered the ticket for the left luggage office and fetched his overcoat. He searched through the pockets with a mounting sense of unease, before it dawned on him that the ticket had been inside his stolen wallet.

"Whatever's the matter, Mr Rushforth?" asked Mrs A. "You look as if you've seen a ghost!"

"Oh, it's only a lost piece of paper – I expect I shall get over it," said MacIntyre, pulling himself together. "Actually, I ought to be going now, or else I'm going to miss a most important appointment. Thank you, dear woman – I'm more grateful to you than I can possibly say." There was an awkward pause, and then he added, "I'm terribly sorry to ask, but could I trouble you for five shillings, for a cab?"

At precisely half past seven by the clock, he approached the left luggage office at Victoria station. He told the attendant that he'd had his pocket picked and had lost the ticket, and described the packages he was to collect in as much detail as he could, insisting that if he didn't get back to his employer with them right away he would be dismissed from his post.

"Please, guvnor. I've the wife and two nippers at home and another one on the way. I've only been in the job a week and I've been laid off three times in the past year already, through no fault of my own. The landlord's getting nasty – he came in the other day when I was at work and threatened my missus. We'll be out on the street if I can't pay the rent again this month. Are you going to snatch the very bread from our mouths for the sake of a scrap of cardboard?"

The attendant listened to MacIntyre's story with a sceptical expression. When he had heard him out, he drew himself up self-righteously and said, "Sorry, mister, it's more than my job's worth. Rules is rules – no ticket, no parcels."

MacIntyre tried to argue, but a queue had formed behind him and people were beginning to get impatient. Threatening the fellow would only attract unwanted attention, and besides, the last thing he wished to do was to get himself arrested for causing an affray.

"Stuff your tickets, then!" he snarled, and walked off.

"You watch your manners, my man, or I'll have you took up on a charge!" the indignant official yelled after him.

MacIntyre did not look round, though he was aware that several necks were being craned to follow his retreat. After half an hour, when there was still no sign of the Scorpions' man, he made up his mind to return to HQ.

# Ten

"Miss Trant, did you manage to record all the details of MacIntyre's account?"

"Yes, sir." I glanced at MacIntyre, who gave me a slow wink that made me look hurriedly back down at my notes.

"There was certainly plenty of interminable detail," Hampson-Smythe commented with a sneer. "Anyone would think you were writing a novel, not filing a report."

"Dear me, the young are so impatient nowadays, don't you find?" MacIntyre remarked mildly, writing a few words in his notebook and underlining them before leaning back in his chair with his eyes closed. Then, without opening his eyes, he added, "We mustn't forget to send something to Mrs A – I don't know what I should have done without her."

The Chief smiled. "Dear old Mrs A – what a thoroughly good sort. She's been helping us for years and she still picks up more useful titbits than all our other informants put together. You're absolutely right, old chap – this time we must make sure she gets a really decent reward for her pains. Please make a note of that, Miss Trant."

Suddenly Liebowitz, who for some time had been staring at the wall with a glazed expression, leapt to his feet and rushed out into the office, leaving the rest of us looking after him in puzzlement. A few moments later he returned, clutching a large envelope. He sat down, took out some papers from inside it and read through them avidly. Then he looked up with a peculiar expression on his pallid face.

"This is most remarkable!" he declared. "MacIntyre, have you read the latest report from head office?"

MacIntyre shook his head. "No, old man. I've been rather busy."

"It might surprise you, then, to hear that your description of Saunders – small, dark, crooked nose, gold tooth, mole on left cheek – is almost identical to the one head office has issued of Henriquez. The only element that differs slightly is the gammy leg – but then he might easily have sustained an injury in the past few days."

"Bravo, Liebowitz!" said the Chief.

"Henriquez?" asked MacIntyre, looking momentarily bewildered.

"Yes – the man that Hunter hoped to befriend in order to establish his alias."

An alias! Here at last was another clue as to the precise nature of Hunter's mission, about which I had been puzzling ever since his departure. No wonder the other men had been so eager to wish him well as he went off: he had been about to venture right into the lion's den; to brave mortal peril in order to infiltrate the Scorpions and gain their trust!

The Chief and MacIntyre exchanged a troubled glance.

"Hold on a minute!" exclaimed the Chief. "Why on earth has Hunter gone all the way to Berlin to track down Henriquez if he's here in London? And how can he possibly have made contact with him? I presume that's what we were meant to infer from that last communication of his. What was it that it said?"

Liebowitz flicked through the papers in front of him and extracted a telegram. "Bagged the duck stop return delayed stop all well," he read, frowning.

"Well, I suppose it's possible that there could be two Scorpions who look very much alike," said MacIntyre doubtfully. "Or head office could have misidentified Saunders as Henriquez – it wouldn't be the first time they've made a mistake of that kind. Or, possibly, dear old Hunter might have bagged another duck altogether!"

"I do wish you fellows would remember that I have spent so many hours generating a code that is almost impossible to break precisely to discourage you from reverting to the sort of cryptic message that can generate just this kind of problematic ambiguity," Liebowitz said.

"Oh, but where's the romance in being a spy if one isn't allowed to be mysterious?" enquired MacIntyre, raising an eyebrow at me.

"It *is* rather odd," mused the Chief. "I'd say it looks very likely that it was Henriquez who recruited you, MacIntyre; in which case, we must hope for an explanation from Hunter soon. Otherwise . . ." His voice tailed off.

I pictured Hunter wandering through the shadowy streets of a foreign city, surrounded by strange sights and sounds and exotic smells. I tried to imagine what it must be like to pretend to be someone else and to know that the smallest slip might plunge you into deadly danger . . .

"Miss Trant!"

Startled, I looked up at the Chief, whose face wore an expression of concern.

"Are you feeling unwell? I'm sorry – this room can get terribly stuffy at times."

"No sir, really, I'm quite all right," I replied, turning red with embarrassment.

"Do you think it was Polti and Henriquez who robbed you?" Liebowitz asked MacIntyre.

"It's impossible to say for sure, but I got the impression that they were much bigger men than those two. Besides, I should be surprised if Saunders – Henriquez –was capable of running off so fast. Whoever they were, they weren't a pair of common or garden rogues; they knew their business too well for that."

At this juncture the telephone on the Chief's desk shrilled discordantly and he went out to answer it. MacIntyre helped himself to some brandy and we sat in silence, listening to the Chief, whose voice carried clearly from the office.

"Yes, speaking . . . I see . . . Thank you. Please send us the details as soon as you can. Yes I will, sir."

He came back into the room and regarded us gravely. "There's been an explosion at Victoria station, near the left luggage office. The luggage attendant and a railway porter were killed and several members of the public were injured and taken to hospital. One or two bystanders received medical aid at the scene. It's a fearful mess – the police have been instructed to scour the area for every available scrap of evidence. Head office will send us a more detailed report later on."

I fought down a convulsive tightening in my throat and my pen dropped with a clack onto the table.

"I knew it!" muttered Hampson-Smythe through gritted teeth.

"I should have shot those swine while I had the chance!" cried MacIntyre, lurching to his feet. "It never occurred to me that one of those packages might contain dynamite. I'll never forgive myself! And the worst of it is, we must wait for another lead before we can find them – you may be sure they won't go back to that house again."

The Chief placed a steadying hand on MacIntyre's arm. "Calm down, old chap. It's absurd for you to blame yourself. My advice is to wait quietly until we get the full report and then we'll decide what needs to be done." Ashen-faced, MacIntyre sank down into his chair.

"So the Scorpions really are on the move at last," said Liebowitz, looking thoughtful.

"Yes," put in Hampson-Smythe, glaring at MacIntyre. "We need to buck up our ideas and catch them before they act again, or who knows what outrage they will commit next?"

# Eleven

The next day the newspapers were filled with speculations as to the identity of the person who had planted the device at Victoria station and the aims of the organisation of which he had been an agent. Some said he was a Fenian, others claimed that he must be an anarchist, while one lone voice insisted that he was obviously a Russian revolutionary, though what motive such a person might have for planting dynamite in an English railway station was not satisfactorily explained. There were conflicting stories from a number of onlookers who had been present at the scene of the catastrophe, and the police and various high-ranking officials in the railway company had also been prevailed upon to comment. Fortunately, MacIntyre's argument with the luggage attendant was not mentioned in any of the reports, though a violent altercation between the same official and another member of the public variously described as "swarthy", "of a Mediterranean complexion" and "Italian" was generally considered to be significant.

At the headquarters of Bureau 8 everything was quiet save for the rattling of my typewriter and the sound of rain pattering on the roof and splashing down onto the cobbles below. The Chief had told us that no action could be taken until he had received further information from head office and we were all impatiently awaiting its arrival. Hampson-Smythe was looking through old newspaper clippings for references to individuals who were suspected of involvement with the Scorpions and Liebowitz was scouring the pages of Bradshaw, investigating the range of places from which the perpetrators of the outrage might have arrived by train. Meanwhile, the Chief sat chewing the end of his fountain pen, as was his habit when engaged in deep reflection. MacIntyre, looking very pale and with a bandaged head, slouched staring into space and I myself was painstakingly typing up the transcript of the account of his exploits that he had given us on the previous day.

Abruptly, MacIntyre got up, stalked over to the Chief and muttered something in his ear. The Chief stood up at once and they both crossed to the meeting room. MacIntyre paused in the doorway and turned to me.

"I say, Miss Trant, could you brew us a nice pot of tea? And I noticed that there were still one or two biscuits in the tin; perhaps you could put those on a plate for us? I rather feel as if I could do with some feeding up."

Five minutes later, armed with the tea and biscuits, I knocked on the door of the meeting room and walked in. Huddled together in a cloud of tobacco smoke, the two men continued talking to one another as if I weren't there.

". . . I still don't understand why he didn't try to warn us. Surely, if he really had managed to gain entry to the inner circle then he'd have heard about the dynamite."

"Come along, MacIntyre – I know you're upset, but I hardly think you're being fair. I understand that all these coincidences have made you suspicious, but one ought to have a little more faith in one's colleagues. I refuse to entertain the possibility that Hunter has betrayed us on such flimsy evidence!"

Dumbfounded, I drew a sharp intake of breath.

"Good gracious – Miss Trant!" exclaimed the Chief.

"Yes, sir?" I said, setting the tray on the table.

"Thank you for the tea. I'm sorry – you weren't meant to hear any of that. Please forget that you did."

"Yes. When one is upset, one sometimes says things one doesn't mean. You must take my remarks with a pinch of salt," MacIntyre added.

"Of course," I replied, meeting his gaze.

I returned to my typing somewhat half-heartedly. The discovery that Hunter had fallen under suspicion filled me with dismay, for in my naivety I had assumed that the ties of trust and loyalty that bound together the agents of Bureau 8 were unbreakable and absolute. I was not especially concerned by the possibility of Hunter's being disloyal, for instinctively I felt sure that he would soon be vindicated; it was simply that I could not bear the thought that MacIntyre was capable of distrusting him.

Suddenly, the shop bell jangled and everyone sat up, bristling with alertness.

"That might be the boy with the telegram, Miss Trant. Please be so kind as to go down and see," said the Chief, who had emerged from the meeting room with MacIntyre. I might have imagined it, but I seemed to detect an unaccustomed coolness in his manner towards me, as if he were still nettled by the fact that I had overheard something that was not my concern. With burning cheeks, I put on my apron and went downstairs. It was indeed the telegraph boy who awaited me, and within a very short time I was handing the envelope he had brought to the Chief, who read the message it contained with a thoughtful frown. Having got to the end, he looked through it a second time, then laid it on the desk.

"Well, chaps, we've got our instructions. They want one of us – they suggest me, in actual fact – to go to Charing Cross Hospital. I'm to interview the Italian who tried to push in at the front of the queue for the left luggage office after MacIntyre had left. Several witnesses have reported that he was rather desperate to pick up some parcels and that he turned quite nasty when the attendant insisted that he wait his turn. He was still there at the time of the explosion, though I'm not sure how badly he was hurt. Miss Trant, I propose to take you with me as my amanuensis, so long as you don't object."

I stared at him in astonishment and relief: my fears had been groundless. The Chief still considered me to be trustworthy after all.

"It will be quite all right, you know – you won't be in danger of any kind. You have a coat with you, of course, and an umbrella?" I nodded. "Jolly good. The rain seems to have let up a bit and it's not far, so there's no reason why we shouldn't walk – I don't know about you, but I could certainly do with a spot of fresh air. You'll need a pen and a notebook, nothing more."

I buttoned up my jacket, thrilling with excitement at the thought that I was about to meet a real criminal, a ruthless man of violence. I pictured a villain with a granite jaw, a cruel mouth and scornful eyes; an individual not unlike Mr Smith, in fact.

"Are you ready, Miss Trant?" asked the Chief, bringing me down to earth with a bump.

"Good luck!" said MacIntyre, handing me my gloves. His blue eyes creased up at the corners as he smiled. "I must say, I do envy you rather. I should like to be going to the hospital myself, but of course the fellow might recognise me and then we'd really be in a scrape."

"Thank you, Mr MacIntyre," I replied, reddening.

"Not 'Mr.' I wish you'd call me MacIntyre like everyone else."

"Yes, of course," I muttered, looking at the floor. "I'll try to remember."

"Splendid!"

Upon our arrival at the hospital the Chief and I were given into the charge of a fair-haired nurse with a long nose and pursed lips, who left us waiting in the entrance hall while she went off to consult her superiors. Though it was not the visiting hour, all sorts of people were passing through: doctors and nurses; patients who had just been discharged or were hoping to be admitted, and visitors seeking the Enquiries desk.

"See anyone suspicious?" asked the Chief. I shook my head. "No, nor do I, but that's not to say there isn't anyone here who's up to no good. The Scorpions will want to get hold of the man before he gives anything away; I'd wager a good deal that they've got scouts on the lookout for our arrival."

I scanned the hall eagerly and met the eye of a youth in a Norfolk jacket, who blushed and turned away. Immediately, he was pounced upon by a large woman with an elaborate hat, who began smoothing down his hair and straightening his collar, scolding him roundly as she did so.

I looked back at the Chief as he resumed, "It is possible that the fellow may refuse to speak to us, at least to begin with; it would be very useful, Miss Trant, if you could record any physical reactions that he manifests during my interrogation – eye movements, twitches, shifting about in the bed – that type of thing. Such details can provide clues for the well-trained observer and I want to make sure the other chaps receive an absolutely full account of what goes on."

The disdainful-looking nurse returned and invited us to follow her with an unsmiling jerk of the head. She led us up several flights of stairs and down a long, echoing corridor which smelt strongly of carbolic, until we came to a halt outside a door guarded by two policemen. She rapped on it three times; after a brief delay the door opened to admit her and then slammed shut again. A few moments later, she reappeared and snapped, "You may go in," before padding off in the direction from which we had just come.

We entered a spacious room, in the middle of which was a bed, flanked on either side by a uniformed constable. The prisoner lay with his eyes shut, breathing quietly, and did not stir when we entered. Before we could approach him, a thin, white-coated man with a bald head and wire-rimmed spectacles came towards us.

"I'm White," he announced.

"Mr Watson," replied the Chief, "and this is my assistant, Miss Stiles."

I shook the doctor's bony hand, trying not to look taken aback at having been unexpectedly awarded a second *alter ego*.

"And how is the patient?" enquired the Chief.

"Oh, he's a lucky man. He's suffering from a number of lacerations due to flying glass, and a broken collar bone, but on the whole he escaped very lightly. As you can see, he's sleeping at present."

"Has he said anything?"

"Nothing of significance; we thought we'd leave that side of things to you."

"Yes, of course. Doctor, I hope you won't object if I ask you to leave us straight away? Time is pressing, you know, and as you can imagine this affair is highly confidential."

"Not at all; of course, I understand completely. I won't be far away if you need me. Good luck!" He disappeared through a door directly opposite the one by which we had entered.

The Chief turned towards the impassive policemen. "Could you leave us too, please?" Immediately, as if by clockwork, they both clumped out of the other door.

As soon as we were alone, we drew closer to the bed. To my surprise, the unconscious man was a youth, who could have been little more than twenty years old. He had a craggy, olive-complexioned face, scored with a multitude of crimson gashes, dark tightly curled hair and thick black brows, which were drawn in towards the bridge of his nose, as if he were frowning in his sleep.

"Hope he speaks passable English," commented the Chief. "My Italian is somewhat rusty. Never mind – we must do our best. Take a seat and make yourself as comfortable as you can, Miss Trant."

Obediently, I removed my coat and perched on a hard wooden chair near the foot of the bed, noticing as I did so that the patient's ankle was cuffed to the iron bedpost. The Chief drew up another chair diagonally across from me, draped his overcoat over the back and stood behind it. He shot me an enquiring glance and seeing that I was already hunched forward over my notebook, my pen poised above the open page, he addressed the prostrate figure on the bed with the cheerful exhortation, "Time to wake up, young man!"

The prisoner gave a groan, but did not open his eyes.

"I know you can hear me, my boy. Everything will be much simpler if you just wake up and talk to us."

The youth made no response.

"Now, now. There's no point in shamming; you'll have to come round sooner or later. Best get it over with, I should think. And besides, you're in a great deal of trouble. We could help you: we're prepared to offer very good terms in return for your information."

The prisoner still lay motionless, but I sensed that he was listening closely to every word that the Chief said.

"Why not give yourself a chance? Your colleagues won't be of much use to you now that you've been caught. You know too much and I'm sure you don't need me to tell you that they won't want to run the risk of your blabbing to the authorities. All you need to do is to give us the information we want and we can protect you, give you a new identity – help you to start a new life." He paused and then added reflectively, "Although I suppose if you were to keep quiet and were sentenced to a good long spell in gaol – which is almost certain to be the case given the nature of your offence, by the way – you *might* be safe for a time."

The youth's eyelids flicked open. He groaned again and shifted so that his head was higher up on the pillow, defiantly fixing each of us in turn with eyes of a faded Sicilian blue.

"Look, guvnor, I ain't interested, right? Now shove off and take your missus with you."

"Very well," said the Chief, standing up and starting to pull on his overcoat. "If that's the way you want to play it. Before we leave, though, you must let me give you some news of an old friend of yours – George Fletcher."

The prisoner's pale eyes focused on him with an expression of alert interest, though he remained silent.

"Two months ago a corpse was discovered in a derelict warehouse near the West India docks. I'm sorry to tell you that it was your pal George."

"Don't talk rot! George isn't dead – 'e's in Canada."

"Oh, that's what you were told, is it? Well, you can comfort yourself with that little fairy story if you like, but if I were you, I'd be very careful about believing anything those associates of yours have said to you. You know, I saw a couple of suspicious-looking fellows loitering around as we came in. I shouldn't be at all surprised if they were looking for you. Mind you, I suppose they might not necessarily want to do you any harm; for all I know, they might be here to provide you with a pension, or to send you over to Canada to join your friend!"

There was a long pause. I looked across at the Chief. He had replaced his coat on the chair-back and sat calmly watching the figure in the bed.

At last the youth demanded, "'ow do I know you're 'oo you say? I've never met you before. You must consider me a softish sort of flat if you think I'm going to trust you!"

The Chief flashed him a beatific smile. "Not at all; your feelings are quite understandable. But you're a closely guarded secret, my man, and much sought after – not least by the gentlemen of the press. Do you really think the hospital authorities would have allowed just anyone to wander into your room? Besides, I don't think you've got much choice about confiding in me, do you? You can start by giving us your name – I don't expect it to be genuine, but a fellow ought to have a handle of some sort."

"You can call me Murphy," the youth replied sulkily.

"Very well then, Murphy – let's go straight to the heart of the matter. What was the real target of that infernal machine?"

"What makes you think they told me that?"

"Come now. We both know you were posted at the railway station to make sure the device got to the right place. We also know that there was another chap who tried to pick up the parcel before you – it's quite possible that he was in the dark about it all, but not you . . . Oh, and I should warn you that it's not worth your while trying to pull the wool over our eyes. If you weren't straight with us, we'd find out before long; all the conditions of our agreement would be rendered null and void and you'd be left to the tender mercies of your fellow Scorpions."

The young man gave a self-pitying sigh. "Very well, I'll tell you what I can – though I think it's pretty low to come at a fellow when 'e's in pain and 'asn't the strength to fight back. My orders was to make sure the parcel was delivered to an address in Cadogan Place by ten o'clock."

"I see," remarked the Chief matter-of-factly. "Which number?"

"'undred and four."

"You're sure that's correct?"

The youth rolled his eyes.

"I suppose something must have gone wrong with the device for it to have gone off so early?"

The prisoner attempted to shrug and winced with a yelp of pain.

"Now, I'd like you to tell me how those instructions were passed to you, and by whom."

"They was sent by 'and – just some kid keen to earn a few shillings running an errand. 'e wouldn't 'ave known nuffing about it."

"So you were asked to wait near the left luggage office at Victoria station to make sure the parcel was picked up, and to deliver it yourself if anything happened to go wrong, is that it?"

"Yes. I s'pose they was just taking care in case the bloke what they'd taken on to do it didn't show, or else weren't up to the job; which it turned out 'e weren't."

"And what was the name of the person who was to be the unfortunate target of this device?"

"I weren't told."

"Hmm. Well, I suppose I'll have to take your word for that. Was this outrage to be the start of an extended dynamite campaign?"

"Search me, guv; I don't know about that kind of stuff."

"Well then, you can tell us what you do know about the Scorpions. For example, what is the structure of the organisation – its chain of command?"

Murphy scowled.

"Or if you prefer, you can begin by giving us the names of some of the members."

"Look 'ere – I never said I was party to nuffing like that."

The Chief shot him a look of stern reproach. "You underestimate me, Mr Murphy; I'm quite well aware that you know more than you're letting on, and to be frank, I find your feeble attempts at deception rather tiresome. Now, who are the top dogs in this gang of yours?"

The prisoner hesitated before confiding in an undertone, "Well, they ain't 'oo you'd expect – though I've only 'eard rumours, mind. They don't let on much to fellers as low down in the ranks as me. There's rich and powerful men controlling the Scorpions. There's several in the govinment, I reckon, and another what's in charge of a bank. But they'll see us working chaps right when the day comes – I know that for a fact, else I shouldn't 'ave worked for them in the first place."

"You're entitled to believe what you like, of course," said the Chief with grave politeness, "but if I were you I should be a little suspicious of the fact that these 'rich and powerful men' were telling me, an ordinary fellow from the East End, exactly what I wanted to hear. However, we won't dwell on that point for the time being. I've heard that the Scorpions have lately begun to attract an international membership. Have you encountered many foreigners in your dealings with the organisation?"

"I've met one or two – wops mostly, and a kraut. The only one I 'ad anything to do with was a little feller from Milan, but neither of us said much about 'ow we come to be there." The youth closed his eyes with a weary sigh.

"Ever heard anything about a man called Stone?"

"No. Nuffing."

"I'm curious to know: why would you risk so much to help an organisation of which you know so little?"

"They pay well, that's one thing, and though you might not think it, they're like me; they want a more just society, a new order where the nobs'll get what they deserve. Bloated scum! Parasites! It's them what keeps the working man down!"

Suddenly the door through which Dr White had gone out opened and he came back into the room, saying briskly, "I'm awfully sorry, Mr Watson, but I'm afraid I'm going to have to ask you to leave now; it's time for the patient to have his medicine."

"That won't take long, will it?" asked the Chief. "We can wait outside."

"I'm afraid it will make him very drowsy. If you haven't finished questioning him, I should say the best thing you can do is to come back later on this evening or tomorrow."

"Very well, we'll be back later. Do please ensure that you exercise the utmost caution in selecting the nurses to attend to this man, won't you?"

"Of course," said the doctor with a queer little smile. "You may rest assured that this fellow is absolutely safe in our hands."

The Chief turned to address the prisoner. "Right-o then, Murphy, we'll leave you for the time being, but we'll be back soon. If I were you I should rack my brains about what else I knew – I'm sure there's plenty more you can tell us. Remember, your chance of clearing out depends upon it!" He picked up his coat and stood by the door while I gathered my things.

As we emerged from the room, two of the four policemen who were waiting outside surged past us and the door clicked shut behind them. In silence, we began to retrace our steps along the corridor. About halfway down, a door was flung open to reveal the nurse who had been our guide. When she set eyes on us, a startled expression flickered across her face and she made a swift motion with her hand, as if to conceal something in her palm. "Good day," said the Chief with a little nod. She shot him a withering glance, locked the door behind her and strode off towards Murphy's room.

"Rather an unpleasant woman, wouldn't you agree, Miss Trant? Not at all like the usual run of her profession. I should say that something was giving her a guilty conscience. Perhaps she's been smuggling laudanum out of the medicine store. Oh, well, White seems to know what he's doing; I dare say he'll keep an eye on her." The Chief gave a little shrug of dismissal, and added, "I thought I'd look in on my old friend Henley before we leave, if you don't mind. We were at school together. He's one of the consultants here – specialises in ailments of the stomach. By the by, just in case it should arise, he's under the impression that I'm a plainclothes detective. It probably won't be mentioned – he knows my work is sensitive and I don't like discussing it – but it's always just as well to have one's story prepared. "

We made our way to the end of the corridor and down several flights of stairs before we reached the ward where Dr Henley had his office. He was a jovial-looking man, with a balding head fringed by wisps of sandy hair, long side-whiskers, ruddy cheeks and a stout figure. He seized his friend by the hand and pumped it up and down delightedly. "Rivers! How splendid to see you!"

A pained expression flitted across the Chief's face. "Please, Henley, do try to remember – the name is Watson."

Henley slapped a hand to his forehead. "Of course it's Watson! So sorry – I always seem to forget."

"Please do try not to, old chap; it's frightfully important, for obvious reasons. Anyhow, it's splendid to see you too. This is my secretary – Miss Stiles."

"Pleased to meet you!" said the doctor, taking my hand with a little bow. "What brings you here today? I don't flatter myself that you've both ventured out in this filthy weather just to see me." There was an awkward pause. "Or perhaps you'd rather not say? Well, there's no need; I've a hunch you've been interviewing the villain that they brought in after the explosion at Victoria. Don't worry – I shan't say a word to anyone! He got off rather lightly, didn't he? I read in the newspaper that they were scraping up pieces of the luggage attendant for hours afterwards."

"Yes, I suppose in the circumstances he was very fortunate. We're going to look in on him again later; your colleague Dr White has packed us off for the time being."

"Oh yes, old Carrots! He was fearfully excited about being put in charge of such a notorious case, you know."

"Carrots? What a peculiar nickname."

"Don't tell me you didn't notice his hair!"

"What hair? The fellow we spoke to was as bald as an egg, wasn't he, Miss Stiles?"

The doctor gave a low whistle. "How queer! There must have been some kind of confusion; perhaps there's another doctor here named White that I don't know about . . ."

The Chief's face hardened and his eyes gleamed with a strange, grim light. "Henley, you must come with us at once," he exclaimed.

We hurried out of the ward and sped back the way we had come. As we approached Murphy's room we saw that the policemen had vanished from outside, and the Chief broke into a run. He banged on the door and then rattled the handle, but to no avail. He pressed his ear against it and listened for a moment, straightening up just as Henley and I arrived breathlessly behind him.

"Step back! I'm going to break it down!" he commanded.

"Don't be too hasty, old chap," said Henley, laying a hand on his shoulder. "They might simply have moved the patient to another room after you left."

"I can't afford to rely on that possibility, I'm afraid," returned the Chief. "Stand clear."

He took a few steps back and launched himself against the door, ramming it with his shoulder. It shuddered in its frame but did not budge. He hurled himself at it a second time, wrenching it from its hinges with a great burst of splintering wood. He whisked a revolver from his inside pocket and flicked off the catch, then crept into the room. We waited in tense silence until he reappeared in the doorway and beckoned us in. I saw at once that the room was deserted: the bed was empty and the door behind it stood wide open.

"Do you think they escaped through that door?" I asked.

"Not much chance of that," the Chief replied with an unhappy laugh. "Take a look."

I crossed the room and looked through the door: it opened onto a store cupboard.

"That infernal fellow who passed himself off as Dr White must have been hiding in there, listening to every word," said the Chief. "Well, it looks as if the Scorpions have got their hands on poor old Murphy after all; I wouldn't be in his place for anything."

"But surely the policemen . . ."

"Whoever those men were, Miss Stiles, I'm afraid that they were not policemen," said the Chief sombrely.

"What on earth have they done with the real White?" demanded Henley in dismay.

"Oh, I've a pretty good hunch about that. Come with me." The Chief led us back down the corridor, halting outside the room from which the nurse had emerged earlier on.

"I don't suppose you happen to have a key to this door, do you, Henley?" he asked. The doctor shook his head. "Very well then, I'll have to run the risk of being accused of causing wilful damage to hospital property for a second time. I jolly well hope your matron doesn't have a hot temper!"

The door flew open after the first carefully aimed blow and Henley and I followed the Chief into a room very much like the one we had just left. On the bed lay an unmoving shape covered with a sheet, which the Chief twitched away to reveal a man's head, crowned by a shock of red hair.

"That's White all right!" exclaimed Henley, hurrying over to the bed.

"He's a goner, I'm afraid," said the Chief.

I moved a few steps closer and stood looking on as the doctor drew the sheet further back, then unbuttoned White's shirt to expose a pale torso.

"He received a heavy blow to the temple," Henley muttered, lifting the hair from the corpse's forehead. "It's unlikely that it killed him, but it would have been enough to knock him out. No, from the look of him I should say that he was poisoned. See, here on his chest – this looks like a mark left by a syringe!"

"They must have knocked him unconscious to keep him out of the way, then stolen his clothes and afterwards decided not to run the risk of his being able to tell us anything by getting rid of him altogether. We were right to be suspicious of that nurse, Miss Stiles."

"There will have to be a post-mortem, of course, but I'd lay a hundred to one that's exactly what happened. Poor White," said Henley, pulling the sheet over the dead man's head with a sigh. "He couldn't have been more than thirty, and he hadn't long been married."

"Poor old White indeed," echoed the Chief. "Come along, Miss Stiles. I say, whatever's the matter?"

Speechlessly, I pointed at a motionless hand that stuck out from underneath the bed.

"Well, I'll be . . . Henley, come and look at this!"

The two men crouched down and peered into the darkness.

"Help me to wheel away the bed, Henley. Miss Stiles, I advise you not to look!"

Despite the Chief's injunction, I could not resist stealing a glance over his shoulder. What I saw made my stomach twist with horror and I hastily averted my eyes. Sprawled on the floor, his white coat splattered with blood like a butcher's, his bloody spectacles lying smashed at his side, was the bald-headed impostor. A syringe had been rammed into his eye and its handle reared up from the socket as if he were performing a bizarre balancing trick. His face was frozen in an agonised grimace, the lips pulled into a snarl, exposing yellowing teeth.

"Whatever does it mean?" I asked. "Surely Murphy wouldn't have had the strength . . ." I began to shake violently and felt my legs fold under me. Just in time, the Chief took my arm and led me towards the door.

"For the present, my dear," he said with a frown, "I am as puzzled about the matter as you are."

# Twelve

The Chief and I were obliged to wait at the hospital while the police conducted a thorough and ultimately fruitless search of the premises, and we did not arrive back at headquarters until late in the afternoon. MacIntyre had gone home complaining of a headache, so once the Chief had apprised the others of all that had occurred a delighted Hampson-Smythe was despatched to Cadogan Place to investigate the intended target of the Scorpions' bomb.

He had not returned by the time I left the office and, since the next day was a Sunday, I did not see him again until Monday morning, when I came in to find him writing laboriously.

"Good morning," I said, smiling. "Did you find out anything interesting in Cadogan Place?"

He regarded me for a moment with a pursed-up expression before replying, "I'm afraid I'm not at liberty to disclose that information to you, Miss Trant."

Stung, I went to hang up my coat. I had just begun to sort through some papers when a sequence of knocks sounded on the door. Liebowitz got up to open it and MacIntyre breezed in.

"Good morning all!" he called, walking straight over to Hampson-Smythe. He leant across the desk and said something in a confidential tone, which caused the younger man to roll his eyes in disgust.

MacIntyre addressed him again, more urgently, and this time he got to his feet with a great show of reluctance, and they both went into the meeting room.

Ten minutes later Hampson-Smythe emerged with a sulky expression, followed by MacIntyre, who approached my desk whistling "Ev'rything in the Garden's Lovely".

"Time for breakfast, Miss Trant," he remarked, producing a brown paper bag from the inside pocket of his jacket with the air of someone doing a conjuring trick. "Do come and have a cup of tea!"

"I ought really to finish filing these documents," I said doubtfully. "The Chief has asked . . ."

"Oh, the Chief won't mind a bit. Besides, he's out on business somewhere and I want to talk to you!" he said, leading the way to the kitchen.

He shut the door and pulled out a chair, saying, "Now sit down my dear – I'll put the kettle on." Once everything was prepared to his satisfaction he opened the paper bag and offered me a currant bun – which I declined – before devouring three of them himself in quick succession. Then he dropped several sugar lumps into his tea and stirred it vigorously.

"So, Miss Trant, now that the more pressing matters have been dealt with, may I ask what were your impressions of the events that occurred at the hospital on Saturday?"

Surprised that he should take the trouble to seek out my opinion, I endeavoured to give him as precise and detailed an account as I could. He listened attentively, intermittently scribbling in his purple notebook and nodding every now and then as if what I was saying confirmed various suppositions of his own. After I had recounted the discovery of the two bodies and the hopeless efforts of the police to find the nurse who had conducted us to Murphy's room, he sat reading over what he had written, delicately removing crumbs from his moustache with his finger and thumb.

"You know, Miss Trant, you really have been a tremendous help," he said, lifting his piercing eyes to mine. "Not many people would have remembered so many details."

"Thank you. I'm glad that what I said was of some use," I responded, and took a sip of cold tea.

MacIntyre lifted the lid of the teapot and glanced inside it before saying in a low voice, "It's a shame that Smythe wasn't able to find out more the other day. He spoke to the housekeeper, but all she would say was that her master, a Professor Robinson, went away unexpectedly on the seventh of September, the day before the explosion, and hasn't been seen since. I'm going to go over to Cadogan Place myself to see what else I can dig up; I'm sure the young chap did his best, but he isn't accustomed to working in the field. If the Chief comes back could you let him know, discreetly, where I am? I wouldn't mention anything to Smythe."

A floorboard creaked and we both turned round to see Hampson-Smythe standing in the doorway.

"Wouldn't mention what?"

"How long have you been standing there? You must have crept in jolly quietly!"

"Well, given that I appear to have walked in on a discussion that directly concerns me, it's a good thing I did. Now what is it that you don't want me to know about? You've no right to keep me in the dark." He turned and scowled at me. "And as for you, Miss Trant, I thought better of you than to find you closeted away in here, plotting."

"That's enough!" MacIntyre roared. "You've overstepped the mark; I won't allow any man, particularly one who calls himself a gentleman, to address a lady disrespectfully in my presence. Now, apologise to Miss Trant!"

Hampson-Smythe mumbled a sulky apology, his eyes fixed on the floor.

"If you must know, Smythe, I'm going to Cadogan Place to have a look around."

"You can't do that! The Chief asked *me* to pursue the investigation – if anyone is to go back, it ought to be me! You have no right ..."

"Now, Smythe, don't be unreasonable." MacIntyre got up and walked out of the kitchen, saying over his shoulder, "I've been in this game for a good while, and if I hadn't had to go home you know very well that the Chief would have sent me to the house in the first place."

Hampson-Smythe growled an incomprehensible reply and stood in the kitchen doorway, watching with clenched fists as MacIntyre put on his overcoat.

"I shouldn't be more than an hour or two," he called as he strode out of the office. "Ta-ta!"

There was a moment of stillness, during which the sound of footsteps descending the metal staircase seemed to fill the room. I glanced anxiously at Hampson-Smythe, who looked ready to launch himself in pursuit; however, to my great relief, as soon as the shop bell jingled to signal MacIntyre's departure he stalked back to his desk, muttering rancorously under his breath.

"Is there someone in the shop?" asked Liebowitz, looking up from the telegram he was deciphering. He removed his monocle and rubbed his eyes; his shoulders drooped wearily and his face still wore the distant, glassy expression that it habitually assumed when he was wrestling with a particularly fiendish code. I explained MacIntyre's errand as discreetly as I could, for I was uncomfortably aware of Hampson-Smythe's simmering presence just across the room.

"I see," said Liebowitz, as if his mind were engaged with more important matters. He added vaguely, "I thought Smythe had already done all that."

I glanced across at the young man's studiously impassive back and mouthed an emphatic "*Yes*".

Liebowitz, however, failed to respond to the note of warning in my voice. "Ah well, I'm sure MacIntyre has excellent reasons for what he's doing; there is no man I would trust more to break down a seeming dead end. You know, I really think that I could be on the trail of something remarkable here, Miss Trant. The messages that I've been working on were intercepted by an agent in Berlin and I've a hunch that there may be a direct connection to the Scorpions. Perhaps they will provide us with the breakthrough we need . . ."

Suddenly, there was a loud smash and I looked round with a thudding heart to see that a piece of chemical apparatus had toppled from Hampson-Smythe's desk and lay in fragments on the floor. Cursing in a furious undertone, he strode into the kitchen and returned with the dustpan and brush.

"I hope it wasn't anything important," offered Liebowitz, glancing over his shoulder.

"Oh, what does it matter?" Smythe shot back and, in the instant before he turned his head away, I seemed to catch the gleam of tears in his eyes.

I tried my best to bring my mind to bear on my work, but the atmosphere in the room was charged and unsettled like the air just before a thunderstorm, and I felt too unnerved to concentrate properly. From the corner of my eye, I could see Hampson-Smythe sitting at his desk with a book open in front of him, gazing blankly at the wall. Liebowitz was still working feverishly, but every now and then, to my discomfiture, he would stop and regard me with the same air of reflective consideration that he might have exhibited had he been pondering the purchase of a useful but awkwardly shaped piece of furniture.

About an hour after MacIntyre's departure, the shop bell rang and I put on my apron and hurried downstairs. Standing at the till was a boy in a post office uniform.

"Telegram for Mr Watson," he said.

"Mr Watson is out at present, but I will ensure that he gets it as soon as he returns," I replied.

"Very well – sign here, please."

I took the telegram up to the office and placed it on the Chief's desk. Neither Liebowitz nor Hampson-Smythe asked what it was and I reluctantly returned to my typing.

The hours dragged by until at last there was a knocking on the door and I looked through the peephole to see MacIntyre. He walked in and sat down without speaking, and started scribbling in his notebook. My eyes strayed towards Hampson-Smythe, who had abandoned all pretence of working and was staring moodily at the usurper of his cherished project.

Suddenly, he flung his chair back and stormed over to him,

exclaiming, "Look here! I should think you might at least tell me what you found out, instead of sitting there with that smug expression on your face!"

MacIntyre gave a sigh and allowed the notebook to close around his forefinger. "What's the matter, Smythe? I suppose you can see how busy I am?"

"I'll tell you what the matter is, you pompous oaf! I've just about had enough of you wading in with those great feet of yours and messing things up. If the Chief had let *me* go to the trade union meeting, I can assure you that the bomb would never have been planted in the first place. And yet *you* choose to doubt *my* competence!"

MacIntyre removed his finger from the pages of the notebook and stood up.

"My dear chap, please don't excite yourself like this. I have absolutely no desire to question your competence; on the contrary, I am in fact building on the findings that you obtained."

Hampson-Smythe eyed him fiercely. "Well, perhaps you'd be good enough to share your conclusions with me?"

MacIntyre gave a regretful shrug. "Sorry, Smythe old fellow; simply can't be done."

"Why not?"

"The information is too sensitive at this stage. I need to find out what the Chief has to say about it before I pass it on to anyone else."

"So now you're implying that I'm not to be trusted?"

"Don't be a fool, Smythe – you know that our work is highly confidential . . ."

At this, Hampson-Smythe launched himself towards MacIntyre and struck him hard in the face. Liebowitz leapt to his feet, but before he had crossed the room MacIntyre had seized his assailant by the wrist, spun him over and flung him to the ground, where he lay gasping for breath.

I looked on, aghast, as Liebowitz handed MacIntyre a handkerchief, which he held up to his bloody nose while they both stood gazing down at the prostrate Hampson-Smythe.

"Go home, boy," said Liebowitz, with an unfamiliar steeliness in his voice, "and make sure you've recovered your temper before you come back. I don't want to see you again before tomorrow."

The other man lay silently, as if debating within himself whether to argue. Eventually he scrambled to his feet, and without looking at any of us he took down his hat and overcoat from the hatstand and left, slamming the door behind him.

MacIntyre walked over to the mirror and tentatively examined his nose.

"Well, thank heaven it's not broken!" he remarked and, meeting my horrified regard in the reflection, added, "Would you mind fetching me a basin of warm water, Miss Trant? There ought to be some left in the kettle from earlier on."

By the time I returned with the water the thudding of my heart had subsided and I was feeling somewhat calmer. Liebowitz had gone back to work and MacIntyre was sitting in his shirtsleeves, with the bloodstained handkerchief pressed to his nose. I set down the bowl next to his elbow and he began to dab awkwardly at his face with the sodden cloth, spattering a thin trail of blood across his shirt.

He dropped the handkerchief back into the water. "I say, Miss Trant, I hope you don't think it's a fearful imposition, but would you be so kind as to bathe my nose for me?"

As I worked I realised afresh how tall he was; even when he was sitting down I scarcely had to stoop to reach his face. Cleaning the caked fronds of his moustache required considerable concentration and unconsciously I bent more closely towards him, taking in as if for the first time the elegant contours of his long limbs, his tapering fingers, the sensitive flare of his nostrils, the humorous curl of his lips. The pale lids and lashes of his closed eyes seemed astonishingly vulnerable and I was overcome by a most improper longing to lean over and kiss them. Appalled, I let the handkerchief fall into the bowl with a splash and, with a queer feeling of breathlessness, I stepped back to examine his countenance for any lingering traces of blood. As soon as I did so his eyes sprang open and all at once I felt horribly self-conscious, as if I had been caught in a forbidden act.

"Thank you, my dear. You would make an admirable nurse." He smiled at me and our eyes met, sending a little quiver of excitement along the upmost portion of my spine.

There was a rapping at the door and I scurried across to answer it, blushing fiercely. It was the Chief.

"Good afternoon, Miss Trant!" he said, crossing to the hatstand to hang up his coat. "Everything all right?"

"No, sir, it's not!" exclaimed Liebowitz, getting to his feet.

"Don't worry, old chap; I'll explain everything," said MacIntyre, walking across to the Chief and placing his palm between his shoulder blades.

"Is there something the matter with your nose, MacIntyre?" asked the Chief. Then his eyes turned to the bowl of bloodied water. "What's that?"

"Nothing to worry about, sir," said MacIntyre, propelling him into the meeting room and closing the door.

Liebowitz took a few steps as if he were intending to go after them, then sighed and returned to his desk. My gaze moved restlessly about the room and alighted on the telegram still lying unopened on the Chief's desk. I hesitated, glanced at Liebowitz, who was sitting hunched over a book, then went to pick it up.

I knocked at the meeting room door and waited a few moments before it was opened by the Chief. "Yes, what is it, Miss Trant?" he asked, rubbing the crease between his brows with his thumb.

"This telegram arrived for you this morning, sir. I thought it might be urgent."

"Thank you. Let us hope that it doesn't contain bad news." He tore open the telegram, glanced at it, and walked across to Liebowitz. "We are using the third volume of Gibbon at present, aren't we?"

"That's right, sir." Liebowitz rummaged around among the papers on his desk and unearthed an ancient-looking volume bound in green leather, which he handed to the Chief. "You do remember how the cipher works?"

"Yes, I think so. Thank you." The Chief took the book back to his desk and began flicking through the pages, stopping every now and then to write something down. I went over to the filing cabinet with a handful of documents and had just filed the last of them when MacIntyre appeared in the doorway of the meeting room.

"Miss Trant, could you come in and take down my report? I . . ."

"Well, thank heaven for that!" exclaimed the Chief, drowning out the rest of his remark. "Hunter's in the clear!"

"What does he say?" asked Liebowitz, hurrying across to him.

"Yes, do tell!" said MacIntyre, coming up behind them and peering down over the Chief's shoulder. After a moment he pursed his lips and gave a long whistle. "So he didn't warn us about the explosion at Victoria because he had no more idea it was going to happen than we did. Well, that's a great relief. One rogue agent at a time is more than enough for any organisation."

"Don't be facetious!" snapped the Chief with uncharacteristic sharpness. "No doubt Hampson-Smythe will be back once he's had a chance to cool down."

MacIntyre's eyes widened and then his face composed itself into an expression of contrition.

"Sorry, sir, of course you're right – and I don't mean to make light of the situation. It is a relief to have heard from Hunter, particularly in light of subsequent developments. Suppose we all go into the meeting room and talk this through?" Then, seeing me hesitate, he added, "You too, Miss Trant – your skills will be invaluable."

We all followed MacIntyre into the meeting room. The Chief took his seat at the head of the deal table and placed the palms of his hands together, pressing his index fingers to his lips and gazing thoughtfully upwards.

"The Scorpions have been dormant for all these years since the Arrowsmith affair, and now the first real sign of renewed activity on our shores turns out to be part of an internal squabble. It really is quite extraordinary."

"And somewhat reassuring that the act of violence wasn't targeted against the general public – or even an individual from outside the organisation," commented Liebowitz.

"Indeed. And now that Hunter is aware that Henriquez is in

London, presumably he also knows that he belongs to the faction that wanted to assassinate this Professor Robinson of Cadogan Place. Can you cast light on any of this, MacIntyre?"

"Yes sir, I believe I can; well, perhaps a little gleam or two," MacIntyre said, opening his notebook. "Are you ready, Miss Trant?"

I nodded. He held my glance for a moment and then smiled in a way that made me catch my breath and look swiftly down at my pen, which was suspended, quivering, above the page, ready to take down every word.

MacIntyre was a natural storyteller and as he related the details of his investigation of Professor Robinson's house, it was hard to resist being transported by his thrilling account. Fortunately, however, the years that I had spent working for Mr Plimpson had taught me to concentrate on the task at hand – though then it had been boredom that had set my mind wandering rather than the draw of a well-told tale – and the transcription that I eventually put into the Chief's hands was once again accurate in every particular.

# Thirteen

MacIntyre's Story

On the way to the house in Cadogan Place, MacIntyre called in at his lodgings to pick up a battered leather bag which contained a candle, a box of matches, half a dozen firecrackers, some kindling and a rag soaked in paraffin. He also changed his clothes and dug out a letter of introduction that had been written for him by a master bookbinder, who happened to be an old friend. Before leaving, he scrutinised his face in a small square of mirror which hung on the wall and was rather perturbed to see that the bruise above his left eye had ripened to an amorphous blot of lush greens and purples. He did what he could to cover it up with a stick of flesh-coloured greasepaint, then took up his bag and set out, whistling.

He reached Professor Robinson's house without incident, and once he had made sure that he wasn't being observed he slipped down into the area yard. Then, with great speed and precision, he constructed a little heap of twigs, stuffed the firecrackers and the rag inside and set the candle on top. From the length of wax remaining, he judged that he had an interval of about fifteen minutes before the whole lot went up in flames. Having made a few fine adjustments to the positioning of the twigs, he scanned the street again, ran up the steps and made his way round to the back door.

His knock was answered by a pretty, dark-haired maid, who rather pertly enquired after his business. He claimed to have been instructed to collect some books for rebinding, showed his friend's letter as evidence, and eventually persuaded the reluctant girl to escort him to the professor's study. "But you'll have to be quick," she said. "And don't let none of the other servants see you, or you'll be out on your ear. When he's at home, the professor never lets no one in his study."

He followed her along an echoing stone passage with doors opening off on either side. Voices drifted in from a room that was out of sight, accompanied by a clashing of saucepans and a rattling of crockery. There was a savoury smell of cooking in the air and it made him feel rather hungry. They went through the door that led onto the back staircase and ascended two flights of stairs before coming to a halt on a half-landing. The maid signalled to him to wait and crept up the next set of steps, then looked round and beckoned him on.

They passed through a long corridor and entered a drab apartment which smelled strongly of stale cigar smoke. It was impeccably tidy; not a scrap of paper had been left on the desk, which stood in the alcove of a bay window overlooking the street, and the books that lined the shelves were severely regimented. The mustard-coloured walls were hung with maps and a single photograph, which MacIntyre went over to scrutinise at closer range. It showed a group of four men wearing flowers in their buttonholes and a young woman dressed as a gypsy.

"That's new!" remarked the maid, walking up behind him. "I dusted in here not two days ago and I'd swear it wasn't there then. Blimey! Don't the professor like to rearrange his pictures and what not! The number of times I've come in and found it all changed. He's very funny about this room is the professor – he insists on being here when I come in to clean and he watches me like a hawk."

"Is one of those men in the photograph the professor?"

"Bless you, no! Why, the professor . . ." She stopped abruptly, as if suddenly recollecting herself, and snapped, "But you've got no time to stand there gawping! Be quick and find your books, before someone comes along and catches us."

She moved over to the doorway and stood watching while he

pretended to scan the shelves. He consulted his notebook as if he were checking off a list, selecting every now and then a book that looked more dog-eared than the rest, and putting it to one side. After he had assembled a pile of four or five volumes, he glanced at his watch; twenty minutes had gone by. Perhaps his little incendiary heap had already been discovered and dismantled; or perhaps, despite all his precautions, the candle had gone out. In either case the whole enterprise would be scuppered.

Even as he wondered what to do next, the air was rent by a series of explosions. They both hurried over to the window and saw flames shooting up from the area below. With a stern injunction that he should stay where he was until she came back, the girl hurried out of the room, closing the door behind her.

Almost immediately, the sound of voices and running footsteps began drifting up from outside. MacIntyre set about picking the lock on the desk drawer, for there was not a moment to lose; he calculated that after the cause of the detonations had been discovered the diversion would keep the maid occupied for, at most, five minutes. Fortunately, the lock gave without too much trouble. Inside the drawer were numerous bundles of correspondence arranged in neat rows and he started leafing through them eagerly. However, to his disappointment, the letters were all dry and businesslike; many of them seemed to concern the acquisition of new exhibits for the British Museum or to theorise interminably about some obscure historical point, and he soon realised that he wasn't going to find anything of interest there. He poked around a bit more and discovered that the drawer had a false bottom, which was released by a little catch in the far right-hand corner; underneath it was a cavity containing a large brown envelope and some notes written in a peculiar alphabet. He thrust them all into his bag, replaced the secret panel and laid the letters neatly over the top. He made a hasty examination of the maps tacked up on the walls and just had time to see that they all showed different stretches of the south coast and were dotted with red, green and yellow pins before he became aware that the commotion outside had died away.

When the maid came back in, she discovered him with his back to the room, gazing pensively out of the window.

"Marvellous weather, ain't it? It's hard on a fellow to be kept indoors by his work on a day like this," he said, without turning round.

"Quick-sharp now – off you go!" she hissed, hastening up to him. "Miriam's on the warpath. She's all stoked up – I wouldn't put it past her to pin the blame on you for that mischief outside. If we hurry, I can let you out the front door; we're less likely to be seen if we go that way."

MacIntyre slipped the books into his bag and they trotted along the landing. As they passed the door to the servants' staircase they heard the creak of a heavy tread moving upwards. The maid shot him a startled look and dragged him through the nearest door, shutting it carefully behind them. "That's Miriam. I knew it wouldn't be long before she came up to find out what I've been doing, the nosy cow! We'll have to wait here till she goes downstairs."

MacIntyre saw that they had entered a room in which all the furniture was swathed in brown calico. The walls were covered in a dark green paper, there was a large fireplace framed with decorated tiles, and a number of architectural engravings hung on the walls. A pungent odour of Turkish cigarettes infused the air and one of the sash windows stood wide open.

"That's queer!" the girl remarked, sniffing. "Who's been smoking in here? This room's never used except for when the professor has visitors to stay. Well, whoever it is, won't he just catch it from Miriam if she finds out! It's perishing cold, ain't it? I suppose the cheeky blighter opened the window to get rid of the stink."

"I'll close it, shall I?" said MacIntyre.

"All right – but do it quietly, else they'll know we're in here."

The window sash had been pulled up as far as it would go. MacIntyre stuck his head outside and saw that there was a drop of twelve feet or so down to the pavement below; it would not have been difficult for a man to climb out, hang from the exterior ledge and let himself fall, if he had wanted to escape in a hurry. He withdrew his head and closed the window just as the girl whispered, "She's gone downstairs again – we'd better be quick!"

He pointed at a crumpled piece of paper in her hand. "What's that you've got there?"

"Oh, just some rubbish off of the sofa."

"Mind if I have a look?"

She passed it to him with a shrug and watched impatiently while he smoothed it out. Several strange characters, vaguely reminiscent of ancient Egyptian hieroglyphics, were scrawled on the page, together with a sketch of a pyramid surmounted by a single human eye.

MacIntyre thought at once of the documents that he had found in the secret compartment in the desk drawer. "Does this belong to the professor?" he enquired.

"Cor, you're a nosy beggar! How should I know?"

"Mind if I hold on to it as a keepsake of our adventures together?"

"If you like. It's no use to me. Now do come on; you must go before they all start looking for me."

They crept out of the room, along the landing and down the main staircase without encountering a soul. The maid unbolted the front door and stepped aside to let MacIntyre out. He thanked her warmly, then turned and hurried straight back to HQ with his spoils.

# *Fourteen*

"*A*nd have you come to any conclusion about your findings?" asked Liebowitz with a frown.

"Well, as a matter of fact I do have one or two observations to make," said MacIntyre, stroking his moustache. He turned a page in his notebook, cleared his throat, and began to read out loud.

"First: we know that Professor Robinson went away suddenly on the day before the explosion at Victoria, apparently without leaving a forwarding address. It seems likely that someone warned him that he was the intended target of the device. Who was it? Second: the existence of the secret compartment, used to conceal various documents, implies that the professor has something to hide – very possibly his involvement with the Scorpions."

At this, Liebowitz gave a sceptical growl, but said nothing.

"Third: I should like to have a second look at the photograph of the four men in evening dress and the woman dressed as a gypsy fortune-teller. It may not be of any particular significance – I must say, they looked to me rather like the members of an amateur dramatic society – but one never knows; in my experience the least promising objects sometimes turn out to provide the most telling clues of all. Fourth: the maps on the study walls . . ."

"They were maps of the south coast, you said? That suggests a maritime connection. What do you think, Liebowitz?" asked the Chief.

Liebowitz jumped and turned a blank face towards him. "Yes, sir?"

"Is there something the matter? You've been fidgeting about ever since MacIntyre started giving his report."

"I'm sorry, sir. I think I took my coffee a little too strong this morning."

"Well, let that be a lesson to you for drinking such filthy stuff! But doesn't this support the evidence you picked up from the Mannheim telegrams, about the smuggling of weapons from the European mainland?"

"It's certainly possible," replied Liebowitz with a shrug. "But don't you think that Hunter could have been mistaken about this faction business? It was only in July that those policemen were murdered in Berlin, don't forget – and that was the first sign of concerted activity from the Scorpions since Arrowsmith was executed in ninety-six. They haven't had time to fall out with one another! If you ask me, the professor could well be working for someone else. Or, possibly, he has unintentionally become involved in matters of which he has no understanding. In either case, the Scorpions would certainly have objected if they thought he was poking around in matters that didn't concern him – and no doubt they considered that those packages of dynamite would signal their displeasure with suitable clarity."

"But you said earlier that you were relieved that the dynamite was intended for one of the Scorpions' own men."

"That was before I heard the evidence. I'm not denying that Robinson is connected in some way with the Scorpions, but the link seems to me to be a tenuous one and it would be foolish for us to waste time trying to trace him when there are so many other avenues that we need to explore."

I had never heard the taciturn Liebowitz be so voluble. I glanced at MacIntyre and he raised a meaningful eyebrow.

"I'm afraid I disagree," returned the Chief with a grave look, before turning to MacIntyre. "So you didn't pick up any pattern in the arrangement of those coloured pins?"

"No, I'm afraid not – except for the fact that they all seemed to be positioned on fairly sizeable towns. And a number of them were a good distance from the coast, which rather scuppers the smuggling theory." There was a brief pause before MacIntyre looked down at his notebook and continued, "Anyhow, the fifth point I have to make concerns the maid's claim that the professor is continually rearranging his study, which does seem odd. Of course she could have been exaggerating, but still . . . Then there's also the fact that her master doesn't admit visitors into the room and won't allow his servants to enter it without supervision. I suppose that could be attributed to eccentricity." He looked pointedly at Liebowitz. "However, it seems to me yet another indication that the professor has something to hide.

"Sixth: who was in the sitting room just before the maid and I went in? He can have been up to no good, given that he appears to have left so precipitately. And yet if he didn't want to be detected why leave such obvious traces of his presence behind?"

"Are you sure it wasn't just one of the domestics, enjoying a cigarette where he had no business to be?" asked the Chief. "Just because the window was open doesn't mean that he jumped out of it; he could have left the room while you were still in the study and gone down the front staircase to avoid bumping into any of the other servants."

"I suppose so," said MacIntyre grudgingly. "However, though I can't explain why precisely, I've still got a feeling that there was more to it than that. Anyhow, let's move on to item seven: the notes written in cipher that were concealed in the professor's desk and the scrap of paper covered in almost identical characters, which one infers must have been dropped by the professor and not by the intruder, as appeared to be the case at first."

MacIntyre removed several sheets of foolscap from a leather satchel at his feet, then took his wallet from his jacket pocket and plucked out a scrap of paper about two inches square. "I don't pretend to know much about these things, but I'm certain I've seen a cipher very like it before," he said, pushing the documents across the table towards Liebowitz.

I strained my eyes, trying to work out whether the characters bore any similarity to those on Smith's postcards, but I was too short-sighted to perceive anything more than a vague blur and I was afraid that if I asked to look at them more closely I might appear overly curious. So much had happened during the past few days that I had had no opportunity to ask Liebowitz about the card I had given him, but now I resolved anew to follow the matter up as soon as I could find a suitable opening.

Liebowitz removed his monocle and rubbed his hand wearily across his eyes. "It's perfectly possible that you have seen something similar to this, old man. But you see, as I think I've explained to you, many different ciphers share a superficial likeness, which can lead the amateur astray. You needn't look so displeased – naturally, I will take the precaution of comparing it to some specimens of ciphers that the Scorpions have used in the past before I attempt to decode it." He reached out and pulled the documents towards him, flicking through them with a preoccupied expression before putting them to one side.

MacIntyre leant over and removed something else from the satchel.

"I've saved the most perplexing detail until last," he said, handing a large brown envelope to the Chief, who opened it and took out a photograph.

"What the devil . . ." he exclaimed.

"My thoughts exactly," MacIntyre responded.

The Chief gave the photograph to Liebowitz, who replaced his monocle, peered at it closely and returned it to MacIntyre.

"Care to have a look, Miss Trant?" asked MacIntyre, passing it to me.

The picture showed a fair-haired girl sitting at a café table. I gazed at it in astonishment; the young lady in the picture bore a striking resemblance, was even, perhaps, identical, to the girl in the photograph on Tom Hunter's desk.

"Do you recognise her?" he enquired. I nodded. "I thought you might. Her name is Hetty Bartholomew; she's Tom Hunter's fiancée. I don't know much about her except for the fact that her father is a clergyman in some out-of-the-way place near Ely. As to why the professor should have her photograph in his study . . ."

"Suppose the professor is a Scorpion, as Hunter believes. In that case it might mean that they have found out Hunter's real identity; that they propose to blackmail him by threatening to harm Miss Bartholomew," said the Chief, with an air of rising agitation.

"But we aren't certain of that by any means. It seems to me much more likely that Robinson is an outsider who has somehow contrived to antagonise the Scorpions," Liebowitz objected.

"I still say that Hunter is in a better position to understand what happened than we are, and he seems pretty convinced that the explosion was the result of an internal dispute. And whoever Robinson is, the fact that he has a photograph of Hunter's fiancée in his possession is worrying, to say the least. We must try to warn Hunter that he could be in danger – I'll write a telegram at once," said the Chief, getting up and hurrying into the office. "I only hope that he gets the message in time."

# Fifteen

There was so much to think about that the journey back to the boarding house seemed to take no time at all. Like MacIntyre and the Chief, I felt pretty certain that Professor Robinson was a Scorpion, and it seemed to me that the fact that he was in possession of a photograph of Hetty Bartholomew could mean only one thing: he must have begun to suspect that the dashing young man who had recently joined the Scorpions' inner circle was not all that he appeared to be. There seemed little doubt that he intended to use the photograph of Miss Bartholomew to put pressure on Hunter – perhaps to extort a confession or to control his actions. None of us knew quite how serious the danger was, however, for we could not be certain how fully developed Robinson's distrust of Hunter had become. Had the professor somehow learnt that he was a government agent? Or was his suspicion much vaguer and more ill-founded than that? Had he communicated his misgivings to anyone else before his abrupt departure from Cadogan Place? And where had he gone? Even before I had left the office, Liebowitz had already been set to work on the encrypted documents from the professor's study which, the Chief and MacIntyre hoped, might furnish some answers to these crucial questions. Liebowitz himself, however, still stubbornly continued to insist that Professor Robinson was not a Scorpion at all.

Though I had seen Hunter only on that first day, he had made a deep impression on me, for in his looks and manner he seemed to me to be the living embodiment of one of those dashing heroes that feature so commonly in popular adventure stories. I was almost equally fascinated by Hetty Bartholomew, his mysterious, golden-haired fiancée, and soon drifted off into a long and complicated fantasy in which Hunter abandoned his mission and returned to England to rescue her from deadly peril. It was not until I put my key into the front door that I remembered to be apprehensive about Mother. The arthritis in her hands had worsened over the past few days and her fingers had become so stiff and swollen that she could scarcely do anything for herself. Helplessness always made her appallingly bad-tempered and I had been driven to the limits of my patience by her scolding and fretting. Therefore, when I entered the sitting room to find her bent over the writing desk, labouring away with her pen, I was greatly surprised and not a little relieved.

As I came in she sighed, ripped the sheet of paper she had been writing on into tiny shreds and let them fall into the wastepaper basket.

"What time is it? Aren't you back very early?" she asked, turning towards me.

In fact I was rather later than usual. "No, Mother; it's nearly time for dinner," I said, glancing at the clock on the mantelpiece. "Are your hands feeling better?"

She looked down at them vaguely, as if they didn't belong to her. "Yes, I suppose so – it hadn't really occurred to me."

"Is there something the matter?"

There was a moment's silence before she said, still examining her hands, "Something remarkable has happened, but if I tell you about it, you must promise not to scold me for being foolish."

"Of course I won't. What is it?" I asked, steeling myself for the worst.

Mother had always been prone to fads. Usually her obsessions were fleeting and fairly harmless: a desire to learn a particular style of calligraphy said to be practised by the ladies at Court, for example;

or a face cream which claimed to restore the glow of youth to a faded complexion. Most recently, she had squandered several shillings on a nutrient called Plasmon, which was promoted by its manufacturer as containing all the necessary elements for renewing muscle, brain and nerves, and she had persuaded Mrs Hodgkins to use it in her baking. Save for the bitter taste that it imparted to everything to which it was added, the nutrient had demonstrated no other perceptible effect and at last, after a month or so, the caprice had worn itself out.

Mother picked up a piece of paper from her desk and held it out to me. "This came in the post this morning," she said.

The document proved to be a handbill, printed in an ornate script. It read, *To proprietors and managers. If you want to draw the people nowadays you must give them something new and novel. Here it is – Madam Coraline, Medium and Clairvoyant.*"

"Mother, really! You surely don't give any credence to such nonsense!" I exclaimed in exasperation.

"Margaret, I am not a fool – I am perfectly well aware that there are plenty of charlatans in this world. My first instinct was to throw the advertisement away and to think nothing more about it. But you see, there was something else in the envelope." She passed me a square of stiff paper. When I looked at it more closely I saw, to my astonishment, that it was a crude watercolour portrait, framed in blue card.

"Is this supposed to be you?" I demanded.

"Of course it is!"

"And this 'Madam Coraline' was the one who sent it?"

"I suppose so. No other name was enclosed."

"How ridiculous!" I said, giving it back to her.

"Yes, but there was another one, and it was that which . . ." Mother heaved a shuddering sigh and put her face in her hands. When she looked up again, I saw the glistening trails of tears on her cheeks. I stooped down awkwardly and squeezed her shoulders, then leant across the desk to pull out a sliver of dark blue card that was peeping out from beneath her writing case.

A tremor ran through me, as if someone had suddenly struck me hard in the chest. I was holding a painting of my dead father – the resemblance was unequivocal, though like the other portrait it was done in a slapdash and uneven style. I started to shake and Mother took the picture away from me and placed it face down on the desk.

"I'm sorry, Margaret. I didn't want to upset you, but I've been driven almost out of my wits with wondering why this Madam Coraline should have gone to the trouble of painting the portraits and sending them to me. And how can she know what I look like? Or your father?"

I turned away and went over to the window to gather my thoughts. As my initial surprise and bewilderment began to fade, I grew increasingly convinced that the portraits were no more than a cheap trick. I had no idea what could be behind it, but I was determined that my mother should not be drawn in.

"Mother, listen. You must promise me not to allow yourself to be duped by this nonsense. I want you to throw the portraits away."

She hesitated for a moment and then, to my surprise, dropped the paintings and the handbill into the wastepaper basket.

"You needn't worry – I won't do anything foolish," she said stiffly. "And besides, Madam Coraline didn't give me her address. Now, do go down to supper – I find I have quite lost my appetite."

I went down to dinner alone and upon my return I found Mother perched rigidly on the sofa, her hands knotted in her lap, her eyes closed.

Her eyelids fluttered open when she heard the door shut and she regarded me with a dazed expression. "I'm so tired, Margaret. Put me to bed."

I assisted her across the room, wondering anew at how light she was; her bones seemed to lack density, as if years of unhappiness had gnawed them away. I helped her to get ready for bed and tucked the sheets tightly around her. She lay limp and unmoving like an exhausted child, and when I went out her eyes followed me, huge and dark in her shrunken face.

*

Next morning I awoke before dawn, and as I lay drowsing my mind began to drift back over the events of the previous day. I wondered how Hampson-Smythe was feeling now that he had had an opportunity to cool down. Very likely he was dreading his return to the office; he was such a touchy young man that it would be very difficult for him to swallow his pride and admit that he had behaved badly. I hoped that MacIntyre wouldn't be too hard on him; I even pictured myself having a quiet word with him to that effect, and at the thought of doing so I felt my cheeks redden. I tried to summon up my first impression of MacIntyre as a diffident, stooping, eccentric creature, but my imagination baulked, for it was wholly incompatible with my present awareness. Instead I found myself dwelling on the intense gentian-blue flash of his eyes, on the humorous lines that bracketed his mouth and the earnest, intimate tone of his voice when he had thanked me for bathing his nose.

At a quarter to seven I went into Mother's room and found her awake, lying on her back with her eyes fixed on the ceiling. I asked how she had slept; in reply, she sighed and turned her face away. She made no objection when I started dressing her, but maintained an unnerving silence throughout breakfast, right up to the moment of my departure.

I stooped to kiss her papery cheek, wishing she would utter one of the criticisms or admonitions with which she customarily sent me off to work.

"Mother, don't be angry about last night. You must realise that I am only concerned for your well-being."

"Really, Margaret, I'd quite forgotten about that," she said briskly. "I merely slept badly and I have a headache – there's no need for you to make such a fuss. Now hurry along, or you'll be late!"

This flash of acerbity was somewhat reassuring and I turned and went out before she lost her temper in earnest.

It was a gloomy day with a bitter wind blowing and dark clouds scudding across a pale sky and I shivered in my thin jacket, wondering if I would ever manage to put aside sufficient money to buy a warmer one. The tram was crowded and the other passengers looked wan and bad-tempered. An irritable little man wearing an overcoat that was too big for him jabbed me in the back with his umbrella and a stout lady in furs stepped on my toe. I alighted on Tottenham Court Road with a sense of relief and drew several deep breaths of the dank air.

"Margaret, is that you? How extraordinary!"

I froze with astonishment; standing before me was Anna, Aunt Sophie's only daughter.

The last occasion on which we had seen one another had been at my father's funeral. She was a year younger than me and I remembered her as an impish schoolgirl with darned stockings and wisps of dark hair escaping from her plait. Now she was elegantly turned out in a moss-green walking suit of the latest fashion and the glossy loops of her hair were coiled beneath a natty little feathered hat. Her face and figure had filled out to a dimpled plumpness and her formerly sallow cheeks were rosy with good health, yet I knew her at once from her mischievous, treacle-coloured eyes and her lopsided grin. She put down her umbrella and stood gazing at me for a moment, then threw her arms around me. I submitted somewhat self-consciously to her embrace, aware that passers-by were turning to look at us.

"My dear! What an astonishing stroke of luck!" she exclaimed, stepping back and taking both my hands in hers. "I'm on my way to Oxford Street, to do some shopping. I'm only in London for the day —my husband has been posted to Jaipur, our things are to be shipped over in a few days, and there are still one or two oddments I simply must have. Are you going anywhere in particular? Can you spare the time to join me? Do come – we could have such a cosy morning together!"

"I'm terribly sorry, Anna, but I'm afraid that I'm on my way to work," I replied, sounding colder than I had intended.

A look of confusion flitted across her face. "Oh, I see. I had no idea . . . How admirable of you to earn your own living! Well, I mustn't get you into trouble by keeping you, then. But I simply can't leave London without talking to you properly. Are you engaged for luncheon?"

"No." I was feeling shy, but she appeared to mistake my nervousness for hostility.

"You know, I did try very hard to trace you after Mother died, but you left no forwarding address at your old house, and . . ." She stopped, her face stricken with concern.

"Oh, Margaret, how thoughtless of me! It's been so long now that it never occurred to me that you might not have heard. I'm so sorry! Please don't cry! If it's any comfort, she was terribly fond of you, and I'm sure she would have got over that ridiculous quarrel with Aunt Mariah. I found a letter addressed to you among her things after she died – I've never opened it, but I'm quite sure that it must contain an explanation, or an apology at the very least. Oh, do have luncheon with me! There's so much I want to talk to you about."

I explained, rather incoherently, that I was terribly sorry about Aunt Sophie and dreadfully pleased to see her, but must press on or I would be late for work. I suggested a teashop where we could meet for luncheon, gave my cousin an awkward kiss, which missed her cheek and landed on her nose, and hurried away with my emotions in turmoil.

Liebowitz, who was alone in the office, raised his hand in an absent gesture of acknowledgement as I walked in.

"There are some documents to be typed on your desk," he informed me without looking up from the telegram he was studying. "The Chief has gone round to Hampson-Smythe's lodgings and MacIntyre is searching for Miss Bartholomew."

I fleetingly considered asking him whether he had had an opportunity to look at Mr Smith's postcard, but found that I didn't have the heart to do so. I hung up my jacket and paused to tidy myself up in front of the mirror. My face looked plain and faded and for the first time I noticed a network of tiny wrinkles at the corner of each eye. I took off my hat, which was wet through, observing regretfully how dowdy it was, and made a vigorous and imperfect attempt to pin back my hair.

I sat down and began the painstaking task of typing a coded letter on the old-fashioned machine. Try as I might, I was unable to curb the giddy racing of my thoughts and, having made three false starts on the first sentence, I surrendered the attempt and sat clasping my hands in my lap.

Though I had not seen my aunt since I was a girl, the news of her death was a terrible blow. Passing time had not diminished my affection for her; indeed, over the years I had come to perceive her as a kind of good fairy possessing all the powers of sympathy and understanding that my own mother lacked. I recalled my childish hurt and incomprehension at her failure to reply to my last few letters, and the idea that she had written to me after all, but had died before she had had an opportunity to send the letter, brought forth a hot rush of tears.

I fled into the kitchen and closed the door, and for several minutes I lost myself in a storm of weeping. Then, abruptly, I became aware of the hum of voices in the office. I lifted my head from my arms, drew a deep, shuddering breath and went over to the sink to bathe my eyes. I was patting my face dry with my handkerchief when I heard the door open and close again.

"Miss Trant! Is something the matter?"

It was the Chief. I smoothed back my hair and replied, "No, not really; I've got rather a headache – it sometimes helps if I splash cold water on my temples."

"Turn round please, Miss Trant."

I did so, keeping my swollen eyes cast down to the floor.

The Chief shook his head, tutting gently. "Now now, my dear lady, I am a married man and therefore sufficiently experienced to recognise the signs of weeping when I see them. Come here and sit down."

He waited until I was seated, then took the chair opposite. "Are you able to tell me what the matter is?"

In a high, uncertain voice, I began to describe the unexpected meeting with my cousin, but as soon as I mentioned my aunt I broke down.

The Chief passed me his handkerchief and, waving aside my apologies, said, "We are all human, Miss Trant; it's only natural for you to be upset. Of course you must meet your cousin for luncheon, and don't hurry back – however invaluable you may be to us, I expect we shall manage without you for a few hours." He patted my shoulder and returned to the office.

I waited until my tears had dried up completely before going back to my desk. With the dreary, emptied-out sensation that follows a prolonged bout of crying, I resumed hammering out the letters, but my fingers were slow and clumsy and by the time I had finished it was time to get ready to go and meet Anna.

The rain had stopped and a yellowish mist hung over the greasy-looking streets. The pavements were thronged with office workers taking their luncheon break and I arrived slightly late at the Aerated Bread Company on Oxford Street, where my cousin and I had arranged to meet. Anna was sitting at a corner table next to a potted fern, craning her neck to look around the crowded tea room. As soon as she saw me approaching, she waved eagerly.

"Thank heaven!" she exclaimed, getting up and kissing me on both cheeks, in the French manner. "I felt sure you had been forbidden to come."

"I'm terribly sorry; I had no idea it would take me so long to get here," I replied, dropping a flurried kiss on her cheek, which was smooth and soft and emanated a delicate scent of face powder.

"Oh, it doesn't matter in the slightest. I was early – I ran out of errands and besides, I was so looking forward to seeing *you*."

She gave me a radiant, charmingly crooked smile and I was struck afresh by the way that flashes of the gawky schoolgirl were revealed in the countenance of the beautiful woman. She handed me a menu. "Do have a look – I'm simply ravenous! Naturally, you must allow me to treat you."

I attempted to protest, but she remained insistent. "My husband, George, has simply pots of money. I know it's vulgar to mention such things, but then you are a relation, so perhaps it's not quite such a *faux pas*. Of course, I would have married him even if he had been a pauper – he really is such a darling – but it's far jollier that he happens to be so comfortably off."

130

At that moment the waitress came over. I was not particularly hungry and ordered only soup and a pot of tea. My cousin began a conversation with the young woman about the competing merits of the different kinds of cake and I turned my gaze to the busy street beyond the plate glass window. After a short time I sensed that I was being watched and looked back to find that Anna was scrutinising me with childlike openness.

"It's frightfully modern of you to go out to work and support yourself, Margaret; I'm sure Mrs Pankhurst would approve. You have an air of independence and . . . resilience that we closeted females who are merely kept by our husbands utterly lack. I noticed it as soon as I laid eyes on you. Do tell me about your work – I should so much like to hear all about it."

I was tempted to snap that I would far rather have had the expensive education and the freedom to travel that she had enjoyed, rather than the obligation to support my mother and myself which had been forced upon me at such a tender age. Instead, I gave a concise description of the hearing appliance shop and the duties as a clerk and typist that, officially, I was supposed to practise, though it was a fiction that I felt rather ashamed of and I found myself wishing fervently that I could tell her the truth about Bureau 8. She enquired after my mother's health and about the place where we lived, and though I tried to put as good a light on our circumstances as I could, she saw through my evasions and reached out to squeeze my hand, murmuring, "Poor you."

It was not until we had finished eating and Anna had pushed aside her coffee cup that I finally summoned the resolution to ask her about the circumstances of Aunt Sophie's death. She hesitated for a moment, and then said, "I'd rather hoped you wouldn't ask, but I suppose it's natural that you should want to know. I'll tell you what I can, but it's a strange story, Margaret, and there's a great deal that I can't explain, even now." She paused, clearly reluctant to talk about what was evidently still a distressing topic, but after a moment she drew a resolute breath and continued, "After Uncle Arthur's death, Mother was not at all herself. She seemed to be avoiding me and she began to spend more and more time alone. I thought at first that it was simply grief – I had read about such things in novels and I assumed that she would be healed by the tender flow of passing time and so forth. I expect you know that she was terribly fond of Uncle Arthur. He used to come to see her sometimes, without Aunt Mariah's knowing. He regarded Mother as his confidante – she once let slip that he couldn't talk to my aunt about his difficulties because of her delicate nerves. I wasn't supposed to tell anyone about his visits – they said that it would cause a dreadful fuss if your mother ever found out about it."

Anna shot me an anxious glance, as if fearful that she had offended me, then picked up her napkin and began to twist it in her hands. I felt relieved that she was not looking at me, for I was aware that my puzzlement must be showing on my face. I should never have suspected that Father and Aunt Sophie had been at all close; indeed, whenever I had seen them together, they had been rather distant with one another.

My cousin gave a sigh and resumed her story. "Anyhow, time failed to do its work and Mother became increasingly preoccupied and withdrawn. It wasn't just that she was upset about Uncle Arthur's death; she seemed to be furious about something. When I tried to ask her what was wrong she was very snappish and quite unlike herself. Then she started slipping out in the evening without telling anyone about it. It happened three or four times at least and on the last occasion she didn't get home until after midnight; Mrs Jacques and I were fearfully worried. I crept out onto the landing when I heard the front door and I shall never forget the way she looked: as if she had the weight of the world on her shoulders. Of course when she saw me she pretended to scold me and told me that she'd been having supper with a friend, but I knew that she wasn't telling the truth.

"And then came the quarrel with Aunt Mariah. I know they used to squabble about silly little things, but to break with her own sister so completely, and after she had just been widowed – I couldn't understand it! But Mother was so stubborn. She told me that I would have to trust her, that there were good reasons why we couldn't see either of you again, and she refused point-blank to say anything further on the matter." She fell silent and turned her dark eyes away, swallowing convulsively.

In a blaze of revelation it occurred to me that the quarrel between Mother and Aunt Sophie might not have stemmed from sisterly rivalry over money and status, as I had always believed. What if Mother had found out about my father's visits to Sophie and, in the frenzy of her grief, had accused her sister of committing an unforgivable betrayal? Perhaps therein lay the "good reasons" that had led my aunt to sever all ties with Mother and myself?

"She died six months after your father's funeral, almost to the day," Anna went on. "Her illness was very sudden and unexpected; she fell ill on a Tuesday and by Friday of the same week she was dead." She breathed a long sigh, gave her napkin one final, violent twist and tossed it onto the table. "Afterwards there was a great deal of fuss because the housekeeper, Mrs Jacques, went to the police claiming that one of the servants, a stable lad who had gone missing on the day after Mother died, had been poisoning her, and indeed the post-mortem showed that there was an abnormality of some sort – I have never understood precisely what –in her blood. The matter was not absolutely clear-cut; apparently it was still quite possible that her death could have been brought about by natural causes. Mrs Jacques was so pressing in her accusations that she persuaded the police to try to trace the stable lad, but they never found him; he appeared to have vanished into thin air."

"Do you really believe that your mother was poisoned?" I asked.

"Oh yes, I have no doubt about it; if you had only seen the way she looked when she was ill then I'm sure you would have thought so too. Nevertheless, she remembered you right at the very end. On the day before her death, she gave me the letter I told you about and made me swear that the only person who would ever read it would be you. I've never spoken to anyone else about its existence; not to the police, not even to George. I tried and tried to find out where you were living, Margaret – I was absolutely desperate. But it was no good. If only I had thought to ask Mother for your address." Anna smiled sadly and for a few moments we sat without talking, our hands clasped firmly together.

"And what about the housekeeper; did she stick to her story?" I asked at last.

"Well, that was another tragedy; she died not three weeks after Mother's funeral; fell headlong down the cellar stairs and broke her neck. Poor Mrs Jacques." Anna shuddered. "Oh, that was a dreadful time."

"But why on earth should anyone have wanted to kill Aunt Sophie?"

"Who can say? She was so well liked, I find it impossible to imagine."

"And no one was ever arrested for the crime?"

"No. I've always thought the fact that there was no absolutely firm evidence meant that the police were not as determined in following things through as they might have been. And besides, as you say, there was no clear motive. When the investigation began to tail off I started saving up to pay for a private detective, but of course nothing ever came of it. And now that I'm really in a position to employ someone to look into the matter, I'd rather let sleeping dogs lie."

At this juncture the waitress returned to our table, and when Anna had settled the bill we emerged from the restaurant into the clamour of the busy thoroughfare and began to walk in the direction of Tottenham Court Road. Anna glanced at the clock in a stationer's window and exclaimed, "Half past already – how dreadful! I must get back home." She reached out and caressed my cheek with her gloved hand. "Dear Margaret! I have so enjoyed seeing you again; you haven't changed a scrap! Now, do give me your address; I'll post Mother's letter on to you as soon as I get home."

She handed me a little crocodile-covered notebook and a pencil, and I wrote down my address and gave it back to her.

"Thank you! You'll give my best wishes to your mother, won't you? There's a hansom over there just setting down a passenger;

134

I must run! Goodbye, darling!" For an instant I was engulfed in her perfumed embrace and then she was gone.

I turned to watch as she got into the cab, and stood waving goodbye as it swung into the road and whisked her off into the distance. Suddenly, I became aware of a tall thickset man gazing across from the opposite side of the street and my heart leapt into my throat; surely it couldn't be Mr Smith? A butcher's van rattled along the road in front of me and by the time it had passed the familiar-looking figure had vanished. Shaking my head at my own foolishness, I turned and made my way back to HQ.

# Sixteen

s I mounted the stairs to the office, I found that I was shaking, as if with exhaustion. I stammered an incoherent reply to the Chief's enquiry as to how I had got on and moved uncertainly towards the hatstand.

"Go home, Miss Trant," the Chief instructed, taking me gently by the shoulders and guiding me to the door. I tried to protest, but he interrupted me before the words were out of my mouth. "Go home and rest, and we'll look forward to seeing you bright and early tomorrow morning." I was too tired to summon up any coherent objection and surrendered to being escorted downstairs and out of the shop.

I had not been able to shake off the nagging conviction that it *had* been Mr Smith who had stood watching me from the other side of the road as I had said goodbye to Anna and, having taken my seat on the tram, I found myself plagued by the suspicion that he might have followed me. I glanced about surreptitiously at the passengers sitting around me, then stood up and scrutinised the faces behind, as if I were seeking an acquaintance. Having satisfied myself that Smith was not on the lower deck, I felt compelled to ascertain that he wasn't hiding upstairs. Of course he was nowhere to be seen and I returned to my seat, averting my eyes from the curious glances of the other passengers. I rested my head against the window, struggling to reflect upon all that Anna had told me, but my mind felt woolly and a dull ache had started to throb behind my temples, and after I got off at Finchley Road I decided to walk about for a while to clear my head.

The fog had lifted; the gas lamps blazed out through the dusk like beacons and the curtained windows of the houses glowed with a homely light. As I paced along, I soon started to feel better and I began to think back over my conversation with Anna. Two trains of reflection trailed round and round in my head, intertwining and circling one another, like the dual strains of a single melody: first, how curious it was that Aunt Sophie had died so soon after my father and in similarly obscure circumstances; and second, the discovery that she and my father had been such close friends. The fact that this friendship had been concealed from my mother filled me with a conflicting welter of thoughts and emotions, some of which I could scarcely bring myself to put into words. Of course, it was true that Mother's nerves had always been fragile, and much as I regretted my father's refusal to confide in her I found it perfectly understandable. As to the precise nature of what it was that he had been compelled to hide and whether this enigma had had any bearing on his death or my aunt's, I found myself unable to form a definite conclusion.

I could not help thinking how strange it was that, at a time when a thrilling new future was opening out before me, phantoms from the past had begun to rise up with such remarkable frequency. First had been the old photograph that Mr Plimpson had given me, the one in which he and Father wore lilies in their buttonholes. A few days afterwards, the Whitehall official who had interviewed me for the secretarial post at Bureau 8 had shown such a curious and inexplicable knowledge of my personal history that I had found it positively unsettling. Then, only yesterday, those peculiar watercolour portraits of my parents had arrived out of the blue, shaking Mother so profoundly that she had been driven to speak to me directly about my father for the first time since his death. And despite my professed certainty that the paintings were the work of a cheap swindler rather than the expression of some supernatural agency, I too had found them thoroughly unnerving.

And so, even before my chance encounter with Anna, many long-buried recollections had already been set stirring and I had begun to puzzle, for the first time in many years, about the events leading up to Father's death. My cousin's disclosures had brought my memories of that period still more painfully to life and yet, at the same time, had served only to intensify the uncertainties that prevented me from understanding precisely what had led to that final disaster. All of this lent a sharper edge to my curiosity about the letter my aunt had written me on her deathbed, and as I made my way through the damp, leaf-sodden streets I felt increasingly sure that it alone would cast light on events and motivations that at present still lay smothered in obscurity.

When I reached the boarding house Mother was already dressed and impatiently awaiting my arrival. As soon as I opened the door she rose from the sofa and hobbled towards me, and I saw at once that she had worked herself up into one of her fits of resentment.

"About time! I ask little enough of you and yet you are incapable of coming home at the hour that you are expected. Clearly, you can have no conception of how it feels to be shut up alone in this room day after day with no one to talk to. And then, when I do feel well enough to go downstairs for dinner, I am obliged to wait for you. Well, when I'm gone I dare say you might wish that you had behaved differently. Now hurry up and wash your hands; Minnie will be wondering where on earth we are."

When we entered the dining room, the Krackewiczs and Mr Smith were already sitting at the table and Mrs Hodgkins was clearing away the soup plates. As soon as she saw us she exclaimed, "Oh, there you are, Mrs Trant! I waited for as long as I could, but the soup was getting cold. There is a little left, though it won't be very hot."

Mrs Hodgkins had been very liberal with the salt cellar and, if anything, the tepid, congealed cream of cauliflower soup tasted even worse than it looked. Mother was able to plead a poor appetite, but under the landlady's beady eye I felt obliged to choke down every drop. My lately acquired secrets weighed heavily upon me; yet, wrapped up in my own thoughts as I was, I could not help being aware of

Mr Smith's brooding presence, which seemed to cast an atmosphere of constraint over the whole company. Irma Krackewicz smiled at me across the table every now and then, but she and her husband ate in silence and Mother, picking desultorily at her food, seemed more concerned to reacquaint herself with St Sebastian than to respond to the landlady's short-lived attempts at conversation. All in all the meal was a tedious and joyless occasion, as all social gatherings in that house tended to be, and I only mention it here because of two small incidents that later proved to be significant.

The first of these occurred while Mrs Hodgkins was ladling out the tapioca. Krackewicz leant back in his chair to stretch and for the first time I noticed a ripe purple bruise on his forehead, which had hitherto been covered by his hair. Perhaps I stared harder than I had intended, for, catching my eye, he flashed me a white-toothed grin and remarked, "Do you know how I receive this hurt, Miss Trant? Come now, I invite you to guess!"

His wife turned towards him and shook her head. "Not at dinner, *mon cher*!"

"Irma, you do not understand the English character; to discuss one's health is most interesting. Is that not correct, Mrs Trant?"

My mother shot him a venomous look, but to my relief made no other response. Krackewicz kept looking at me as if he were waiting for me to answer his question and so I suggested half-heartedly, "Perhaps you banged it on a piece of scenery at the theatre?"

"Ah, no – if that was all then I should not trouble to tell."

"I should say that you were hit on the head by a policeman's truncheon at one of those infernal socialist rallies that you and your wife are so fond of," growled Smith, startling us all.

"Actually, no," said Krackewicz with such a pointed sneer of disdain that it would not have surprised me very greatly if Mr Smith had lashed out and given him another bruise to match the first. Instead, he merely snorted and began noisily spooning up his tapioca.

"Indeed, it concerns a friend what belongs to you, Miss Margaret," Krackewicz went on, flinching as Irma nudged him hard in the ribs with her elbow. "*Kochanie*, there is no need. Miss Margaret likes to hear news of old friends, I am sure; though if you knew all, *mademoiselle*, I think that you would not hold to such an acquaintance. Come now, you know to whom I am referring?" he asked with a wink, determinedly ignoring his wife, who continued to glower at him. Thoroughly baffled, I shook my head.

"It is this scoundrel Plimpson, of course. A little after our first meeting, of which I told you, he offered me to do some work for him; I will not say what, for I gave my promise, and I am a man of honour, even when I am treated bad. But you must understand I would never agree to this work at all, though the wage is good, only that he tells me it is to help the cause of the working man. Yesterday, after I finish my work at the theatre, I am in a café to wait for my wife and of a sudden a stranger, a big fat man with a red face who I have never seen in all of my life, comes to me and punches me, here. He says, 'That's for Plimpson,' and he walks away as calm as he can be. You must imagine how I am feeling!"

"How dreadful!" I exclaimed.

Krackewicz shook his head reflectively and his voice dropped as he continued, "I have not seen Plimpson, not yet; it is too far to go when I am so busy. But in a few days I will find him and then we will see what he says to me!" His dark eyes blazed fiercely and he brandished his fist in the air, causing my mother and Mrs Hodgkins to exchange scandalised glances.

At this juncture Mr Smith stood up and plodded out of the room without a word, and almost immediately the Krackewiczs made their apologies and left. I excused myself a few moments later and as I passed into the hallway a diminutive figure suddenly appeared from the kitchen corridor and whispered, "Excuse me, miss."

"Yes? What is it, Becky?" I asked, looking down at her in surprise.

"I know I shouldn't ought ter speak to you like this, but I didn't know what else to do. What it is, is this: I fink Mr Smiff is up to no good. I tried tellin' the missus about it, but she only boxed me ears, and since then it's got worse and worse. I noticed there was somethin' strange about the gentleman when I first come 'ere and it's not just the way 'e looks neither, though that sends shivers up me spine. No,

I've seen 'im watchin' the 'ouse from across the street lots of times. 'e pretends to go out, but then 'e stays 'ere, skulkin' around. 'e writes fings down as well – the uvver day 'e dropped this out of 'is pocket as 'e was goin' upstairs. I never learnt me letters, but it don't look like normal writin' ter me." She handed me a crumpled piece of paper covered in strange hieroglyphs, similar in appearance to those on the postcards. There was one symbol in particular that I felt certain I had seen before: a tiny pyramid topped by a human eye, which was drawn at the bottom of the page. "I know I shouldn't say nuffink and I don't know what 'e's up to ezzackly, but it's gettin' so I can't 'ardly sleep at night for fear we'll all be murdered in our beds."

Her green eyes were those of a frightened child and I patted her shoulder clumsily, casting around for some words of reassurance. Before I could say anything, however, Mrs Hodgkins roared out, "Rebecca, is that you?" and she went scurrying into the dining room, leaving me staring thoughtfully at the crumpled piece of paper in my hand.

So Mr Smith, as well as the mysterious sender of the postcards, was in the habit of using a cipher. And if he had been watching the house when I was out at work, it would seem to imply that he was interested in the doings of some of the other boarders and not only me. Becky's suspicions lent weight to my earlier misgivings that Smith was engaged in illicit business of some kind, and I resolved to take the paper to Liebowitz and to tell him the truth about the origin of the postcard, in the hope that he might be able to cast some light on the matter.

After Mother had gone to bed I took out the only two photographs of my father that I possessed from their hiding place in my bottom drawer. I put aside the portrait of my parents that I had kept in my desk at Plimpson and Co. and bent to examine the second picture, the one showing Father and Mr Plimpson sporting lilies in their buttonholes. My father was smiling broadly at the camera, but there was a trace of unease in his glance which filled me with a profound disquiet. I wished that I had been more pressing when I'd asked Mr Plimpson about the lilies. After all, they were flowers one usually saw at funerals, yet here they were being flaunted as jauntily as carnations at a wedding.

A fragment of the song that Father had been so fond of drifted through my mind:

*Her cheeks that once glowed*
*With the rose tint of health,*
*By the hand of disease had turned pale,*
*And the death damp*
*Was on the pure white brow*
*Of my poor lost Lilly Dale.*

How I had lingered over those lines when I was a girl, wallowing in the sweet sadness that they had aroused in me. But now the words summoned up the image of my aunt on her deathbed and I felt a hard knot of tears rise into my throat. Hastily, I put the photographs away, telling myself that it was pointless to speculate any further about the events leading up to my father's death until I had read my aunt's letter.

# Seventeen

The following morning I showed the paper that Becky had given me to Liebowitz. He glanced at it with a wrinkled brow before handing it back, remarking, "Ah, more of the same nonsense, I see, Miss Trant."

"So you have had time to look at the postcard I gave you?" I asked, unable to suppress the note of eagerness in my voice.

"Yes, of course, but I didn't think it worth mentioning; the whole affair is clearly a practical joke of some kind. Who is he, this friend of yours? He must think himself very clever."

"Oh, he's not a friend," I said quickly. "When I gave you the postcard I said that he used to lodge in our boarding house; in fact he still lives there. I felt I ought not to have interfered with his post, you see, but now it seems justified. The maid who found that piece of paper told me yesterday evening that this man has been behaving very oddly, creeping about and spying on the house; and I'm sure he's been following me. What did the postcard say?"

"It was a mixture of arcane references, some pure gobbledegook and a few unpleasant obscenities; I shan't trouble to repeat any of it to you."

"And don't you think that the scrap of paper that the maid found might be different?"

"I would wager a great deal that it is not. In my opinion your 'spy' is a harmless eccentric and I should advise you to pay him no further heed. Here – give me the paper and I'll get rid of it for you." He snatched it away and handed me a plate and two cups. "Could you take these things into the kitchen? And after that the Chief would like to speak to you; he's in the meeting room."

After washing up the crockery, I poured myself a glass of water and stood sipping it, staring reflectively at the glowing embers in the stove. Liebowitz's manner had struck me as strangely unconvincing. It occurred to me that he might have discovered something significant that he did not wish to share with me, which would explain the alacrity with which he had confiscated Becky's sheet of paper. I resolved that despite what he had said, I would keep as close a watch on Mr Smith's activities as I could from now on.

The Chief rose to his feet when I entered the meeting room and indicated the empty chair opposite. "Please, Miss Trant, do sit down. I hope you're feeling better. "

"Yes, much better, thank you, sir."

"Miss Trant, I have a proposal for you. It is not within the usual remit of your duties, but I hope that you will agree to it nevertheless. As you may have gathered, we are extremely concerned about the safety of Tom Hunter's fiancée, Miss Hetty Bartholomew. MacIntyre has already made some initial investigations into her whereabouts and has drawn a blank; rather a baffling one as a matter of fact. Hampson-Smythe's storming off like that has put us into a dashed awkward position. It's looking increasingly unlikely that he is merely lying low until he gets over his fit of bad temper – he was seen leaving his lodgings carrying a suitcase – and to be missing an agent, particularly at a time of crisis such as this . . . well, as you can imagine, it poses a risk. We're a man short, and, to make matters worse, we're obliged to spend precious time trying to trace Hampson-Smythe. Which brings me to my request, Miss Trant: would you be willing to go to Little Garton to look for Miss Bartholomew?"

I stared at him for a moment, scarcely able to believe my ears. Then I exclaimed breathlessly, "Oh, yes, please! That is, of course I should be very happy . . ."

The Chief got to his feet and held out his hand, grinning broadly.

"Congratulations, Miss Trant!" he declared. "Unofficially at least, you are now not only Bureau 8's first secretary, but our first female agent!"

I stood up and shook the Chief's hand, dizzied by the realisation that the hopeless daydreams I had cherished for so long had, incredibly, come to pass: all at once I had been snatched up out of my pedestrian existence and thrust into the heart of a sensational adventure story!

"Now, to the details of the investigation," the Chief continued, gesturing for me to sit down. "The main purpose of your visit is to ascertain that Miss Bartholomew is safe, but we would also like you to establish whether she knows anything at all about Hunter's real line of work. She ought not to, of course, and you will have to exercise the utmost care and discretion in trying to find out." The Chief chewed his upper lip for a few moments before continuing, "MacIntyre's most recent enquiries have thrown up one or two questions with regard to Miss Bartholomew. Ten to one there's nothing to be concerned about, but, naturally, it's important that we make sure that she is all that we believe her to be. Do you understand me, Miss Trant?" The Chief fixed his shrewd brown eyes upon mine and I was reminded that beneath his jovial exterior lay unknowable depths.

"Do you mean that Miss Bartholomew is not to be trusted? That she might have been deceiving Hunter in some way?"

"As I say, it's very unlikely, but I cannot deny that MacIntyre's coming upon her photograph in the professor's house has made us all uneasy. Let us hope that your visit to Little Garton will set our minds at rest." The Chief looked away and moved decisively over to the door of the meeting room, as if he did not wish to discuss the matter any further. "I'll fetch Liebowitz so that he can give you more detailed instructions," he said, and went out.

I glanced around at the hundreds of architectural plans, diagrams, scrawled notes, formulae, newspaper clippings and maps that were pinned up on the walls of the meeting room in a disorderly fashion, one on top of the other, reflecting that there must be layers upon layers of them and that if they were unpeeled one would discover the history of the Bureau's previous investigations beneath, like archaeological remains. After a minute or so, Liebowitz came in, looking rather put out, and without any preamble sat down and began to read aloud from a page of notes.

"One: tomorrow morning, you will travel by train to the village of Little Garton, near Ely. There you will present yourself at the rectory, where Miss Bartholomew lives with her parents.

"Two: you will carry out this mission in the persona of a distant maternal cousin of Mrs Bartholomew, Miss Abigail Wenlock. Miss Wenlock is twenty-seven years of age and has recently become engaged to a Mr Henry Johnson, the son of a prosperous clothing manufacturer. She is a resident of Bradford in the West Riding of Yorkshire and she and Mrs Bartholomew have never met. Though Miss Wenlock is relatively genteel, it would be advisable for you to shorten your vowels a little in order to play the part with greater conviction.

"Three: if Miss Bartholomew is not at home you are to make every effort to find out her whereabouts. You must do your best to divine whether any explanations that you are given in this regard are true or false.

"Four: if Miss Bartholomew is at home, as we hope and expect, then you must attempt to gain her trust by speaking to her about your engagement. You might invent a few confidences about your betrothed; I'm sure you know the kind of thing better than I. Try to provide every encouragement for her to reciprocate, and we must hope that she will let slip some clue as to where she believes Hunter is at present. It's even possible that he might have written to her, in which case you must do your utmost to get a look at the letters. You must take care, however; under no circumstances should you arouse her suspicion by questioning her too eagerly, though you might attempt to lead the conversation in the right direction. And of course you must make no reference whatsoever to the real nature of Hunter's work. You should also be aware that the rector disapproves of his daughter's intimacy with Tom Hunter and may very well be ignorant of the fact that the two of them are engaged.

"Five: try to find out whether Miss Bartholomew is conscious of having been watched or followed. You might share the story of your eccentric fellow boarder – suitably adapted, of course." He paused, raising one eyebrow, and I felt myself blush.

Having concluded without once meeting my eye, Liebowitz handed me the list of instructions, bidding me to commit it to memory and then to burn it. I followed him into the office and sat down at my desk to read it over. Naturally, I was delighted to be working "in the field", but I must acknowledge that I was also terribly excited by the prospect of satisfying my curiosity about the beautiful Miss Bartholomew. The one thing that cast a dark shadow over the whole enterprise was the thought of informing Mother that I would be absent on business overnight, or possibly even for a few days; she had been so unpredictable lately that I had no idea how she would react.

I did not arrive home that evening until six and so was obliged to put off breaking the news until after dinner. Mother excused herself from the table as soon as the main course had been cleared away, and pretended not to notice when I followed her upstairs. She would have gone straight to her room had I not caught her by the arm and asked her to sit down for a moment. I proceeded to tell her the cover story with which I had been furnished by Liebowitz: that I was obliged to stay for a day or two at the house of an unmarried aunt of Mr Flowers on a business errand, about which I was deliberately vague. If she had been more herself she would undoubtedly have plied me with questions; as it was she merely sighed and remarked, "I'm going to bed. No, you needn't trouble about coming in to help me – I shall be quite all right."

I watched her limp towards her room, wondering whether I ought to go after her despite her insistence to the contrary. In the end, however, I went to get Father's old leather travelling bag out of the cupboard and began to pack my things.

When I went in to say goodbye the next morning, Mother groaned and pulled the eiderdown up under her chin. It was almost ten o'clock, for my train did not depart until after eleven, and I tiptoed towards the bed, seized by an anxious foreboding that she might be ill after all. Without opening her eyes she snapped, "For heaven's sake, Margaret, off you go! I'm perfectly capable of looking after myself – in fact it will be a relief to be alone for a few days without your fussing!"

"Goodbye, Mother," I said, turning away. I closed the bedroom door gently behind me, then picked up my bag and left the apartment without a backward glance.

# Eighteen

## MacIntyre's Story

MacIntyre had told me that he was the only one of Tom Hunter's colleagues to have met Miss Bartholomew and he had done so but once, just a few days after Hunter had joined their ranks. Hunter seemed pleasant and good-humoured, but he was guarded about his private life and MacIntyre knew almost nothing about him. He had resolved that he would watch and wait until he had gathered sufficient information about this latest recruit to lay any uncertainties to rest.

Then, one crisp spring twilight when he was returning home after a stroll in Hyde Park, he had happened to walk past a little restaurant in a cobbled backstreet close to Lancaster Gate. He glanced inside and immediately noticed Hunter, deep in conversation with a very pretty young lady. He entered the restaurant at once, spoke quietly to the waiter in attendance and approached the table.

"Good evening, Hunter," he said, giving the young woman his most dazzling smile.

Hunter looked up at him with an expression of horror, which was instantly transformed into one of polite welcome.

"Good gracious! Well, what a surprise!" he exclaimed, standing up and shaking MacIntyre's hand.

"I'm terribly sorry to intrude upon you like this, old chap," said MacIntyre ruefully. "I feel now I oughtn't to have done it, only I happened to see you with this delightful young lady as I went past and I simply couldn't resist."

"Mr MacIntyre is one of my colleagues – at the office," Hunter told his companion, looking exceedingly ill at ease.

"Tom dear, where are your manners?" she asked with a reproachful glance. "Mr MacIntyre, I must apologise on behalf of my fiancé. My name is Hetty Bartholomew." She looked up at him with a charming smile and held out her hand. MacIntyre bent over and kissed it.

"Enchanted to meet you," he said, before turning to address Hunter with a wink. "So this is the famous Miss Bartholomew, about whom we have heard so much. Do you know, my dear, he can scarcely stop talking about you."

"Really?" remarked Miss Bartholomew, regarding her fiancé with an expression of fond amusement. "How very extraordinary of him!"

"Do you live in this part of London, Miss Bartholomew? It's a very pleasant district."

The couple exchanged glances. "No, as a matter of fact I live with my parents in Little Garton – a village near Ely. My father is rector of a country parish and things are terribly quiet there, but I am fortunate enough to be able to stay with friends in London whenever I wish."

At this moment the waiter had approached, bearing a tray on which were set two dishes with silver covers, and MacIntyre had bade them good evening and left.

He had passed a few yards down the street and then ducked into the shadow of a gateway to wait, smoking one cigarette after another to stave off his hunger pangs. He thought about leaving several times, but it was a pleasant evening to be out, he had nothing else to do except to go home to his supper and then to bed, and anyway his curiosity was not yet fully satisfied. At last, after nearly an hour, Miss Bartholomew and Hunter had appeared, walking arm in arm, their heads bent close together in conversation. He proceeded to follow them, keeping at a cautious distance. After about five minutes, they turned into a broad, well-lit street. MacIntyre hung back as they ascended the steps of an elegant villa and were admitted by a tall man who, so far as he could tell from such a distant vantage point, was a butler. Hunter had not re-emerged, so MacIntyre had made his way home.

The following day, Hunter had placed a photograph in a silver frame on his desk. "My fiancée, Miss Bartholomew," he had told his colleagues, but divulged nothing else. As soon as an opportunity presented itself, however, he took MacIntyre to one side.

"I'm dreadfully sorry about last night, old man," he said in a low voice. "I hope you didn't think I was being rude, but it was such a dashed awkward position to be in. You see, I've told Hetty that I work for the civil service and I was in agonies in case you might let something slip that would give me away. I hate having to lie to her as it is."

"You needn't have worried, but I'm sorry too – it might have been wiser if I had restrained my curiosity and left the two of you alone."

"Well, it's a blessing in disguise really," said Hunter, lowering his eyes with a self-conscious smile. "I wasn't quite sure before how private we were expected to be with one another; you know, about our home lives. But I thought it might be all right, now that you've met Hetty, if I brought in a photograph; I did so hate feeling as if I ought to pretend that she didn't exist. Thank you, by the way, for digging me out of that particular hole – Hetty was pleased to be told that I don't forget all about her when I'm here."

"Don't mention it, old chap; all part of the service," said MacIntyre. "When's the wedding?"

"Oh, not yet," said Hunter, looking uncomfortable. "To tell the truth, there are a few difficulties – with Hetty's father, chiefly – but I'd rather not talk about that, if you don't mind."

So when MacIntyre had found the photograph of Miss Bartholomew in Professor Robinson's study he had consulted the Chief and Liebowitz, and it was agreed that their first course of action would be to send him to pay a morning call at the Bayswater villa.

In daylight, the house looked even more imposing than it had done at night. A pair of gorgeous decorated urns stood at the top of the flight of polished marble steps that led up to the front door, and the building was surmounted by a curved parapet, edged by an ornate balustrade which, MacIntyre told me later, reminded him of the splendours of the Italian Riviera.

A tall, Slavic-looking butler had opened the door and addressed MacIntyre in a foreign accent that he couldn't place. "Good morning, sir. How may I help you?"

"Good morning. My name is Mr Hearne. I am trying to find a distant relation of mine, who I understand is acquainted with the people who live in this house." As MacIntyre was speaking, he looked past the butler and saw a grand, red-carpeted staircase. Just at the point where it curved out of sight stood a pair of feet in black Oxfords.

"What is your friend's name?" demanded the butler, intercepting MacIntyre's wandering gaze.

"Miss Hetty Bartholomew," said MacIntyre, glancing up once again at the unmoving feet.

"I'm sorry, sir. I have never heard of anyone of that name." The feet suddenly disappeared, but the butler's face remained impassive. "Good day to you, sir," he had said, and without giving MacIntyre a chance to say anything else he had closed the door.

# Nineteen

*J*alighted from the omnibus at King's Cross brimming with nervous excitement. I had not been in a railway station for many years; indeed, the last occasion on which I could remember travelling by train had been just a few weeks before Father's death, when my parents and I had gone to see Aunt Sophie in Wade. Young and heedless as I was then, I had none the less been aware that the conversation among the adults was strained, that my father was silent and uneasy, and that my mother appeared to be unaccountably angry with my aunt. Though it would have saddened me to know that I would never visit my aunt's house again, I would not have found it altogether surprising.

I had forgotten what busy places railway stations can be; I had to push my way through the surging crowd to the ticket office, where I took my place in the queue behind a round-shouldered fellow in a tweed suit who had arrived just ahead of me. All around swirled the roar of conversation, the clamour of hurrying feet, the rumble of luggage trolleys and the mingled cries of flower sellers and newspaper vendors. Father was very fond of quoting Blake's lines about the world that is contained in a grain of sand, and as I looked about me I reflected that one could say much the same thing of an English railway station.

Once I had bought my ticket, I consulted a timetable and hurried along to the platform for the Cambridge train, ignoring various encouragements to "buy my sweet posies", "read the blood-curdling tale of the Derby butcher" and – this one accompanied by a plucking at my sleeve – "give us a shillin', miss – I lost my leg in Africa and can't work." I got on the train and walked along until I found an empty compartment in a second class carriage, stowed my bag in the luggage rack and settled down with the latest number of the *Strand Magazine*, which I had been unable to resist purchasing from a stall near the ticket office.

The journey proved to be a slow one. The train kept grinding to a halt between stations, standing still for up to twenty minutes at a time. If I had not had the magazine to distract me, I should probably have been terribly frustrated by these erratic stops and starts, but as it was my thoughts flitted contentedly from Miss Caley's thrilling exploits to vivid imaginings of the scenes that lay ahead. I pictured myself being ushered into a cosy parlour to discover the Bartholomew family sitting companionably in front of a blazing fire. Mrs Bartholomew would be knitting clothes for the poor, the rector would be nodding over a book of sermons and Hetty herself would be sewing lace onto a petticoat for her trousseau, her pretty cheeks tinged pink from the heat. They would be surprised to see me, no doubt, but very happy to welcome an unknown relation; at least such was my fond supposition. Eventually, towards the end of the journey, the train picked up speed, and I closed the *Strand* and sat gazing out at the flat countryside sailing past beneath an iron grey sky until, after about ten minutes of swift, uninterrupted progress, we began to slow down again on the approach to Cambridge.

There was a forty-minute interval before the next train departed, for we had arrived at Cambridge very late and I had missed my original connection. I was exceedingly hungry, and I purchased a tongue sandwich and a bottle of lemonade from the refreshment counter before making my way to the ladies' waiting room to eat my luncheon. By the time I boarded the branch-line train that was to take me to Little Garton it had begun to rain, and the light was growing increasingly dreary.

The train puffed slowly on its way, stopping frequently at

deserted-looking stations where no passengers seemed to get on or off. I gazed out at the vast expanses of black soil, broken up only by the occasional line of spindly trees, at the scudding rain-clouds and the dark forms of crows wheeling overhead, feeling suddenly lost and unsure of my ability to carry out the task with which I had been entrusted. I sought to distract myself by thinking about what MacIntyre would say if he were sitting beside me in the carriage, but every remark that came into my head sounded like a line of stilted dialogue from a romantic novel and I soon desisted, overcome with irritation at my own foolishness. Really, in a woman of my age, a woman with significant and pressing responsibilities, this kind of thing was not only ridiculous and undignified; it was a dereliction of duty!

I was the only passenger to leave the train at Little Garton and the station was deserted, but when I made my way out onto the high street, there were a number of villagers walking along in the thickening dusk. Having asked for directions from a pleasant-faced countrywoman, I was very soon turning down a narrow street that ran along one side of the church and coming to a halt in front of some tall iron gates. My heart was beating hard, but I was unable to work out whether this was due to excitement at the prospect of meeting Miss Bartholomew or nervousness lest I should fail to play my part with sufficient conviction. Taking a deep breath, I walked through the gates and down the long gravel path to the rectory. I stepped into the dank stone porch and pulled on the bell rope, producing a discordant jangling which could be heard echoing through the house, and waited for several minutes before I heard the sound of footsteps and the door was wrenched ajar.

"Who's that?" a female voice demanded. Taking care to shorten my vowels as Liebowitz had suggested, I apologised for my intrusion and explained that I was Abigail Wenlock, a relative of Mrs Bartholomew's. After a moment's hesitation the door opened just wide enough to admit me. I found myself standing in a windowless passageway next to a tall, stooped woman whose face was thrown into shadow by the flickering candle that she carried in her hand.

"Well, this is a surprise, I must say. You had better come into the parlour, Cousin Abigail," she said, so quietly that I could scarcely hear her.

I followed her down the passage and into a cheerless apartment which was pervaded by a stale, damp odour, as if it had gone unused for some time. Mrs Bartholomew told me that her husband was in his study writing next Sunday's sermon and invited me to sit down on a lumpy horsehair sofa while she went to fetch him. She did not offer to take my bag or my coat; the former I laid down at my feet and the latter I kept on, for there was no fire in the hearth and indeed my hostess was herself wrapped up in a thick black shawl. While I waited, I gazed out through the French windows onto a shadowy lawn bordered by a high laurel hedge, ruefully reflecting how different my reception had been from the one that I had envisaged.

The door opened and Mrs Bartholomew came back in, accompanied by a lean, silver-haired man wearing a dog collar. I stood up as he approached and he clasped my hand in his, remarking, "My wife and I have been married for nigh on thirty years but, extraordinary as it may seem, I never knew that she had any relatives living in Bradford." His grave brown eyes betrayed not the least hint of suspicion and I felt a twinge of remorse that I was obliged to deceive him.

"We will soon be having supper – you may join us if you wish," his wife said coldly.

As if seeking to compensate for her ungracious manner, Mr Bartholomew smiled and added, "We are simple country folk, but if you don't object to sitting down to a plain dinner in plain surroundings, then you are most welcome."

So it was that I found myself eating boiled mutton, cabbage and potatoes with these sombre people, who were so utterly different from my imaginings. The dining room, like the parlour, was not in the least congenial. The walls were papered in an indistinct pattern of dark greens and browns, and were adorned with several grimy-looking engravings on religious themes, though here at least the dank chill was somewhat ameliorated by a meagre fire burning in the grate.

So far there had been no sign or mention of Hetty, but then Mrs Bartholomew asked what had brought me to that part of the world and I replied that I was on my way to see an aunt on my father's side who had been recently widowed and was considering moving back to Bradford to be among her family, which seemed to provide an opportunity to ask Mrs Bartholomew about *her* family. I steeled myself, and enquired whether her daughter was perhaps staying with friends.

Her mouth fell open. "Whatever do you mean, cousin?" she faltered.

Aware that I had made some terrible error, I gabbled, "I'm sorry, it's merely that I would very much like to meet . . . Hetty, isn't it? I believe she is not so far from my own age."

Mrs Bartholomew gave a strangled cry, burst into tears and fled from the room. Her husband stood up, breathing heavily, and passed his handkerchief over his eyes before addressing me with a sorrowful look.

"I'm sure that you didn't come here to cause distress, Miss Wenlock, but I'm afraid that is what you have done. I am astonished you did not know that our poor Hetty died of scarlet fever more than seventeen years ago, when she was but three years old. Her death has been the great tragedy of our lives, for we have never been blessed with any other children, though we have longed for them very much. However, one must learn to endure the trials the Lord thinks fit to send us."

"I don't understand!" I blurted out in astonishment. "Hetty is engaged to an acquaintance of mine and I have a friend who has met her. I have seen her photograph!"

The rector's face darkened with suspicion. "Who are you?"

I felt my cheeks begin to burn. "What do you mean? As I told you, I am a distant cousin of your wife's. I . . ." I allowed my voice to tail off, aware of how unconvincing I sounded.

"My wife has never heard of you. Even so, we trusted you and took you into our home, and now I discover that you have lied to us. It will take Eleanor weeks to get over this. Her whole life – both our

157

lives – have been blighted by the loss of our daughter. All these years I've tried my best to comfort her, but . . ." He lowered his head as if he were close to tears.

"I'm so sorry to have distressed you," I said, appalled. "Clearly there has been some terrible misunderstanding. I will leave at once."

I got up and took my coat from the chair-back on which I had draped it before we had started eating, but to my surprise and dismay the rector grabbed me by the arm. "No!" he exclaimed through clenched teeth. "There is something I must show you first."

He propelled me out of the room, barely allowing me the opportunity to pick up my bag. Still gripping my arm, he strode out of the house, down the driveway and through a lych-gate that led into the churchyard. By this time, darkness had fallen and moon-light cast an eerie sheen over the headstones. As we hurried along a gravel walk which ran round the side of the church, a small creature – a mouse or a vole – scurried across my path and I gave a little shriek, which caused Mr Bartholomew to turn and look at me. When I glimpsed his face I felt quite frightened; he was deathly pale and his eyes blazed with a fury I did not wholly understand.

He stopped outside the vestry door, which was of sturdy oak studded with nails, and fitted a large iron key into the lock. He turned it with some difficulty and pushed open the door, which yielded with a low grinding sound. Quailing somewhat, I followed him into the shadowy interior, which was illuminated by the ghostly rays of moonlight that filtered in from a high, narrow window to the left. The place reeked of mildew and stale mice droppings. On the opposite wall was a warped wooden press on whose door several surplices were hooked, and next to that was a set of pigeonholes crammed full of papers. The rector lit a candle which stood on a table in front of the pigeonholes and took a bunch of keys from his pocket. He crouched down and unlocked the door of the press, then reached inside it, moving his wrist as if he were twisting a dial to and fro.

"We used to keep the registers loose inside the press, but now they are in an iron safe," he said dully, without looking round. "The vestry clerk had been nagging me about it for years; he said they weren't secure in such a rickety old thing, and of course he was right." He pulled out a large, heavy-looking volume in brown leather covers and laid it on the table next to the candle. "This is the parish register."

He opened the book and I drew closer. At first I couldn't see what it was that he was indicating, but then I realised that he was pointing to the remaining sliver of a page which had been cut away close to the spine. I raised my eyes and saw that he was scrutinising my face with ferocious intensity.

"Well?" he asked.

"The page has been removed."

"Yes! It was the first page on which the burials carried out in the year 1888 were listed. Can you guess why I noticed it before anyone else?"

For a moment my mind was blank and then it struck me: 1888 must have been the year in which his daughter had died.

The rector seized me by the shoulders and shook me hard. "I think that you know something about this. Have you any idea what agony has been caused? To lose her once and then . . . this!"

I truly believe that if my courage had failed me at that awful moment I would have found myself spending the night in a police cell. However, I drew a deep breath and discovered, to my great astonishment, that I possessed a capacity for quick thinking under pressure of which, hitherto, I had been utterly unaware.

I laid my hand on Mr Bartholomew's arm and looked him straight in the eye. "Sir, you must believe me when I tell you that I have come here with an honourable purpose. You were right; I am not related to your wife, nor is Abigail Wenlock my real name. However, the people who have sent me wish only to redress the wrongs that have been committed. I came here not to insult your daughter's memory, but to uncover a truth that may save a man's life."

The rector frowned and moved away from me. "Do you mean that you are working for the police?"

"Yes, in a manner of speaking."

"Can you tell me anything more?" I shook my head, and he passed a hand wearily across his eyes. "I don't know why I should believe you when you have deceived us so cruelly already; but there is something in your face that persuades me to trust you against my better judgement. I had planned that you would not leave here until you had confessed to your trickery and explained the reasons for it. I have achieved the former, but I see now that even if I were to press you you would refuse to explain yourself any further."

I nodded in mute confirmation of this assertion, feeling that I had already said far too much.

With an air of defeat, Mr Bartholomew closed the register, replaced it inside the safe and then locked the door of the press.

"Very well. All I ask before you go is that you write to me and tell me the truth about this matter, if you are ever in a position to do so."

"I promise," I replied, lifting my eyes to his. Then I turned and walked out of the vestry. I fully expected that he would restrain me, but when I glanced apprehensively over my shoulder I saw that, though he still stood staring after me, he had not moved a step.

It was not until much later, when I lay tucked up in bed in one of the upstairs rooms of the Red Lion on Little Garton high street, that my mind unbent itself sufficiently from the agony of self-reproach that had gripped me ever since my departure from the church to wonder how it was that the Chief and Liebowitz could have been so gravely mistaken about Hetty's whereabouts. How had it been possible to confuse her with a little girl who had died nearly twenty years before? And did the missing page from the register have some connection with the muddle, or was it merely a red herring? I lay awake long into the night, reliving the day's events over and over again, until I felt that Mrs Bartholomew's stricken face must haunt me for ever.

The woman in the photograph on Hunter's desk could not be Hetty Bartholomew of Little Garton Rectory. In which case, who was she?

# Twenty

The journey back from Little Garton passed without incident. I arrived in London shortly after noon and went directly to HQ. I had pictured the three men hanging breathlessly on my every word as I sat recounting my findings at the head of the table in the meeting room, but the reality was not quite as momentous as I had hoped; to my disappointment, MacIntyre wasn't there and the Chief and Liebowitz lounged on either side of my desk in the office listening carefully enough, but without the awed expressions that I had envisaged. They were, however, extremely taken aback to hear that Mr and Mrs Bartholomew's daughter had died before her fourth birthday, and when I told them about the missing page from the parish register they turned to look at one another as if they had both been struck by the same thought.

"False papers!" exclaimed the Chief.

Liebowitz nodded ruefully in agreement. "When I examined the civil records there was no documentation of the child's death, I'm certain; they must have tampered with those as well. We've been duped all right!"

"Poor old Hunter. She must have been briefed to gain his trust, which suggests that the Scorpions were suspicious of him from the first," said the Chief. "I suppose we will have to let him know at once, though it's cruel news to impart in a telegram. We must hope that he has time to get out of Germany before the trap is sprung."

"Do you mean that Miss Bartholomew is a Scorpion? That she has been deceiving Hunter all along?" I asked, appalled. I felt as if the glamorous young woman who had figured so prominently in my daydreams had betrayed me too. To think that I had pictured her as a virtuous beauty, waiting faithfully at home for her dashing lover to return. What a fool I had been!

"I'm afraid so," replied Liebowitz with a grave look. "Do you suppose he has told her anything, Rivers? It might explain . . ."

"Can you imagine Hunter blabbing? Why, he'd never spill official secrets, even under torture! No, though I hate to apportion blame without proof, I should say that it is more likely to be Hampson-Smythe who is responsible for any slippages of information that may have taken place."

At that moment a rhythmic volley of knocks sounded on the door and, at a nod from the Chief, I went across to open it. MacIntyre's tall lean body filled the doorway.

"Good afternoon, Miss Trant. I'm so glad you're back – I wasn't sure you would be just yet," he said. His eyes rested on my face for an instant longer than mere politeness would have allowed. "Was Miss Bartholomew at home?"

"I'm afraid there have been some rather unfortunate developments on that score," said the Chief, coming towards us. "Miss Trant, could you please type up a report of your investigation in Little Garton while Liebowitz and I apprise MacIntyre of all that he has missed."

I started to type, relishing the fact that I was composing my own account rather than merely transcribing the words of others. After a few minutes, a distracted-looking Liebowitz came out of the meeting room, took down his hat and coat and left the office without saying a word. I glanced after him, wondering what was wrong, then shrugged and went on with my typing. I found it much more difficult than I had supposed to express myself with accuracy and concision and ended up rewriting the opening paragraph three or four times before I was reasonably satisfied with it. I grew so absorbed in what I was doing that I didn't notice the Chief and MacIntyre coming back in, and when I became aware that MacIntyre was standing beside my desk I jumped in surprise.

"Ah! You have an artistic sensibility, I see," he remarked, gesturing towards the crumpled sheets of paper in the wastepaper basket with a smile. "Only a true storyteller would take such pains over her words."

"I'm afraid that I am being very slow," I muttered, turning red.

"I shouldn't worry – you'll find that it soon gets easier with a bit of practice. Now, I'm terribly sorry to interrupt you, but if you don't mind I should very much like to talk to you. I expect you could do with a cup of tea after your journey – in my experience travelling by train makes one's throat frightfully dry. What do you say?"

A few minutes later we were sitting at the kitchen table, and MacIntyre was telling me that while I had been in Cambridgeshire he had returned to the house in Bayswater to try his luck again, but had found the place deserted. "An old lady who lived across the street said there had been a great upheaval on the previous evening and she had heard from one of her servants that the people who lived there were going away for good. I've been puzzling about it ever since, but now you've discovered that 'Hetty Bartholomew' was using a false identity all along everything starts to make sense."

He took out a paper bag from the inside pocket of his jacket and tipped its contents into the biscuit tin, which he held out to me.

"Would you care for some shortbread? Do take more than one. I've already succumbed to temptation, I'm afraid – they're awfully good."

I began nibbling away at a biscuit and he gave the tea a final stir then poured it out.

"Now, I suppose we ought to get down to business," he said, leaning back in his chair and edging it away from the table a little. "This morning I had a sudden idea – I don't know why it didn't occur to me before – that Professor Robinson must have an office in the British Museum. I got myself up as a scholarly-looking type – my idea was that I could claim to be looking for some research papers that Robinson and I had been working on together – but it was easier even than that; the spectacles and the tweed suit were enough to get me in with no questions asked."

I nodded, wondering why it was necessary that MacIntyre should pass such details on to me.

"I don't suppose any of your relations were ever in the acting line, Miss Trant?"

I looked at him in astonishment. "In the theatre, do you mean? No. Why on earth should you think that?"

"Not even as a hobby?"

"No, I don't think so."

"Hmm, well – it was rather a long shot. I thought that they might be members of a theatrical troupe. Still, perhaps you could have a look at it in any case – you might spot something that the rest of us have missed."

He shuffled through the pile of documents he had with him, pulled out a photograph and handed it to me. I gazed at the picture open-mouthed, utterly baffled as to how it could have come into his possession.

"Do you recognise someone?" MacIntyre asked gently.

I paused, trying to catch my breath. "Yes – one of those men is my father," I said wonderingly, "and the man standing next to him is my former employer, Mr Plimpson."

"And the others?"

I looked at the photograph again. "I've never seen either of the other men before, I'm certain of that," I said slowly. "However, the gypsy woman does look vaguely familiar, though I can't place her. And besides, she's so heavily made up that it's impossible to tell what she really looks like – I might well be mistaken about recognising her. Where did you get this?"

"I found it in the desk drawer in Professor Robinson's office."

"How very odd," I remarked, feeling more puzzled than ever. "Before I left the firm, Mr Plimpson gave me a very similar photograph, though it was only of him and my father. I did try to ask him about it, but he wasn't terribly forthcoming. Do you have any idea why they're wearing lilies?"

"Lilies?"

"Yes – the men are all wearing lilies in their buttonholes. This picture was taken from a greater distance, so it's more difficult to see – but in the one I have at home it's quite clear."

"Lilies . . . now that reminds me of something, but I can't seem to think what it might be. I'll leave it to mull, Miss Trant; I'll let it simmer. Now, that's one of the most important pieces of advice I can think of for a young agent like you, just starting out on her career: if there is something niggling at you, some half-remembered memory or association, leave it to mull – you'll find that the answer will come to you when you least expect it. I'm afraid I can't explain exactly *why* it works – that's more in Liebowitz's line if you're interested, which I'm not – but it's a strategy that's never failed me yet. It would be worth your while to apply it in the case of our mysterious gypsy – you may find, eventually, that you do remember her after all." I knew that MacIntyre was flattering me, but even so I could not help feeling a sense of pride and excitement that he should see fit to describe me, ordinary Margaret Trant, as an agent in my own right.

"And of course, the other invaluable maxim for today's up and coming secret agent is . . ." he rummaged around in his pocket and then, with a grin, brandished a box of Deer Head damp-proof matches, about which was wound a length of twine, "always remember to carry a box of matches and a piece of string! Here, keep them. I've got plenty more where those came from." He pressed the twine-wrapped matchbox into my palm and, as our eyes met, I felt a tingling sensation along the back of my neck. Breathing rather hard, I looked away and put these essential, if somewhat peculiar, offerings into my skirt pocket. For a few moments the air seemed to radiate with a silence more intense than any I had previously experienced; then, abruptly, MacIntyre made a prolonged attempt to clear his throat.

"Biscuit crumbs," he explained hoarsely, pouring himself some more tea. "Would you care for another cup, Miss Trant?"

"No thank you," I replied, looking down at my hands.

MacIntyre dropped several sugar lumps into his tea and drank it down with a sigh of satisfaction. "Ah, that's better!" he exclaimed. "Now, this photograph from Professor Robinson's office is identical to the one on his study wall at home, which, according to his housemaid, was put up very recently. Clearly, it's not a new photograph, so it seems reasonable to assume that something must recently have occurred to bring the people in the picture, or the occasion that it commemorates, into the forefront of the professor's mind. Do you have any notion when or where it might have been taken?"

"I should guess that it must be about ten or eleven years old, but as to where – I'm afraid I have no idea."

MacIntyre stood up and peered over my shoulder at the photograph. "Is this one your father?" he enquired, pointing.

"How did you know that?" I asked in surprise.

"I suppose you're a little like him – something about the eyes." He leant towards me as if to scrutinise my face and I looked away self-consciously.

"And this is Mr Plimpson?" His long index finger hovered above Mr Plimpson's moon face. "Did they work together?"

"No, they were friends. My father was an accountant for a firm called Bellows and Tuttle – though he stopped working there a few months before he died."

"What did he do after that?"

"He found a new job almost immediately – he was very excited about it. He thought that it was going to make his fortune, but he was also very secretive, so I'm afraid I don't know much more, except that he had to go away for a while. And then . . ." My voice began to quiver and I broke off.

MacIntyre sighed and remarked with uncharacteristic timidity, "I'm terribly sorry. I realise that this must be a painful topic. Might I just enquire – was your father's Christian name Arthur?"

"Yes," I said, observing his closed, hesitant expression with a shiver of foreboding.

"There was a newspaper clipping in the drawer with the photograph – perhaps the easiest thing would be for you to read it." He took a square of newsprint from near the top of the pile and passed it to me. I skimmed through the first few words of the article before putting it to one side; that was enough to confirm my suspicions about its contents, and I could not bear to read any more.

"The facts are quite correct," I said, keeping my eyes fixed firmly on the table. "My father took his own life. It was said that it was due to financial troubles. He . . ." My breast began to heave and I felt tears welling convulsively into my throat. "I'm sorry," I spluttered, taking out my handkerchief and dabbing wildly at my eyes in a frantic attempt to master my emotions.

"My dear Miss Trant, it is I who should apologise. I thought that the article might be of some relevance to my enquiries, but the chance is so slight that it was not worth upsetting you. I am so dreadfully sorry; please forgive me."

Through a tremendous effort of will, I managed to stifle my sobs and gratefully drank down the glass of water that MacIntyre had poured for me.

"There's just one more question I must ask," he said after a moment or two of silence. "Did your father and Professor Robinson know one another?"

In my semi-hysterical state, the question struck me as absurdly funny and I gave a high-pitched laugh. "Oh, no, I shouldn't think so. I should be amazed if Father ever met a professor of archaeology, much less struck up an acquaintance with one." Then I paused, arrested by the sobering thought that MacIntyre's question might imply that he suspected me of concealing the fact that there was a connection between my father and the professor. I looked earnestly into his eyes. "If they had known one another I would have said something straight away, as soon as Murphy told the Chief that Professor Robinson was the real target of the Scorpions' bomb."

"I apologise. I ought never to have doubted you, even for a moment," he said, looking rather shame-faced. "I'm afraid that being in this game for so long has taught me to be appallingly cynical. You mustn't be hurt by my lack of faith – there have been times lately when I've felt as if I am the only person upon whose integrity I can safely rely. Please believe I consider you to be one of the most trust-worthy and dependable people that I have ever met."

He brooded silently for a moment before glancing at his watch with a distracted air. "Oh dear, I really must be going. Miss Trant, it might be some time before we see one another again. I'm obliged to go to Devon for a while; there are signs that the Scorpions intend to gather there." He took one of my hands in his, squeezing it hard. "Do be careful. I do hope that you . . ." He fell abruptly silent and let go of my hand.

"Why should I need to be careful?" I asked in a tone of forced amusement, endeavouring to meet his eye for an instant before looking away. "Surely it should be the other way round; I should be warning you!"

"Oh, there seem to be more reasons now than ever," he said vaguely. "I'm sorry, I don't mean to worry you – the Chief will explain things in his own time. Don't tell him I said anything – I shouldn't like him to think I'd been indiscreet." Then, before I could focus my thoughts sufficiently to question him further, he patted my cheek, picked up his papers and strode out of the kitchen.

I followed MacIntyre into the office and sat down at my desk, watching with a hollow feeling as he got his coat and hat and bade the Chief and Liebowitz goodbye. There was a round of back-slapping and hearty good wishes, as there had been on the occasion of Hunter's departure for Germany, and then, just as I had become convinced that MacIntyre was going to leave without bidding me a proper farewell, he paused in the doorway and turned to look back at me.

"Goodbye!" he said so quietly that I only understood the word from the movement of his lips; and then the door closed behind him and he was gone.

# Twenty-One

## MacIntyre's Story

It was not, of course, until much later that I heard the full story of MacIntyre's subsequent activities, but in pursuit of chronological accuracy I shall set them down in their appropriate place in this narrative. MacIntyre's reports were never dry and in endeavouring to render every detail as faithfully as I can, I hope to recapture something of the style in which he himself might have related the account, were he now here to do so.

MacIntyre was a man who liked to take care of his appearance, and the sensation of being grimy and ill-kempt ruffled his temper and filled him with a longing to be sprawled in a steaming bath. Moreover, he had been obliged to shave off his moustache in the line of duty, a sacrifice which had left him feeling oddly vulnerable and depleted. As he stepped down onto the station platform a biting wind blustered in from the sea, threatening to carry off his hat, cutting through his overcoat and bringing to his sensitive nostrils the odour of salt. For a short time he loitered in the shelter of the station wall, examining the dirt that had sullied the usually pristine half-moons of his fingernails and cursing under his breath. Despite his lofty stature and the fact that he had arrived at a small country town where strangers were out of the common run, the passengers who filed past paid him little attention, for he possessed that facility, so valuable to one of his profession, of being able to blend effortlessly into his surroundings.

At last, having made a cursory attempt to clean his fingernails with his penknife, he picked up his suitcase and made his way up to the road. A squat, balding man wearing a dog collar stood waiting in front of a row of adjoining cottages, a Gladstone bag at his feet. He glanced up at MacIntyre and then looked impatiently at his watch.

"Blessed fellow said he'd be here by five past and it's nearly a quarter to!" he exclaimed. "If there's one fault I cannot abide, it's lateness! Indeed, I'd even go so far as to call it a vice; yes, quite decidedly, a vice. What view do you take on the matter?" He addressed MacIntyre as if he were an old acquaintance whom he wished to engage in theological discussion, fixing him with his one good eye while the other, which was glass, seemed to gaze out over a hedge on the far side of the road.

"I should agree, of course," MacIntyre returned, doffing his hat politely.

"Ah, I see that you're not from these parts," the clergyman observed, regarding him with interest.

MacIntyre held out his hand. "Jonathan Rankin – Jonny."

"Mark Crawley." The tight corners of the clergyman's mouth twitched into a polite smile.

"Pleased to meet you. Yes, you're quite right – I've come down from Surrey to do a spot of fishing. Oh, and I'm supposed to be looking in on a protégé of my mother's at the local sanatorium."

"I hope the case is not too serious?"

MacIntyre grinned. "No indeed – he's lately got a job there as under-gardener. A lad from our village who's trying to better himself – he's become an unfortunate victim of Mother's passion for good works. Do you know the people who run the sanatorium?"

The clergyman's eye swivelled towards MacIntyre again, ranging over his tall, spare form. "No, I'm afraid not. Not part of my flock, so to speak."

"And where is your flock, if you don't mind my asking?"

"Oh, I'm staying at the Ham Stone hotel. A group of us will be gathering there over the next few weeks – we're amateur palaeontologists and we've chosen this delightful spot for our annual expedition. I've come down early, to enjoy the sea air. I've had too much of it this afternoon, however. I came in on the train before last and I've twice missed the chance of taking the charabanc into Seacombe because I'm waiting to be picked up by our president's chauffeur, who is, as always, abominably late."

"So I've missed the charabanc too?"

"'Fraid so, old chap."

"Any idea what time the next train comes in?"

"'Fraid not. I'd love to offer you a ride, but we're picking up three friends on the way down."

"Not at all. If I start walking, someone else is certain to pass me on the road. I dare say the exercise will do me good."

At this juncture their conversation was interrupted by the keening of an engine climbing a steep incline, and a moment later a shiny motor car came roaring over the brow of the hill and drew to a halt outside the station. A uniformed chauffeur leapt out without troubling to turn off the engine, opened the door for his passenger to climb in, stowed away his luggage and jumped nimbly back into the driving seat. The vehicle shot off at top speed, throwing the clergyman off-balance as he turned to wave at MacIntyre's fast-diminishing figure.

"Goodbye, Reverend Mark Crawley – until we meet again," the putative Jonny Rankin muttered to himself before turning away and marching off down the hill, suitcase in hand, his coat-tails streaming out behind him.

Merrivale Sanatorium is a charming little place in summer and the beauty of the views alone would do much to set any invalid on the road to recovery. On the autumn afternoon on which MacIntyre walked through its tall iron gates, however, the aspect that it presented was somewhat bleak and forlorn. The magnolia trees on the far edge of the grounds were bedraggled and dripping, and the flower borders, which in June were glorious with colour, were drab and muddy and contained only a few sparse pieces of greenery. For a short distance he traversed the long gravel driveway that led up to the sanatorium, his shoulders hunched against the cold, before veering away up a steep slope towards a potting shed covered in peeling green paint. The raw wind blew drifts of leaves across his path and stung his eyes, and he dabbed at them with a pocket handkerchief that flapped about like a red pennant. He came to a halt a few yards from the top of the rise, pursed his lips and emitted a low, tuneful whistle, which was immediately snatched away by the gale. He advanced towards the cluster of pine trees that sheltered the shed, trilling away with great zeal, and at length the door opened and a rangy, blond-bearded gardener peered out with a cautious expression. As soon as his eyes fell upon MacIntyre, he grinned and beckoned him inside.

"You're here at last!" he exclaimed, stowing away the suitcase and pulling a stool up to the stove so that MacIntyre could sit down. "I was beginning to wonder what had become of you."

"I've just walked six miles from Queensbridge. I thought you might be able to get away to meet me at the station."

"Not a chance, I'm afraid."

"So, you young scoundrel – what news?"

The young man, whose hooded, penetrating eyes seemed somewhat out of place in the face of a gardener, looked serious.

"You go first. Do the Chief and Liebowitz still believe that I stormed off into the blue?"

"Oh, yes. You're very much *persona non grata* at HQ, dear boy."

The young man's face fell. "I suppose it was foolish of me to expect anything else," he said. "Still, you can't imagine what hard work it's been, pretending to be such an unpleasant, incompetent, jealous . . . nincompoop for all these months. Why, by the end of it I felt as if I wouldn't be able to stop. What was it my nanny always used to say? 'If you pull a nasty face like that, my boy, you'll be stuck with it when the wind changes.'"

"Poor old Smythe, it has been hard on you," said MacIntyre with a sympathetic grimace. "You made a jolly good show of it, though – almost too good at times." He felt his nose ruefully.

"Yes, I'm terribly sorry about that – I've felt guilty ever since. You see, we'd been planning my departure for such a long time – well, I really didn't mean to hit you so hard, but in the heat of the moment . . ."

"Don't worry, dear boy. I'm a tough old bird – I didn't sustain any lasting damage." MacIntyre took out his cigarette case and offered it to Hampson-Smythe, who shook his head. "Actually, Smythe, there is one thing you can do to make up for assaulting me. I don't suppose you can lay your hands on a wee dram to warm our cockles? That wind is the very devil."

"Any excuse!" said Hampson-Smythe with a look of fond indulgence. "I do indeed have a little something," and with a flourish he produced a silver hip flask from the pocket of his overalls and passed it to his companion, who took several long pulls before handing it back with a contented sigh.

"Thanks, old boy – that was just the ticket! You'll have to do something about that flask, though. If you get caught with a museum piece of that kind, they'll think you've filched the family silver."

The gardener looked at the elaborately engraved flask with a frown. "But this little gem belonged to my grandfather. It's an heirloom!"

MacIntyre removed a dead leaf from his hair, regarding his companion with an expression of weary exasperation.

"Oh, very well. I suppose you're right – I'll try to find another," Hampson-Smythe conceded with an air of reluctance, before taking a swig of whisky and stowing the offending article away.

"Never mind, Smythe – at least you've made a grand job of the beard. It suits you. How's your country accent?"

"Oh, I tend to mumble rather a lot – I still haven't quite got into my stride. But no one seems to notice."

"Well, let that be a valuable lesson to you, young fellow – so long as you perform with confidence, most people will believe anything you want them to. Now, why don't you tell me your news?"

"Very well. I've kept a written log, as you advised. I'll just fetch it." Hampson-Smythe stood up and, from among a cluster of watering cans on the far side of the shed, retrieved a battered tube resembling the case for a portable telescope. He unscrewed the top and pulled out a roll of papers, remarking in an apologetic tone as he handed it over, "There haven't been that many developments since I got here."

MacIntyre turned his attention to the log, delicately fingering the bare flesh above his upper lip. Hampson-Smythe took down a pipe from a rack that hung, somewhat askew, on the wall of the shed and filled it from a tobacco pouch he pulled out from his trouser pocket. He sat down, struck a match against the side of his stool and began to puff away conscientiously. At the sound of the fizzing match, MacIntyre looked up.

"I see you're determined to play things by the book. I tend to use Woodbines when I'm obliged to take on the part of a working man – filthy stuff, but I've never felt comfortable smoking a pipe and of course it's details like that which, if you get them wrong, have the potential to arouse suspicion." He gave an appreciative chuckle. "Actually, the pipe rather suits you, especially with that beard – you've quite a Parisian air about you, like a painter starving in his garret."

Hampson-Smythe shot him an indignant glare and turned to stare out through the glistening beads of drizzle strung across the window pane. After mulling for a few minutes over his pipe, he enquired, "What do you think of that fisherman's story?"

MacIntyre paused to skim through the concluding lines of the log before responding, "This fellow who saw a couple of foreign geologists looking out at the sea with binoculars? It hardly suggests that they were spies signalling to the German Imperial fleet."

"Or Scorpions," sighed Hampson-Smythe.

"I believe fossil-hunting is a very popular pastime here. I met a chap at the station . . ."

"Actually, MacIntyre, that was just the fisherman's point. Usually geologists are to be found much further along the coast, towards Lyme Regis."

"Well, there was certainly something peculiar about the fellow

I met, even though he was wearing a dog collar. Crawley, he said his name was – we must keep an eye on him. However, evidence of that type – my intuition or your fisherman – is much too flimsy to go on. Nevertheless, we mustn't despair. My Lambeth contact insists that there is to be a conference of men from the higher ranks somewhere near Seacombe."

"He's heard a *rumour.* I still think it's very odd that they've chosen an out of the way place like this."

"I expect they have their reasons – privacy for one. No one would think of looking for them down here. Besides, that contact has always been very reliable before. And don't forget the corroborating evidence – we've now heard that the Scorpions are going to be congregating somewhere on the south coast from three separate informants – two others since Wilson first tipped us the wink. And then yesterday in Professor Robinson's office at the British Museum, what did I find in his desk drawer? A copy of Bradshaw with the corner turned down to mark the timetable for the Queensbridge branch line!"

"You don't think the professor has travelled down here?"

"Why not? I expect he's come early, in plenty of time for the conference."

"But the Scorpions wanted to assassinate him!"

"A *faction* of the Scorpions, dear boy," MacIntyre corrected him. "Besides, we only have the word of that wretched fellow who landed up in hospital for that. A lowly minion like him could easily have been lied to so that the perpetrators could cover their tracks. I have a suspicion that the explosion at Victoria was not an accident at all. Somebody planned it – perhaps even Robinson himself. That's where this business of factions comes in – the more radical wing of the Scorpions is getting restless."

"And the newspapers played straight into their hands by making such a fuss about the explosion and giving them plenty of free publicity," said Hampson-Smythe excitedly. "And no doubt before long they'll try to do it again. Isn't that precisely what happened in the eighties?"

"Very good, Smythe!" said MacIntyre, giving him a little flourish of applause. "I should say that you're absolutely right – with one important reservation, however. Of course, you're too young to remember first hand, but in the eighties the Scorpions' strategies were rather different. The violence was always targeted at important public figures – politicians, a diplomat or two, a powerful banker, scions of the European nobility – not members of the ordinary population. Potentially, if they really were to continue to perform such outrages in busy public places, the current situation could become far more dangerous."

"But what can we do about it?" cried Hampson-Smythe, getting to his feet and clenching his fists as if he wished that there were a Scorpion on whom he could take out his frustration then and there.

"Sit down, Smythe. You must remember that you are here for very good reasons. Until we are able to rely unreservedly upon the discretion of our colleagues, we must continue to carry out this investigation with the utmost caution."

"But is there nothing more that we can do?" asked the younger man gloomily.

"We must watch and wait. I will continue to report back to HQ. We will do everything we can to root out the traitor in our midst without arousing his suspicion."

Hampson-Smythe removed his pipe from his mouth, scorching his fingers on the bowl. "Ouch! Blasted thing!" he exclaimed, putting it down in disgust. "I must say, to have my confidence in the other fellows undermined like this has really knocked me for six. Sometimes I wonder whether it wouldn't be better simply to place our trust in their being good chaps and forget about all this intrigue. I feel like a fearful cad, having to lie to them and to sneak about . . ."

"Ah, you've just reminded me," MacIntyre interrupted, drawing a postcard and a rather crumpled piece of paper from his pocket. "Speaking of sneaking about and being caddish, I found these on Liebowitz's desk."

Hampson-Smythe took the card and examined the cipher that was scrawled on the back with a furrowed brow. "I don't understand. Why are you showing me these? Isn't it Liebowitz's job to decode messages of this sort?"

"Well, one might think so. However, though I am by no means such an expert as he is, I have sufficient knowledge to perceive that this is a most unusual and fascinating cipher. Being the enthusiast that he is for such things, doesn't it strike you as the least bit suspicious that he hasn't mentioned these communications to any of us?"

"Well . . ."

"You're unwilling to think badly of Liebowitz, which of course is quite natural. However, it might interest you to know that I myself have come across several pieces of paper and other miscellaneous articles, including on one occasion a wall, covered in just this type of hieroglyphic. As you may remember, I discovered further examples during my visit to the professor's house – and I rather suspect that one of them was the calling card of an uninvited visitor who was up to no good."

"But then why should this mysterious person want to draw attention to himself?"

"Oh, showing off, of course, dear boy. The bounder is always one step ahead – he wants to make sure that we know it."

"Is this fellow a member of the Scorpions, do you suppose?"

"Very possibly."

"You think that all the messages were written by the same individual?"

"Perhaps."

"And you're sure all of them are in the same code as this?"

"I've seen sufficient examples now to be almost certain that they were."

"So are you proposing that we should regard the suppression of these items as evidence that Liebowitz has betrayed Bureau 8 to the Scorpions?"

"I hope not. It's conceivable that he simply no longer trusts us either and is following his own line of inquiry, just as we are."

"You mean that he too might suspect that a spy has infiltrated Bureau 8?"

"Why not? It's perfectly possible that we're not the only ones to have noticed that fate's begun to play her cards with a remarkably heavy hand."

"I must say, it sets my teeth on edge, that queer feeling he gives one of always seeming to be watching, as if he's waiting for some slip."

"I think that's just his way, Smythe – though I shan't deny that at times his behaviour is, frankly, rather odd. For example, the Chief was in the middle of telling us what Miss Trant had discovered at Little Garton when he muttered some excuse about having to meet a contact of his and rushed off." MacIntyre paused to light a cigarette. "But Liebowitz has always been rather eccentric – he's far too wrapped up in what's going on in that brilliant brain of his to pay attention to the effect that he's having on other people. However, we've been over all this before."

"And he still insists that Robinson isn't a Scorpion? Don't you think that's rather peculiar?"

"It certainly adds fuel to the fire. I must admit, I don't understand why he's so adamant about it. Nor do I see why he should continue to reject Hunter's explanation about its having been a faction of the Scorpions that was responsible for the explosion – unless he knows something we don't and is deliberately keeping it from us."

"Do you know, there was part of me that couldn't help being disappointed when it turned out that Hunter hadn't betrayed us to the Scorpions after all. Of course, it would have been a dreadful shock – he's always been such a jolly good chap – but at least it would have cleared away this ghastly cloud of suspicion hanging over all of us."

"You got my telegram about Miss Bartholomew?"

"Yes. Poor old Hunter – what a dreadful blow it will be when he finds out!"

"I haven't been in touch with HQ since yesterday, so I don't know whether he's replied to the Chief's telegram. I dare say they'll let me know as soon as there's any news." MacIntyre heaved a deep sigh and allowed his eyes to close.

"Are you sure that we're doing the right thing, MacIntyre?" asked

Hampson-Smythe, looking anxious. "I still think it might have been better to confide in the Chief."

"About Liebowitz? Come come, Smythe – you're allowing yourself to be taken in by Rivers' fatherly exterior. You may never have seen it, but believe me, that man has a side to him that is utterly cold and ruthless. I know you think that I'm being absurdly cautious, and perhaps I am, but experience has taught me that you can never truly know another person – I'm always suspicious."

"So you don't even trust the Chief? What about me?"

MacIntyre gave a short, humourless laugh. "I trust you as much as I do anyone, dear boy. It's fortunate that you were away in Ireland last year at the time of the Twelve Trees affair, or I should have been suspicious of you too."

"And Miss Trant?"

MacIntyre's face lit up. "Ah, there we do have a possible future ally. If I were the kind of man to rely purely upon instinct, then I should say that she is someone we can trust absolutely. However, being the cynical fellow that I am, I will continue to tread with caution."

"I think you have rather a soft spot for her."

"There are various factors that suggest that Miss Trant will end up playing an important role in this business," remarked MacIntyre with a glance of lofty disdain.

"You've turned as red as a beetroot, old fellow!" Hampson-Smythe laughed. "Anyhow, what do you mean by 'an important role'? Why ever should Miss Trant be of such significance?"

"All in good time, Smythe, all in good time. I need to get the matter straight in my own mind before I start discussing it."

"So where does that leave us?" asked Hampson-Smythe, tapping the smouldering ashes from his pipe into a small flowerpot.

A troubled expression settled on MacIntyre's face. "Well, until we know for certain whether or not there is a double agent at Bureau 8, I'm afraid we must continue to conceal the fact that we are working together."

The two men regarded each other grimly and the shed was filled with the sound of the wind, rising like a banshee about its walls.

# Twenty-Two

Mother seemed positively disappointed to see me back so soon.

"I thought you were going to be away at least until tomorrow," she grumbled when I came in. She did not show any interest in the story I had prepared, nor did she manifest the avid curiosity about the domestic arrangements of Mr Flowers' aunt that I had anticipated. She maintained a subdued demeanour throughout dinner, and when we returned to our apartment she went immediately to her room.

I sank down onto my bed with a sigh and lounged against the wall, staring into space. My conversation with MacIntyre had left me in a state of uncertainty, and despite my sternest efforts I was unable to stop thinking about him. However many times I told myself that he would adopt the same tone of intimacy in addressing any young woman of his acquaintance, I could not prevent myself from reviewing everything that had passed between us in minute detail, alternating between the tentative hope that he might be growing to care for me and the gloomy conviction that he was not.

The only thing that had the power to distract me from these tortured reflections was my puzzlement about the photograph and the newspaper article that MacIntyre had discovered in the professor's office. I had no idea who the two unknown men in the picture might be, but I found myself unable to shake off the suspicion that

I had seen the woman before. "Leave it to mull," I told myself, feeling tears rise swiftly to my eyes at the recollection of the half-serious, half-humorous tone in which MacIntyre had given me this advice. I pressed them away with the palms of my hands and plunged on stubbornly through my chain of reasoning. Even if Father and Professor Robinson had once known one another, which seemed to me exceedingly unlikely, it had been many years since they had last met. What could possibly have brought that old photograph to the professor's attention once again? And more fundamentally, why would a man like the professor, a well-respected scholar and possibly a high-ranking Scorpion to boot, have held on to a newspaper clipping about the death of an ordinary accountant for such a long period of time? Here, I mused, was another phantom drifting up from the past, giving rise to yet another mystery; one that seemed even more obscure and inexplicable than the rest.

Troubled by restless thoughts, I lay awake long into the night and arrived at HQ the next day feeling listless and rather sorry for myself. I didn't have time to dwell on my tribulations for long, however; I had scarcely hung up my coat when the Chief bounded up to me.

"Good morning, Miss Trant!" he said briskly. "You're looking a trifle pale, if you don't mind my saying so. I hope you're not feeling ill?"

"No, I slept rather badly, that's all. I'm sure I shall feel better as the day goes on."

"I do hope so – in fact I'm rather relying upon it. Could I have a word with you, about something important?"

I followed him into the meeting room, where he sat down at the deal table and indicated that I should do likewise.

"I don't know whether you've had an opportunity to read the newspapers this morning?" he asked.

I shook my head.

"Ah, then I doubt you will have heard. Yesterday afternoon there was an explosion at a café in Berlin. Three people were killed and many more were injured. Shortly afterwards, a letter was delivered to the chief of police in the city. In it, the Scorpions claimed responsibility for the atrocity, designating it 'an act of protest against the absurdity of the established order'. We have yet to hear from Hunter, but as soon as we do, we will work with head office to formulate a strategy to track down the perpetrators. So far it's unclear whether we're dealing with a faction again, or with the organisation as a whole, but whoever they are, I'm afraid that after all these years of being more or less inactive they really do mean business – and it is our job to stop them." He paused for a moment as if waiting for me to speak, but I was too taken aback by the tidings of this latest manifestation of the Scorpions' ruthless zeal to offer any comment.

"You are an observant young woman and I am sure you will have noticed that our investigations into the activities of the Scorpions have reached something of an *impasse* since the explosion at Victoria," the Chief went on. "They might stage another attack in this country at any time, and with Hampson-Smythe still missing and Hunter and MacIntyre engaged in important work elsewhere there are only the three of us to man Bureau 8's operation here in the capital – rather a tall order, I'm sure you will agree. I explain all this to enable you to understand the full magnitude of the crisis that we are currently facing, for I am about to ask you to throw yourself into the fray.

"Last week I received a call from head office, during the course of which it was intimated that a gentleman with whom you are closely acquainted may be engaged in business dealings with the Scorpions. How deep this involvement is, and whether or not it is unwitting, we have yet to ascertain. We have been monitoring this individual's activities for a number of years; he has been implicated in various suspicious episodes which have come to the attention of the police and have been passed on to us, though nothing has ever been proved. I hope it will not shock you too greatly my dear, if I tell you that the person of whom I speak is your former employer, Mr Plimpson."

I felt the blood drain from my face and mouthed weakly, "Plimpson?"

"Yes, I'm afraid so."

"I was in sole charge of his paperwork; there is absolutely no possibility that he could have carried on any illicit business without my noticing." Even to my own ears I sounded unconvincing.

"Are you sure about that, Miss Trant? What if the particular items concerned had been logged using a cipher?"

I stared at him, thinking of the men I had seen watching the windows of the office; of Mr Plimpson's terror at the prospect of being hunted down by some "disreputable" individuals with whom he had been doing business. Guiltily, I recalled all the little slips and contradictions that I had been wont to dismiss as products of my employer's poor memory and haphazard approach to managing his affairs. And yet, was it possible that the Chief could really be referring to the tedious, blustering little man I had known? The ineffectual fellow who, it had always seemed, was incapable of making a decision unless he consulted me first, though he invariably pretended afterwards that he had not done so? If Mr Plimpson really had been working for the Scorpions then he had strayed far beyond the petty wrongdoing of which I had occasionally suspected he might be guilty. I found it scarcely credible that he could have been capable of organising unlawful transactions on such a grand scale behind my back, let alone that he had been sufficiently cunning to evade detection by cataloguing them in code.

"We want you to go over to Plimpson's office to find some papers for us and to bring them back here. Of course, any additional information that you can dig up in the process would be extremely welcome. Can you do that without arousing his suspicion, do you think?"

I considered carefully for a moment, then replied with a quiver of mounting excitement in my voice, "I should very much like to do it, sir, and I'm pretty certain that I can deal with Plimpson easily enough. However, if his wife is there, things will be more difficult."

"We're in luck, then. According to the latest report, she hasn't been seen near the premises for several days."

"Really? Have they quarrelled?"

"I should imagine she's gone to oversee business elsewhere; I believe she is very much the 'Co.' of Plimpson and Co. nowadays.

Anyhow, if it's convenient, we would like you to go over to Deptford as soon as possible."

"Yes sir, of course."

The Chief's ruddy face broke into a grin. "Good! And you may henceforth consider yourself officially appointed as Bureau 8's first female agent. I'm afraid that for the time being at least we will have to ask you to continue with your secretarial responsibilities, but you will be remunerated with a further two pounds each month." He produced a small red leather case from his pocket and flipped it open with a swift, sudden movement. "You had better take this."

I gave a gasp of consternation.

"No need to worry, Miss Trant; it's merely a precaution. Do you know how to use a weapon of this kind? As you can see, it's a small model, especially designed for a lady."

I shook my head. The Chief took the revolver out of its case and opened it up.

"When the weapon is fully loaded, each of these six cylindrical chambers will contain a bullet cartridge; that gives you six shots before you need to reload." He snapped the two halves of the gun together with a skilful flick of his wrist. "To shoot, you simply pull the hammer back, so, and then pull the trigger." There was a faint click. "Of course, when it's loaded you need to be prepared for a much louder noise. Now you try, my dear."

I took the revolver with trembling hands, and after two or three attempts managed to master the shooting mechanism to the Chief's satisfaction.

"That's very good, Miss Trant. Now, I want you to imagine that I am about to launch a lethal assault on you. Wait a moment – I'll stand on the other side of the table." He moved across and struck the exaggerated pose of a pantomime villain: hands on hips, chin thrust into the air. "Now, aim the gun at my chest!"

I held up the revolver, pointing it in more or less the right direction, but my hands shook so hard that I had to bring it down again straight away.

"Come along, my dear, you can do much better than that."

I drew a deep breath and gritted my teeth in determination, thinking of Miss Wade, renowned among her fictional counterparts for being a crack shot. My hands steadied themselves. I pushed my spectacles towards the bridge of my nose, looked along the barrel of the gun towards the Chief, pulled back the hammer with my thumb and released the trigger. The Chief stumbled to the floor, clutching his chest in mock agony.

"Bravo, Miss Trant!" he exclaimed, getting to his feet and coming towards me with a gratifying air of being genuinely impressed. "Unless I'm very much mistaken, you shot me right in the heart. You clearly possess a natural facility for handling firearms, my dear. Now, if you'll just pass the gun to me, I'll insert a round of ammunition, so that it's ready to fire – watch carefully!" With practised ease, he opened the barrel and filled each empty chamber with a bullet cartridge. "There we are. You won't have any trouble opening the case in an emergency – it's been specially designed so that you can unfasten it with one hand." He returned the gun to the case and closed it, then demonstrated the opening mechanism before passing it to me. "Do keep it out of sight, unless you have occasion to use it."

For want of a better place I put the case into my skirt pocket, feeling a momentary thrill of excitement to think that *I*, Margaret Trant, was now an armed government agent!

However, in the next instant I was overcome with a wave of crippling apprehension. It is one thing to be tantalisingly close to realising one's dream and quite another to find that it has been fulfilled and that the reality of all that one has longed for is staring one in the face. It seemed to me that there must be hundreds, perhaps thousands of women who would be much better suited to espionage work than I, and I suggested as much to the Chief; after all, the consequences of failure could be deadly, not only for me, but for many others besides.

"Nonsense, Miss Trant!" he exclaimed. "You have more than proved your mettle already. We don't have time for such qualms, I'm afraid. Now I can't give you any written instructions – it would be too great a risk – so listen carefully. We need you to obtain two letters from a steel manufacturer, Hertz und Mann. The firm is based in Cologne and an informant in that city has uncovered evidence that the Scorpions have recently established a cell there. According to him, the letters contain encoded references to a shipment of weapons about to be smuggled into the London docks. We have suspected Plimpson of having a connection with this kind of activity before, but this is the first time there has been a prospect of finding any concrete proof."

With a feeling that I was being hemmed in by coincidences on all sides, I explained to the Chief that Krackewicz had recently done some work for Mr Plimpson and had claimed that, as a consequence, he had been attacked by a complete stranger. Was it possible that he had been unwittingly drawn into the circle of my former employer's nefarious business dealings? The Chief listened thoughtfully to what I had to say, but did not seem as surprised as I might have expected.

"When you have been in this game for as long as I, my dear lady, you will discover just how numerous are the extraordinary workings of chance that we encounter every day. We are all mere pawns being manipulated by the hand of fate. What you say about this fellow Krackewicz is interesting, however; perhaps when a suitable opportunity arises you could probe into the matter a little more deeply? Now, let me write down the address of Plimpson's office for you."

It was not until I was on the train to Deptford that it occurred to me to wonder how far back Mr Plimpson's business relationship with the Scorpions might go. He had been a close friend of my father; perhaps he was the mysterious catalyst that had brought Father and Professor Robinson together? And if that had been the case, there still remained the baffling question: for what purpose?

Two hours later, I found myself walking in a dank drizzle through Deptford, an area of London with which I was wholly unfamiliar. It was immediately clear that Mr Plimpson had indeed been obliged to establish his new headquarters in a less salubrious part of town than that to which he had formerly been accustomed; the streets were grimy and the crowded rows of houses were ugly and run-down. Little ragged children peeped curiously out of doorways and stair-wells, blowsy women gossiped with babies at their breasts, and shabbily dressed men lounged about, eyeing me speculatively as I passed by.

Plimpson's business premises were located beside a deserted-looking dockyard in a narrow, tumbledown building next door to a public house. I climbed the rickety stairs to the office, beset by tremors of nervous anticipation lest Mr Plimpson should see through the story that I had carefully refined during the train journey or, worse still, that his wife might have returned, for I had no doubt that she would suspect me of having some underhand purpose in mind as soon as she laid eyes on me. I knocked on the door, which hung crookedly on its hinges, leaving a yawning gap at the top of the frame. There was a pause, followed by the scraping of a chair and the sound of footsteps moving over creaking floorboards, before a voice quavered, "Who is it?"

"It's me, Mr Plimpson, Miss Trant."

"Miss Trant? What the devil . . .?" There was the grinding sound of a key being turned with some difficulty in the lock and the door edged open a few inches.

"It really is Miss Trant!" Mr Plimpson muttered to himself, opening the door a little further to admit me. "Well, I'll be . . . Whatever brings you out here?"

He locked the door behind me as soon as I stepped inside. I struggled to conceal my disgust, for the air was rank with the odours of perspiration, stale whisky and tobacco smoke. The blinds were drawn and the office was lit by a single oil lamp, yet the squalor of our surroundings was plain enough. While I stood staring in dismay at the drifts of paper, empty bottles, scraps of food and half-open packing cases that littered the floor, Mr Plimpson brushed past me unsteadily and sat down at his desk.

Now that his face was in the light, I was greatly struck by the alteration in his appearance. His skin was puffy and raw-looking, his thinning hair stood up in wild grey tufts and his eyes were bloodshot and swollen as if he had been weeping. He drew out his mother-of-pearl cigarette case, lit a cigarette with a trembling hand and took a long swig of whisky before declaring, "Well, Miss Trant, my dove has flown. You see before you a broken man, Miss T, a broken man."

He tipped his head despairingly into his pudgy hands. "I still don't know what drove her to run away. It's true we've had a few business troubles . . . nothing too serious, you understand. And she had some objections to my taking on a new partner, but she knew that I'd no choice, the markets being as they are at present." He handed me an envelope reeking of cheap scent. "She left a note. Perhaps, being as you are one of the fairer sex, you can tell me whether she was really afraid of him, which she never mentioned, or whether she was just trying to spare my feelings and, quid pro quo, using him as her excuse. No need to be shy, Miss T – I should like you to read it."

Feeling very uncomfortable, I slipped the letter out of the envelope and adjusted my spectacles. It was penned in Plimpson's favourite plum-coloured ink in a clumsy, ill-formed hand. The paper was limp, as if it had been pored over many times, and a number of the words were blurred, though whether this had resulted from the spilling of tears or merely of whisky it was impossible to tell.

*My dear Plimmy,*

*This is not an easy letter to write and after you have read it I sinceerly hope that you will find it in your hart to forgive me for what I am about to do. The last thing I shuld wish wuld be to upset you for tho you have your faults I know you have allways been sinceer in wanting to do the best for me and in loving me so truley.*

*I have had to go away for if I was to stay both our lives wuld be in grate peril. You know I think the bisness to which I refer. If you take my advice you will do that man's dirty work no longer for it is that which has landed us in our present trubble.*

*It brakes my hart my dear husband to do this but it is the best thing for us both. I wish you to know my Plimmy that I will*

*allways wear my wedding band for it is solid gold like your hart*
*and will serve to remind me of you.*

*With deerest and most everlasting love from your adoring*
*little dove –*

*Aggie*

*PS I have taken the money from the safe. Its not much and I know*
*that you will not object for as you have said on so many occashuns*
*– whats yours is mine also. A.*

I handed back the letter, avoiding Mr Plimpson's look of beady
expectancy. He stuck out his lower lip and blew a sorrowful sigh
through his moustache. "I've gone over and over it but I just cannot
bring myself to understand what made her go off like that. It's not as
if she doesn't love me – that's clear enough from the letter, wouldn't
you say, Miss T?" he asked, throwing me a pleading glance.

I felt obliged to nod, though it seemed to me that Miss Hagger
– Mrs Plimpson – was one of the coldest and most calculating
women alive. "Solid gold like your heart", indeed. No doubt that
ring had been whisked down to the pawnshop as soon as she had
set foot outside the office!

"Are you able to tell me who this man is that she's so afraid of?"
I enquired.

Mr Plimpson mopped at his forehead with his handkerchief.
He glanced cautiously around the room and confided in a voice so
low that it was almost a whisper, "I've got myself in too deep this
time, Miss T. I was a fool even to agree to see the fellow – I'd done
business with him before and I knew he was a charlatan. To tell the
truth, it was Aggie who persuaded me to give him a hearing; he'd
charmed her as he seems to do all the women, though I shall never
understand it – oily little . . ." He drained the last of his whisky and
poured himself another glass before abruptly changing the subject.
"But you never told me what brings you here?"

I took a deep breath and came out with the words that I had
already rehearsed to myself several times. "As a matter of fact, Mr
Plimpson, I have a favour to beg of you."

"I'll be happy to do anything I can for you, my dear, for old times' sake," he said with a munificent air, then added hastily, "Of course, my financial situation is currently very precarious indeed; it's only temporary, but I'm afraid that for the time being a loan would be out of the question."

"Oh, I haven't come to ask for money," I assured him, amused by the swiftness with which the look of wild panic died from his face.

"No, no, of course not! I never suspected such a thing," he protested, mopping his brow again with the handkerchief which, I observed, was greatly in need of laundering. "Well then, what can I do for you? You needn't be shy about asking, you know."

"You are very kind. The truth is, towards the end of the period when I was working for you I entered into correspondence with a member of my family of whom my mother greatly disapproves. I am ashamed to own it, Mr Plimpson, and I hope that you will forgive me, but I filed those letters away with some of your papers; at the time it seemed the safest place. I was so overcome by emotion at being obliged to leave the firm that I forgot all about their existence until some weeks afterwards, by which time you had moved and I had no straightforward means of tracing your whereabouts. Recently an acquaintance of mine let slip that he knew you and was kind enough to give me your address. Today is my half day, and so . . ."

"Who the devil told you where I was?" bellowed Mr Plimpson, with a flash of his old irascibility.

For a moment I was speechless; then I said the first thing that came into my head. "It was Mr Krackewicz," I faltered, fearing that I might have made a fatal error.

"Krackewicz, eh? The devious beggar! Who has he been talking to, to get hold of my address? He certainly didn't get it from me."

"I don't know, sir – he said you wouldn't mind. I'm terribly sorry; I wouldn't have come here and disturbed you like this if it hadn't been so important to me." I took my handkerchief out of my reticule and dabbed at my eyes, adding, "I can't bear the idea of anyone else's ever seeing those letters."

As I had hoped, Mr Plimpson's gentlemanly instincts came to

the fore; he stood up and patted me awkwardly on the shoulder with his perspiring little hand. "There there, my dear; come now, pray don't distress yourself. Of course you must have your letters back. And you needn't worry; no one has set eyes on them. To tell the truth, I haven't had a chance to sort out my correspondence properly since you left the firm." He gestured towards a pile of packing cases that lined one wall of the office.

"I see. And are the boxes arranged in any particular order?" I asked with a sinking heart.

"I've put all the most recent items together in the top of one of the cases for the time being, but I'm afraid that everything is still rather muddled. Things haven't been the same at Plimpson and Co. since you left, Miss Trant. No, they've not been the same at all." He gave a melancholy sigh and collapsed into his chair. "I hope you won't mind if I allow you to look for the letters yourself; I don't expect I'd be of much use anyway."

"Thank you, sir; you're very kind. There's just one more thing. I've been thinking about my father a good deal of late. There are still many things I should like to know, but it upsets poor Mother dreadfully if I mention him. You and he were good friends, weren't you?"

Plimpson gave another sigh. "Indeed we were, my dear. Those were happier times."

"As a matter of fact, I've been wondering about the lilies in the photograph you gave me."

An expression of alarm flickered across his face. "Oh, they're not worth troubling your head about, Miss Trant. I shouldn't like to have to explain that kind of thing to a lady, you know."

I suspected that he was not being entirely truthful, but there was a discouraging gruffness about his tone which made me reluctant to persist for the time being in case he was alerted to the fact that I was not so naïve as I pretended to be.

I walked over to the packing cases, taking a proper survey of the office for the first time. The walls were cracked and blotched with damp patches and the unvarnished floorboards were adorned with a moth-eaten bearskin rug; there was no sign of the old Turkey carpet, and I imagined it must have been sold or pawned. A number of empty whisky bottles were scattered about and a mouldy loaf of bread stood on top of the cupboard, together with assorted buttons, handbills, nails, inkbottles and other miscellaneous scraps and oddments. I felt almost tearful as I looked around; all those years of hard work spent fighting against the swelling tide of disorder, and now this!

I turned to the packing case closest to me, which was the only one that had had its lid removed. I had scarcely begun to examine the first bundle of letters, however, before I was startled by a loud banging at the door.

At once Plimpson shot to his feet, his eyes bulging with dread, and held his finger beseechingly to his lips. "Shh! It's *him*! Don't make a sound; he mustn't know we're in here."

There was a moment of tense silence before the banging resumed again, accompanied this time by a thunderous, well-spoken voice.

"Plimpson, you cowardly dog, open the door at once or I shall break it down!"

Mr Plimpson cast me a despairing glance.

"Who is it? You had better let him in," I hissed, shoving the letters into my skirt pocket and feeling below them to open the little leather case that I carried there.

Plimpson shook his head vigorously. "No! You don't understand! You don't know what a monster like that is capable of!"

There was a resounding thump, as if the man outside had flung himself against the door.

"Go away!" yelled Plimpson. "I tell you, I've nothing to say to you!"

"Well, I've plenty to say to you, you devil!" There was a loud crunch of splintering wood and the door burst open, admitting the irate person of Mr Peters.

For a moment he stood still and stared at me in blank astonishment. Then hastily assuming an air of composed politeness, he took hold of my hand and kissed it, exclaiming, "Well, well, my dear Miss Trant! What an unexpected pleasure!"

I gazed at him wordlessly. His face and figure were as youthful as I remembered, though since I had last seen him his hair had turned completely grey and there was a hardness in his countenance and an expression of ruthless cunning in his eyes which had evaded my recollection altogether.

"It really is charming to see you again after so long," he continued. "I only deplore the circumstances that have brought us together." He glanced scornfully at Plimpson, who was cowering behind me. "However, your erstwhile employer and I have some very important business to transact, so I hope you will forgive me if I ask you to leave us now."

An image of MacIntyre coolly confronting three violent men in that derelict house in the dead of night flashed through my mind and I said firmly, "I'm sorry, but I believe that Mr Plimpson would like me to stay."

Mr Peters raised his eyebrows in surprise. "You may not know it, Miss Trant, but these days I own Plimpson lock, stock and barrel; he'll do as he's told."

I drew a deep breath and said icily, "Mr Peters, so far as I remember, you are a gentleman. I have come some considerable distance to see Mr Plimpson and I am not at present ready to end my visit. I hope that you have not changed so greatly that you would force me to leave before I am willing."

Peters gave an amused chuckle. "Well, I must admit that I am impressed, Miss Trant; you would never have stood up for yourself like that in the old days. Of course, you were younger then . . . and rather attractive in a dowdy sort of way, as I recollect. However, sorry as I am to be obliged to insist, you really will have to go."

He seized me by the shoulders and began to push me firmly towards the door. Almost without thinking, I pulled out my revolver and held it to his neck, forcing him slowly back into the room.

"Miss Trant!" cried Plimpson weakly. "What on earth are you doing? Be careful with that pistol!"

By now Mr Peters was sprawled backwards over the desk, the gun pointing shakily at his throat. We stared at each other, quivering, both of us afraid to move, and all at once I was reminded of that long-ago moment in Mr Plimpson's office when he had leaned over as if he were about to kiss me.

Suddenly, Peters made a grab for the revolver, and as he did so he slipped on a pile of papers and knocked over the oil lamp with a tremendous crash. The air filled with the scent of paraffin and I leapt back as flames began to crackle across the documents that were scattered about on the desk. Peters let out a piercing scream and then, shrieking in agony, began to stagger blindly around the room, consumed in a sheet of flame. Intent on saving him, I tried with all my strength to drag out one of the rugs from beneath the legs of a heavy armchair, until I felt Mr Plimpson tugging at my arm and cried out in desperation, "Quick, help me! He'll burn to death!"

"It's too late," Plimpson cried hoarsely. "Come on, we must get out!" and with surprising strength he lifted me off my feet and bundled me, struggling, out of the door.

# Twenty-Three

aving already been badly affected by his wife's departure, Mr Plimpson was utterly bowed down by the subsequent destruction of his business premises. He sat sobbing convulsively in the office of Inspector Reeves of the Deptford division of His Majesty's Constabulary, clutching my hand in his clammy grasp. We must have presented an extraordinary spectacle: Mr Plimpson with his smutty, swollen face, bawling like a baby and I, dressed in demure secretary's tweeds, flushed and dishevelled; the pair of us stinking of smoke. I made an effort to disengage my hand, for I was loath to convey the impression that our association was a particularly close one; who knew in what skulduggery I might find myself implicated as a result? However, he only clung on all the more desperately and I did not have the heart to persist in shaking him off.

Inspector Reeves was a peevish-looking man, whose charcoal-coloured suit was immaculately tailored to his diminutive form and whose steel grey hair was so meticulously combed that it appeared that each individual hair had been pasted into place. He regarded Mr Plimpson with a look of profound irritation as for the third time my former employer began a spluttering attempt to explain how the fire might have started, before burying his face in his handkerchief.

Drumming his fingers on the desk, the inspector turned to me and asked in a tone of controlled exasperation, "Since Mr Plimpson appears to be rather . . . er, overwrought, perhaps you can answer my question, Mrs . . . er," he consulted his notes and corrected himself, "*Miss* Trant." He glared at me, as if he suspected that I too harboured an inclination to start crying, and I blinked self-consciously, for my eyes were still teary and stinging from the smoke.

I opened my mouth to speak and emitted a guttural croak. Blushing, I gulped down a tepid mouthful of the tea that a junior police officer had made for us upon our arrival and managed to explain in a hoarse voice, "An oil lamp was knocked over and some papers caught alight. The whole place went up like a tinderbox." I began to cough and swallowed the rest of the tea, which somewhat alleviated the raw, gravelly feeling in my throat.

"I see." The inspector extended his neck and pressed his fingertips together to form a steeple beneath his chin, contemplating me with narrowed eyes as if he were determined to procure a confession that I had been responsible for starting the conflagration myself.

Placing my feet so that they were precisely in line with the stripes on the faded rug, I enquired, "Would it be possible for me to make a telephone call to my employer, please, inspector?"

"And who is your employer, pray? I understood that you worked for the gentleman sitting beside you." His whole face twitched and he bared his teeth, which were long and pointed, like a rodent's.

"No, sir – I work for Stein and Flowers, just off the Tottenham Court Road. I used to be Mr Plimpson's secretary, some time ago."

"And what is the nature of your occupation at Stein and Flowers?"

"Some of my time is spent working in the shop, which sells devices for the hard of hearing – ear trumpets and things of that kind – and the remainder of my duties are secretarial."

"Really?" The inspector gave a sceptical snort. "Then why were you with Mr Plimpson today rather than at the shop? I should have thought that Saturday must be a busy day for you."

"I was given special leave to come here in order to reclaim something that belongs to me – some private letters. Mr Flowers agreed that I could make up the time by working late this evening, so they'll be expecting me."

Plimpson blew his nose explosively into a smutty handkerchief and began to moan faintly. "Gone, all gone, everything . . . My dove, oh, my dove."

"Very well, Miss Trant," the inspector sighed. "I'll ask Constable Beamish to escort you to the telephone." He glanced at his watch. "It's past five now – you'd better tell Mr Flowers that your presence will be required here until the end of the day."

He rang a little brass bell on his desk and a few moments later there was a tap at the door and a dark, angular fellow with a deeply lined face came in.

"Miss Trant wishes to make a telephone call to her employer, if you would be so good as to assist her, Beamish."

The constable nodded and his eyes turned in my direction.

"I'll just allow the lady to wash and make herself more comfortable while she's downstairs, sir, if you don't mind. Perhaps it might do the gentleman some good if he was to tidy hisself up as well." There was the faintest hint of admonition in his tone, to which the inspector responded with an uneasy clearing of his throat.

"Yes, Beamish, I dare say you're right. Please send Constable Fairclough up so that he can assist Mr Plimpson."

Despite Constable Beamish's attempts to persuade me that I would be miraculously restored if I would only submit myself to the offices of soap, towels and "a nice bit of hot water", I insisted that I must first of all speak to my employer, or I would end up in hot water of a less pleasant kind. Smiling, he shook his head at my stubbornness. "Very well then, miss – there's the telephone. I'll just go and send Fairclough up to Mr Plimpson and I'll be back in a minute."

I asked the operator to connect me to Stein and Flowers and sat waiting with a thumping heart until the Chief's familiar voice said, "Hello?"

"Yes, hello, Mr Flowers. This is Miss Trant."

"Where's Miss Wade?" asked the Chief with a note of warning in his voice.

"No, I'm afraid not."

There was a momentary pause. "Ah yes, I see. Quite right, quite right. Where are you?"

197

"I'm at Deptford police station. I'm afraid I'm likely to be detained here until the end of the day. Mr Plimpson's business premises have burnt down, and unfortunately there was a casualty."

"How dreadful! Not Mr Plimpson?"

The Chief had drilled me to use the telephone with the utmost caution. "It is such a dangerous instrument; one never knows who may be listening," he had said, and it seemed clear that now was not the best time to launch into an explanation of Mr Peters' identity. "Mr Plimpson and I managed to escape. However, I fear that a client who was with us at the time was not so fortunate."

"Dear me!" There was a moment of silence during which I was able to hear, as if from a great distance, a voice talking on another line. Then the Chief asked, "Did you manage to find what you wanted?"

I plunged my hand into my skirt pocket and discovered to my great relief that the bundle of correspondence I had snatched up at the moment of Mr Peters' arrival was still there. I also felt the more solid shape of the revolver, which I must have thrust on top of it when the fire started, although I had no recollection of doing so. Throwing a wary glance at Beamish, who had returned from despatching Constable Fairclough upstairs and was sorting through some papers with his back towards me, I fumbled it back into its case while I talked.

"We had to leave in rather a hurry, as you can imagine. I . . . I will ensure that I record the account in full at the earliest opportunity."

"I understand. We shall look forward to seeing you tomorrow morning. And as my aunt Betsy always used to remind me, 'least said soonest mended'– I have found it to be an invaluable precept when dealing with public servants of all kinds."

"Goodbye, Mr Flowers."

"Goodbye, my dear. We have every confidence."

I replaced the receiver and stood up, fortified by the Chief's faith in me.

Constable Beamish showed me to a tiny room, scarcely more than a cupboard, in which there was a bar of grimy-looking soap, some threadbare towels and a large tin bowl, which served as a washstand. He left me for a few moments while he went to fetch a jug of hot water and I took advantage of the opportunity to glance at the papers in my pocket. I skimmed through the letterheads, looking for the name Hertz und Mann, but to my great disappointment it was not there.

At the sound of the constable's step, I hastily bundled the documents away. He put down the steaming jug of water next to the bowl and said, smiling, "I'll leave you to get on. You'll be able to find your own way upstairs?"

I assured him that I would and turned away to pour the hot water into the bowl. I scrubbed at my face, hands and neck until my flesh felt tight and smarting and the water in the bowl had turned black. When I re-entered the inspector's office, I saw that Mr Plimpson had also made his ablutions, though a charcoal-coloured smear was still etched across his forehead. His own clothes, which had been badly singed, had been replaced by an ill-fitting suit of shiny, greenish cloth, which lent him the air of a petty criminal. He looked up at me and winked one bloodshot eye.

"I've told the inspector about Simpson. Poor chap – very clumsy of him to knock over the oil lamp like that. But then I suspect he'd been drinking; wouldn't you agree, Miss Trant? Poor old Simpson – not the man he once was." Plimpson darted a sly glance at me. "I hate to speak ill of the dead, but I shouldn't wish to hinder your inquiries, inspector. He was terribly in debt and I suspect that he was making use of the names of acquaintances in order to obtain loans. I myself have received at least ten or twelve demands for payment from tradesmen of whom I've absolutely no knowledge, and last week a bailiff came round. He was a most unpleasant chap – I sent him away with a flea in his ear. Really, for a man in my state of health it's been most unnerving. I've enough to keep me lying awake at night without this. It took me a while to piece it all together, and then today I confronted Simpson with it and . . . well, he can be very violent when roused. I don't suggest that he knocked the lamp over intentionally, mind, but he'd been drinking and he was in a temper, and I suppose you can imagine the rest."

It was hard to tell whether the inspector was swallowing these fabrications, for his face was expressionless. His eyes, however, were fixed upon Mr Plimpson like gimlets.

"So you believe that Mr Simpson – a client of yours? – was practising fraud?" he asked.

"I'm afraid so, yes," Plimpson admitted, lowering his gaze.

"And we are to presume that he was burnt to death?" the Inspector continued.

"Yes, I should say it was a certainty. His clothes caught fire."

"Do you know whether he had any close relatives? We will need to contact his family."

"So far as I am aware, he was alone in the world. Poor, troubled soul – may he rest in eternal peace!" Mr Plimpson raised his eyes heavenwards and made a small genuflection.

The inspector jotted something down in his notebook before asking, "Were the premises insured?"

Plimpson's face crumpled and he shook his head mournfully. "I believe Aggie – my wife – had all that in hand; though of course the documents must have been destroyed in the fire, together with everything else."

"Where is your wife, Mr Plimpson?" queried the inspector, baring his teeth in a smile that failed to reach his eyes.

Plimpson plunged his head into his hands and started a meandering explanation of the circumstances of their first meeting, and my thoughts drifted off to the ill-spelled missive with which Aggie had announced her departure.

Abruptly, I understood that I must prevent Plimpson from referring to her claim that she had run away because she was afraid of Mr Peters. So far he had depicted "Simpson" as a pitiable wreck of a man, a drinker who had been driven to commit fraud in order to pay off his debts. It seemed to me that Inspector Reeves was the dogged type and that once set upon the right trail he would never give up, however hard one might try to shake him off. I had heard sufficient complaints about the clumsiness of police methods by now to realise that a full scale inquiry must be prevented at all costs;

if the Scorpions were alerted to Bureau 8's investigations at this juncture, it might prove disastrous.

"Excuse me, Mr Plimpson," I interjected, interrupting a sentimental account of the day of his engagement, "I know it must be difficult for you to address your mind fully to the inspector's question. I do hope that you won't be offended if I take it upon myself to spare you the trouble and answer for you. Inspector, Mr Plimpson's wife has deserted him. She left him a note, which I read earlier this afternoon, in which she states that she is leaving him due to irreconcilable differences and is never coming back."

"Did the note give any more detailed indication of Mrs Plimpson's intentions?" Reeves asked, scrutinising my face before jotting down a few words in his notebook. Plimpson sat gazing at me as if I had reached out and slapped him. I returned his stare, willing him to realise that it would be in his own interest to say as little about his wife as possible.

"Miss Trant?"

"I am afraid she does not want to be found, inspector. The letter gave no clue as to her whereabouts, and it seemed clear that the reasons for her departure were purely between Mr Plimpson and herself."

To my great relief Mr Plimpson did not contradict me, but covered his face with his hands and began to sob again.

Inspector Reeves closed his eyes for several moments and drew a deep breath. Then he glanced at his watch and snapped his notebook shut.

"That will have to do for now. I take it that you've left your address with Constable Beamish, Miss Trant?" I nodded. "And you, Mr Plimpson? Do you have somewhere to stay? We will need to contact you as soon as a more thorough examination of your premises has been undertaken."

Mr Plimpson dabbed at his eyes and blew his nose with a loud honk. "You won't find anything, inspector, I'm afraid. The place has been burnt to the ground."

"That may very well be, sir, but nevertheless we must have your address."

"I'll give you the address of my lodgings, then. Do you have a pen?"

The inspector tore a leaf from his notebook and held out his pen. Plimpson got up and bent over the corner of the desk, shaping his letters with the laborious concentration that I remembered so well.

"There!" He handed the pen and paper to the inspector and sat down, shaking his head. "I haven't been back to the place since she left – I've been sleeping in the office. I suppose I've no choice now." He let out a long sigh. I craned my neck to catch sight of the piece of paper with Mr Plimpson's address on it and swiftly committed it to memory. The inspector intercepted my gaze as I looked up, and narrowed his eyes.

"Well, that concludes our business for today; thank you for your help. Good evening." He stood up, shook hands with each of us with an identical flick of the wrist, as if he were discarding something unpleasant, and ushered us out of the door.

On our way out we passed Constable Beamish. He nodded to us and enquired with a look of fatherly concern, "Will you manage all right getting home, miss? Deptford ain't what it was ten years ago; it's not the sort of place where a young woman should be walking alone after dark."

"Don't worry, my man, this good lady will be quite safe with me," Plimpson assured him, puffing out his chest. "I shall accompany her to the railway station and wait with her on the platform for the train."

"Very well, sir, if you say so," Beamish responded, throwing my protector a sceptical glance before turning to me, his face softening. "Goodbye, my dear. Just you take care."

"I will. And thank you for your kindness!" I called back as Mr Plimpson led me towards the door.

Outside, the air was cold and damp, the darkness thickened by a soupy fog. I had lost my coat in the blaze and began to shiver. Glancing at my watch I saw that it was only a few minutes past seven, though it felt much later.

Taking my arm, Mr Plimpson steered me into a side street, quickening his pace so that I was obliged to break into a run to keep up with him. We passed a gaggle of sailors swigging from a bottle and as we hurried by they broke into raucous laughter, one of them yelling something coarse-sounding and incomprehensible that inspired the others to even louder roars of mirth.

"I'm sorry, Miss Trant," puffed Plimpson, picking up speed. "I'm afraid one doesn't find a very desirable class of person in this vicinity. Alas, I have come down in the world – temporarily – and it is a sorrow to me, a great sorrow. However, such are the vicissitudes of fickle fortune. Here we are. Would you like me to see you onto the platform?"

He looked so cast down by the prospect that I shook my head. "I'll be quite all right now, thank you."

"Yes, I expect you will." He hesitated. "Might I ask how you came by that revolver?"

"It belonged to my father."

"Ah yes, of course. You must be careful, Miss T. It wouldn't be advisable for you to make a habit of carrying a dangerous weapon like that around with you. What would you have done if the police had found it?"

"Of course, you're quite right," I acknowledged, looking as innocent as I could. "I merely frightened myself at the prospect of having to travel such a long distance on my own. I see now that I was foolish. Might I ask you a question before I go?"

"That depends on what it is," he replied, raising one eyebrow in a show of jocularity.

"I know you said you didn't want to talk about that photograph – the one with the lilies – but it really has been puzzling me . . ."

"My dear Miss Trant, I don't understand why you're so interested in that picture. I was a sentimental fool to give it to you; I certainly didn't mean to cause you any anxiety. It commemorates the completion of a business agreement. Your father was rather down on his luck at the time; I have always been one who will stop at nothing to give a friend a helping hand."

"But the lilies . . ."

He leant towards me, and I tried not to flinch from the sour smell of whisky on his breath. "The lilies were a practical joke, nothing more. And that really is all I can tell you. Now, isn't that your train I hear?"

"Goodbye, Mr Plimpson!" I called to his retreating back and, without looking round, he raised a hand in farewell.

# Twenty-Four

y the time I got back home it was after ten and I was some-what cheered to find that, against my expectations, Mother was already in bed. I put away Mr Plimpson's letters in my portfolio; they had seemed innocuous enough when I had read through them at Deptford station, but I comforted myself with the possibility that they might be written in code. Then I hid my smoke-infused clothes and combed my hair with Witcham's dry shampoo before clambering into bed. Despite my exhaustion I slept fitfully, for my dreams were lit with a flickering, lurid glow and echoed with the sound of Mr Peters' screams as he raced to escape the flames that were consuming him.

I awoke with the beginnings of a cold. After eating a hurried breakfast of bread and milk I ventured into Mother's room with an apologetic air, expecting her to demand an immediate explanation for the unprecedented lateness of my return home. However, in the end it was I who broke the silence with a faltering explanation that I had had to stay behind to catalogue a very large, last-minute order. She made no comment, and even when I confessed that I had had my coat stolen from a tea room while I was having luncheon she scolded me as if her mind were elsewhere, then instructed me to fetch her black woollen cloak from her wardrobe. My heart sank, for it was an unbecoming garment, which she had worn during the first few winters after my father's death as if she were doing penance for surviving him. When I tried it on, it smelt of mothballs.

"That will do very well, Margaret. It will be perfectly serviceable for another year at least," Mother said.

I bit back my objections, though I resolved to purchase a replacement at the earliest opportunity.

"Now, why are you standing there with your head in the clouds?" she demanded, dragging her legs out from under the eiderdown with a weary sigh. "Go and put the cloak in your room – and then I suppose you had better fetch the Bible."

Mother and I did not usually attend church, but she insisted that I read her fifty Bible verses before breakfast on Sunday mornings. "I'm afraid I shan't be able to read to you until later on," I said, avoiding her eye. "Mr Flowers has asked me to go into the shop this morning."

I had anticipated that she would object violently to this proposal, but to my surprise she merely gave a tight little nod and got back into bed.

"I don't approve of working on Sunday, as you know. And I don't understand why it should be necessary when the shop is closed," she remarked, pulling the eiderdown up to her chin with another sigh. "However, you've become so headstrong since you started this new job of yours, I shan't trouble to argue with you. If you can spare the time, you might get down the Bible from the shelf and leave it on the table – I shall read the verses myself."

I arrived at HQ feeling old, dowdy and tired. Despite my failure to obtain the letters from Hertz und Mann, the Chief was tremendously encouraging and heaped me with praise for my initiative in snatching up the papers when Mr Peters came in, and for managing the police interview without giving anything away.

"We'll let Liebowitz have a go at decrypting those documents and then we'll bring in Plimpson for questioning," he declared. "Thank you for coming in, Miss Trant. I do hope that you have a pleasant day. Oh, and since yesterday must have been exceedingly taxing for you and you've had to put yourself out again this morning, you must have a little holiday tomorrow."

I opened my mouth to protest and he held his finger to his lips.

206

"No, not another word! I shall expect you to stay at home – and make sure that you put your feet up and have a good rest!"

"Sir, really, I'll be quite all right . . ."

"That's enough, Miss Trant. Now put your cloak back on and off you go. We'll see you on Tuesday morning."

The Chief's benevolence only served to persuade me that I was eminently dispensable, and I began to wonder whether his kind words had been intended to disguise the fact that I had been tried as a secret agent and found wanting. Before long I was sunk into deepest gloom by the conviction that all my dreams of heroism and adventure had fallen away into dust.

Then, halfway up Tottenham Court Road, inspiration exploded inside my head like a firework. I would go back to Mr Plimpson tomorrow and ask him directly about the letters from Hertz und Mann! I felt sure that I could persuade him to tell me all about them – and the photograph too – if I were sufficiently cunning. And if not, then perhaps the sight of my revolver would induce him to talk.

It seemed likely that I would find Mr Plimpson at home in the early evening, so I prepared the ground for my departure by informing Mother that I had been granted a half-holiday on Monday and would not need to be at the shop until the afternoon. She was delighted to hear that I was to be compensated for the extra hours I had worked over the weekend, and found so many chores for me to do that I ended up leaving the house much later than I had originally intended.

Therefore, though I had hoped to inspect the ruins of Mr Plimpson's business premises before going round to his lodgings, by the time I reached Deptford it was evident that it would be unwise to do so, for it was getting dark and the insalubrious character of the district was all too apparent. I heard footsteps running along a nearby thoroughfare and then the sound of a man and a woman passing the other way, quarrelling in raucous voices. The strains of drunken singing drifted towards me from several streets away and I quickened my pace, remembering the sailors who had harassed us on our way to the railway station.

Fortunately, it did not take me long to find the house where Mr Plimpson was staying: a ramshackle dwelling on the corner of a narrow lane, with steep, higgledy-piggledy steps ascending to the front door. My heart sank when I saw that the windows were dark; it would be too bad to come all this way only to discover that Mr Plimpson was out. I heard the chink of a coin falling onto the cobbles a short distance behind me and spun round in alarm, fearing some sort of trap. There was no one to be seen, however, and so I climbed the steps and knocked tentatively on the front door.

To my surprise, it drifted open under the pressure of my clenched fist. I called Mr Plimpson's name in a low voice several times, but received no answer. There was something eerie about this and I hesitated, feeling the ardent impulse that had brought me all the way to Deptford beginning to cool. Then I pictured the Chief's sympathetic expression when he had told me to go home and put my feet up – a look that, I felt convinced, had signalled the extent to which my failure to obtain the Hertz und Mann letters had caused me to sink in his estimation – and, drawing a deep breath, I stepped into the poky, stale-smelling hallway.

Hearing, at that moment, men's voices approaching from somewhere further up the street, I hastily closed the door behind me, plunging myself into darkness. My pulse quickening, I edged forward with my arms extended, then turned and moved cautiously to the right, flailing about until my fingertips encountered coarse-textured wallpaper and then the wooden panels of a door.

I stepped out of the suffocating darkness into a room illuminated by the dim parchment-coloured light that filtered in through the uncurtained window. I could just make out the indistinct forms of a table, several chairs and a chest of drawers, all of which lay scattered about with their legs poking into the air at odd angles, as if they had been hurled with great violence in every direction.

My heart began to pound and the blood flashed into my face. I peered around, straining my eyes to discover the silhouettes of intruders crouching in the shadows, and my hand crept towards the leather case that contained my revolver. I could not see or hear any sign of another living presence, however, and so I edged across the uncarpeted floor, my feet crunching over shattered pieces of crockery, shards of glass, splintered fragments of wood and miscellaneous screws and nails.

I came to a halt in the middle of the room, listening with all my concentration, but still I could hear nothing save for the thudding of my heart, the rasp of my breathing and the insistent yowling of a cat in some distant alleyway. I remembered a story in which Miss Wade had entered an apparently empty house at the dead of night, only to surprise a gang of jewel thieves who had discovered that the down-at-heel gentleman who lived there was in fact a Russian prince, still in possession of his family heirlooms. Her quick-wittedness had enabled her to deliver the prince from deadly peril in the nick of time, but unfortunately I couldn't for the life of me remember how she had succeeded in performing such a feat.

I realised that I was very close to losing my nerve; thinking about Miss Wade was merely a means of self-distraction, a smokescreen intended to conceal the possibility that at any moment I might encounter the person or persons capable of wreaking the fearful destruction that was apparent all around me. In a strange way, the insight gave me new strength; for years I had longed to be like Miss Wade, and now that I found myself in a corner as tight as any she had ever been in I was certainly not going to allow my courage to fail, even though the reality had turned out to be so much more harrowing than any of the fictions I had lived through again and again. Assuring myself that the intruders must have fled long ago – surely otherwise they would have intercepted me when I came in – I started calling Mr Plimpson's name. There was no response and I trailed off into silence, feeling the uncanny quiet of the house settle around me once more.

I began once again to creep forward through the debris, but almost immediately there was a dull snap and I stooped to pick up a candle which had broken beneath the toe of my boot. With a sudden flash of recollection, I reached into my jacket pocket and took out the box of matches with which MacIntyre had presented me before his departure to Devon. At the time I had viewed the gift as no more than an affectionate joke, and I had continued to carry it around with me merely as a sort of keepsake; but now I saw that there had been a more serious intention behind it and I marvelled at his prescience. I unwound the length of twine and put it back in my pocket, then struck a match on a chair-leg and lit the candle, which shed a fitful circle of light over the wreckage.

In front of me lay the remains of a carriage clock; the intricate coils and springs of its innards spilled out onto the floor, intermingling with the shattered torso of a china shepherdess. I stepped around it and made my way towards a door which had previously been obscured in darkness. It stood ajar, but when I tried to push it open it wouldn't budge.

"Mr Plimpson?" I whispered, wondering whether he might have attempted to barricade himself out of harm's way. "It's Miss Trant. Are you hurt?"

There was no reply. I pushed the door again, with greater force, and this time it seemed to give way a little. The memory of the Chief breaking down the door in the hospital flickered through my mind, and squaring my shoulders I hurled myself forward. I stood back, rubbing my elbow; the door had scarcely shifted at all. Feeling somewhat crestfallen, but determined to gain entry, I leant my whole weight against it, gritting my teeth with the effort, until I succeeded in creating a gap that was just large enough to admit me. For safety's sake I blew out the candle, pinching the wick between my finger and thumb before placing it in my pocket, and then I flattened myself against the doorframe and squeezed through into the next room.

Almost immediately, my foot struck something soft and I stumbled forward onto the floor, a sharp pain shooting through my right hand. Somewhat shaken, I raised my palm to my mouth, tasting blood. The darkness seemed to press in around me as I sat holding my breath and listening intently, but I could hear nothing save for a steady drip, drip, drip, as if the roof were leaking. I shifted about on the chilly flagstones and began, tentatively, to feel around. All at once I encountered a solid mass and I snatched back my hand, picturing the cold sheen of dead flesh. Trembling all over, I rummaged about in my pocket for the matchbox and candle and, after two or three fumbling attempts, succeeded in rekindling the wick. I glimpsed several vivid crimson smears on my skirt and blouse and gave a scream, but in the next instant I realised that the source of the blood was in fact the cut on my hand. I forced myself to draw several deep breaths, telling myself that I must have been mistaken about the object that my fingers had brushed against in the darkness; after all, it was hardly surprising that my recent ordeals should have caused my imagination to take a morbid turn.

Looking up at my surroundings, I found that I was in a cramped little kitchen with peeling, soot-blackened paper on the walls and a narrow hearth containing a battered stove. I noticed a grubby dish-cloth hanging from a hook on the wall just to one side of me, which I thought would serve to bind my hand until I could find something better. I got up and grabbed hold of it, then sank to the floor again, feeling somewhat light-headed. I did not have the strength to rip up the cloth and so I wound it all the way up my forearm, making a clumsy knot just above the elbow. All the while, the silent, unseen presence of what lay just behind me burned into the back of my head. The horrid temptation to turn round grew more and more compelling, until at last I could resist it no longer and, steeling myself, I struggled to my feet.

At first I did not understand what I was looking at. Sprawled across the flagstones was a bulky object covered in shiny green fabric. A pair of small black shoes stuck up at one end, reminding me suddenly of a guy that Father and I had constructed one fifth of November. My eyes travelled over the bulge of its middle and along a row of buttons before coming to rest on a wide red smile, bold as a mouth in a child's drawing. Looped around this bloody maw was a length of wire, which cut into the corners of the flesh. Puzzled, I noticed a second, smaller mouth, the lips pouting obscenely from the black-purple sheen of a bloated face. With slowly dawning horror, I took in the line of sandy bristles beneath the long, bony extrusion of the nose, and the whites of the eyeballs, which turned horribly into the skull. One arm lay sprawled by the creature's side and in its dead fingers it still clasped a flat box. With a detachment born of utter terror, I stooped to pick it up and stood turning the thing over and over in my hands, mesmerised by the sheen of changing colours. Then, with a hideous convulsion, I realised that I was holding Mr Plimpson's mother-of-pearl cigarette case.

In my confusion it seemed then as if the room were suddenly filled with voices and hurrying figures and I remember crying out again and again before my senses gave way and I plunged downwards into darkness.

# Twenty-Five

MacIntyre's Story

Two days after his arrival in Seacombe, MacIntyre went to the Ham Stone hotel to enquire after the Reverend Mr Crawley. It had rained all the previous day and night, and the steep country lane that led up to the hotel was slippery, pitted with deep puddles and rutted by the passage of farm carts. Gulls wheeled above his head, sailing along on a stiff north-easterly with a raw edge that cut straight through his elegantly tailored overcoat.

He entered the grounds through a pair of rusty, wrought-iron gates, one of which stood open, and traversed a weedy path that wound between straggling box hedges past overgrown flowerbeds, a fish pond green with algae and a broken fountain. The impression of decaying grandeur was echoed and intensified by the building that loomed in front of him. The exterior paintwork was cracked and peeling, several windows were boarded up and the towers that stood at either end seemed to lean in towards one other, like miniature replicas of the famous edifice at Pisa.

MacIntyre entered a dingy reception area with a faded red carpet. Behind a desk on which stood a jade figurine, a woman was going through a box of receipts. The dark hair on her bent head was streaked with grey and when she looked up her forehead was still corrugated in a frown of concentration. He answered her clipped good morning with a grin, held out his hand, which she shook with an air of reluctance, and introduced himself as Jonny Rankin, lately arrived from Surrey for a fishing holiday.

"I'm Mrs Rutherford, the owner of the hotel," she replied, looking him up and down with narrowed eyes. "Would you care to take a room? If so, I can happily accommodate you until the end of the month; after that I'm afraid we're full until the seventeenth of November."

"You are too kind," said MacIntyre, who had his own reasons for wanting to lodge elsewhere. "I only wish that I were at liberty to pass my holiday in such a lovely setting, but alas, I am already enjoying the hospitality of a friend who lives in Seacombe. In fact, the reason I have ventured up here is to return an item which, I believe, belongs to one of your guests." From his pocket he unwound a long muffler knitted in stripes of navy and maroon. "Yesterday, after I got off the train, I happened to meet a clergyman by the name of Crawley. After he'd shot off in his motor car, I noticed this lying in the road."

Mrs Rutherford took the muffler and fingered it with a doubtful expression. "I don't recall seeing the reverend wearing this, though I suppose he might have bought it when he was away. It does seem rather – colourful – for a clergyman; however, I will enquire upon his return."

"Isn't Mr Crawley here at present?"

"No, I'm afraid not."

"Anyone else belonging to his party, then?"

"No. They all left this morning, before sunrise."

"Could you tell me when they'll be back?"

"Oh, not until the conference – and that doesn't begin for several weeks yet," said Mrs Rutherford with a smile which sat ill on her bony countenance.

"Just my luck – I was hoping that Crawley might want to go fishing with me!" exclaimed MacIntyre, improvising wildly. "I realised, after he'd gone, that he must have been at school with a friend of mine. He struck me as an interesting sort of chap, though we only spoke very briefly. Now I come to think of it, he did mention something about a conference; geology or palaeontology or some such thing, isn't it?"

"Yes. It's going to be a very grand affair," said Mrs Rutherford, unbending a little. "Nearly forty gentlemen will be staying here; they've booked every room except for those belonging to our regular guests and quite a number of them will be coming from overseas. They tell me that they're hoping to discover a new kind of fossil; if they're successful then it will make quite a sensation in scientific circles, so they say. And of course the hotel is in just the right spot for them, being so close to the shore."

"Good gracious! What a shame Crawley isn't here; I should like to have asked him more about it," MacIntyre remarked, before sneezing into his handkerchief. "It's a bitter day outside, Mrs Rutherford. I know it's rather early, but I don't suppose it would be possible for me to purchase a hot toddy before I go? I believe I feel a cold coming on."

"Well, the maids are still finishing with breakfast, but I expect that I can manage to do that for you, sir. It's true, the wind up here can be very brisk at this time of year. If you'd like to take a seat in the saloon, I'll bring you your drink in a few moments."

MacIntyre made his way down a long corridor into a room with dark panelled walls on which hung a collection of African masks. For a few moments, he warmed himself before the fire of beechwood that was burning in the grate, then selected a sagging armchair, which stood to one side of the hearth, and turned it round to face the dining-room door. A minute later, Mrs Rutherford came in, set down a steaming tankard on a small table that stood just within his reach and departed without a word. MacIntyre hauled across a wing-backed chair so that it stood at a companionable distance from his own and settled down with a copy of the previous day's *Times* which he had picked up from a nearby sofa. He was just taking the first sip of his toddy when there was a sound of approaching voices and two elderly ladies came shuffling in from the dining room, arm in arm. Casting him sidelong glances of suspicion, they passed out of the door that he had entered by, just as a square-jawed, bespectacled woman followed them through the dining room door. She was dressed in a loose robe-like garment, boldly patterned in purple and vermilion, and was peering intently at a small volume of Byron's poetry. MacIntyre opened his mouth to bid her good morning, but she looked so absorbed in her reading that he resolved not to trouble her and took up the paper instead.

He had finished skimming through the stories on the front page when he heard the sound of footsteps moving across the creaking floorboards once again and looked up to see a stout, brassy-looking woman dawdling past him with a coy smile and a toss of her head. He took refuge behind his newspaper, and had reached the letters page before a young couple drifted in, cooing absorbedly to one another. Concerned that his hopes of discovering more about Mark Crawley were rapidly diminishing, he cleared his throat to address them, but desisted when he met the gaze of a white-haired gentleman with a reddish countenance and a handlebar moustache who had entered just behind them. The man bade him a gruff "Good morning" then sat down on the sofa, took a pipe from the inside pocket of his tweed jacket and proceeded to fill it.

"I say, is this yours?" MacIntyre asked, holding up the news-paper.

The old man nodded and replied without looking up, "That's quite all right. You're welcome to it; it's yesterday's. That's one of the most trying things about living in this godforsaken spot – the papers never arrive until after luncheon."

"Oh, do you live permanently in the hotel?" MacIntyre enquired in a tone of deferential interest.

"Yes, for my sins. You'd think a fellow could do a little better on an army pension, wouldn't you?" said the old man, exhaling a long stream of smoke.

"The name's Jonny Rankin," said MacIntyre, walking over to him and extending his hand, which the military gentleman shook with a firm grip that belied his advancing years. "My father was a captain in the army. Which regiment were you in?"

"Richard Wright-Harris; I was a colonel in the Buffs. And your father?"

"He was in the Twelfth."

"Was he really? I'll come over and sit down with you, lad; it's rather chilly over here away from the fire."

MacIntyre listened patiently while Colonel Wright-Harris gave a long and rambling account of his army days. At last he fell silent and sat gazing ruminatively into the flames. MacIntyre allowed him a few moments to reflect before asking whether he had encountered the clergyman who had been staying in the hotel.

"I suppose you mean the fellow with the glass eye, who's been looking after the invalid? Now, what was his name . . . ? Crawley. And the other is called Charter. Well, the party they're with is a rum lot, there's no mistaking that. I'm told they belong to some geological society or other. Apparently they're going to hold a conference here in a week or two – an international affair, would you believe! Mrs Rutherford, the owner of the hotel, is as proud as punch, but I must say I find the idea of hordes of foreigners trampling through the place and treading sand into the carpets completely intolerable. I dare say I shall clear out to stay with my sister until it's over. Sorry, I don't mean to be rude – is Mr Crawley a friend of yours?"

MacIntyre shook his head. "Oh, no. I merely happened to meet him at the railway station in Queensbridge."

"Well, it's not the clergyman I object to so much in any case. He has a hard enough time of it; Charter may be in poor health, but he's one of the most thoroughly unpleasant individuals I've ever come across. It doesn't surprise me in the least that Crawley got sick of it and went away for a day or two."

"Really? I wonder where he went?"

"No idea, I'm afraid. Charter was more of a nuisance than ever while he was gone. Another young chap came to look after him and he didn't like that at all. I'd overhear him at mealtimes, needling and complaining, and it was all I could do to prevent myself from going

217

over there and giving him a piece of my mind. Then two days ago the rummest one of all turned up. I noticed that Charter was polite enough to *him* . . ."

At this juncture, the colonel was interrupted by the reappearance of one of the old ladies, who remarked, rather querulously, that she appeared to have left her spectacles in the dining room.

"My dear Miss Hepplethwaite," he declared, getting to his feet and fishing in his breast pocket. "I happened to notice them lying on the table and took the liberty of picking them up so that I could return them to you. I can only apologise for being so slow in the execution of my intention. It is entirely the fault of this young fellow here, with whom I have been sidetracked into conversation. I do hope that you will forgive me."

"Of course, Colonel Wright-Harris," fluttered the lady, turning quite pink beneath her face powder. "I'm most grateful to you for taking the trouble."

"No trouble at all. May I introduce Mr Rankin? Mr Rankin, this is Miss Eliza Hepplethwaite, one of two delightful sisters who reside here in the hotel."

"Charmed to meet you, madam," responded MacIntyre, bending low over her hand and causing her wizened cheeks to flush a still darker shade of red.

"We were just discussing Charter and his party," remarked the Colonel.

"Oh dear me yes – most unpleasant," said Miss Hepplethwaite, wrinkling her nose. "Why, I still haven't recovered from the fright one of them gave me."

"That was the queer one I was telling you about," Wright-Harris interjected. "Do tell Mr Rankin about it, Miss Eliza. Here, take my chair; I'll fetch another one."

"Oh, very well!" assented the old lady, sitting down and putting away her spectacles in a leather case. "However, you mustn't keep me long. Millicent is waiting for me to come back and read to her, you know."

"I'm sure your good sister won't begrudge us a few minutes of your time," returned the gallant colonel, dragging across another chair and settling down on the other side of MacIntyre. "Do go on."

There was a pause, during which Miss Hepplethwaite closed her eyes and screwed up her face, as if she were trying to solve an intricate problem in arithmetic.

"It was three evenings ago, after dinner," she said at last, looking very solemn. "Millicent had left her handkerchief in the dining room, and when I went to fetch it I saw something that . . . well, I dare say it will sound silly, but I thought at first that I had seen a ghost. You know what they say about Lillian Lauderdale . . . Anyway, there was a tall figure coming towards me through the shadows, and where its face should have been there was just a white blur. I couldn't prevent myself from giving a little scream, and a man's voice said, 'They are bandages, madam.' Then the creature brushed past me and I ran back to my room. I scarcely slept a wink all night. I found out next day from Mrs Rutherford that I had run into a business associate of that unpleasant man, Charter, who had come to bring him some message or other and had already gone away again."

"Did she happen to mention his name?" asked MacIntyre.

"Why, do you think you might know him?" Miss Hepplethwaite enquired, darting him a look of horrified fascination.

"Dear me, no – it's merely that idle curiosity is a terrible fault of mine, I'm afraid."

"I don't know his name in any case. Do you, colonel?" Wright-Harris shook his head. "Anyhow, I must say I'm dreading this conference, if we're to have peculiar types like that roaming the hotel . . . why, we might all be murdered in our beds! I must say, I'm surprised at Mrs Rutherford for allowing it."

The muffled chimes of a grandfather clock drifted in from an adjoining room and Miss Hepplethwaite got to her feet. "Good gracious me – ten o'clock! Millicent will be wondering where I am. Very nice to meet you, Mr Ranking. Good morning, colonel; I expect we will see you at luncheon."

"She must have been a fine woman in her day," reflected the colonel, looking speculatively after her retreating back. "The sister's much frailer, but still they're a pleasant enough pair. I must say I could hardly believe my eyes when I saw that fellow with the bandaged face coming out of Charter's room. Still, as I told you, they're a rum lot."

"What was all that about Lillian Lauderdale?" asked MacIntyre. "Surely she was the American heiress who was murdered in the eighties? I remember the story was in the papers for months."

"That's right. The hotel used to belong to her, although at that time of course it was a private residence; I suppose it would have been her country retreat. It was sold after her death and then Mrs Rutherford's father won it in a game of cards. Of course there's no sign now that the place once belonged to such a grand lady; unfortunately it hasn't been kept in good repair and naturally the furniture and valuables were all shipped back to her family in America. All except for that monstrosity there – perhaps it was too heavy to move with the rest or, more likely, the family didn't want it. It was built especially for Miss Lauderdale – a wedding gift from her fiancé, and as you'll remember, he was the one who murdered her. It's a mechanical piano; it can play by itself. They're common enough now, but I believe this one was unique in its day. I've never heard it play; I should be surprised if it still works."

MacIntyre got up and lifted the lid of the instrument, which was covered in a thick layer of dust.

"I say, I shouldn't touch it if I were you," remarked the colonel. "Mrs Rutherford wouldn't like it."

MacIntyre gave him a deferential nod and lowered the lid at once. Then, having several other avenues of investigation to pursue that morning, he thanked the Colonel for his company, made his excuses and left.

# Twenty-Six

*I* have only the vaguest recollection of awakening in a mottled darkness with my face pressed into some coarse cloth, and of straining unavailingly to lift my head away from its musty smell. "My head has turned to stone," I thought, feeling the motion of carriage wheels beneath me and hearing the murmur of hushed voices before sinking into blackness once more.

When I next came back to consciousness everything was still. A light was shining on my closed eyelids and when I opened them I found myself looking up towards the white glare of a street lamp. I became aware that I was lying on damp grass, next to a clump of shrubs that bordered a weedy path. The night was icy cold and I was shivering, so with a great struggle I raised myself into a sitting position.

I surveyed my surroundings with disbelief, which was swiftly succeeded by a mounting sense of horror as I realised that by some uncanny agency I had been transported home, to our landlady's front garden! I sat there panting as if I had just run a hundred yard dash, utterly baffled as to who could have brought me there. I thought back to the moment when I had slipped into insensibility, but the recollection was so hazy that I was unsure whether there really had been anyone else present in Mr Plimpson's kitchen, or whether I had been hallucinating. Though I told myself that perhaps some passers-by might have heard me screaming and come into the house to investigate, my mind leapt stubbornly to the disconcerting possibility that the murderer himself might have been skulking in the house ever since my arrival. Yet if that had been the case, why should he have gone to the trouble of transporting me across London instead of killing me too?

I gave a shudder; the truth was that any person lingering in such a disreputable district after nightfall was probably up to no good and his motive in bringing me home was unlikely to be altruistic. This dubious individual had discovered me at the scene of a murder. He might easily resort to blackmail, or violence – and the worst of it was that by some mysterious means he now knew where I lived. I racked my brains, trying to recall any conversation in which I might have been led to disclose my address, but my memory remained an obstinate blank.

Suddenly, I was struck by the alarming realisation that the person, or indeed persons, who had brought me back might still be lurking somewhere close by. I felt in my pocket for my revolver and was dismayed to find that it was not there. Terrified that I might be set upon at any moment, I tottered to my feet, my head spinning, and stumbled towards the house. Mrs Hodgkins always hid the spare key under a loose tile, the third one along, just in front of the doorstep. To my relief, I found it there in its usual place, unlocked the door and staggered inside. The shadowy outlines of the darkened hallway shifted giddily as I moved towards the stairs and I felt myself begin to plunge downwards.

It was Smith who found me in a dead faint, my head pillowed on the bottom step. I was lucky, Mrs Hodgkins told me the next day. I might have expected to lie there all night, coming in at such an hour. Fortunately, Mr Smith, who was a light sleeper, had been woken by the sound of the front door closing and had hurried downstairs at once, pausing only to put on his dressing gown.

"He thought you was robbers breaking in," she informed me, in a tone that implied that I had entered with the intention of making off with her valuables. "I told you when he arrived that it would be a great thing to have a man in the house," she added, turning to address my mother, who sat in the armchair adjacent to the sofa on which I was lying down. I had been cooped up with such sour-faced gossip and snide remarks all morning and my patience was wearing thin.

"What about Mr Krackewicz?" I interjected. "He'd already been here for over a year when Mr Smith arrived."

Mrs Hodgkins shot me a withering glare before turning back to my mother. "It had quite gone out of my head, Mrs Trant, but Margaret has reminded me . . ." Mother and the landlady embarked on yet another disapproving conversation about the Krackewiczs' goings-on and I buried my face in the sofa cushions. Almost at once the ghastly image of Plimpson's garrotted corpse swam into my mind and I turned over onto my back with a shudder.

As I lay staring up at the ceiling the carping voices gradually receded and I drifted into a kind of waking dream. Jumbled recol-lections of a mysterious carriage journey passed through my mind in fragmentary bursts. I saw myself shivering on a pile of sacking, heard once again the muttering of gruff voices and pictured a gigantic pair of boots planted just in front of my face. And then I had come to with a start of terror to find myself being lifted through the air.

"Don't worry, Miss Trant, you're quite safe," Smith had said in his unmistakable toneless voice. "I shall take you straight up to your room."

But that had been afterwards; Smith could not have been in the carriage. The boots I had seen had not been his after all. My mind must be playing tricks on me; and yet I could have sworn that his had been one of the voices I had heard while I lay helpless, speeding along through the night.

I became aware once again of Mother and Mrs Hodgkins talking, and with a convulsive effort I stood up and walked towards my room, feeling strangely detached from my own limbs. As I passed the writing desk I brushed against it, knocking off some papers, but before I could pick them up Mother leapt at me with unprecedented vigour and snatched them away, painfully wrenching my injured hand.

"These papers are mine, Margaret, my private correspondence. You have no business to be prying into them." She clasped the bundle jealously to her chest and I glimpsed rows and rows of her looped handwriting, full of crossings-out and false starts, before she whisked it away into her writing case. She took out the little bronze key she wore on a black ribbon about her neck and opened the drawer of a small rosewood cabinet in which she kept her private papers and, I had long suspected, various secret mementos of my father.

Mrs Hodgkins watched with thinly disguised curiosity as she put away her writing things and turned the key. "I'm surprised you manage to write at all, what with your poor hands. If you ever want me to take down any letters for you, I'd be only too happy."

"That's very kind of you, Minnie, but my arthritis has been much better these past few days," Mother replied, easing herself back into her chair. "These new pills Dr Forbes has given me seem to be making a great difference. Margaret, why don't you go to bed? You're looking dreadfully haggard."

"Well, it's hardly surprising, gadding about like that at all hours of the day and night," interjected Mrs Hodgkins.

"I've already told you; I was working. Mr Flowers . . ."

"Flowers indeed!" Mother snorted. "You would be quite justified if you were to take out an action against him. An injury like that . . ."

"Nonsense, Mother! I explained last night; it was my own inexperience that led me into trouble. The errand took much longer than it ought to have done. And then after I fell over and cut my hand, I simply lost my head – it was dark and I couldn't think which direction to take, and I wore myself out walking round and round in circles. I didn't have any money for a cab and by the time I had managed to drag myself home . . . I suppose I must have fainted from sheer exhaustion."

"Yes, so you said. But it's not your job to be running errands like that – you should have refused to go." Mother looked at the landlady, widening her eyes in exasperation. "Do you know, she would have gone to work this morning if I hadn't stopped her, though she was barely fit to stand! And even then, the only way I could persuade her to stay at home was by agreeing to send Becky to the post office to telegraph to her employers that she was ill. And *they* are the ones responsible for the dreadful state she's in. I've told her she ought to hand in her resignation!"

I refused to rise to this bait, which Mother had dangled before me several times already that morning, for naturally I was wary of being drawn into any sort of discussion about my future at Stein and Flowers. The same cautious impulse had led me to reject my initial inclination to slip a veiled reference to Mr Plimpson's demise into the message that I had written out for Becky once it had become clear to me that I really wasn't well enough to go to the post office myself. The thought of having to delay even for a short time the delivery of the unhappy news made me very uneasy, but I could think of no alternative.

"What *I* don't understand is why her employers should have supposed that she would be a suitable person to view the premises for a new shop in the first place. Why, she's no experience of any kind!" said Mrs Hodgkins, standing up and smoothing down her skirts with the expression of pained forbearance that she reserved peculiarly for my benefit. "Well, Mrs Trant, I must go. It's nearly time for luncheon and I promised Mr Smith particularly that I'd do him a nice cold platter, as a little thank you for his trouble. Is there anything I can get for you?"

"No thank you, Minnie; we shall manage quite well." There was a moment of expectant silence before Mother frowned at me and added, "It was good of you to take the trouble to look in on Margaret."

The landlady compressed her lips. "Never let it be said that I don't know my duty, Mrs Trant. I know kindness should be its own reward, but I must say it would have been nice to have had some thanks from them as is its object. Mind you, it's no more than I would have expected. Good afternoon." And, with a sniff, she flounced out of the room.

As soon as the door had closed behind her, Mother gave an exclamation of contempt. "Pah! The presumption of the woman! Taking it upon herself to thank him! I should have thought she'd have seen through that fellow by now. Hero indeed! Why, I wouldn't trust Mr Smith so far as I could throw him! And you, Margaret – I thought I'd brought you up to have better manners. Couldn't you have thanked Mrs Hodgkins yourself?"

I sighed, but said nothing. Suddenly, her face softened and she reached out her gnarled hand to touch my cheek. "Now come on, you poor girl – off to bed with you! You'll feel much better after you've had a good sleep."

At that moment there was a knock at the door.

"Come in!" Mother called, and I looked round expecting to see Mrs Hodgkins or Becky. To my surprise, however, the door opened to reveal the towering figure of Mr Smith. His gaze ranged past Mother and came to rest on me.

"Good afternoon," he remarked in his deep, expressionless voice. "I won't intrude but for a moment. I hope you have recovered from your ordeal of last night, Miss Trant?"

I nodded, shrinking beneath his hooded scrutiny. "Yes. Thank you very much for . . ."

"Not at all. Only too glad that I happened to hear the door. But after I had taken you upstairs I went down to make sure the front door was properly bolted and found this on the floor – it must have dropped out of your pocket." He held out a flat rectangular object: Mr Plimpson's cigarette case. He stepped forward to hand it to me and I forced myself to take it. "Thank you, Mr Smith," I murmured.

He gave me a long, searching look which sent a shiver down my spine, and then, without another word, he turned and went out.

As soon as he had gone Mother took the cigarette case from me and began to examine it. "What's this, Margaret?" she enquired, opening it up to look inside.

"It belongs to Mr Plimpson . . ." I trailed off in astonishment, for all at once her face had grown strangely contorted.

"Liar!" she hissed, flinging the case down onto the table with a

226

crash. "You're covering for that man Smith! I have always suspected him of some involvement – no doubt he was sent here to spy on me! And to think that he has had the impudence to use you as a tool! Your poor father . . ." And ashen with rage, she spat into my face.

I froze, quite beside myself with horror. Surely I must have slipped unknowingly into another dream? I looked at Mother's hands, which gripped the chair-back so tightly that her knuckles were white. How could she? My own mother! Fighting back tears of humiliation, I took out my handkerchief and scrubbed the spittle from my cheek.

"You are quite brazen then – you make no attempt to defend yourself?" she panted, quivering with emotion. "How could you do it, Margaret? How could you?"

"Mother, what on earth do you mean?" I demanded. "This cigarette case belongs to Mr Plimpson, surely you heard what Mr Smith said just now? He brought it up because he found it on the floor last night and realised that it must have fallen out of my pocket."

"I see. And how did it come into your possession in the first place?"

"I don't remember," I replied untruthfully.

"You're lying! I suppose the three of you – you, the Pole and Smith – are in some sort of conspiracy, though why you should choose to drag poor Mr Plimpson's name through the mud I cannot imagine."

"Please, Mother, you must believe me. I am absolutely ignorant of whatever it is that you are accusing me of."

"So you have the temerity to claim that *this* is something of which you have no knowledge?" She shoved the cigarette case into my reluctant hands, fixing me with a penetrating stare while I made a helpless pretence of examining it, turning it to and fro so that the hidden colours in the mother-of-pearl gleamed as they caught the light. "Open it!" she barked.

I held the case against my chest with my injured hand and manipulated the clasp with the other until the two halves parted to reveal a tarnished silver interior, still containing several of Mr Plimpson's cigarettes. Inhaling the familiar smell of his tobacco, I felt a lump rise into my throat.

"Mother, you're not accusing me of taking up smoking?" I objected with forced levity, swallowing back my tears. "Really, I would never do anything so unladylike."

"There!" she cried, jabbing a crooked finger towards the case.

I looked at the spot she had indicated and perceived that a device had been engraved into the metal. I peered at it, but could not discern anything more than a faint blur. However, I was beginning to suspect what it might be, and I decided that the best way to discover whether I was right and, if so, how much Mother knew was to maintain my pretence of ignorance.

"What is it?" I asked. "My eyes aren't strong enough to make it out."

"Don't try my patience, Margaret; you know quite well what it is!"

"Mother, I can't see it," I insisted. "*You* must tell *me* – what is it?"

"Never!" she thundered. "I will not utter that word in this house! After your father . . ." Here she stopped abruptly, lowering her eyes as if she felt that she had said too much.

"If it concerns Father then surely I have a right to know," I retorted, feeling my face flare with passion. For a long moment she stared at me, as if she were attempting to divine my thoughts; then she gave a long, shuddering sigh.

"Very well," she said with an air of wounded dignity. "I see that I have been mistaken. Naturally I find it upsetting to be reminded of that terrible time. And I acknowledge that I may have allowed myself to be carried away by the strength of my feelings. I'm sorry, Margaret. I should be grateful if you would oblige me by not referring to this matter again." She turned and limped away into her room, looking frail and shrunken.

I removed my spectacles and peered at the cigarette case once again, but the device that she had pointed out was no bigger than the tip of a fingernail and my eyes really were much too weak to make it out with any clarity. Feeling rather shaky, I went into my bedroom and locked the door. I pulled out my bottom drawer, lifted up the neatly folded piles of underclothes inside it and removed the old chocolate box in which I kept my most treasured belongings.

I eased off the lid and took out a magnifying glass in a green leather case. It had belonged to my father and I held the lens to my cheek, feeling the glass warm under my skin and remembering the rainy Sunday afternoons that we had passed browsing companionably through his collection of rare and antique coins. I used to pretend that it was the magical eye of a Cyclops, and I can still vividly recall the wonder of it when the intricate details of each design were revealed with miraculous clarity through the circle of glass. Sometimes there would be an even greater treat in store, for Father was adept in the creation of all kinds of games and puzzles. My favourite among these pursuits were the treasure hunts, for which he wrote intricate clues on doll-sized pieces of paper that he placed in various nooks all over the house. I would follow the trail that he had set, magnifying glass in hand, pretending that I was a great detective solving some fiendish crime. The conundrums were often much too difficult for me to unravel, for he took a boyish delight in exhibiting his own cleverness. He would tantalise me for a while by throwing out all kinds of obscure hints and red herrings, before entering with great zest into an elaborate explanation of how each of the ingenious clues had been constructed.

I opened the cigarette case, releasing the haunting odour of Mr Plimpson's tobacco once again, and held the magnifying glass over the minute symbol that had been impressed into the metal. At first it looked like an elaborate letter Y, then like a character from the Greek alphabet, but at last the image shifted abruptly into view. My intuition had been correct – it was a scorpion! The first thing that occurred to me was that I had stumbled upon confirmation of the Chief's suspicions about Mr Plimpson after all, and then I fell to wondering how my mother had come to be familiar with the device and why her reaction to it had been so violent.

Suddenly, the dark misgivings that had troubled me from the moment Mother had started hurling her hysterical accusations crystallised into an unshakable certainty: in some manner that I did not yet understand, the Scorpions had been responsible for my father's death.

# Twenty-Seven

*I* spent the remainder of the afternoon lying on my bed, drifting in and out of a fitful slumber, and by the evening I felt strong enough to go down to dinner. Afterwards, Mother and I sat at opposite ends of the sitting room, each absorbed in our separate occupations. For the first time in many months the condition of her hands was sufficiently improved to allow her to knit; she was making a matinee jacket for one of Mrs Hodgkins' grandchildren, while I reclined on the sofa with a book from the circulating library. Our silence was not, however, a companionable one, for I had no doubt that she blamed me for driving her to an undignified loss of self-control, and my own thoughts were awash with a host of wild and disquieting speculations.

There was a loud knock at the door and we exchanged startled glances, momentarily forgetting our enmity.

"Who's that?" Mother called.

"It is I, Krackewicz. I must speak to Miss Margaret at once."

Mr Krackewicz had not been at dinner and his absence had evidently caused his wife considerable anxiety; she had made none of her usual conversational endeavours and every time Becky's footsteps had approached the door she had looked up as if hoping that it might be her husband.

Before I could think how I ought to reply, Mother had put aside her knitting and hobbled over to the door. She bent down and pressed her mouth against the keyhole. "My daughter is unwell," she enunciated loudly and with exaggerated clarity. "She cannot speak to you at present."

Overwhelmed with irritation, I moved towards her and she glanced back at me, pressing her finger to her lips.

"It is most urgent, madam," Krackewicz persisted. "I should not have disturbed you else. Please, when am I able to speak to her?"

Ignoring my mother's frown of disapproval, I called out, "It's quite all right, Mr Krackewicz. Excuse me, Mother." And I pushed past her and flung open the door.

Krackewicz's face was flushed and beaded with perspiration, the ends of his cravat had come untied and dangled loose, and he was breathing heavily, as if he had been running. He strode into the room, seized my uninjured hand and clasped it in his hot fingers, gazing at me with an expression of intense urgency.

"Miss Margaret, I am so glad to find you here! Where is Plimpson? You must tell me at once! It is a matter of the most grave importance!"

"I don't . . . that is, he . . ."

"Mr Krackewicz," Mother interjected, drawing herself up to her full height. "I informed you just a few moments ago that it is inconvenient for us to see you at present. Your lack of consideration is absolutely extraordinary!"

"I am most sorry," said Krackewicz, still addressing me. "You see . . ."

"It is utterly outrageous that you should have intruded yourself into the apartment of two unprotected ladies! It has been made abundantly clear to you that you are not welcome here. Now, please leave."

"Excuse me, Mrs Trant," Krackewicz replied with steely coldness. "I know well your dislike to my wife and myself; you do not like that our ways belong to foreign lands, I think. But I come here to your room because I must. I cannot help but to do so." He turned back to me. "My dear miss, once again I must give my most true apology to come upon you when you are sick." His eyes darted to my bandaged hand. "I come only because I must. Please, permit me to explain."

"I shall ask Minnie to send for the police!" cried Mother, turning scarlet with rage.

"Mother, you'll bring on one of your attacks," I said. "I have no objection to helping Mr Krackewicz – indeed I shall be very happy to do so – and I'd prefer it if you would refrain from interfering."

There was a brief pause, during which I began to wonder whether I might have gone too far. Perhaps the shameful memory of her earlier fit of temper served to restrain my mother, however, for suddenly the anger died from her face. "Very well, on your own head be it!" she muttered, and then she tottered into her own room, slamming the door behind her.

Krackewicz breathed a sigh of relief. "Now, Miss Margaret, please sit and I will tell you all."

I sat down in the armchair, but Krackewicz remained on his feet. He radiated an intense nervous energy, and as he told his story he paced up and down, gesticulating wildly and coming to a dramatic halt every now and then to give emphasis to a particular point.

"This afternoon I have been at my work, at the Majestic. I am painting the most charming scene of a garden when I hear a footstep and a swish of skirts. I look round and I am surprised to see Aggie Hagger . . . Mrs Plimpson. She asks me if I have seen her husband.

"At once I remember this fellow who comes – pouf! – from nowhere and hits me in my face. 'That is for Plimpson,' he tells me: I, a man innocent of any wrong! Thinking of this, I am angry. I throw down my brush and the crimson paint splashes onto Mrs Plimpson's dress, and I tell her that I only wish I *had* seen this scoundrel, her husband; then perhaps I can pay back for the insult that I have received, all thanks to him.

"I am most fierce, and Mrs Plimpson takes out her handkerchief and puts it to her eyes. She tells me I would not be so cruel if I knew that last Saturday *Plimmy's* office has burned to the ground. She has seen it – it is nothing but a heap of ashes! At first she thinks him dead, but then she speaks to a neighbour who sees her husband going off in company with a lady. Mrs Plimpson, she is most dramatic – she is like the heroine in one of your absurd English plays – in despair to discover all at once that her dear Plimmy has betrayed her with another!"

Krackewicz shot me a piercing sideways glance. I felt myself turn scarlet, and fixed my eyes on the toes of my house shoes as he continued, "I pick up my paintbrush and go back to my work. I ask her why she does not go to the police. 'They will tell you where is Mr Plimpson,' I tell her. But oh no, she insists to me she cannot do this – she cannot speak to them. I ask her why not, but she is stubborn and will not answer me.

"I put down my brush again, for I see by now that she will not go until I listen to what she wishes to tell. She makes a tight mouth, like she tastes a lemon, and then she says that this woman, she is *you*, Miss Margaret. She says *you* have tried to steal her husband! When I hear this it is so absurd I cannot help but to laugh and at this she becomes most fierce and stamps her foot. And at this moment that Mrs Plimpson stamps her foot, I hear strange sounds behind us. I turn and I freeze with horror – I cannot explain to you how horrible is this sight. I see a man limping towards us; he shakes and breathes hoarse and wet, as if he is in much pain. His nose and mouth is swelled and twisted. One eye is closed. The flesh is raw and red, like a piece of meat; it bubbles and drips. His lips cannot open themselves and it is difficult to hear his words, but he looks at Mrs Plimpson and seems to speak her name. I see that she is white, so white, and her mouth hangs wide. She cries out to him – she calls him Mr Peters."

I stared at Mr Krackewicz, appalled. This was far worse than I had feared. Peters was still alive! The implications of that realisation were so disturbing that I could scarcely begin to take them in.

"She asks if he has had to him a doctor, but he shakes his head and says there is too much risk to do so. He is very angry. Plimpson has lost some papers. He, Peters, comes to the office to get them and then . . . He tells Mrs Plimpson he burns because of *you*, because you threaten him, with a gun." Krackewicz looked at me as if he expected me to deny such a far-fetched accusation, but I remained

233

silent and so, betraying only a brief flicker of surprise, he continued, "She begs him to go to the police. She calls you a devil; she cries for you to hang! This Peters, he tells her she is a fool; that he is not ready to give himself in just yet, even if she is.

"Mrs Plimpson is very furious with Peters, though she takes good care to turn her face from him, so he will not see. When I observe this, I laugh a little – I cannot help – and this Peters, who pretends I am not there until now, he asks Mrs Plimpson who am I. She tells him I am the Pole who did some translation work for Plimpson. He turns and looks at me with his terrible eye, as if he wishes to kill me. Then he threatens me that if I speak to anyone about this work, most dreadful things will happen. He speaks of my wife . . ." Krackewicz broke off and crossed abruptly to the window, where he stood staring out for a few moments. He blew his nose loudly, and when he turned back to face me his dark eyes shone with tears.

"Mr Krackewicz, I'm so very sorry . . ."

"I tell him that I know nothing!" Krackewicz exploded before I could go on. "This is a job of work I do for Plimpson because he obliges me to do it. I take no notice of these letters – I remember nothing of which they say. But he will not listen to me – it might be that I am not there. He tells Mrs Plimpson she must go now with him. She wants not to do this, I can see. She says she will try to find her husband, but Peters laughs a most terrible laugh and he tells her he thinks she will not find her Plimmy no matter how hard she looks. Then they go out and I come here at once to find you, my good friend, Miss Margaret. For myself I have no fear, but I will not allow that he hurts Irma! Plimpson must speak to Peters – he must tell I am an innocent man and know nothing. Where is Plimpson, Miss Margaret?"

"I am afraid that Mr Plimpson is dead."

"I feared this!" he cried. "From all that Peters speaks, I feared it! It must be that Peters kills him!"

The directness of the accusation affected me like a blow. Mr Peters, a man whom I had once imagined myself to be in love with, a murderer? And yet even during that distant period when I was under his spell, I had perceived that something sinister lurked beneath his outward charm. Perhaps Krackewicz was right; certainly, everything he had told me indicated that, directly or indirectly, Peters could well have been responsible for Mr Plimpson's grisly execution.

Before I could frame a response, Mother's bedroom door opened and she came limping towards us.

"You have more than outstayed your welcome, Mr Krackewicz," she announced with a frown. "I insist that you go now!"

Krackewicz gave a curt nod. "I know all I need. I will stay no further." Then he turned to me and said in quite a different tone, "Thank you, my dear Miss Margaret. You are a good friend to us." And with a little bow of gratitude, he went out.

# Twenty-Eight

*D*espite the ordeals of the previous two days I slept a deep, dreamless sleep and awoke feeling almost myself again. Though my injured right hand was less sore, the wound was still seeping and I was obliged to ask Mother to dress it with a clean bandage. She did so grudgingly and with an awkwardness deriving from the slight rigidity that continued to linger in her finger joints despite the doctor's pills, grumbling to herself all the while about my callous and undeserving employers and my foolishness in returning to work so soon. It was evident that she had not yet forgiven me for witnessing her outburst over the cigarette case, for she would not meet my eye, nor did she address me directly with a single word. I too remained silent, though I could scarcely restrain my impatience with her fumbling, for I was particularly anxious not to arrive late after my day's absence.

As it turned out, I got to HQ somewhat earlier than usual to find that neither the Chief nor Liebowitz had yet arrived. There were no letters waiting to be typed, so I went over to Hampson-Smythe's desk and glanced along the spines of an assortment of manuals about toxic substances until my eyes alighted on a slim scrapbook containing old press clippings relating to the Scorpions. With the sense that I was doing something forbidden, I opened it and began to read an article from the *The Times* about the daring escape of a notorious Scorpion from Dartmoor Prison which had occurred two weeks previously. At that juncture I had not yet heard the name Marcus Stone. Nor did I have the opportunity to discover the nature of the crime for which he had been imprisoned, for I had read only a few lines when I heard a key turning in the lock and the door was flung open.

I started guiltily and replaced the scrapbook next to a battered-looking tome entitled *Opiates and the Mysterious East*.

"What are you doing, Miss Trant?" Liebowitz demanded, in a tone that implied that I must be up to no good.

"Nothing," I faltered. "That is, I was looking at some press clippings. I wasn't quite sure what I ought . . . since no one else . . ."

"Oh, I think you know what you're doing all right!" he snapped back with an unpleasant sneer.

I stared at him in bewilderment.

"So you thought you'd go behind our backs and pay a little visit to Mr Plimpson after hours, did you?" he demanded. "What did he have to say for himself? Not a great deal, I should imagine, in his present state."

"I . . . yes, I did go to see him. How did you know?"

Liebowitz's thin, hunched form bristled with outrage.

"A woman matching your description was seen entering his house on Monday evening, by a neighbour. It's fortunate for you that the Chief was able to persuade the police not to take you into custody, or you'd have found yourself back in Deptford police station pretty smartly." His bushy eyebrows drew together in a frown. "It wasn't press clippings you were looking at just now, was it? You've been passing on our secrets to Plimpson, haven't you? And now that he's dead you have found someone else to give them to! By Jove, that's remarkably quick work, Miss Trant, even for someone as efficient as you!" I gazed at him in horror, then sank down at my desk and burst into tears.

The familiar pattern of knocks rang out and Liebowitz whirled round to open the door.

"Good morning! Lovely day!" the Chief exclaimed brightly.

Then his gaze fell on me. "What the devil? Liebowitz! Take off your coat and get on with some work!" Footsteps creaked over the floorboards and I felt the pressure of a hand on my shoulder. "Miss Trant . . . my dear, you and I will go into the kitchen for a little talk."

While the Chief made a pot of tea I struggled to regain my composure. By the time he had set out the tea things on the table I had stopped crying, though my cheeks were tight with dried tears and my eyelids felt gritty and swollen. I tried to smile when he passed me the best teacup – the only one without a crack – but my face seemed to have stiffened and would not move in the way I wanted it to.

"I take it you have heard the sad news about Mr Plimpson?" he enquired.

I nodded, not yet able to trust myself to speak.

"Liebowitz was very wrong to upset you like that. I suppose he accused you of being a traitor?"

I nodded again, unable to meet his gaze; I could not help feeling that the ease with which he had divined the nature of Liebowitz's attack suggested that he too suspected me.

"Miss Trant!"

I looked up at him and for an instant his brown eyes seemed hard and soulless. It struck me that beneath his kindly exterior he was ruthless to the core and that I had taken his integrity for granted without knowing anything about him. The world seemed to fall away from me and I felt a flutter of panic. Then he smiled and the dizzying, disorientating moment of doubt passed. He reached out and laid his hand over mine, and all at once I felt heartily ashamed for having mistrusted him.

"You must excuse him; he hasn't been himself of late. I suspect that he was merely testing you – he was harping on about some new-fangled interrogation technique only the other day. I'm sure he knows that you are far too honourable to betray us, whatever temptations might be thrown your way."

"Temptations?" I asked, watching the Chief stir three lumps of sugar into my tea.

"For the shock," he explained, ignoring my question and pushing the cup and saucer towards me. "Now I think it would be best, Miss Trant, if you tell me, at your own pace, what you were doing in Deptford on Monday evening."

And so I began; falteringly at first and then, as I fell under the spell of his patient, listening gaze, more and more urgently. When I had finished, he reached across and squeezed my uninjured hand.

"My dear Miss Trant, please accept my most sincere apologies. You are a gem of the finest cut! I am appalled that either of us entertained even the slightest doubt of your integrity and I shall ensure that Liebowitz knows it forthwith. Please don't blame yourself for losing the revolver; of course it is always unfortunate when these things happen to fall into the hands of the wrong people, but that may not have occurred in this case – let us hope not. If it makes you feel any better, I should estimate that the number of weapons that MacIntyre has mislaid during the course of his career would furnish a small arsenal! And I shouldn't trouble too much about this idea of yours that an unknown person brought you back from Deptford either – it seems to me very improbable. No, I should say that it's much more likely that the shock of finding Plimpson like that brought on an episode of amnesia and that those cloudy memories of yours were just hallucinations. I have heard of such cases. The most important thing is that you got home safely."

All at once I felt a tremendous sense of relief; all the previous day those secrets had brooded over me like a thundercloud and now the cloud had melted away into air. I pictured myself soaring like an eagle, far up in the pale blue heavens; the Chief didn't believe that I was a traitor – or a failure – after all!

"I was particularly pleased that you felt able to speak to me about your father," he went on with careful deliberation. "One of the things that made Liebowitz suspicious, you see, was a newspaper article about the death of an Arthur Trant which, you may be surprised to learn, MacIntyre found in Professor Robinson's study. Of course, that proves nothing, but then, knowing too that Horace Plimpson was an old friend of your father . . ."

I nodded, rather perplexed that MacIntyre had failed to inform the Chief that he had already spoken to me about his discoveries at the professor's house. I considered mentioning his lapse and then decided against it, for I judged that it was unlikely to be of any importance and did not wish to be thought guilty of telling tales.

"At present we have no evidence to suggest that Plimpson's connection to the Scorpions was anything other than a recent one; still, the fact that your poor mother was so upset about that cigarette case does suggest that there might be some previous association. And then there is Plimpson's mention of the business agreement that the photograph commemorates and his claim that he helped your father out of some difficulties towards the end of his life. There might be something in that."

A suspicion that had been nagging away at me ever since I had first found out about Mr Plimpson's involvement with the Scorpions came sweeping with sudden insistence to the forefront of my mind.

"Sir, was I brought in to Bureau 8 by design? Because it was thought that I might know things about the Scorpions, because of Mr Plimpson and my father?"

"My dear, believe me, we were as astonished to find out about these connections as you. We had nothing to do with your recruitment – you were simply sent to us by head office. Though come to think of it, I suppose it's possible that they sought you out, on account of the fact that you had worked for Plimpson."

Fleetingly, I recalled the newspaper containing the advertisement for the secretarial post at Bureau 8 that had been shoved into my hand as I was getting onto the tram after my last day at Plimpson and Co., and the probing questions about my family which had so surprised me at the Whitehall interview.

"But if they had known of your father's having any involvement with the Scorpions, then I have no doubt they would have informed us." He looked at me as if he hoped I might have some comment to make, but I could think of nothing to say and so he went on, "This Mr Peters, who you say might be responsible for Plimpson's murder; do you suppose that's his real name?"

"I'm afraid I don't know. I never had any reason to think that it wasn't, but then really I knew very little about him."

"Never mind. If you do remember any details that could be of relevance, though, please make sure that you pass them on to me at once." He pushed his cup aside and stood up. "I'm so glad that we have had this conversation, my dear."

"So am I, sir – very glad indeed," I replied.

We went back into the office and he beckoned Liebowitz into the meeting room. I sat eyeing the door, my stomach churning with anxiety, but when Liebowitz emerged a few minutes later he walked straight over to me and held out his hand. I shook it without hesitation, though with my left hand because of the wound on my palm, and he gave me an abashed smile. "I'm afraid I've made rather a fool of myself, Miss Trant. Please forgive me."

"That's quite all right – one cannot be too careful in such matters," I answered, noticing that he had removed his monocle and that without it his face looked much softer.

The rest of the day passed quickly and pleasantly. Liebowitz insisted on doing all the typing until my hand was healed, and so I was able to concentrate my energies on the project of sorting out the pigeonholes, with which I made very satisfactory progress. The three of us went out for luncheon at the Lyons teashop, an unprecedented treat, and I began to feel as if some of the camaraderie that I had glimpsed in my first few days at Bureau 8 had been restored.

That evening when I arrived home I discovered that there was an envelope addressed to me on the hall table. Turning it over to look at the sender's name, I saw with a thrill of excitement that it was from my cousin. I slipped it into my pocket and was about to hurry upstairs when the dining room door opened and Becky scurried towards me.

"Excuse me, miss! I've somefing to tell you, if it's convenient."

"Of course," I replied, though I was thinking impatiently of the letter in my pocket.

The maid looked at the floor and shuffled her feet about, blushing to the tips of her ears. "I feel a real booby, now it comes to sayin' it.

241

But I've been worryin', miss, and I fought you'd like ter know. All it is, is, when you fainted and Mr Smiff found you on the stairs, I don't believe 'e was in bed like 'e said 'e was. Me winder looks out onto the area steps, as you know, and I'm a light sleeper – if someone comes in late at night, I 'ear the door, 'owever quiet 'e is. Any'ow, I was already awake – I'd been woke by next door's dog barkin' – and I 'eard someone creepin' up the steps. I peeped out and saw Mr Smiff go in. Then about five minutes later I 'eard some footsteps, not so quiet this time, and looked out again and it was you. It was bright moonlight and I could see at once you looked poorly, and besides, it ain't like you to come in so late. I fought I'd come up to see if you was all right, but the kitchen staircase is terrible dark and I couldn't find a candle straight off, and when I got there Mr Smiff was bendin' over you and when 'e 'eard me 'e looked up, real startled like, and took 'is 'and away quick, as if 'e'd been going frough your pockets or somefink. 'e told me ter go back to bed – said 'e'd been woke by the door and 'ad found you in a faint and was takin' you to yer muvver. I felt bad about it afterwards, but I was fit to peg it from fright, if you'll excuse the expression, miss, and did as I was told. Next fing I know, Mrs H is makin' out like 'e's some kind of 'ero for findin' you, but I fought it best to keep me mouf shut until I could speak to you about what was best to be done."

"Thank you, Becky. You were absolutely right to tell me. But I think we ought to keep this to ourselves for the time being, don't you?" Determined not to show how unsettled I was by her disclosures, I smiled at her and she grinned from ear to ear.

"I'll keep watchin', miss. I see a lot, for no one takes any notice of me. I'll tell you straight off if I see anythin' else, shall I?"

"Yes, Becky, please do."

"Right you are then, miss," she said, bobbing a curtsey, and she trotted off towards the kitchen stairs.

I trudged up to our apartment, filled with dismay and revulsion at the idea of Mr Smith pawing at me while I lay unconscious. Had he really been going through my pockets, as Becky had suggested? And if so, had his motive been mere curiosity or something more sinister? I did my best to persuade myself that it must have been the former; that he had taken the cigarette case on an opportunistic impulse and then, having thought better of it, returned it to me, claiming to have found it on the floor. Nevertheless, the fact that he had concealed the truth about coming in late was in itself suspicious. He couldn't be worried about incurring the landlady's wrath, surely?

At the door of our apartment I forced myself to set aside these speculations, filled with irritation that I had been wasting my time attempting to decipher the impenetrable motivations of a man like Smith. Though it wanted fifteen minutes until six o'clock, I found Mother sitting on the sofa with her knitting, already dressed to go down to dinner. She responded to my "Hello" without lifting her eyes from the half-completed matinee jacket and I walked directly into my room and locked the door. My breath began to come quickly and all thoughts of Mr Smith were swallowed up in my eager desire to read the long-awaited letter from my aunt.

I took out Father's ivory-handled paper knife from the chocolate box and slit open the envelope rather awkwardly with my left hand. Inside was a note from my cousin, which I will not go to the trouble of reproducing here, and a second sealed envelope, on which my name, *Margaret Trant*, was printed in faded ink. By now my hands were trembling so much that I could scarcely hold the paper knife and I scrabbled about dreadfully before I managed to extract a single sheet of paper, which had been folded several times. I smoothed it flat, then sat down on the bed, filled with dismay. For in the last hours of her illness, my aunt's neat, bold hand had deteriorated into a series of illegible squiggles.

I peered at the letter in hopeless incomprehension until I was interrupted by a knock on the door.

"It's time for dinner, Margaret. Whatever are you doing?"

I had eaten a hearty luncheon, and besides, I felt sick to the stomach with disappointment.

"I've a dreadful headache," I said faintly. "I think it would be best if I lie down and try to sleep. Do you mind going downstairs without me?"

"I suppose I shan't have to mind!" Mother replied. "I knew you oughtn't to have gone back to work so soon after your accident. Shall I fetch the camphor bottle before I go?"

"No thank you; you don't know where I keep it and you'll keep everyone waiting. I'll find it myself."

The door handle rattled from side to side. "Why have you locked the door?"

"I didn't mean to," I replied, yawning. "Good night, Mother."

There was a short silence before she said, as if it cost her a great deal to make the admission, "I'm sorry for the way I behaved, Margaret – it was very wrong of me. Seeing that emblem again after all these years was a terrible shock, but I ought not to have acted as I did."

I bit back my words of forgiveness and sat listening to the heavy, muffled sound of her breathing, until I heard her sigh and limp slowly from the room. Though I felt a twinge of guilt for having shunned her apology, I was not tempted to go after her. Our reconciliation could wait a little while longer; I was too desperate to make sense of the letter to be able to put it to one side, even for a short time.

I stared at the impossible scrawl for several minutes before it occurred to me that I might make it out it more readily with the aid of Father's magnifying glass. And indeed, to begin with, it did prove to be of great help; within half an hour I had managed to puzzle out the first few lines.

Just as I was beginning to flounder into difficulties again, I heard Mother come back in. The floorboards creaked as she moved about the apartment, there was a rustling of papers, and then, after a few moments, her bedroom door clicked shut. I turned my attention back to my aunt's indecipherable script, yet though I strained my eyes unmercifully over the remaining paragraphs, I succeeded in making out only a few additional words. The fragmented text that follows is the end result of all my efforts.

*Dearest Margaret,*
*By the time you read this I will be dead. . . . matters that I should have left well alone . . . cost me my life and have done no good . . . do not . . . mistakes.*

*. . . Terribly sorry . . . schism . . . be impossible . . .*
*. . . father . . . suspicious of . . . responsible. . . . confided that*
*. . . safe*
*. . . secret . . . ledger . . .* <u>piano</u> *. . . Lily . . .*
*Lily . . . beware . . .*
Sophie

The thought that my aunt had roused herself from her deathbed to write a missive I could not read filled me with pity and sadness. It was clear that she had intended to warn me about something, but what was it? While the inference of the opening paragraph was clear enough, there were whole sentences in the middle where I had been unable to distinguish a single word.

I read through the transcription again with a mounting sense of frustration. Who was this "Lily" who was mentioned twice? Could she have hurt my father in some way? Or perhaps my aunt was alluding not to a woman at all, but to a flower, like those worn by my father and Mr Plimpson in the photograph? More baffling still was the reference to a piano. Why ever should she mention such a thing? Yet the word was written relatively clearly and had been underlined.

I looked at my watch; it was after eleven, my head now really was aching and I was utterly exhausted. I put the letter away in my box of treasures and began to undress, humming to myself to buoy up my spirits. The melody was so familiar that it was not until after I had turned out the lamp and climbed into bed that I realised I had been singing "Lilly Dale", my father's favourite song.

*I go, she said*
*To the land of rest,*
*And ere my strength shall fail,*
*I must tell you where,*
*Near my own loved home,*
*You must lay poor Lilly Dale.*

# Twenty-Nine

## MacIntyre's Story

Attired in mackintosh and sou'wester, MacIntyre made his way through driving rain to the garden shed at Merrivale. Hampson-Smythe had taken shelter from the downpour and was sitting on a deckchair by the stove, whittling away at a piece of wood with his feet resting on an upturned flowerpot, when he heard his fellow agent's knock and leapt up to let him inside. MacIntyre removed his sodden outer garments and handed them to Hampson-Smythe to hang up, then sat down in the deckchair that his colleague had left vacant.

The younger agent pulled up a stool and enquired with great eagerness, "Have you had a letter from HQ?"

"Indeed I have – and it contains one or two very interesting pieces of news." MacIntyre cleared his throat and broke into a fit of coughing. "Curse this wretched cold! You don't happen to have a drop of that brandy still about, I suppose?"

Hampson-Smythe produced a battered flask from inside a flowerpot and handed it to his colleague, who regarded it with an expression of disgust.

"I say, what's this?"

"Don't you remember? You told me to get rid of the other one. You said . . ."

"Yes, I know very well what I said. I hope you made sure that you rinsed out the paraffin thoroughly before you refilled this one."

"But it never had paraffin in it. I bought it from . . ."

"All right Smythe, calm yourself. I was only teasing you." MacIntyre took a swig from the container and wiped his lips with his handkerchief. "It isn't as agreeable as drinking from the family heirloom, but never mind!"

He handed the flask back to Hampson-Smythe and withdrew a pouch fashioned from a fragment of tarpaulin from his breast pocket. From this he removed an envelope, inside which was a large sheet of foolscap covered in his own slanting script. "It took me simply ages to decode – mainly because the Chief's appalling scrawl was more difficult to puzzle out than the cipher itself."

"I wonder why he didn't get Miss Trant to type it?"

"I'm afraid poor old Rivers is just as weighed down by suspicion as we are."

"What has Miss Trant done to make him distrust her?"

"Oh, it's nothing *she's* done. I suspect that he's decided to make it a general policy to keep his cards close to his chest. He appears to think that Liebowitz has been behaving rather oddly." MacIntyre handed Hampson-Smythe the letter. "Here, read it for yourself."

*Tuesday, 26th September, 1905*

*My dear MacIntyre,*

*I do hope this finds you in good spirits and invigorated by the sea air. You may perhaps have looked to hear from me sooner, but new developments have descended upon us thick and fast and it would be impossible to convey all that I have to tell you in a telegram.*

*To proceed first with the most recent piece of news: this morning we had a communication from Hunter, in which he insists that despite our discovery that "Miss Bartholomew" is an agent of the Scorpions, he is determined to remain in Germany for the foreseeable future. He is absolutely adamant that his cover has not been compromised, since she is apparently still in England. Furthermore, he assures us that he will be safe so long as he keeps out of her way. I know that Hunter is relatively inexperienced, but I should never have supposed that he could be so naïve. I sent a pretty stiff reply, telling him not to be such a headstrong young fool and that if he refuses to come back we will have to report him to head office as a rogue agent. Let us hope that he sees sense before it comes to that; if he gets kidnapped by the Scorpions, one dreads to think of the possible consequences for our operation.*

*In answer to your query regarding the true identities of those individuals going under the names of Charter and Crawley: of the latter I can as yet tell you nothing – one suspects that he was too recently recruited for us to find any trace of him in our files – but in Charter's case we have been more successful. Liebowitz has managed to discover that Mr Charter's real name is Augustus Harding. As you may recall, Harding was a crony of Stone and Arrowsmith during the eighties and, in common with several other senior Scorpions, departed to reside on the Continent (Germany to be precise) after Arrowsmith was sentenced to death. According to head office, various agents have monitored his activities over the years until, at the turn of the century, he was diagnosed with an incurable wasting disease and the surveillance was ended.*

*I will come to the man with the bandaged face a little later. Our "invisible man" (did you ever read that story by Wells?) is more famous even than Harding. Before I unmask him, however, there are a number of important facts with which I must acquaint you.*

*As I promised in my telegram, I am now in a position to give you some further particulars regarding Horace Plimpson's death. The first person to come upon his body was our own Miss Trant, who went round to his lodgings on the evening of Monday, 18 September, hoping to press him for more information.*

For various perfectly valid reasons, which I will not go into here, we knew nothing of his demise until we received a telephone call from head office on the Tuesday morning, informing us that his landlord had summoned the police after discovering the house in a state of disarray and his tenant on the kitchen floor with a length of wire pulled tight around his throat. As you know, the garrotte is the tool that the Scorpions tend to favour for punishing anyone who is suspected of turning traitor, and I'm sure you will agree that one need not look beyond their ranks to discover the perpetrators of this hideous crime. However, I can be still more specific about the culprit and his motivation than that.

We have learnt from Miss Trant that in the days leading up to his death Mr Plimpson was being threatened by a man whom she knew as "Mr Peters", an erstwhile business associate who was present at the time of the fire that razed the Deptford business premises to the ground. Peters was thought to have burnt to death in that fire, but an acquaintance of Miss Trant's insists that he spoke to him three days later. Miss Trant assures me that this fellow, Krackewicz, is reliable, and since there is at present no evidence to contradict his story, for the sake of argument let us assume that he is telling the truth. Miss Trant has confirmed that when she encountered him on the night of the fire Peters was already very angry with Plimpson and considered himself to have been severely wronged by him. How much more infuriated he must have been after Plimpson had abandoned him to perish in a burning building! I doubt that Mr Peters' hands held the garrotte, but I strongly suspect it was his tongue that gave the order to kill.

According to Mr Krackewicz (whom we intend to bring in shortly for questioning), Peters' face had been very badly burnt. It does not demand a great deal of ingenuity to infer that "Peters" and our "invisible man" with the bandaged face are one and the same. Even I, old duffer that I am, was able to deduce so much. It took Liebowitz's quick brain to work out the rest, however, and I must say that it would have been quite

249

beyond my powers to have done so. So far as I understand it, the clue was given to him by Miss Trant, who asserts that when she first started working for Plimpson, about ten years ago, Mr Peters was a close business associate of her employer and a regular visitor to the office in Tottenham Court Road. However, it appears that within six months the two men had a serious disagreement, which resulted in Peters storming out in high dudgeon. Miss Trant did not see him again until they met last week at the premises in Deptford. Some peculiar flash of inspiration has persuaded Liebowitz that Mr Peters' extended absence can be explained by the fact that he was in gaol. You see, the quarrel with Plimpson occurred at about the time Marcus Stone was taken into custody on charges relating to the murder of Lillian Lauderdale, and what's more, "Mr Peters'" reappearance coincides with Stone's escape from Dartmoor prison. The association with Augustus Harding that your inquiries have uncovered lends further ballast to Liebowitz's theory that "Peters" and Marcus Stone are one and the same, for, as you know, Stone, Harding and Arrowsmith were as close as brothers in the old days. The point that settles it to my mind, however, is that apparently the name Peter is derived from the Latin word for rock; a very pretty piece of word-play, as I'm sure you'll admit. It is at such times that I wish I had been more studious when I was at school!

Liebowitz is insisting that for the time being the fewer people who know of the connection between Stone, Hagger and Plimpson the better, so we haven't informed Miss Trant about any of these developments as yet. I don't see what harm it would do to enlighten her myself – her discretion can be relied upon absolutely – but Liebowitz is being rather difficult at present, in all sorts of ways, and I did not think it worthwhile to argue the point.

Undoubtedly, Stone's escape will have given new momentum to the Scorpions' revival, but they are still desperately short of funds. Yesterday, Liebowitz decoded a telegram intercepted by our operative in Mannheim which indicates that they are hoping to *obtain a new source of income by selling British secrets to the German government. Who can say how many Scorpions there are treading the corridors of power – and of course it only requires one such traitor to pose the direst threat to the nation's security. It is a great shame that we can no longer turn to Hunter to follow the matter up in Berlin; we will have to rely on the material that the Mannheim operative sends us.*

*It seems increasingly clear to me that the resurgence of the Scorpions has been brought about through the influence of one individual. His strategies so far – the bomb, the negotiations with the Germans, the conference – all suggest that he is a man of over-arching ambition who will stop at nothing to achieve his aims. It may be that this designing genius is one of the men already known to us, but they are all members of the old guard and I must say that at present I'm inclined to go along with Liebowitz's theory that there is someone else; that it is new blood that has set England's dark heart beating once again. If we can apprehend this unknown individual, together with Stone and Harding, then I would wager Miss Lauderdale's fortune that we can put an end to the Scorpions once and for all. If we fail, there is little doubt that the security of the nation will be gravely breached.*

*It is evident that the impending gathering is to be a decisive moment, one that will determine the success or failure of our entire operation. We must ensure that we are thoroughly prepared, so that when the time comes to move in and arrest the leaders there is no room for error. You must start laying the groundwork now. Stone and his cronies may well come back to the hotel in advance of the others; keep a regular watch and inform us at once of any developments.*

*Have you made any progress in the search for Professor Robinson? So far, I'm afraid, we've been unable to obtain a more concrete description than the one you were given by the clerk at the British Museum. I went back to the house and questioned some of the servants, but their impressions of their employer's appearance were all equally vague. It appears that Robinson is one of those nondescript individuals who could be extremely successful as a secret agent. And to make matters worse, according to his housekeeper the professor was peculiarly superstitious about having his photograph taken – wouldn't allow it under any circumstances – and so we're unlikely to uncover any further ...*

*I have just resumed writing this, having been interrupted by a telephone call from head office. It consisted mostly of a long rant from R12, who berated me for the slow progress made by Bureau 8 so far, threatening us with all kinds of dire consequences if we don't produce some results soon. The main grievance seems to be that we are allowing ourselves to be distracted by "extraneous divagations", for example our attempt to locate Professor Robinson, at the expense of "more important matters". They are still fuming about Hampson-Smythe, and despite all our efforts they continue to insist that we haven't tried hard enough to find him; apparently we will have to wait at least three months before they can recruit anyone to take his place. It seems that we are to receive the blame for every unhappy accident that befalls this investigation: the perfidy of "Miss Bartholomew"; the explosion at Victoria; even poor Plimpson's death which, according to R12, we might have prevented by acting more decisively to take him into custody after the fire. One might suppose that Liebowitz would share some of my indignation at head office's making Bureau 8 the scapegoat for everything that goes wrong, but he was quite sharp with me when I pointed out the injustice of it all.*

*I must say that he has been growing rather distant of late. He's driving himself into the ground through overwork, though he becomes prickly and evasive when I try to question him about what exactly it is that he's been doing. He's also been out of the office a great deal, which is very unlike him; do you remember how we used to joke that if he weren't careful he would end up taking root at his desk? In the past few days I have scarcely seen*

252

*him; I suspect that he's been staying here overnight to catch up with his paperwork, snatching forty winks at his desk and then going out again early in the morning. When I ventured to enquire what he was up to, he told me – very brusquely – that he was pursuing the investigation, and would say no more. Then, at teatime, when I asked him whether he wanted any cake, he exclaimed, "Cake? No, I do not want any cake! Confound it all, you people . . ." and then broke off and started scribbling away again. Of course, the remark might have been perfectly innocent, but the tone of those words "you people" really took me aback; it was as if he were overflowing with scorn for all of us.*

*Please don't imagine that I am accusing Liebowitz of being a traitor. I suppose what I'm trying to express is an intuition that his loyalty has shifted away from us. Towards what or whom I cannot say; perhaps only towards himself. Nevertheless, with you, Hampson-Smythe and Hunter gone, I should feel as if I were working entirely on my own if it weren't for Miss Trant; I can't tell you how thankful I am that head office instructed us to take her on.*

*Though it pains me to put the warning into plain words, please be careful about which communications you choose to share with Liebowitz. I hope very much that my suspicions amount to nothing, but it will do no harm to make caution your watchword in dealing with every aspect of this affair.*

*Yours, with warmest regards,*

*Anthony Rivers*

*Postscript: with regard to Professor R, I shouldn't pay too much heed to R12's suggestion that he can be discounted. Head office has made mistakes of this sort in the past and I'm inclined to believe that he might be of use to us in the future – possibly as a double agent.*

Hampson-Smythe put down his pipe and met MacIntyre's eye. "Perhaps you were right about Liebowitz after all," he said with a downcast air.

"Yes, perhaps. But Liebowitz is forever getting wrapped up in one thing or another and I for one have always found him rather difficult to fathom. It sounds as if the Chief is under a great deal of pressure from head office; it may simply be that his anxiety is making him see things that aren't there. Or, of course, it might be a double bluff."

"The Chief would never turn traitor!"

"It does seem unlikely," MacIntyre agreed, twirling a broken piece of garden cane between his long fingers. "But one always has the sense that Rivers is holding something back."

"Well, that's to be expected, given his position."

"Yes, I know that, and you're probably right. However, I can't be certain of it, and until I am I'm afraid that, much as it pains me, I shall continue to hold on to my suspicions."

The younger man heaved a sigh. "What do you suppose he meant about Robinson?"

"That business about becoming a double agent, do you mean? Well, if Murphy – the man injured in the explosion – was telling the truth about the destination of those packages of dynamite, then Professor Robinson is in a very dangerous position indeed. I suppose the Chief thinks that if we can bring sufficient pressure to bear – offering him protection and so forth – we might manage to persuade him to act as a double agent. However, as I said before, there's a strong possibility that our friend Murphy was lying. In which case the professor's reasons for leaving London so abruptly are probably entirely unconnected with the explosion."

"Do you suppose that he might have come to Seacombe to make preparations for the Scorpions' conference?"

"Even if he did, he may no longer be here. The trouble is that the description I was given by that fellow at the museum is so vague that it could fit almost anyone – middle years, middle height, slightly balding . . . why, either of us might have spoken to the man without having been aware of it!"

"It might have been Mark Crawley!" Hampson-Smythe exclaimed.

"Ye-es – though one would think that someone would have mentioned the glass eye. But it might, for example, have been that other fellow who came to the hotel to keep Harding company while Crawley was away. However, we just don't know, and unless we can obtain some more definite information there's little point in speculating any further."

There was a brief silence, during which Hampson-Smythe took up his pipe again and lit it.

"It sounds as if Hunter is being rather rash," he remarked, blowing out a long stream of smoke through his nostrils.

"Perhaps," said MacIntyre, looking sombre. "However, let us suppose, just for the sake of being bloody-minded, that Rivers *has* betrayed us. In that case, if Hunter was starting to become rather too successful in Berlin, it would suit Rivers very well to find an excuse to bring him back. Really, we've heard very little about Hunter's doings – I don't think Rivers has been passing everything on to us."

"But it was the Chief's idea to send him out to Berlin in the first place, wasn't it?"

"No, it was Hunter's. But Rivers might have agreed to it, knowing that he could control the flow of information through to the rest of us. And of course it would suit him very well for us all to believe that Bureau 8 is on top of things because we have an agent out there, at the heart of the Scorpions' operation."

"Do you really believe that about the Chief, MacIntyre?" said Hampson-Smythe, wrinkling his brow.

"It's one possible theory. And no, I don't quite believe it – at least not yet."

The two men sat looking thoughtful for a few moments. Then, as if under the influence of a dawning inspiration, MacIntyre burst out, "Of course! Why ever didn't I see it before? It *must* be more than mere coincidence, the Scorpions choosing to hold their conference in such an out of the way place as Seacombe – and in Lillian Lauderdale's old house to boot! And since they don't tend to be sentimental chaps and – according to Rivers at least – they're terribly short of funds, I should say that there's only one explanation."

Hampson-Smythe screwed up his face, as if he were trying to will the answer out of the air. "They're hoping to find Miss Lauderdale's lost fortune!" he said at last, with a look of triumph.

"*Voilà!*"

"So where do you think the money is hidden?"

"In a Swiss bank account, I should imagine."

"Don't be facetious, MacIntyre. Don't you think that the money might be in the hotel itself?"

"No. If that were the case, it wouldn't take a gathering of more than thirty men to find it. I suspect that it's not the money itself they're looking for, but some clue to its whereabouts. And they're not entirely sure it's here, or they would have held the conference sooner. I should say that the main significance of the event is symbolic; it demonstrates to the Scorpions and to anyone else who may be aware of it that the organisation is stronger and more cohesive than it has been for years."

"What kind of clue? Something like a treasure map, do you mean?"

"No, more likely an account book of some sort."

"Surely if the money were in a bank they would have been able to get at it somehow?"

"Not if they didn't know where it had been deposited, or under which name."

"So you think we ought to search the hotel? But how can we do that without arousing suspicion?"

"My dear Smythe, we're not going to search the hotel; we'll get someone else to do it."

"Who?"

"Can't you guess? Why, Miss Trant, of course."

"Why on earth would we do that? Oh."

"My motivations, dear Smythe, are professional, not personal. If we were to arrange for Miss Trant to be employed as a maid in the hotel, then she would be able to come and go more or less as she likes."

"Is there a position vacant?"

"Not so far as I know, but I'm sure that I can charm Mrs Rutherford into taking on one of Mrs Rankin's 'special cases' for the duration of the Scorpions' conference – especially if she knows that dear Mother and some of her friends might want to take a holiday in Seacombe in the spring. The hotel will be so busy that she's certain to need extra help."

"Doesn't it pose a risk that Miss Trant's father had some sort of connection with the Scorpions?"

"Not at all – she'll be working under an alias."

"I suppose that's true."

MacIntyre lit a cigarette and regarded Hampson-Smythe with a reflective frown. "Do you know, I have an instinct that Arthur Trant may prove more significant in this affair than any of us have imagined. For that reason alone I should say that it's better to have Miss Trant here with us in Seacombe rather than in London with the Chief and Liebowitz. It may well be that she knows something important without even being aware of it, and if she does you and I must make sure that it is brought to light."

All at once Hampson-Smythe's face was stricken with consternation.

"I say, what about Peters? I mean Stone? It seems pretty likely that he'll be at the conference – surely he'd recognise Miss Trant!"

MacIntyre flung his cigarette onto the floor and ground it under his heel with a look of bitter frustration.

"D–n! What a fool I am! That didn't even occur to me. Of course, you're right – it would be far too dangerous to bring her here!"

"Not to worry, old chap – we'll find another way," said Hampson-Smythe, clapping him on the shoulder. "And you needn't get too heartsick over it – I dare say you'll see Miss Trant again before too long!"

# Thirty

*D*espite my best efforts, I got no closer to discovering the significance of my aunt Sophie's letter during the days succeeding its arrival. Though I spent hours studying it with the magnifying glass, I could make out not a single character more, and the connotation of the words that I had managed to decipher remained obstinately opaque. Initially, I considered asking the Chief or Liebowitz to look at it, but the pace of the investigation had picked up again and they were both frantically busy. Furthermore, Liebowitz appeared to be holding himself increasingly aloof and had quite suddenly begun to spend a great deal of time out of the office. It was a development that, I sensed, worried the Chief, and this increased my reluctance to take up any of his valuable time with what I still assumed was a personal matter. Then something occurred that was so shocking and unexpected that it blotted the letter out of my mind altogether.

On the morning in question I came out of my room to find Mother already fully dressed and sitting at her writing table, poring over a piece of paper. As soon as she heard me come in she started guiltily and shoved it under her blotter.

"Good morning," she said, turning towards me. To my dismay, I saw that her eyes were unnaturally bright and that her cheeks were stained with a hectic flush.

"Mother, are you ill?" I asked, hastening over to feel her forehead.

She batted my hand away in irritation. "Don't fuss, Margaret; I'm perfectly all right. I woke early and didn't feel like lying in bed, so I thought I'd catch up with some correspondence. Now, hurry along and eat your breakfast or you'll be late for work. You needn't trouble about me; I'll have something later."

I had fallen asleep again after the alarm had sounded and it was too late to make tea, so I gobbled down a piece of bread and marmalade and put on my coat. Then I stooped to kiss Mother goodbye, inhaling the faint, familiar scents of lavender face powder and coal tar soap that rose from her skin.

"Are you sure you're all right?" I said, looking down at her flushed face with a feeling of uneasiness.

"Whatever is the matter with you this morning?" she demanded, frowning, though I noticed that she did not meet my eye. "Now off you go, or you'll be in trouble with Mr Flowers."

Glancing at my watch I saw that it was indeed very late. "Very well," I said with a sigh. "Make sure you send for Mrs Hodgkins if you start to feel ill. Your sal volatile is on the chest of drawers in your room."

Her pale blue eyes regarded me queerly for a few moments, as if she were struggling inwardly with some pressing dilemma. Then, with an abrupt motion, she turned to her writing desk, unlocked the drawer and took out a fresh sheet of paper. "Goodbye, Margaret," she said, reaching for her pen.

I picked up my portfolio and went out, pausing in the doorway to look back at the frail, crooked figure hunched over the desk. "Goodbye!" I called, but she was so absorbed in what she was doing that she didn't seem to hear.

My anxiety about Mother soon faded as other matters rose up to demand my attention. Liebowitz was not in the office, but he had left a very large pile of telegrams on my desk, together with several exceedingly lengthy coded reports. Fortunately by this time my injured hand was almost healed, but none the less I knew that even if I were to type at my fastest rate, I would not be finished until well into the afternoon.

The Chief spent the day moving back and forth between his desk and the meeting room, and several times I looked up to see him staring into space with a thoughtful frown. I made myself as unobtrusive as I could, for it was clear that he was engaged in work of the utmost urgency and importance. At half past four he picked up the telephone receiver, glanced in my direction and put it down again.

"You look as though you've had rather a long day of it, my dear," he said. "Have you finished typing the documents Liebowitz left for you?"

I nodded. "Yes sir, just a few minutes ago."

"That's excellent. In that case, you deserve to go home early."

"Are you certain there's nothing else for me to . . ."

"No, really, Miss Trant – you've done quite enough for today. I only hope all this typing doesn't seem too tedious after your recent adventures. However, you needn't worry; I dare say we shall find something more exciting for you to do before long."

I looked at him eagerly, waiting for him to say more, but he only smiled enigmatically. And so I got up to fetch my coat, and made my way back to St John's Wood, lost in speculation about what my next mission might involve and utterly forgetful of Mother's peculiar behaviour earlier in the day.

The first thing I noticed when I opened the door to our rooms was a slight smell of gas. Then, a fraction of a second later, I saw Mr Smith crouching on the floor. He moved aside and stood looking down at my mother, who lay bunched and twisted, like a rag doll that has had its limbs bent out of shape. Even now I can picture her blotchy, distorted face as vividly as if it were still before me: her eyes bulging blindly, her lips gobbling silently, a froth of saliva dropping down her chin. And then, within a matter of seconds, a hollow stillness stole over her and settled upon her countenance like a mask.

Smith's great bald head tilted and the pinpoints of his pupils fixed upon me.

"She is gone, Miss Trant," he said, and then he let go of Mother's hand, took me by the arm and led me to the sofa, pressing my shoulders to make me sit down. I struggled to resist him and my breath caught in my throat as I cried out that he must let me go to her.

"No," he said with quiet insistence, "there is nothing to be done, let me assure you. I have seen that look many times before and it is the end – she is at peace now."

Feeling suddenly limp and exhausted, I dropped onto the sofa and rested my head against a cushion. Mother lay on her side with her back towards me, and from the angle at which I was sitting it looked as if she had surrendered to a whim to take a nap on the floor.

"I'm so very sorry, Miss Trant. It must be a dreadful shock. Here, this will help," said Smith, removing a flask from his jacket pocket and holding it out to me. I declined, but he continued to press it on me until I gave in. The rum scorched my throat and made me splutter, but I felt its warmth coursing through me and took another sip before giving back the flask. Smith lifted it to his lips and gulped voraciously, his Adam's apple bobbing in his meaty neck, then wiped his mouth with the back of his hand.

"Sit still while I send for a doctor. Don't touch her on any account, not until the death certificate has been signed," he commanded, his eyes fixed on a spot somewhere above my head. "Potentially compromising circumstances," he added, then turned and went out.

Left alone in the stony presence of death, I sat motionless, swallowed up by the sensation that I was trapped in some nightmare from which I could not wake. At last I stood up and, trembling all over, tottered across to Mother's prostrate body. I gave a shudder at the sight of her eyes bulging glassily in her livid countenance and knelt down to close them, before I remembered Mr Smith's prohibition and snatched my hand away. I attempted to retreat from those terrible, staring eyeballs, rolled back halfway into their sockets, but was overwhelmed by a sudden giddiness and slumped to the floor. I could not summon up the energy to get up again and so I lay there with my face buried in my hands, longing for the relief of tears that would not come. Several minutes passed before I heard the sound of footsteps ascending the staircase; not Smith's heavy tread but the creaking leather of Mrs Hodgkins' new shoes, and with a great effort I staggered to my feet.

The landlady, who looked very white and tearful, paused in the doorway, as if she did not quite know where she was. Then, seeing me standing in the middle of the room, she hurried over and pressed me to her bony chest.

"Oh, my dear, what a terrible thing! Your poor mother! To think she's been took in my house!" Then all at once her whole body convulsed and she emitted a little scream. "Oh my! Her eyes! Why didn't you close them?" And before I could stop her, she stooped and pulled down Mother's eyelids.

"Mr Smith said we oughtn't to touch her," I said dully.

"We couldn't leave her like that! It's not respectful!" she retorted, and then she paused, sniffing the air. She went across to examine the gas burner on which Mother and I were accustomed to boil water to make tea, but apparently finding nothing amiss she turned back to me with a sigh. "Poor Mrs Trant – why, she was only three years older than I am! She was a good friend to me, Margaret – I hardly know what I shall do without her!" She sank down into the armchair and held her handkerchief up to her face, weeping noisily. I sat on the edge of the sofa and stared straight ahead, overcome by an empty feeling of disbelief, as if I were viewing the scene from a great distance.

After a short interval, the sound of carriage wheels drifted in through the open window and the landlady straightened up with a loud sniff, dabbing at her eyes with her handkerchief. "That'll be the doctor!" she exclaimed, slipping across to stand behind the curtain, from which vantage point she was able to watch the physician's progress up the garden path without being seen from outside. It was not until later that it occurred to me how strange it was that the window had been open at all, for Mother had always lived in dread of catching a chill and had insisted upon keeping the windows shut, even in the height of summer.

A minute later there was a tap on the door. I had been expecting Mother's usual physician, Dr Andrews, but the man who walked in was a stranger, a complacent-looking fellow with ginger side-whiskers and a stomach that bulged in his waistcoat like a great pumpkin. He was accompanied by Becky, who froze in the doorway when she caught sight of my mother's huddled body, her eyes as wide as saucers.

"Thank you, Rebecca!" snapped Mrs Hodgkins, and at once the maid sprang to attention and scurried off like a frightened rabbit. The doctor shook Mrs Hodgkins' hand and introduced himself as "Miller". I made an effort to stand up, but my legs gave way beneath me.

"Don't trouble yourself, Margaret," said the landlady. "I shall make sure everything is done properly." She turned to address the doctor. "This is Mrs Trant's daughter, Margaret."

"May I extend my deepest sympathies," he said, giving me a courteous nod before looking back at Mrs Hodgkins as if he thought she would prove the more reliable source of information.

"Poor soul, she had suffered ill health for years! Of course, I did what I could for her, but there is only so much . . ."

The landlady rambled on while the doctor began his examination. I turned away and squeezed my eyes shut, for I could not bear to watch while Mother was poked and prodded about by a stranger.

After what seemed a very brief interval I became aware that the doctor was standing over me, looking very solemn. "Your mother died of heart failure. Unfortunately, for a woman in her state of health such an occurrence is not at all uncommon."

"But what could have brought it on? Do you think she had a fright of some kind?" I asked, thinking of Mr Smith.

"According to the gentleman who came to fetch me she was alone in her room all day. He was alerted to the calamity by a cry and the sound of something crashing to the floor. Such an attack might have come on at any time. Of course we cannot say for sure, but it is probable that there was no external cause whatsoever. I will move the body for you before I go. If I might ask where . . ."

"Into her bedroom," said Mrs Hodgkins, assuming a proprietary air. "I will attend to the other necessaries myself. I dare say Margaret will assist me."

"No, madam," Dr Miller interjected, "I think it will be best if

Miss Trant goes to bed. She is in a state of shock and must rest. Here is something to help you sleep my dear."

I thanked him, and ignoring the landlady's peevish look I accepted the little vial of liquid and retired to my room, locking the door behind me.

I lay on my bed, listening to the noises from the next room. I heard the doctor bid Mrs Hodgkins goodbye and then, after an interminable interval during which I did my best not to think about the preparations that must be going on in my mother's bedroom, there was a sound of creaking shoe leather, followed by the banging of the main door, and then silence.

I don't believe that I have ever felt as lonely as I did at that moment. I got up and crept through the darkened sitting room into Mother's bedroom. She lay with closed eyelids and her hands folded on her breast. Death had changed her face and made of it a pinched waxwork, weirdly shadowed by the lamp that Mrs Hodgkins had left burning at the foot of the bed. The stillness was so intense that my presence seemed an intrusion and after less than a minute I backed out of the door and returned to my room.

My father was gone, and my aunt; my cousin was on her way to the other side of the globe, and now Mother was dead. I wept for all of them, crying so hard that I thought I should suffocate with misery. At last, when my face was clammy and swollen and my eyes were dry and smarting, I drank down the sleeping draught. It may seem strange, but nevertheless it is true that my last waking thought was not of any of those dear lost ones but of MacIntyre, who I wished with all my heart was by my side.

# Thirty-One

The funeral was held in the same church that had seen my father's service. Just as it had then, the light inside seemed bleak and meagre, seeping in through the stained glass and settling like dust. Even Mrs Hodgkins' tearful eulogy sounded strained and flat. While she stood at the lectern, wringing her hands, Mr Smith slipped in and sat in a pew at the back. By some uncanny means I seemed to sense his presence before I looked round and saw him, pale in his black coat, his impassive gaze fixed upon the altar. At once I was swept back to the moment when I had opened the door to find him crouching over my dying mother like a gigantic vulture and I turned to the front, struggling to dispel a lowering sense of dread.

Mrs Hodgkins blew her nose with a thin, trumpeting sound and returned to her seat, and the vicar began to intone the Lord's Prayer. I pictured Mother lying inside the coffin in her best dress, her eyes staring up at the ebony lid like two blank blue stones, and for an instant I thought I must cry out and protest that they could not take her away and bury her in the cold earth. Then I heard the door of the nave clap shut and looked back to see that Mr Smith had gone. I heaved a sigh of relief, but for the remainder of the service I was unable to shake off the uneasy feeling that Smith's unexpected appearance in the church had been some sort of warning; that he was biding his time, watching and waiting until the moment came for him to reveal his true hand.

I had been sleeping badly, and the night after the funeral was no exception. I lay awake into the small hours, and when finally I sank into sleep I had the most extraordinary and horrifying dreams, from which I awoke with a violent start to see the bleached light of dawn glowing through a gap in the curtains. I was too afraid of my own thoughts to lie in bed for long and so, despite the earliness of the hour, I dressed, made myself a pot of tea and drank it at the little table in the sitting room, feeling limp, unfocused and without any purpose in life. I had telegraphed to inform the Chief of Mother's death on the morning after it had occurred and he had responded immediately with a telegram in which he had expressed his condolences and instructed me that I must not think of coming into HQ for at least a fortnight. Now, nine days later, the thought of languishing at home in solitude filled me with despair, yet I knew that I was still in no fit state to go back to work.

Two days slipped by, during which I did not set foot outside our apartment and spoke to no one except Mrs Hodgkins. The Krackewiczs had sent a brief and ungrammatical note of sympathy, but they had not appeared at the funeral, and did not come to see me now. Becky was in bed with a bad attack of the quinsy and the landlady was extremely put out by all the extra work that had fallen to her as a consequence. Three times a day she came grumbling up the stairs to bring me my meals on a tray, a privilege for which I had to pay a considerable supplement, though the food was invariably cold and of even worse quality than that which was served in the dining room. I ate little and was aware that I had begun to lose weight. I could not summon the concentration to read and spent hours drifting listlessly from one window to another, gazing out at the changing quality of the light.

On the third day, having slept a little better, I decided to start sorting out Mother's possessions. I put off entering her bedroom until about halfway through the morning, for I had not been inside it since the night of her death. Now, more than a week later, it smelt stale and unaired and I went over to the window and pulled down the sash. As I was turning back towards the wardrobe, my gaze fell on the little walnut dish that stood on the bedside table. In it lay a bronze key, threaded onto a long black ribbon. My heart began to beat with a fierce excitement that broke upon me like a revelation; like something from another, half-forgotten life. This was the key to the rosewood cabinet in which Mother had locked away all her private papers. She had guarded its contents jealously, but once or twice I had glimpsed the interior and I was aware that, as well as business documents, it contained several yellowing bundles of letters tied up with ribbons and a number of intriguing boxes and tins. I had never trusted her insistence that she had burnt all the photographs of my father and got rid of his possessions, and had always cherished the hope that there might be at least one or two keepsakes secreted among her things.

I went back into the living room and stood looking at this potential Aladdin's cave for a moment. The prohibition against touching it had been instilled in me so strongly that I felt as if I were about to commit some terrible violation, and when I reached out to put the key into the lock my hand was trembling. Nevertheless, I drew a deep breath and opened the door.

But the shelves were empty, save for a few scraps of paper and a length of crimson ribbon. I wondered whether my mother might have hidden her treasures elsewhere or, acting upon some uncanny presentiment of her death, destroyed them. Outlandish as it was, this last possibility did not seem quite out of the question, for she had been unusually subdued and distracted during the last weeks of her life, and on several occasions I had caught her reading pieces of correspondence which she had hastily attempted to conceal from me. I removed the morsels of paper and was about to consign them to the wastepaper basket when I noticed that there was something written on one of them. I peered at it more closely and in that instant my blood seized: it was marked with a pyramid and a human eye; the same symbols that I had seen on Mr Smith's postcards and on the creased slip of paper that Becky had given me. Could this be further evidence that my father had had some involvement with the Scorpions? With shaking hands, I smoothed out the paper and went to fetch my writing case, for I felt as if I ought to inform the Chief of this latest development at once.

Later that afternoon, as I sat looking out of the window, wondering how it could be that I felt so weary after a short stroll to the postbox, there was a knock on the door of my room.

"Come in!" I called, and Irma Krackewicz entered, throwing an anxious glance over her shoulder.

As soon as she had closed the door behind her, she came up very close to me and scrutinised my face. Then, as if satisfied, she squeezed one of my hands and said, "Nikolas is wrong – you cannot be a friend of this creature. You have the eyes of a good woman and I do not believe you are a friend of such persons – *c'est impossible, n'est-ce pas?*"

I shook my head in confusion, colouring up under her steady regard.

"I am so sorry for the death of your mother," she continued. "And I regret very much that I do not come to you. But such terrible things have happen we are in fear of our lives and Nikolas says we must not speak to no one. And now, this evening, we go to Warsaw." To my surprise her big dark eyes brimmed suddenly with tears. "Nikolas says it is *impossible* to stay in London. I say please we must go to Paris, but he tells me it is too near and we will not be safe. Since two days he is took by some mans who say they are policemans. They ask many questions and he tells them nothing but he thinks they must try to take him again."

I gestured for her to sit down in the armchair and took a seat on the adjacent sofa.

"Can you tell me what has happened to bring all this about?" I asked, with a strong sense that I could predict her answer.

Irma dabbed at her eyes with her handkerchief and drew a deep breath. "I think you know, my husband meeted a strange man, a friend of Madame Plimpson. It happen when Nikolas is making the painting at the *théâtre*. I do not know how to say, this man – *il a menacé* Nikolas when he discover he has work for Monsieur Plimpson.

He is telling Nikolas he must not speak of this work or terrible things is happening. Two days since, I am receiving a letter – it say I must not tell I seen Madame Plimpson near this house or I will be kill. Nikolas says it is too great danger and we must go." She paused and reached out to take my hand, gazing solemnly into my face. "He says she come here to see you. Please, *ma chère*, tell me if this is so."

"Mrs Plimpson? Here? Why ever should she want to call on me? When was it that you saw her?"

Irma reflected for a moment before replying, "It is a week before last Thursday – I am going to the café, for to meet Nikolas. It was afternoon; perhaps a little after four o'clock. She see me come out of the house and then she turn and she walk away without to speak. I think then she will not come here after all. She wear her costume and so it can be perhaps she goes next to the *théâtre*."

A week last Thursday was the day on which Mother had passed away.

"I didn't get back until after five that afternoon," I informed her, shuddering at the recollection of that terrible homecoming. "And if it was me she came to see, she didn't leave a message. If only Becky weren't ill, she might be able to tell us whether or not Mrs Plimpson came to the door."

"I see Becky – she is not in her bed today. But, Margaret, we must not tell no one that Madame Plimpson comes here."

"Don't worry; Becky can be trusted, I promise you," I said. "Wait here for a moment and I'll fetch her."

I found a wan-looking Becky polishing the dining room table and whisked her upstairs before Mrs Hodgkins could catch us. When she saw Irma sitting in the armchair, she turned to me in surprise. "Oh, I fought you wanted ter ax me about Mr Smiff!" she exclaimed, before her hand flew to cover her mouth and she turned scarlet with confusion.

"It doesn't matter, Becky," I assured her. "As a matter of fact, Mrs Krackewicz and I wanted to ask whether there were any visitors to the house on the Thursday afternoon that my mother . . ."

"The day Mrs Trant was took?"

I nodded and Irma gave a little gasp. "I did not know this! Forgive me, Margaret – I had forgot it was this day!"

"That's quite all right," I said, trying to smile. "Do go on, Becky."

The maid looked down at her feet and fidgeted uneasily with her apron.

"I was goin' ter tell yer, honest I was – only wot wiv bein' poorly and that, I've not 'ad the chance."

"I quite understand, Becky – you couldn't help being ill. You can tell us about it now."

She nodded, darting me a look of gratitude. "Mrs H was out at 'er sister's and she told me not to open the door to no one cos she'd sent a leg of mutton wot was rotten back to the butcher and she didn't want 'im comin' round creatin' when she weren't 'ere to tell him wot's wot. I 'eard the bell go as I was settin' down to me lunch, but I didn't go up on account of wot I was told. It went again and then I 'eard voices and nipped upstairs to see wot was goin' on, but they was already gone. It was Mr Smiff's voice wot I 'eard – and 'e was talkin' to a lady."

"What time would you say this was, Becky?" I asked.

"I couldn't say ezackerly, but I was late on account of 'avin' to clean a stain off the dinin' room carpet wot wouldn't come out, so I should say about 'alf past four."

"Did this visitor go away at once?" Irma enquired.

"No. I fought it was a lady visitin' Mr Smiff, wot he didn't want no one to know about on account of Mrs H's rule that single gentlemen ain't permitted female company in their rooms. But then I 'eard somefink from upstairs. It all seemed rarver queer to me, miss, so I went up to find out wot was wot. As I was goin' past your door, I 'eard voices and, beggin' yer pardon, I stopped ter listen. You won't say nuffin' to the missus? Only if she was to find out I'd been listenin' at doors, she'd lay into me somefing rotten."

"We wouldn't dream of doing such a thing, Becky," I said, thoroughly taken aback by the dual revelation that my mother had had a visitor so shortly before her death and that Mr Smith had lied to Dr Miller about it. "Please, do go on."

"Well, the door weren't quite shut – it weren't open wide enough for me to see nuffin', but I could 'ear quite well. Yer muvver seemed to be expectin' the lady – they was talkin' about some letters they'd writ each uvver – they was concernin' your farver, miss, beggin' yer pardon." She darted me an anxious look and added, "There was some talk of spirits and such. Mrs Trant's nerves was playin' 'er up and the lady tried to give 'er brandy to calm 'er down. She didn't want it to begin wiv, but the lady said as 'ow they wouldn't get no joy from the spirits unless yer muvver was in a proper state to receive 'em and in the end she give in and drunk it. She didn't like it much, said it 'ad a queer smell, but the lady poured 'er anuvver glass and she drunk that too. Then yer muvver says she's feelin' giddy, but the lady weren't listenin' . . ." Becky broke off, seized by a violent fit of coughing. I poured her a glass of water and tried to persuade her to sit down on the sofa, for she looked very pale.

"Oh, no, miss, I couldn't," she said, wiping her eyes with the hem of her apron and gulping down the water. "Wot would the missus say if she was ter come in and catch me? No, I'd rarver stand, if it's all the same to you. Now where was I? Oh, yes. The lady sez she'd lay 'er alphabet on the table and they'd best to get on, for she'd somewhere else to go. Yer muvver 'ad to give 'er Mr Trant's weddin' ring. She didn't sound well at all by then and I was in 'alf a mind to go in to 'er. But then the lady starts to make these funny sounds – sighin' and mutterin' – and she speaks in a different voice, sort of gruff and foreign-soundin', and arst for Mr Trant to come. There was a clatterin' sound and then a music box started up. Mrs Trant cried out when she 'eard that. And then the lady's voice changed again – it was more genteel-soundin' and low, like a man's. She sez yer muvver 'as a secret and she must give it up or else. Yer muvver starts to cry and then I 'eard a creakin' behind me – from the cupboard on the landing it sounded like. It give me a terrible fright – and so I run down ter me room. I s'pose there weren't no one there really, but all that talk of spirits and such 'ad played on me nerves. Any'ow, I sat down on me bed to get me breaf back and I was so tired, miss, that before I knew it I was fast asleep and didn't wake till I 'eard the bell – and *that* was the doctor wot 'ad come to see about your poor muvver, miss." She looked uncertainly from one of us to the other. "You ain't angry wiv me, are you, miss?" she asked.

"Quite the reverse – you've been most helpful, hasn't she, Mrs Krackewicz?"

"Indeed! *Merci, ma chère*," said Irma, giving her a dazzling smile.

"Now you'd better hurry back downstairs, Becky, before Mrs Hodgkins misses you. And take this." I scooped a threepenny piece from the jar on the table and slipped it into her palm.

"Why, fank you, miss!" she exclaimed, wide-eyed. Then, making an awkward little curtsey of gratitude, she trotted out.

As soon as the door had closed behind her, Irma rushed over to embrace me, engulfing me in the heady fragrance of attar of roses.

"Oh, Margaret! This bad woman is with your mother when she becomes ill! Is it this talk of spirits what kill her?"

"I don't know what to think," I said numbly, still struggling to take in the implications of all that the maid had said. "At any rate, the visitor can't have been Mrs Plimpson . . ."

"But no, I believe it is! In the *théâtre*, Aggie is *une clairvoyante*!"

With a peculiar sense of inevitability, everything fell suddenly into place. "And her stage name is Madam Coraline," I said flatly, remembering the handbill that had been sent to my mother together with the watercolour portraits of her and my father.

"Indeed," said Irma, frowning in puzzlement. "But I do not know she does also private work. Did you know your mother is making the *séance*?"

I shook my head. "No – I had no idea."

Irma consulted a little silver watch, which she wore pinned to the lapel of her jacket. "*Alors!* I must go!" she exclaimed. "I am so sorry I cannot stay to speak more, but we must not be late or the ship sails without us. You must have care, *ma chère* Margaret. If these bad mans come, you must tell the police – it is of no matter after we depart." She paused and fumbled with the clasp of the jade necklace that she wore about her throat, before pressing it into my hand. "*C'est un souvenir* – you are always most kind. You are the only friend we have at this house."

I was greatly touched by this impulsive demonstration of her affection, but did not feel that I could accept such a valuable present and said so.

"You must take!" she insisted. "I am – how do you say? – offend if you refuse me."

She looked so upset that I did not have the heart to persist in my refusal. "Thank you," I said. "I'm sure nothing that I have ever done merits such a generous gift, but I'm very grateful to you all the same. I hope very much that we shall see one another again."

"Perhaps," she said with a melancholy smile, adding more briskly, "I must go – Nikolas is waiting. *Au revoir!*" And she turned and hurried out, leaving behind her a lingering scent of roses.

After Irma had gone, I sat trying to piece together a coherent account of the events that had occurred on the afternoon of my mother's death. Now that I knew the truth about Madam Coraline, the affair of the watercolour portraits was revealed in a fresh and more sinister light. I realised that it must have been Mrs Plimpson's intention to persuade my mother to participate in a séance from the beginning and saw with new eyes Mother's furtive letter writing, long silences and inexplicable changes of mood during the period leading up to her death. I had no doubt that she had been suffi-ciently credulous to believe in the possibility of conversing with my father's spirit from beyond the grave; as one who had spent the last decade brooding over the past, she would have been only too ready to be won over by Mrs Plimpson's cynical inventions.

It would have been perfectly in character for Mr Plimpson to pique his wife's curiosity by boasting about mysterious doings in his past and then to pull himself up short when he realised that he had said too much. Perhaps he had hinted at my father's connec-tion to the affair, and Mrs Plimpson had latched onto my mother as being the most likely source of information about it – in which case she was almost certain to have been disappointed in the end, for according to my cousin it was Aunt Sophie, not Mother, in whom my father had confided.

So Mrs Plimpson had conceived her elaborate plot to draw my

mother in, and had clearly been well on the way to achieving her object when Mr Plimpson had been murdered, and with him any lingering hope his wife might have cherished that he would eventually tell her what she wanted to know. Something so important that she had taken the trouble to come to the house, in the character of Madam Coraline, to extract it from my mother. But what was it?

It was then that I remembered the photograph that MacIntyre had found in Professor Robinson's office, and with a shock of realisation I understood why the gypsy woman sitting at the front of the picture had seemed so familiar. Aggie Hagger, as she had been in those days, had been present on that mysterious night. She had probably been involved with the Scorpions since well before her marriage.

I walked across to the window and stood gazing out at rooftops bathed in the crimson glow of the setting sun. My conviction that the Scorpions had played a part in my father's death remained as strong as ever, and I now felt a deepening certainty that the organisation was in some way responsible for my mother's sudden demise. If Mrs Plimpson had come to the house with the intention of uncovering information on the Scorpions' behalf, it was possible that once she had got everything she could out of Mother she had decided to get rid of her rather than run the risk of exposure. But questionable as I knew Mrs Plimpson's morals to be, I could not quite bring myself to believe that she was capable of resorting to the cold-blooded murder of a helpless invalid. Could it really be that Madam Coraline's hocus-pocus had been too much for Mother's feeble constitution, as Irma had suggested?

That evening, when Mrs Hodgkins came up with my tray, she breathlessly informed me that the Krackewiczs were gone for good and good riddance to them. She seemed disappointed that I was neither surprised nor pleased by this momentous news and soon left in disgust, muttering that she had been a fool to expect that I would take an interest in anyone other than myself.

A few seconds later she poked her head back into the room. "There's a letter on the tray that was delivered by hand this afternoon," she informed me haughtily, looking down her long nose. "And before you ask, I don't know who brought it – it must have been posted through the door while I was having my nap."

I glanced down and saw that there was indeed a large square envelope tucked underneath my plate. The landlady continued to watch from the doorway, as if she were waiting for me to open the letter.

"Thank you, Mrs Hodgkins," I said firmly and, scowling, she closed the door with a bang.

I examined the unevenly written superscription, *Miss M. Trant*, and then slit open the flap of the envelope with my knife. Inside was a ticket for the second house at the Hoxton Alhambra on the following evening and a handbill proclaiming

### Madam Coraline
WORLD FAMOUS MEDIUM AND CLAIRVOYANT
Will shortly be Appearing at the Hoxton Alhambra
MARVEL! At Golden Dawn her Red Indian Spirit Guide
WONDER! As she converses with the Departed and be
ASTOUNDED at her Uncanny Predictions of the Future!

On the back of the bill was a note written in emerald-coloured ink, in an unsightly scrawl which was immediately familiar. It is still in my possession, and what follows is an accurate copy.

*Alhambra Music Hall*

*9th October, 1905*

*Dear Miss Trant,*
*Water has gone under the brij since last we saw one another. As you will know I have lost my Plimmy which tradgedie has blited my life – the world is a barren dessert to me wivout that good sole to serve as my starff and comfort. I can no longer bare even to use his name, for it is so sorowfull to hear it spoke. I was also most sorry to hear of your mother's sad demize and it is to this end I now write for I have some*

275

*informashun in that regard which it will be much to your advantidge
to learn. I enclose a complimentry ticket for the show tomorow nite in
which I will be apeering in my character as Madam Coraline World
Famous Medium. If you will kindly come to wotch Ill be waiting to
receeve you in my dressing room after. You must wotch the show furst
mind if you wish to learn the secret.*

*With affecshunate regards
Aggie Hagger (Plimpson as was)*

I read this epistle with a mounting sense of disbelief. The
audacity of the woman was quite astounding! How dare she send
me her affectionate regards and pretend to be sorry for my loss after
she had preyed so ruthlessly on my mother! And yet I could not
help thinking that if she *had* been responsible for my mother's
death, she would surely have preferred to avoid drawing attention
to the fact by issuing such an invitation as this. I began to wonder
whether, perhaps, she really did know something that might help to
unravel the mystery surrounding my mother's last moments. She
might even be in possession of evidence that condemned Mr Smith;
evidence that would enable me to set about making a credible case
against him. I realised that I was prepared to make almost any
sacrifice in order to discover more about the puzzling occurrences
of that fateful afternoon, even if it meant venturing unchaperoned
into a boisterous music hall and worse still being subjected to a
private audience with the vulgar and condescending Miss Hagger.

# Thirty-Two

The following evening I left the house before six, intending to arrive in plenty of time to get to my seat before the crush. However, when I turned the corner into Penn Street shortly after seven o'clock, the pavements were thronging and I hung back for a few moments, observing the scene. From every side came the cries of theatre-goers calling to one another excitedly across a sea of bobbing hats. It was a cold night and the air burnt the tips of my fingers inside my gloves and made my cheeks tingle. I looked around at the host of lively, expectant faces which, bathed in the whitish glare of the street-lamps, had assumed a strange and exotic night-time splendour, and quite unexpectedly I felt my spirits rise. I began to realise that my prolonged confinement in the dreary boarding house had done much to contribute to the building sense of gloom and foreboding by which I had lately been so oppressed and I resolved to try my best to enjoy the evening's entertainment and to forget about the undesirable encounter that awaited me at the end of it.

I edged forward into the crowd, clutching my reticule tightly in case of pickpockets, and joined the queue that had formed in front of the theatre. Its façade was decorated in the Moorish style, mimicking its grander counterpart in Leicester Square. There were pillars, a balcony, an ornamental staircase and even some small minarets decorated with crescent moons. The principal entrance was sheltered by a rather ramshackle porch with a rusty iron roof supported by cast iron columns with ornamental capitals, and was lit on either side by blazing Saracenic lanterns.

I stood waiting outside the theatre for about ten minutes and when at last I passed into the cramped entrance hall, I was shivering with cold. Outside, I heard a man yelling "Oi, cobber! Look where you're going!" and glanced round just in time to see a tall, broad-backed figure disappearing into the crowd. A chill went through me and I strained my neck to look after him, but he was already gone. A fat man smelling of whisky and onions shoved past me and I moved further into the interior, assuring myself that I had merely succumbed to a fit of nerves and that it was absurd to suppose that Mr Smith could have followed me all this way without my having detected him. Resisting the urge to look behind me, I skirted the circular ticket-booth, which was surrounded by a gaggle of chattering customers, and handed my ticket to a cheerful girl with a wall-eye, who sat on a stool a little way off to one side. She directed me up a narrow flight of stairs and at the top I was met by a boy with gilt buttons and oiled hair. He scrutinised my ticket before leading me along a red-carpeted corridor to a door in the wall, which he opened with a little bow. I peered inside and saw only darkness, though I could hear the hum of loud conversation drifting up from below. "Where is the audience?" I asked.

The boy regarded me with a puzzled look before replying uncertainly, as if he weren't sure whether I was pulling his leg, "You're in a box, miss – you'll see 'em all clearly enough once you get in." He lowered his voice. "A gentleman come in last night and asked me to see that you got these." He handed me a pair of opera glasses.

"What was the gentleman's name?" I asked in surprise.

The boy shrugged. "He didn't say, miss."

"Did he mention me by name?"

"No, miss – he just said to give 'em to the lady what would be sitting in this partickler box tomorrer night, which is you. He said with his best wishes and he hoped you would stay until the interval at least."

"Are you certain they were intended for me?"

"Quite as sure as I can be, miss, in the circumstances."

I stepped through the doorway into the box. Breathing in the scents of dusty upholstery and polished brass, I felt a sudden stirring of nostalgia, recalling the occasion when my parents had taken me to see the Drury Lane pantomime *Humpty Dumpty*, starring Marie Lloyd and the comedian Little Tich. My throat tightened and my eyes welled with tears as I pictured myself sitting with Mother and Father on either side of me, all three of us entranced by the marvellous spectacle unfolding before us. I bit my lip, sternly batting the memory away, and sat down on a throne-like chair with gilded edges and scarlet plush upholstery. The gilt was chipped and the gorgeousness of the plush was somewhat spoilt with wear, but I was very pleased to have been accommodated in such solitary splendour and leant over to look at the mass of heads in the stalls below me. The theatre was already warm with the combined heat of hundreds of bodies and I removed my coat, reflecting that in summer the atmosphere must be sweltering. I looked across to the gallery and remarked a hand pointing in my direction and then several faces turning excitedly my way; as the privileged occupant of a box, I appeared to be an object of curiosity and speculation for a good number of the assembled mass of spectators. I was struck by the unpleasant realisation that at least some of the interest I aroused might be of a more salacious kind; after all it is not the done thing for a respectable woman to go out unaccompanied at night. Hastily, I stood up and withdrew into the shadows, where I remained until the show began.

At last the house-lights dimmed and the footlights blazed. I returned to my seat and held the opera glasses to my eyes, but I could only manage to see through one of the lenses and put them to one side. A tall, strapping man stepped out from behind the curtain; with his top-hat, tails and dark curling moustache, he reminded me of the illustration of a ring-master in one of my childhood storybooks. He waited for the cheers that had greeted his appearance to fade away before declaring in a deep, mellifluous voice, "My lords (are any of you in tonight?), ladies and gentlemen – good evening! The Hoxton Alhambra is one of the *last great* halls in London – one of the *few* to keep the good old customs alive. And I am that rare beast – a *chairman!*" This was answered by a trickle of laughter. "Though all around me my fellows are falling *extinct*, I am still going strong in the name of my father and grandfather, who was chairmen of this very theatre afore me, though that was in the days before the old place burnt down and they built it up again, all new and three times as grand. So look sharp, ladies and gents, for you see before you the *king* of this handsome palace – *Jimmy Jolly!*" He flung up his arms on either side like wings and took a deep bow to a round of applause before continuing, "Prepare to be *astonished* by the best programme of entertainment ever to be laid on by the management of this theatre, or by any other in London town. I guarantee, you will *laugh*, you will *cry*, you will gasp with *amazement* at the *tremendous* acts that follow. And without further ado, I would like to introduce those *delightful* young lovelies from across the water in Dublin: *Bert O'Connor's bewitching Irish Indian Maids.*"

The curtain rose and he moved to stand at the far right-hand side of the stage, gesturing flamboyantly towards five young women dressed as squaws, with black plaits dangling over each shoulder, feather head-dresses and smiling faces smothered with reddish-brown greasepaint. Behind them was a gaudy backdrop depicting wigwams and totem poles. The orchestra struck up a melody and the girls started to trill "Barney You're Full of Blarney" to the accompaniment of a series of curiously sedate dance steps. I could not help reflecting on the strangeness of these Irish singers dressing up as Red Indians to lend their act a touch of glamour, but so far as I could tell by looking at the other spectators, no one else seemed to think it in the least bit odd.

The song ended with a short burst of clapping and the Maids began another, more sentimental number. I picked up the opera glasses again and examined them, hoping to discover the cause of the obstruction. One of the lenses was loose, and when I pressed it it fell out into my hand. With a thrill of surprise, I saw that a piece of paper had been wedged into the casing. I drew it out, unfolded it and held it up to catch the light from the stage. Written in bold capital letters was the instruction CO-OPERATE WITH HAGGER, BUT DON'T TELL HER TOO MUCH. I read it again, trying to puzzle out who could have written it. I had informed no one at Bureau 8 about Aggie's message, for I had perceived the purpose of my visit as a personal one, rather than what I now suddenly recognised it to be: a potential opportunity to open a new line of inquiry into the Scorpions' activities.

The Maids' act drew to a close and they curtsied to enthusiastic applause before trotting off in a line, waving brightly in unison. Though several voices were raised demanding "More!" they did not return. Instead the chairman announced the entrance of "Mr Pip Squeak, the funniest strongman on the boards". The curtain went up to reveal a colourful painting of a circus tent flanked by roaring lions. A sickly-looking fellow with strands of carrot-coloured hair smoothed across his bald pate entered, flexing his muscles and tripping over his own feet. His act elicited a few faint giggles from the audience to begin with, but swiftly palled. Someone in the gallery gave a derisive shout and soon raucous jeers and catcalls began to rain down from every quarter. To the accompaniment of uproarious laughter, booing and hoots of derision, the unfortunate strongman shouldered his false dumbbells and limped off into the wings.

The chairman gravely begged to remind the ladies and gentlemen present that they *were* ladies and gentlemen and that the Hoxton Alhambra was a high-class establishment, where rowdy behaviour of the kind just witnessed would not be tolerated.

"Ain't it jist?" bawled a coarse baritone voice from the gallery. "Well, in that case I should say there's a few females sitting up 'ere wiv me what has strayed in and ought to be asked to leave, cos if they're ladies I'm the ruddy Prince of Wales!" The speaker was hastily shushed by those around him and with a scattering of chuckles and a few indignant murmurs from the women in his vicinity, the audience settled down to watch the next turn.

Whenever the chairman stepped onto the stage my heart began

to beat more quickly in the expectation that Madam Coraline would be announced, but I was repeatedly disappointed. Pip Squeak was followed by a troop of performing dogs with ruffles about their necks, and then a large ape in a flowered dress and a magnificent picture hat who took afternoon tea as daintily as any lady. When it was all gone, she waddled to the front of the stage, lifted up her skirts and curtsied several times, blowing kisses to the audience and chattering with delight before scurrying off into the wings on all fours, to thunderous clapping and cries of 'Bravo!' I knew that it must be nearly time for the interval and that the second half was entirely taken up by "Doctor Walter Westleigh, Bloodless Surgeon and Electric Healer", the act at the top of the bill. I began to wonder whether Aggie's note might have been a practical joke of some kind or even part of a scheme to get me out of the house, and I felt a twinge of dread at the possibility that I would return home to be confronted by some new misfortune.

And yet, I reassured myself, it seemed unlikely that someone would have gone to the trouble of inserting the instructions into the opera glasses unless Aggie Hagger really was going to appear. I scrutinised the faces turned intently towards the stage in the hope that I might recognise the person who had left me the mysterious message. My gaze came to rest on a tall man in a wide-brimmed hat and my stomach gave a sickening lurch. For a few panic-stricken moments I became convinced that Mr Smith had followed me into the theatre after all; then the man turned his head and I saw, with a spasm of relief, that it was someone altogether different. However, I found it impossible to shake off the creeping sensation that Smith was lurking somewhere in the auditorium, was perhaps concealed in my own box, and, though I knew that I was being ridiculous, I could not rest until I had got up and peered into every corner, and opened the door to look up and down the corridor outside.

By the time I sat down again the cheers for "Miss Julia" were at last fading away and the chairman stood looking out into the audience with his finger held to his lips. "And now, ladies and gents, we have the last act before the interval," he proclaimed in a stage whisper. "It's a very strange and remarkable turn, and if any of you ladies – or gents – are of a nervous disposition I should advise you to leave the auditorium now." He waited for a moment, but of course nobody moved. "Very well – you have been warned! May I present the world-renowned . . . Madam Coraline!"

Up went the curtain, and there, standing at the centre of the stage, was a woman whom, at first, I did not recognise as Aggie Hagger at all. Her plump arms were laden with glinting bracelets and her fingers adorned with gigantic gemstones, which were far too big to be real. She wore long, flowing purple robes and a black wig which tumbled luxuriantly about her shoulders; her lips were painted carmine and her closed eyelids were heavily emphasised with sweeping black lines. Behind her was a dark red backdrop decorated with arcane symbols, and a crystal ball, a wooden box and a pack of cards stood on a table covered with a velvet cloth. She lifted her arms and began to mutter a silent incantation as the strings in the orchestra struck up with a low, ominous sound, like the humming of bees. Then, suddenly, she stumbled forward as if she had been pushed from behind.

"Golden Dawn, my spirit guide, has arrived!" she proclaimed. "He does not always so oblige us, but he tells me that you are a sensitive audience and your minds is open to words of wisdom from the Other Side." She stood very still, as if listening intently, her capacious bosom rising and falling with the rhythm of her swift, panting breaths. Then she began to sway from side to side, her arms outstretched. "There are hundreds of spirits, all crowding round me. I cannot breathe! Golden Dawn, you must tell some of them to go back; there are too many!" She paused and the orchestra fell silent.

"Get on with it, missus – we ain't got all bleedin' night!" yelled the heckler in the gallery, but Madam Coraline affected not to hear.

"Is there a Martha in the audience?" she asked. "There is an old gentleman with white hair what passed away last year wants to speak to you, my dear."

A woman in the third row of the stalls leapt to her feet. "Father, I'm here!" she cried.

"He says that he is helping you through all your difficulties and that the New Year will bring some good news from across the sea. Do you understand?"

"I do!" replied the woman and sat down.

This performance was repeated several times. A man named Gerald was told by his deceased mother that he must not marry a girl called Mary Ann and a tall old lady in the front row of the gallery was informed that her late husband did not approve of her taking in lodgers and she must cease doing so at once or she would come to regret it. Next, Madam Coraline performed tarot readings for several eager volunteers and each time she received an enthusiastic round of applause, leading me to marvel at the credulity of the theatre-going public.

At last she gathered up the cards and cupped a hand dramatically to her ear. "Ah! Golden Dawn has told me that there is a very important message for someone here in the audience tonight." She opened the lid of the wooden box and the thin, tinkling notes of a familiar melody began to spill out into the hush of the auditorium. I felt a prickling up and down my spine; the tune was that of my father's favourite song, "Lilly Dale". Madam Coraline raised her arm and pointed in my direction and at once my eyes were dazzled by a bright light shining into my face.

"The message is for Margaret – I believe that's the name of the lady sitting all alone up there," she announced.

Hundreds of eyes turned to look at me and I was overcome by the sensation that one occasionally experiences in a bad dream, of being unable to move or speak.

"*Is* your name Margaret?" she demanded, with a hint of that shrillness I remembered so well from our encounter at Mr Plimpson's office.

I swallowed hard and choked out a reply. "Yes."

"Margaret, I'd like you to come down onto the stage. If you will step out of your box, one of the ushers will be with you in a moment to show you the way. Give Margaret a round of applause, ladies and gentlemen – she will be with me on the stage in a very few moments." There was a burst of clapping and I stumbled out of the box with a pounding heart.

Lounging against the opposite wall of the corridor was the boy with gilt buttons who had given me the opera glasses. When he saw me, he straightened up and strode off purposefully, calling over his shoulder, "This way, miss." He led me downstairs into the empty lobby and over to a red velvet curtain, behind which was a door marked *Private*. He fitted a key into the lock and opened it, and I followed him down several passageways and through a series of doors until we arrived at the area immediately behind the stage.

"If you wait over there, miss, Madam Coraline will tell you when to go on," he informed me, pointing towards the wings. I walked past a pair of whispering stagehands in caps and aprons and picked my way among hampers containing props and discarded items of costume towards the darkness at the edge of the stage. I peered out at the vast crowd before which I was shortly to appear and felt myself begin to shake. Somewhere behind me I heard a dog bark and a woman's voice telling it angrily to be quiet, followed by a loud yelp.

A few feet away, Madam Coraline was intoning over her crystal ball. "The clouds've parted again –I see a child's face, a little boy. He's smiling!" This was followed by a murmur of appreciation from the audience. "Don't worry, my darling, you and your husband will soon be blessed with a son." At this there was a tumultuous burst of weeping and several female voices muttered words of comfort.

Just then, I detected a movement in the wings on the opposite side of the stage. To begin with I thought it was one of the stagehands, but when I peered into the darkness I saw a long, emaciated silhouette which seemed to shift and winnow like a blade of black light. I tried to look away, but my gaze was irresistibly drawn back towards it and I stood, gripped by a dreadful fascination, until the spell was broken by Miss Hagger's voice calling me onto the stage.

I stepped, blinking, into the glare of the footlights, sensing rather than seeing the dark mass of the audience before me. All at once, I was overcome by the realisation that I would be obliged to talk about my father in front of all these strangers. It seemed an unbearable invasion of my privacy, but it was too late to turn back and so I gritted my teeth and walked across the creaking boards of the stage to Madam Coraline. She opened the lid of the musical box and the melody of "Lilly Dale" tinkled out again.

She turned her back to the auditorium and gave me a shrewd, somewhat scornful glance, then suddenly her jaw went slack and her eyes became glassy and she veered round to face the front again, stretching out her arms in an exaggerated gesture of welcome, which set her bracelets clinking and her flowing sleeves tumbling back from her wrists. With a sepulchral moan she declaimed, "Arthur Trant! You have come to this place with a message for your daughter Margaret." A loud rap rang out, causing the audience to gasp. "Golden Dawn tells me it concerns a secret – a secret what you entrusted to your daughter's keeping before your most tragical death." She paused as if listening to an ethereal voice, her eyes rolling wildly in their sockets, and seized my hand in her small, dry grasp. I felt the points of her nails digging into my palm. "Your father's name was Arthur, was it not?" I nodded. "He wants you to know that the time has come for you to share his secret with them as needs to know. Can you do that?" Recalling the instruction to co-operate, I nodded again.

Suddenly, there came a crash from backstage. The man whom I had seen in the wings had moved closer to the stage and in doing so had knocked over a stack of chairs. From where I now stood, I had a clear view of him and blinked several times, for I thought at first that the light must be playing tricks with my vision or else that one of my nightmares really had come to life. He wore a patch over one eye and his countenance was horribly mottled, and ridged and seamed with scar tissue, so that it looked as if his skin had melted and then unevenly congealed, like candle-wax. I don't think I would have recognised him at all had I not recalled Mr Krackewicz's description of Mr Peters' ruined face. To my horror, I saw that he was aiming a revolver directly at Miss Hagger's back.

"Mr Peters is there!" I whispered with a sensation of rising panic. "He has a revolver!"

She nodded calmly and said in her stage voice, "Your father says he must go now, but he wants to tell you he's sorry and he hopes you forgive him. You must be glad for him, as he has gone to a better place. Ladies and gentlemen, thank you! I hope that I have succeeded in bringing comfort to some grieving hearts."

There was a swell of applause and the curtain came down, after which several things occurred in quick succession. There was a series of clicks as Peters attempted to fire his revolver. Then, ascertaining to his disgust that it did not contain any bullets, he cursed loudly and flung it to the floor. Almost simultaneously, there was a resounding crash and the lid of one of the vast wicker hampers that stood in the wings was flung back. Out of it leapt a small, dark-haired man whom I recognised, to my astonishment, as Liebowitz. Mr Peters started to sprint away, there was the sharp report of a gunshot, and he plunged to the floor, clutching his ankle in agony.

Liebowitz sidled forward, pointing a pistol at Peters' head. "Don't be alarmed, Miss Trant," he said. "Everything will be explained to you in due course." Then he turned to address Aggie.

"Thank you, Miss Hagger; you did very well. You will find an envelope containing the money in your dressing room. I trust that you will hold to the terms of our agreement?"

She nodded, her eyes fixed upon Peters, who was writhing about on the floor.

Jimmy Jolly approached, wiping his brow with his handkerchief. "What's going on?" he demanded. "That bang sounded just like a gunshot from out there – I thought we was going to have a bloomin' stampede." He broke off as his eyes fell on Peters' agonised form and then latched onto Liebowitz's pistol.

"Don't worry, sir," Liebowitz reassured him. "Everything is quite proper and above board. I am a police detective and that fellow there is a wanted man. Marcus Stone, I place you under arrest."

"Stone?" I cried out in bewilderment.

"Yes, Miss Trant. Didn't they teach Latin at your school? Get up!"

He jerked the prisoner to his feet and removed a pair of handcuffs from his pocket, but it was already too late. Stone's head lolled forward on his chest, a smear of white foam spilling from his blistered lips.

"D–n! Cyanide!" ejaculated Liebowitz in disgust. "We'll never get anything out of him now! Where's Hagger?"

But Aggie Hagger had vanished.

# Thirty-Three

The next day I rose early despite having got home after midnight. It was a bright October morning and the air was as pure and invigorating as ice-water. I walked briskly to the Finchley Road, my cheeks tingling with the cold, and felt a faint stirring of the sense of hopeful exhilaration that had swept me along during my first weeks at Bureau 8. The tram was not quite so crowded as usual and the faces of the other passengers, bathed in the dappled play of sunlight, seemed more receptive to the beauties of the world and less weighed down by the cares of the daily round.

I approached the entrance to the shop, humming snatches of an air that I had heard at the music hall on the previous evening. Before I could enter, however, Liebowitz burst through the door, setting the bell clanging, and dashed towards Tottenham Court Road. He seemed not to see me and when I called after him he did not turn round.

Somewhat taken aback, I entered the shop. In the bright sunlight, the dust and cobwebs that covered the cluttered interior seemed to lie more thickly than ever and the hearing trumpets and other assorted contraptions looked like artefacts that had been abandoned for centuries in some long-hidden tomb. Ascending to the office, I found the Chief hunting through a pile of papers on his desk.

"Miss Trant!" he exclaimed with a smile. "I hoped that we might see you today, though of course I did not presume to expect it. How are you, my dear? I was so sorry to hear about your mother."

"Thank you, sir. I am quite well in myself," I replied. "I thought that you might want me here, after everything that happened yesterday evening."

"Yes, of course – how thoughtful of you."

"I saw Liebowitz on my way in – he seemed to be in a great hurry."

The Chief mopped at his flushed face with his handkerchief, a gesture that reminded me unexpectedly of Mr Plimpson. "Liebowitz seems to have mislaid an important document. Apparently, it contains the key to one of those infernal ciphers and he can't get any further without it. Between you and me, Miss Trant, I think he's driving himself too hard. He's been behaving very oddly."

"He has been looking extremely tired."

"Well, perhaps it is only tiredness," the Chief said doubtfully.

"I must admit, I was astonished when he leapt out of that basket last night," I remarked, hoping that the Chief would explain how Liebowitz had come to be at the theatre.

"Yes, but what a shame he didn't manage to get to Stone before he poisoned himself. And then to have allowed Hagger to go rushing off like that. Good heavens, those tartars at head office are going to be furious. And to have permitted Hagger to use you as bait without giving you any indication of the danger you were in was outrageously irresponsible. I can only apologise on his behalf."

"I'm sure he must have had good reasons for what he did, sir. I imagine that if I had known all about it, I would have found it very difficult to behave naturally."

"I suppose his aims were laudable enough," the Chief admitted with a sigh. "You see, in the past few days it's emerged that Aggie Hagger was definitely working with Stone; all that nonsense about being afraid of him was concocted for Plimpson's benefit. Liebowitz saw through it somehow and managed to bribe her to betray him – Stone, I mean . . ." He broke off, frowning, and then added stiffly, "Though I'm afraid I'm not at liberty to tell you any more about that." His eyes darkened and he seemed to withdraw into himself for a few moments. I watched him uneasily, wondering what had caused him to clam up so abruptly.

Then all at once the shadow passed from his face. "You are aware of course that Stone – Peters, as you knew him – was one of the leading lights of the Scorpions in the eighties and played a key part in Lillian Lauderdale's murder?" he said, eyeing me keenly.

"Yes, sir, though it is a fact that I anticipate it will take me some time to get used to. Speaking of the Scorpions, did you get my letter?"

The Chief's forehead wrinkled in bewilderment. "Letter? No. When did you send it, Miss Trant?"

"I posted it on Monday afternoon. It ought to have been here by now."

"How unfortunate!" he said, looking thoughtful. Then he glanced up at me as if recollecting himself. "Goodness me – fancy my keeping you standing here so long! I'm sorry, Miss Trant. Do sit down and tell me what your letter said."

I told him about the scrap of paper bearing the hieroglyph of the pyramid and the eye that Smith had dropped and Becky had given me, and about the identical device that I had found in the locked cupboard in which my mother had kept some of my father's old papers. And then, as so often happened when I was talking to the Chief, I found myself saying a great deal more than I had intended to. All my suspicions about Smith came pouring out: the coded postcards that he had been receiving for months, Becky's account of his peculiar behaviour on the occasion when I had fainted on the stairs, his lie about Miss Hagger's visit and the fact that he had been alone with Mother in the moments just before her death. The Chief listened attentively, his mouth set in a grim line. When I had finished speaking, he rifled through a pile of documents and extracted a slip of paper on which were written several characters that I recognised at once as being of the same type as those on Smith's postcards.

"That's it! That's the cipher they were written in!" I exclaimed.

The Chief's frown deepened. "You're sure that the cipher is identical?"

"Yes, sir, I have seen sufficient examples of it to be almost certain."

"And you say that you passed a couple of these cards on to Liebowitz and he told you that they were a practical joke?"

"Yes, but I received the impression that he hadn't looked at them properly; he was very busy and his mind was on other things."

"Perhaps," said the Chief, looking away. "I will ask him about it. However, we won't dwell on it now." He sat up straighter and his eyes cleared. "The important thing is that your suspicions of Smith are fully justified; it looks to me as if the Scorpions posted him in your boarding house to keep an eye on you. You see, your theory that the Scorpions played a part in your father's death is quite correct, though there is rather more to it than that, I'm afraid. Liebowitz did manage to get at least one useful piece of information out of Miss Hagger before he let her slip through his fingers. Do you recall telling me that on the last occasion you saw Mr Plimpson, he claimed to have helped your father by finding him a job at a time when he had run himself into debt?"

"That was certainly what he implied, sir."

"And am I right in thinking that your father was an accountant by profession?"

"Yes."

"This might come as rather a shock, my dear, but according to Miss Hagger, the person whom Mr Plimpson persuaded to employ your father was Stone's confederate, Richard Arrowsmith; the man who married Miss Lillian Lauderdale and then murdered her."

I shook my head. "How ridiculous – she must have been lying! She took a dislike to me as soon as we met. It's all nonsense; nothing more than a malicious slander!"

"She claims that for all these years Stone has cherished the suspicion that your father was privy to the whereabouts of Miss Lauderdale's missing fortune, though of course it was only after his escape from gaol that he was able to act upon it. It seems that he concocted a plan whereby Hagger would use her stage character, the medium, Madam . . . I can't recall the name, to extort the secret from your mother. After that stratagem failed, they sent you that invitation to the theatre. Stone was to be there, waiting. If Lieb-owitz hadn't uncovered the plot beforehand, I shudder to think what might have happened."

I felt a surge of anger that set me trembling. "Do you suppose they planned to kill my mother all along?"

The Chief leant across the desk and placed his warm hand over mine. "I am going to ask a tremendous favour of you, my dear, but first I will do my best to give an honest answer to your question. The doctor informed you that your mother died of heart failure, isn't that right? Was he your mother's usual doctor?"

"No, I'd never seen him before. Mr Smith went to fetch him."

"I see. Well, of course that does suggest the possibility that he might have been a fraud. However, we will return to that in a moment. Am I right in thinking that your mother had been in poor health for some years?"

"Yes."

"So the first hypothesis that we must take into account is that both the doctor and the diagnosis were genuine. On the other hand, perhaps your mother's heart failed because Hagger, or indeed Smith, intimidated her; literally, frightened her to death. The third possibility, it seems to me, is that she was poisoned. Of course, if Hampson-Smythe were still here, he could tell you much more about that kind of thing, but I do know that there exist certain poisons that possess the capacity to induce heart failure, which are almost impossible to detect. The maid told you that Hagger gave your mother brandy to drink, you say?"

"Yes. When I knelt down beside her – afterwards – I could smell it."

"It's perfectly feasible that the alcohol was used merely as a means of loosening her tongue, but I won't deny that it might also have been a convenient method of administering a poison such as arsenic. Even if your mother was poisoned, however, and that is by no means certain, it may well be that the doctor determined the cause of death in good faith; after all, there was nothing in the circumstances to dictate that he ought to suspect foul play."

"But why would they have to kill her?" I asked, the words sinking down to form a dry clot in my throat.

"No one can say what passed between the three of them. Smith, or Hagger, or perhaps both, might have felt compromised in all sorts of ways. Or perhaps the order came from Stone. These people are not like you and me, Miss Trant – they are utterly ruthless and will do anything to get out of a difficulty.

"Now, the favour that I wish to ask you is this: don't go to the police. It would be very distressing for you – there would have to be an exhumation and so on – and there are ninety-nine chances out of a hundred they wouldn't find any evidence. And then, with regard to our current investigation, such an enquiry would of course stir up a veritable hornets' nest."

I swallowed hard, finding myself suddenly on the verge of tears. "Of course, I'll do whatever you think is best."

"Thank you, my dear." The Chief squeezed my hand and then sat back and looked at me solemnly across the width of the desk. "You are in great danger, Miss Trant. It is not safe for you to remain in London. You have two choices: either you can take a nice long holiday at some foreign spa, or you can venture right into the dragon's den."

"I'm afraid I don't quite understand . . ."

"Personally I should recommend the first alternative, but MacIntyre has been particularly pressing, and . . ."

"MacIntyre?" I asked, my pulse quickening.

"Yes. As you know, he has been doing some investigative work on the Devon coast. The Scorpions are planning to hold a conference in a hotel in a little seaside town called Seacombe . . ."

"Seacombe?" The name was familiar, but I could not immediately work out why.

"Yes. Have you been there?"

"No."

"Well, that's a relief; it might have put the whole plan in jeopardy if you had. Now, MacIntyre has exerted his charm to persuade the owner of the hotel – a Mrs Rutherford – that it would be an invaluable experience for one of his mother's protégées if she were to be employed there during the busy period of the conference. You see, the poor girl is an orphan who wishes to better herself. She has just lost her place as a parlour maid, though through no fault of her own, and to compound her misfortunes her fiancé, a valet, has deserted her. I thought that was laying it on a bit thick, but apparently Mrs Rutherford swallowed it without any trouble."

I nodded eagerly, on tenterhooks to hear how all this related to me.

The Chief took a bite from a half-eaten wedge of seed cake which had been sitting on a saucer just in front of him and munched on it with a reflective expression. He swallowed and continued, "MacIntyre is down there in disguise as Jonathan Rankin, a chap from Surrey, who's in Devon to do a spot of sea-fishing. The fictional Mrs Rankin is the benefactress of the unfortunate young woman, Louisa Jones, alias Miss Margaret Trant." He lifted the cake to his lips again and then put it down before he had taken a bite. "I do apologise; how rude of me! Would you care for some cake?"

"No thank you," I answered, buoyed up by a swelling undercurrent of excitement. "Are you proposing that I should undertake a new assignment?"

"I must say, I don't like it; it seems much too dangerous. However, the fact of the matter is that MacIntyre has had very little success in gathering information so far and he is concerned that his vigilance might have begun to arouse suspicion. Whereas, if *you* were working as a maid in the hotel no one would suspect you; you'd be in an ideal position to gather intelligence. Naturally, we both knew that the plan could never be put into practice unless Stone was safely out of the way. But now that he is dead there is no possibility that he will turn up at the conference and recognise you. And as for Mr Smith, it's most unlikely that he will be in Seacombe – only the higher ranking members are to attend. Besides, as a precaution we could easily concoct enough diversions to keep him occupied in London for months on end." He gave a heavy sigh. "Nevertheless, I should have continued to resist putting the proposal to you – particularly so soon after your bereavement – had it not been for the fact that the investigation looks likely to stall, and at this juncture that would almost certainly prove disastrous."

"I should like to do whatever I can to help!" I exclaimed impulsively, my delight at the thought of being in the field as an agent once again surpassed only by the soaring happiness that I felt at the prospect of seeing MacIntyre.

The Chief reached out and patted my hand. "That is very noble of you, my dear. However, you must allow yourself time for consideration before you agree to the suggestion. It is crucial that you understand the risk you would be running."

I thought of the dreary boarding house and Mrs Hodgkins' carping and the ever-watchful eyes of Mr Smith.

"I'm sure that a change will do me the world of good," I said fervently.

"And the spa?" asked the Chief with a slight upward curling of his lips.

"Absolutely not!"

"I knew that we could rely on you!" he declared, seizing my hands with a look of fierce approbation that set my cheeks aflame.

I excused myself and got up to pour a glass of water from the jug on my desk. After I had sat down again the Chief handed me an envelope.

"Now for the details," he said. "This contains information about Miss Jones' background and experience, which I have compiled from the outline that MacIntyre provided. Read it through carefully when you get home and then destroy it." He paused to remove a caraway seed from between his front teeth. "Now remember, Miss Jones is not so well bred as Miss Trant, or even Miss Wade. You will need to alter your accent – and make sure that your table manners are not too refined; eating peas with one's knife is by no means unusual at the servants' table. You will receive regular letters from 'Mrs Rankin', of course, and being a dutiful girl you will reply to them promptly, I'm sure.

"Tell your landlady that you are going away for a good long holiday, to recuperate. Take this." He gave me a small leather purse heavy with coins. "It will simplify matters if you pay next month's rent in advance, and you'll need to purchase some suitable clothing. Shall I telegraph to MacIntyre that you will be on the eight o'clock train from Paddington tomorrow morning? Excellent! You will need to change at Exeter and he can meet you at Queensbridge station. Oh, and one more thing – you'd better take this with you in case of any emergency. Do make sure that you keep it well hidden." He opened a drawer in his desk and took out a small object wrapped up in a length of calico, and a leather pouch. "The bag contains spare ammunition. But do remember that if anyone sees the revolver your alias will be destroyed."

"I'll make sure that I don't lose this one, sir," I assured him.

"I hope you haven't been nursing a guilty conscience about that, my dear – as I said to you at the time, these things will happen occasionally, despite our best efforts. Now, do you have any questions?"

All at once I recalled a nagging concern that had been pushed to the back of my mind by the events of the past few weeks. "Have you heard anything from Hunter?" I asked.

For an instant the Chief's face contorted into an expression in which I seemed to read frustration, anxiety and suppressed irritation, before his guard came up and he assumed a look of grave neutrality.

"I regret to say that we haven't received a communication from him for some time. Of course, he is in a very dangerous situation now that his cover has been compromised, and I have sent orders for him to return. Between you and me, Miss Trant, though he is a courageous young man and highly skilled as an agent, he has in the past shown a tendency to be somewhat foolhardy, and I must confess that I am becoming increasingly concerned for his safety. However, I am loath to spare another agent to go after him at this point – certainly not until we are in receipt of more definite intelligence about his fate." The Chief caught sight of my stricken face and flashed me a broad smile, adding in a breezy tone, "You must not be distracted by worries about Tom Hunter, Miss Trant. We require our energies to be concentrated in other directions. And besides, I dare say I am fussing like an old maid, as MacIntyre would no doubt tell me; after all, there is every likelihood that Hunter will be back with us any day. Is there anything else?"

"What about Hampson-Smythe?" I enquired, feeling that I might as well be hanged for a sheep as a lamb.

This time the Chief made no attempt to disguise his anger. "That young fool has cost us more time and anxiety than I care to think of and there is still not a trace of him. Fortunately, we have discovered no evidence that he has betrayed us, but of course we cannot know for sure. Believe me, Miss Trant, when we do find him he will be subject to the severest penalties." He stood up, frowning. "I expect you've got plenty to do before tomorrow. I'll see you out."

We descended the stairs in silence and I began to worry lest I had breached some unspoken code by asking too many questions. However, my anxieties were put to rest when, at the shop door, the Chief wrung my hand in farewell, saying earnestly, "The best of luck, Miss Trant. Make sure that you don't run any unnecessary risks. Bureau 8 must have its secretary returned in one piece!"

I made an excursion down Oxford Street and returned to the boarding house carrying several parcels. These contained two skirts and three blouses made out of cheap material, a second-hand jacket and a hat trimmed with red roses, which was not at all the sort of thing I would usually wear, but I thought it would suit Louisa Jones rather well. As soon as I set foot inside the apartment, I flung down my parcels and opened the envelope containing the additional details about my new persona. The instructions were brief, and having committed them to memory I burnt the document in the grate, grinding down the smouldering fragments with the poker. Once I had satisfied myself that no incriminating scraps were left behind, I went downstairs and knocked on the door of Mrs Hodgkins' private sitting room.

"Come in!" she called. The smile faded from her lips when she saw that it was me and she laid aside a volume entitled *The Foundling Murderess*, with a look that already contained the germ of irritation. "Yes? What can I do for you?"

I told her about my plan to go away and placed a pile of coin sufficient to pay two months' rent on the occasional table that stood by her elbow.

"Well, of course, you must please yourself!" she said with a shrug once she had counted the money, adding in a tone of intense sarcasm, "May I take it that you will honour us with your presence at dinner this evening, seeing as you're able to go out visiting now?"

I considered the prospect of sitting down to eat with Mrs Hodgkins and Mr Smith, and shook my head. "No thank you," I replied. "However, I shan't put you to any trouble – I'll eat some bread and cheese in my room. I still have a great deal to do before tomorrow morning."

"Well then, I shan't keep you," said the landlady, returning to her book with a loud sniff.

I soon forgot all about Mrs Hodgkins and her rudeness, for I had plenty of other matters to command my attention. Naturally, I was troubled by the danger that the Chief had warned me of and locked the door to our apartment from the inside. I tried not to think about the fact that my mother had almost certainly been murdered, nor to brood upon the knowledge that my promise to the Chief meant that the perpetrators of the crime could not, for the time being, be brought to justice. Instead, I staved off the dangerous thoughts that loomed around the edges of my mind like icebergs by directing all my energies outwards, towards the practical task of packing Louisa Jones' possessions.

First, I made a list of all the items that I would need to take with me, organising them under different headings. Next, I laid everything out on my bed, ticking off each item as I fetched it. After that, I began putting them into Father's old travelling bag; but no matter how carefully I folded my clothes and tucked the smaller objects away into odd holes and corners, I simply could not get it all to fit, and I was obliged to unpack everything and start all over again. On the third attempt, having discarded a spare pair of boots and several other oddments, I succeeded at last in getting the bag to close.

It was not until much later, after I had consumed a solitary supper of bread and cheese and was retiring to bed, that I recalled how it was that I had heard of Seacombe before. In a state of considerable agitation, I took out the chocolate box from its hiding place in my bottom drawer. Buried beneath the other keepsakes I found a postcard showing a grand house set in gardens with palm trees and a fountain, and arching across the top in ornate white lettering were the words *Greetings from Seacombe*. When I turned it over, the reverse side was blank and marbled with a yellowish stain. My mind leapt back to the day, shortly after my father's death, when I had come across the card in the pocket of his old winter overcoat, together with a handful of seashells still grainy with sand, and I sank down onto my bed, oppressed by the suspicion that Miss Hagger's allegation that my father had worked for Arrowsmith might have had some truth in it after all.

I lay awake until long after midnight, chasing away uneasy thoughts; memories which, over the years, I had done my best to submerge, as one might sink a shameful secret, weighted with stones, to the bottom of a black lake. When at last I slept, these drowned recollections came clamouring to the surface and I awoke just before dawn, wilting and hollowed out, the tears turning cold on my cheeks. But only one of the images that had poured through my brain remained to haunt my waking mind.

I closed my eyes and once again I saw Father slumped over his desk. Blood was running down the study walls and lay splattered over the cream-coloured carpet like crimson paint.

The note that he had left propped up on the study mantelpiece had said merely, *What's done cannot be undone. Forgive me. A.* It was conjectured by the police and later by the coroner that these words referred to the financial difficulties that Mother and I had mistakenly believed had come to an end. For it turned out that a week before his death Father had withdrawn every penny of the five thousand pounds that had recently been paid into his bank account. Though strenuous efforts were made to trace the money it appeared to have vanished into the air, just as Miss Lauderdale's fortune had and at about the same time.

Even as the true extent of Father's gambling debts had started to become evident, I had grown increasingly convinced that the offi cial consensus about the motive for his suicide was mistaken. I was only fifteen and I had no comprehension of the agonising pressures that might lead a man to take his own life, but it was clear to me that, in fact, the mystery surrounding his death was one that he had not wished to be unravelled. There were no letters, accounts, lists of appointments or memoranda that gave any clue to his doings during his last months. A large quantity of ash had been found in the study grate, but no half-burnt scraps of paper had remained to give him away. According to the police he must have ripped all the documents into tiny shreds before he burnt them and then broken them down further with the poker, so strong had been his determination to keep the state, and more important the precise nature, of his business affairs from being exposed.

In the end, most of our furniture and possessions had had to be packed up and auctioned off in order to pay his creditors, and soon after that we moved into our new lodgings at Mrs Hodgkins' boarding house. On the morning following our removal I received an unexpected parcel, which contained a covering note from the gentleman who had purchased Father's books, explaining that the item enclosed was something that he thought I might wish to keep for sentimental reasons. Wrapped separately, in a sheet of brown paper, was a one-volume edition of *The Last Chronicle of Barset*, a book I had not even been aware that my father possessed. Upon opening it I discovered that the flyleaf bore an inscription in handwriting so minute that I was obliged to use Father's magnifying glass in order to decipher it. It read, *To my dear Margaret, in the hope that your fondness for detective stories will one day prove profitable. 16 September, 1895.*

At first this had puzzled me greatly, for I was well aware that Mr Trollope was not a writer of detective fiction; and then it occurred to me that the deliberate obscurity of the declaration was very much like the clues in the intricate treasure hunts that Father had designed for me when I was a child. When I came upon a slip of paper with a column of numbers written upon it folded up inside the book's leaves, I felt more certain than ever that *The Last Chronicle* was the relic of just such a game; one that Father had abandoned as he had begun to be submerged by the creeping tide of melancholy that had swallowed him up at the end of his life. It had been years since he had constructed one of his treasure hunts, and that he should have embarked on a new one so recently seemed quite unaccountable; until, with a pang, it occurred to me that perhaps he had done so with the intention of reaching out across the immense distance that had opened up between us during the months preceding his death.

I had put the book on the little mahogany bookshelf in my room, reflecting with a tightening of the throat that, now that our separation had become infinite and unbridgeable, Father's carefully designed conundrum would almost certainly remain unsolved. And indeed, I had scarcely looked at it since, for my inclination to avoid all reminders of that unhappy period in my life had grown stronger and stronger as time went on.

Ten years later, the thought of that thwarted gesture of affection still brought tears to my eyes. Brushing them away with the back of my hand, I scrambled out of bed and took *The Last Chronicle of Barset* from the bookshelf. I had kept it as a sentimental token of my father's love for me; it had not even crossed my mind that it might have some bearing on the mysteries surrounding the latter part of his life. Now, however, after the revelations of the past weeks, I saw it in a new and intriguing light. Tense with expectation, I examined the inscription on the flyleaf with Father's magnifying glass and then pulled out the yellowing slip of paper on which he had scribbled the column of numbers. I was tortured by the certainty that I was trembling on the verge of a vital discovery; that if only I could uncover the connection between the words and the numbers I would determine their significance. Yet I found that, try as I might, I could make nothing of them.

I yawned and, glancing at the clock, saw that in another hour or two, it would be time to get up. I was not ready to abandon the puzzle, however, and I picked up my reticule, took out of it an envelope containing my aunt Sophie's letter and the postcard from Seacombe and put the piece of paper inside. *The Last Chronicle of*

*Barset* was too unwieldy to carry with me on the train, and besides, I thought it might seem odd for Louisa to be in possession of such a thing. However, I copied down the dedication that Father had written on the flyleaf and slipped that into the envelope too.

I had got back under the eiderdown and was about to extinguish the lamp when a new thought occurred to me. I leapt out of bed and rummaged about in the drawer until I found the photograph of Father and Mr Plimpson in evening dress. By this time I was more or less convinced that Richard Arrowsmith had been the chief party in the business arrangement that the picture commemorated, and I found its quality of hectic gaiety more disturbing than ever. I looked from one grinning face to the other and all at once I understood, with sickening certainty, the significance of those eerily incongruous flowers. The lilies had been worn as a tacit reference to the unhappy bestower of Father's unprecedented good fortune: Lillian Lauderdale, the murdered heiress.

# Thirty-Four

When I saw MacIntyre coming down the platform towards me I faltered, feeling as if the air had been squeezed from my lungs. He was clean-shaven, thinner than I remembered and more stooped, but at the sight of him I felt a swelling note of joy which threatened to burst forth in peals of hysterical laughter. Catching sight of me, he lifted his arm in greeting and came cantering up to relieve me of my bag. His hand brushed mine, our eyes met for an instant and then, without a word, we started walking in the direction from which he had come, back up towards the road.

There, to my astonishment, standing in front of a row of thatched cottages was a dark green, mud-splattered motor car. MacIntyre cleared his throat.

"She's rather a beauty, isn't she? She's a Panhard, fifteen horse power. She belongs to a fellow I've befriended – a famous writer of detective stories, who's come down to Devon for a spot of peace and quiet. He's rather a queer sort of fish, but I suppose one would expect an author to have his eccentricities, and he's a decent enough chap at heart. I've been getting in some motoring practice along the country lanes hereabouts – it's jolly good fun as a matter of fact." His blue eyes came to rest on my face. "I can't tell you how marvellous it is to see you again!" he exclaimed, beaming.

"I'm very glad to see you too," I replied, feeling as if my voice were sinking away inside me, like water falling onto wet sand.

There was an awkward pause.

"Terribly sorry to hear about your mother."

"Thank you," I said, looking away to indicate that I did not wish to pursue the subject.

"I'll stow this here if you don't mind." MacIntyre put my bag into a compartment at the back of the vehicle, then opened the passenger door and helped me to sit down. "You'd better put this on," he said, handing me a long coat and a hat with a veil, which I substituted for my shabby cloak and tam o'shanter. Then he jumped out and turned the starting handle several times, until the motor spluttered into life

"I thought we'd go for a little spin before I take you down to the hotel," he said, leaping into the driver's seat. "I'd like to hear all about what's been happening in London; the Chief's reports have been rather patchy of late." He adjusted a pair of motoring goggles over his eyes. "Poor chap – I get the impression that his nerves are beginning to suffer under the strain."

The Panhard shot forward and I found myself gripping the edges of the seat.

"Ever ridden in a motor car before?"

"Never."

"It really is terrifically enjoyable, though I admit it does take a little getting used to. And of course it's a marvellous way of seeing the countryside."

We drove on along narrow, winding roads edged by high hedgerows of dark twigs studded with scarlet berries. It was late afternoon and the sky was dotted with veils of white cloud, which were beginning to be tinged pink with the glow of the setting sun. On either side of us unfolded a landscape of rolling hills covered by wintry fields and pockets of bare-branched woodland, burnished in places by traces of autumn leaves. Here and there I saw a farmhouse or a little cluster of cottages, but there were no larger settlements and I felt a marvellous sense of exhilaration to be in the open countryside with MacIntyre, a solid, miraculous presence at my side. We passed a couple of farm carts and once we were obliged to come to an abrupt halt to make way for a farmer driving a herd of cows across the road, but this was the only traffic we encountered during the whole journey.

At last, after about twenty minutes, we began to drop down into a valley and rows of cottages with smudges of grey smoke pluming up from their chimneys started to appear along the roadside.

"This is Barker's Edge!" MacIntyre yelled, the wind catching his words and whipping them away. "There's a cosy little place here, where we can have a spot of tea and talk to one another without troubling about being recognised by anyone."

"That would be lovely!" I exclaimed. And indeed, the prospect of drinking tea in front of a warm fire was a very inviting one, for I had had my fill of the bracing open road and my teeth were chattering with cold. Yet at the same time I felt a strange reluctance for the journey to end, for I was overwhelmed by a kind of excited terror at the idea of at last sitting face to face with this man who had come to play such a prominent part in my thoughts and dreams.

It was market day and the high street was still bustling, despite the lateness of the hour. The sight of the Panhard created something of a sensation. People stared and pointed, and MacIntyre was obliged to sound the horn several times in order to clear the road. Fortunately, it was not long before we drew up in front of a pink house with brightly coloured curtains and a sign which read *Geranium Tea Rooms* in bold black letters.

"Here we are!" said MacIntyre gaily, jumping out of the car and hastening round to help me out. "Excuse me, young fellow!" he called, addressing a boy who had come sidling out of the front garden of one of the whitewashed cottages opposite and was gazing at the motor car with a wondering expression on his chubby face. "I'll give you tuppence to keep an eye on this beauty until we come out."

The boy nodded his head with alacrity. "I'll say, mister!" he cried, and darted across the street.

"Make sure you don't touch anything!" admonished MacIntyre as we went in and the boy, who was striding up and down alongside the car like a sentry, assured him, "Don't you worry, mister; you can rely on me!"

"Now, off you go, the rest of you!" bellowed MacIntyre, waving away the retinue of dogs and small boys who were trotting along in our wake. "I've engaged this young fellow here to look after my motor car and anyone who comes within three feet of it or gives him any trouble will be turned in to the police." At once the little crowd melted away into the shadows.

"I seem to have developed quite a way with small boys," MacIntyre remarked with humorous complacency, ducking his head to avoid a beam as we passed into a snug parlour scented with wood-smoke. "The kitchen boy at the Ham Stone hotel has promised to act as a messenger, should you ever need to reach me in a hurry."

He led me across to a small table by a mullioned window. "May I take your coat?" he asked, removing his own to reveal a chequered Norfolk jacket and a pair of matching knickerbockers. "One must dress the part, I'm afraid," he added, stroking his bare upper lip with a rueful grimace.

Privately, I thought it suited the angular contours of his face to be clean-shaven, but I refrained from telling him so, for I knew that he had been exceedingly proud of his luxuriant moustache.

I will not report the conversation that ensued in any detail, for the reader is already acquainted with the events that had occurred since MacIntyre's departure and the information that he passed on to me will unfold itself in its own good time. For the present it will suffice to say that, warmed by the fire and revitalised by the delicious scones and strawberry jam, I eventually managed to broach the subject of my misgivings about Father's role in the Lillian Lauderdale affair. I found it easier to talk to MacIntyre about it than I had anticipated, but even so my whole attention was absorbed in the effort of putting into words thoughts and emotions that I was still scarcely able to acknowledge to myself. I grew more and more involved in what I was saying, and it was only when I met the impertinent gaze of the waitress who had come to clear away our plates that I became conscious that MacIntyre and I were leaning across the table with our heads in such close proximity that they were almost touching. I stopped talking at once and drew back, my cheeks aflame. I did my best to cover up my discomfiture by turning away to rummage through my reticule for the envelope containing my aunt's letter, the blank postcard from Seacombe, the dedication that I had copied from the flyleaf of *The Last Chronicle of Barset* and the slip of paper bearing the mysterious column of numbers that my father had left inside the book's pages, which I slid across the table without meeting MacIntyre's eye.

There was a brief silence, during which I sat staring down at my folded hands, before he exclaimed excitedly, "Just as we thought! I knew you'd come up trumps, Miss Trant! We've been digging around for weeks down here and haven't found anything nearly so promising!"

"We?" I asked, looking up at him in surprise.

He glanced away, abashed. "Ah, yes. Dear me! This is a trifle difficult. To be truthful, we weren't sure whether this was the right time to tell you; it puts you in such a dashed awkward position – divided loyalties and so forth. But now that you're here and after you've been so wonderfully frank with me, I should feel a frightful cad if I were to keep you in the dark." He fell silent for a moment, as if deep in thought. Then his brilliant blue eyes locked onto mine and once again I felt the colour flooding into my cheeks. "Perhaps it would be best if I took you to meet my friend; explanations can become so fearfully complicated and they give too much potential for misunderstanding. Besides, unless I'm very much mistaken, I suspect that that waitress is waiting to shut up shop."

Outside, darkness had fallen and the frost was beginning to bite. The chubby-faced boy was shivering with cold; nevertheless he had stuck stoically to his post by the motor car. MacIntyre pressed a sixpence into his palm, and he examined it wide-eyed with delight. Then, with an elated "Thank you, mister!" he dashed across the road and out of sight. MacIntyre opened the passenger door and swung me up onto the cold leather seat.

I could not help noticing that since suggesting that I meet his mysterious colleague, MacIntyre had become rather tense. We began by exchanging one or two polite remarks, but it was hard work to sustain a conversation over the din of the engine and once we had left the town we both fell silent. Despite the cold I began to find it increasingly difficult to stay awake; several times I felt my head nodding onto my chest and jerked it back again, only to realise, after a few minutes had passed, that it was lolling forward once more. At last I drifted off into an uneasy slumber, from which I was roused by MacIntyre shaking me gently by the shoulder.

"We've arrived, Miss Trant. We'll leave the motor out here, just off the road, so as to avoid attracting any unnecessary attention."

Drowsily, I forced myself to move, caught my foot in the travelling rug and stumbled out of the motor car. I might have taken a bad fall had MacIntyre not caught me.

"You must be thoroughly exhausted; let me help you," he offered, linking his arm through mine, as if it were the most natural thing in the world. My heart began to beat more quickly and suddenly I felt wide awake. We passed through some tall gates and began to traverse a gravel path. In the middle distance I could make out a large building with rows of illuminated windows, but almost at once we veered off in another direction and started to squelch uphill across a damp lawn. We had taken only a few strides when MacIntyre came to an abrupt halt and for a moment we both stood staring up at the star sprinkled sky.

"Ye stars, that are the poetry of heaven!" he murmured, gesturing at the glimmering constellations that arched above our heads. Then, without exchanging another word we continued walking towards a faint glow of light emerging from between the silhouetted outlines of some tall pine trees.

As we drew closer, I saw that the light shone from the window of a large potting shed. MacIntyre gave a low whistle and an instant later the shed door opened and a fair, bearded young man in a gardener's uniform stood staring at us in consternation.

"I know I said I wouldn't, old chap," said MacIntyre, "but I've changed my mind. There's nothing else to be done, in the circum-stances."

"You'd better come in then," said the man, stepping aside, and with a jolt of recognition I realised that I was looking at Hampson-Smythe.

I froze, utterly perplexed, and turned towards MacIntyre for an explanation.

"Do you trust me, Miss Trant?" he enquired, regarding me with earnest intensity.

"Of course I do," I replied, feeling as if the world had been turned upside down.

"Well, come into the warm – Smythe's got a first rate stove in there – and we'll explain everything."

I allowed myself to be ushered into the shed, which was indeed rather cosy, though somewhat cluttered with gardening tools, flowerpots and other horticultural paraphernalia. Hampson-Smythe urged me to sit down in a deckchair which stood next to the stove, but I felt that to accept would be to place myself in rather an undignified position and so instead I perched on a low three-legged stool, on which I could at least sit properly upright.

"I don't understand!" I exclaimed, gazing at Hampson-Smythe in bewilderment. "I thought that you . . . The Chief thinks —"

"That I am a traitor," said Hampson-Smythe. "And of course he has good reason for believing so. But what he doesn't know is that the rivalry between the two of us, the punch, the quarrels – all of it was pure pretence. In truth I have only the greatest admiration for MacIntyre."

"But what made you do such a thing?"

"Because, my dear," MacIntyre broke in, "over a period of nearly two years we have come to suspect that Bureau 8 has been infiltrated by a disloyal element. Time and again, our investigations have been thwarted by some unhappy accident or quirk of fate. To give just one example, you may remember, a little over a year ago, that there was a spate of robberies from grand country houses, in which a number of extremely valuable jewels were taken. I succeeded in gaining the confidence of one of the thieves, a fellow called Edgely, and various remarks he made seemed to point to the fact that the thefts had been organised by a cell of Scorpions then active in Germany. When one views the enterprise in the light of recent events, it seems probable that it was expressly designed to raise funds for the campaign that, even at that time, was being planned against the British mainland.

"Edgely let it slip that the next theft was to take place at Twelve Trees, the country estate of Lord and Lady Bellingham. I decided to lay a trap, but the thieves didn't appear, and when I went looking for Edgely to find out what had gone wrong he had vanished without trace. It was pretty clear that someone had let the cat out of the bag – but who?

"The only people that I had taken into my confidence were the Chief, Liebowitz and Hunter; Smythe's father had been taken ill and he was away in Ireland and knew nothing about it. I'd been scrupulously careful not to give myself away to the thieves; it seemed pretty clear that either one of the other three had betrayed me directly to the Scorpions or, at the very least, there was someone at Bureau 8 with a dashed loose tongue.

"It was a dreadful thing to face up to, but I couldn't see any other explanation for it. As time went on and the unlucky coincidences multiplied, it began to seem more and more likely that one of us was passing information to our enemies. And now that Hunter has been in Germany for so long – and it would be practically impossible for him to keep fully abreast of our operations here from such a distance – it's started to look rather as if it must be either the Chief or Liebowitz."

"The Chief!"

"Believe me, I am as loath to think ill of Rivers as you are, Miss Grant, but it is possible for even the best of men to be led astray. One could argue that he has been rather too keen to emphasise the fact that Liebowitz has been behaving suspiciously. I'm afraid it is not entirely out of the question that he has been deliberately misleading us in order to deflect attention from his own actions."

"But Liebowitz *has* been behaving oddly!" I insisted. "And he has been very secretive about the lines of investigation that he is following.

I told you that he didn't say a word about his plan to arrest Stone at the music hall. The Chief was absolutely furious about it!"

"And it might mean that Liebowitz no longer trusts the Chief."

"Don't worry, Miss Trant – MacIntyre is only playing devil's advocate. It's a favourite pastime of his," Hampson-Smythe interjected, fingering the bowl of an unlit pipe which he appeared to have adopted as part of his disguise.

"He's quite right, I'm afraid. I do have a natural indication to be bloody-minded," said MacIntyre, getting up and stretching. "*Mea culpa*, Miss Trant. And please do forgive the two of us for having deceived you; you may rest assured that from now on we will both be entirely open with you."

He stepped over a roll of wire netting and came to crouch down by my side. "In the spirit of openness, would you object if I pass on to Hampson-Smythe the general outline of the information that you gave me about your father?" he whispered, his warm breath tickling my ear.

I drew away from him, my sinews tightening with resentment. How could he have failed to realise that I had confided in him as a dear friend; someone whom I thought I could trust? And though I understood why it was that I had been kept in the dark about the plot that he and Hampson-Smythe had cooked up, I could not help feeling a sense of hurt and betrayal, which was deepened by his obtuseness. The idea of having to look on while he communicated to Hampson-Smythe the miserable details of Father's last week filled me with dismay, but after a brief hesitation I concluded that even this humiliation was preferable to the awkwardness of refusing my consent, and gave a stiff nod.

MacIntyre straightened up, his knee joints clicking, and turned to Hampson-Smythe. "It seems that we were right about Miss Trant's father. The unfortunate fellow does indeed appear to have been tricked into working as Arrowsmith's accountant. One suspects that he did not realise the full import of what he had been asked to do until it was too late. Yes, if anyone knew where Lillian Lauderdale's money was hidden, it was Arthur Trant. In the end I believe that it was his heroic refusal to give up that knowledge, and his desire to protect his family, which drove him to take his own life."

He stopped talking and met my eye. I had feared that his words would expose my father as an unscrupulous petty criminal, but I had been wrong to think that he could be capable of such gross insensitivity; he was far too subtle and intelligent a man for that. Insensibly, my resentment faded, and I only wished that I could still believe in his version of events, one in which my father was cast as an innocent pawn. But ever since that moment in the dead of the previous night when I had finally understood the awful significance of the lily that Father was wearing in the photographs, I had been forced to face up to various long-held doubts which hitherto I had striven to suppress. There were certain recollections that I had stopped short of confiding to MacIntyre earlier that afternoon, not because I wished to conceal anything from him, but because I was still struggling to establish their meaning and implications in my own mind.

Perhaps he sensed some of this, for he gave me a searching look before saying, "For the reasons that I have suggested, Mr Trant did his utmost to destroy all evidence of his involvement with Arrowsmith. Fortunately, however, there remain a few clues that he overlooked, or was unaware of, and these Miss Trant, with great presence of mind, has brought with her. Would you mind, my dear?"

I extracted the envelope from my reticule and MacIntyre passed it to Hampson-Smythe.

"You do realise that the house on that postcard is the Ham Stone hotel in an earlier incarnation?" he said, turning back to me. "Did you know that it was once owned by Lillian Lauderdale?"

"I had no idea!"

"What's more, Arrowsmith inherited the house after his wife's death and remained resident there until his arrest, more or less; one assumes that he wished to keep himself out of the public eye. It may well be that your father stayed at the house while he was working on Arrowsmith's accounts, Miss Trant."

MacIntyre moved across to Hampson-Smythe, who was already standing at one of the cluttered work benches, studying my aunt's letter with a magnifying glass. I listened in silence as the two men bent their heads over the documents with solemn concentration, murmuring to one another now and again with some new observation.

My back had begun to ache and I was starting to wish that I had sat in the deckchair after all when Hampson-Smythe startled me by bursting out, "I say! Do you think the piano that Miss Trant's aunt mentions in the letter might have something to do with that strange instrument in the saloon at the Ham Stone hotel? After all, it once belonged to Miss Lauderdale . . ."

"It's rather a long shot, old chap, but I suppose anything's worth a try. Miss Trant, you might see whether you can get a look at it without anyone's noticing? It's one of those peculiar instruments that plays itself – you'll know it when you see it. Who knows, there may even be some correspondence between the column of figures your father wrote down on that bookmark of his and the notes on the keyboard!"

"I'll do my best," I said, though privately I considered that the possibility of my discovering anything of significance was very remote.

"Would you mind if I hang on to these papers for the time being? There are one or two avenues I should like to explore a little further, and besides, if by chance anyone at the hotel does decide to go prying through your things, it would be safer. I'll make a copy of the numbers for you – it won't take a jiffy." He took a pen and notebook from the inside pocket of his jacket and began to scribble furiously.

"Would you care for a drop of brandy before you go, Miss Trant?" said Hampson-Smythe, producing a battered metal flask from inside a flowerpot. I shook my head.

"I insist that you do, my dear," said MacIntyre, screwing the cap on his fountain pen before ripping a leaf from his notebook and handing it to me. "You're white as a ghost; if you turn up at the hotel looking like that Mrs Rutherford will think that I've tricked her into taking on an invalid." He took the flask from Hampson-Smythe, poured some brandy into a tin cup and placed it in my hands. "Now drink up, there's a good girl!"

I did as I was told, and almost immediately I felt a fiery warmth begin to radiate through my throat and stomach.

"We'd better be off, Smythe," said MacIntyre, taking a long draught from the flask before extending his hand to help me to my feet.

"Goodbye, Miss Trant," said Hampson-Smythe, looking so good-natured that I marvelled to think that I had ever considered him to be sly and sulky. "I'm so glad that you know the truth at last. Best of luck at the hotel – and please be careful; there are some very dangerous men staying there at present!"

# Thirty-Five

*I*n the lobby of the Ham Stone hotel there hangs a painting of the house during its glory days in the 1880s. It must have presented a wonderful spectacle then, with its towers and wrought-iron balconies, its flagpole bearing the newly designed Lauderdale crest, its rows of windows flashing in the sunlight, and its gardens of palm trees and vivid exotic flowers looking out onto the wide blue expanse of the ocean.

After Arrowsmith's execution, it was purchased from the Lauderdale family by a foreign gentleman who wished to develop it into a first class hotel. Unfortunately, the gentleman was an invet-erate drinker and gambler, and after the initial round of alterations had been completed, he realised that he lacked the funds to carry out the next stage of his plans. It was not long before he rid himself of his difficulties by staking the property at cards and losing it to a ship's captain named Rutherford.

Captain Rutherford had just returned from a voyage to the Indies and was eager to abandon his seafaring life for good. Though he possessed neither the will nor the necessary capital to construc the splendid establishment of which his predecessor had dreamed he managed to scrape together enough money to fit out the Ham Stone in an altogether simpler style. Its spectacular location, just a few hundred yards from the edge of the cliffs, brought in a satisfactory number of visitors over the summer months, and gradually he accumulated a core of year-round boarders who provided him with a stable source of income. He did not trouble to preserve the building's external fabric, however, and by the time of his death, less than a decade after it had first come into his possession, the hotel had fallen into a sad state of neglect.

It was inherited by the captain's daughter, Mrs Rutherford, who had already proved herself indispensable as a housekeeper and, during the period of the captain's last illness, as the manager of the hotel. She was a tall, spare individual with a deeply lined face and coarse black hair streaked with grey, which she wore coiled tightly into a bun. She had never married; the honorific had been adopted purely as a bulwark to her fearsome personal dignity. All the domestics at the hotel lived in mortal terror of incurring her wrath, and as we went about our work we were perpetually listening for her brisk tread lest she should catch us out in some error we were not even aware of making.

Mrs R, as we referred to her when she was out of hearing, could not afford to employ anywhere near enough servants to meet the demands of running such a large establishment. There were three maids (Janet, Sarah and myself), a cook and a kitchen boy and between us we were responsible for the upkeep of some forty rooms and for answering the demands of a rapidly increasing number of guests. We were on our feet from dawn until late into the evening, scrubbing and polishing, cleaning windows and laying fires, peeling vegetables, waiting at meals and washing plates, and after the first day of my employment I fell into bed aching, exhausted and full of doubts about how long I should be capable of continuing this fatiguing second life.

Janet Rogers, a squat little thing with a crooked shoulder, imparted as much as she knew of the history of the Ham Stone and its inhabitants in brief snatches as we went about our work. She was of that type who will happily chatter on about themselves and their own interests for hours on end and, to my immense relief, she displayed no curiosity about my background or opinions whatsoever. She confirmed that the hotel was unusually busy; ordinarily no more than nine or ten of the rooms were occupied and nearly all of those by permanent residents who used the place as a boarding house. By and large, these were persons of faded gentility and included among their number a retired army colonel with an impressive handlebar moustache, two old ladies known as the Misses Hepplethwaite and the forty-five-year-old widow of a northern clothing manufacturer who spent her days out on the cliffs painting florid seascapes. There were also a travelling salesman of patent remedies and a former parlour maid who had come into some money, both of whom were rather looked down upon by the other long-term guests. Janet echoed their disdain and was extremely scathing about the sales-man's common manner and the dreadful airs assumed by the quondam maid, "that ridiculous Miss Blaby".

The news that an international society of geologists wished to use the hotel for their annual winter conference had been the cause of considerable excitement. Mrs Rutherford had made it known that the geologists intended to commemorate the thirtieth anniver-sary of their society's founding with a splendid banquet and that an Italian chef and his two assistants would be coming down from London especially to prepare the meal, a piece of news that had soured Cook's already uncertain temper and rendered the lives of the other three a misery. It was generally understood that the society had decided to congregate in Seacombe rather than any of the more popular resorts because, during a memorable fortnight more than twenty years ago, they had discovered no less than seventeen rare fossils in the vicinity, or so they claimed. I found it surprising that no one had disputed this assertion, for that stretch of shoreline is not especially renowned for its palaeontological riches. Of course, I was well aware that the "geologists" in question were seeking something far more valuable and elusive: Arrowsmith's missing hoard of money.

On the day that I started work there were already fifteen Scorpions staying at the hotel, and by the end of the following week their number was expected to exceed thirty. The free and easy manner in which they milled about the place laughing and joking, the earnestness with which they pored over geological journals in the draughty mildewed conservatory, the open-faced geniality with which they greeted the other guests at mealtimes, was something marvellous to behold. I overheard one of the Misses Hepplethwaite remarking to Colonel Wright-Harris that, flying in the face of all her expectations, the "dear scientists" had brought a breath of new life to Seacombe, and I should quite possibly have agreed with her had I not known that in locked rooms and deserted nooks all over the hotel the discussions did not concern ammonites and high tides, but death and dynamite and bloody insurrection.

MacIntyre and I had arranged to meet on Wednesday afternoon, which was my half day, and I was determined to have something substantial to report before then. Yet by Tuesday I was beginning to despair. I had been able to eavesdrop on only the most innocuous of conversations, and though I had kept a sharp lookout out for incriminating documents, maps, or other suspicious-looking items while I was cleaning the bedrooms I had found nothing. Nor had I had a chance to investigate the player piano as MacIntyre had requested. Sarah was responsible for the upkeep of the saloon where the instrument was kept, and though I passed by it several times a day on my way to and from the dining room, I was always with Janet and had not been in a position to examine it unobserved.

On Tuesday after supper, as we came through the saloon pushing a trolley laden with dirty plates, Janet saw me turn my head towards it and screwed up her pasty, lopsided little face. "Whatever is it makes you so interested in that old piece of scrap? It ain't a real piano, you know, and it don't work. I expect Mrs R only keeps it cos she thinks it gives the room a touch of class – she's got ideas above her station that one, if you ask me. Look at all those picker-ninny masks and pots and statues and suchlike that she insists on cluttering up the place with, just so as she can say to the guests that her old father was a sea captain what collected them on his voyages. She don't consider *us* and what a trouble they are to clean. That piano's even worse; just you thank your lucky stars you ain't responsible for polishing it as Sarah is; what with all them finicky bits of carving, it's a devil to keep the dust off."

Sarah, who was walking behind us carrying a basket of soiled napkins, gave an exclamation of dismay. "Oh, I knew there was something I'd forgotten! I never have time to do that piano proper, but Mrs R don't seem to notice, so lately I haven't taken the trouble at all. Only this morning one of them foxil-hunting gentlemen says to her, 'What a vey fain specimen of an early player piano, whay I've never seen one qwait like it afore – pway mudum, where do it come fwum?' 'Well,' she says, 'it's been here since the eighties and once belonged to Miss Lauderdale,' and you should have seen his eyes light up and his big grin when he declares all his friends will be *most* interested to hear that and does it work? Mrs R says, 'Most regrettably, no,' and he says, 'What a shame to see it in such a *dusty* state, but it is a wemarkubly fain piece of furniture in any case.' Then Mrs R glares at me and when he's gone she lays into me like you wouldn't believe and when she's finished with me I'm shaking like a leaf. It was all I could do not to start crying, only I wouldn't give the old cat the satisfaction. Only then it was time to begin setting for luncheon and things have been so busy all afternoon I forgot all about it. Freddie's supposed to be calling round for a drink and a bite to eat after the dinner things are cleared and I suppose now I shall miss him, cos I shall have to clean the horrid thing or Mrs R will have my guts for garters." Sarah's large, pale green eyes filled with tears.

"Freddie is her young man and he don't get round here much of an evening –his mother's sick and usually he's wanted at home," Janet explained in hushed tones. Then as we descended the kitchen stairs carrying the trays of plates that we had removed from the trolley, she added in a vehement whisper, "I don't suppose Mrs R would take so long getting that dumb waiter mended if it was her having to carry piles of plates up and down stairs. If it's not done before the banquet, I don't know how we're to manage!"

I made a vague murmur of agreement and allowed her to waddle into the scullery ahead of me.

"I'll polish the piano," I said, turning to Sarah.

"And why would you want to do that?" she demanded, giving me a suspicious look.

"You needn't worry – I don't want nothing!" I assured her. "You may not think it to look at me, but I know how it feels not being able to see your young man when you want to more than anything. I was engaged for a while before I came here, though it's broken off now. Besides, I don't mind a bit of dusting – I'd only go upstairs and mope otherwise."

"Stop chattering, youse girls!" yelled Cook, surging towards us. "There's work to be done and the rest of us haven't time to stand waiting about for lazyboneses like the pair of youse!"

As we scurried towards the scullery clutching our respective burdens, Sarah whispered, "I'm sorry I was short with you, Louisa. I didn't know you'd been engaged – you are a dark horse and no mistake! If you really don't mind polishing the piano, I'd be very much obliged to you – I'll find a way to pay you back, I promise."

By the time I tiptoed into the saloon, duster in hand, it was shortly after ten o'clock. The air was scented strongly with cigar smoke and there were a number of empty glasses scattered about on the tables but, to my relief, the room was deserted. A row of African masks glared down at me forbiddingly. The fire had gone out and the oak-panelled walls and tobacco-coloured carpets and curtains, which had looked quite cosy under the illumination of a blazing hearth, now created an atmosphere of murky gloom, which the feebly burning gas mantles did nothing to alleviate. It was a poor light for dusting and a worse one still in which to search for clues to the whereabouts of the missing money, particularly for someone as short-sighted as I am. Nevertheless, I was aware that such an opportunity might not arise again for some time and I set to work, scrutinising the piano's mahogany casing as I went for any cracks or seams that might indicate the existence of a hidden compartment.

Having polished the mahogany until my arm was aching, I opened the lid of the keyboard. The keys were thick with grime; evidently Sarah had taken the trouble to clean just the visible surfaces of the instrument. Thinking it unlikely that I would be overheard, I played one or two jangling notes and then quietly picked out a melody, which I recognised only as it was forming beneath my fingertips; it was "Lilly Dale".

I was so absorbed in sounding out the notes that I did not notice that someone had entered the room until a well-bred voice enquired, "What are you doing?"

I wrenched away my hand and looked round in surprise.

"Well?"

I gazed speechlessly at the young woman who stood regarding me with a quizzical expression, for there was something intensely familiar about that face with its composed doll's lips and wide, thickly lashed eyes.

"There *is* such a thing as a lady geologist, you know, though of course I am aware that we're a rare species," she remarked with an amused smile.

"I'm sorry, miss," I said, colouring up. "I'm doing nothing I shouldn't be – only dusting."

"How remarkable – it sounded to me as if you were playing the piano. What was the melody? It's very pretty," she said, dimpling.

With a shock of recognition, I realised who she was.

"I'm sorry, I can't recall, miss," I replied, shutting the lid.

The young lady's fingers closed around my wrist and she scrutinised my face with an intensity that caused my cheeks to burn. "Where did you learn to play the piano?" she demanded.

"My father, miss. He was a piano tuner. But he died." Perhaps the fact that I was thinking about my own father as I said this lent the lie an air of conviction for, after a brief moment of consideration, she nodded and let go of my arm.

"Don't let me interrupt you," she said, still looking at me thoughtfully. "I only came in to find a pack of cards."

"I've done now. Goodnight!" I replied, snatching up the duster.

"Perhaps . . ." she began, but before she could finish the sentence I had darted past her and out of the door.

I hurried away as fast as I dared, my heart crashing against my ribcage like a trapped bird. I had set out to discover a clue to the whereabouts of Miss Lauderdale's vanished fortune and instead I had stumbled upon a ghost. For the person I had just encountered was the double of the young lady in the photograph on Hunter's desk: the officially deceased Hetty Bartholomew!

# Thirty-Six

MacIntyre had chosen for our meeting place an old watch tower which overlooked Sharples Cove. I left immediately after luncheon, in plenty of time to cover the half mile distance, or so I imagined. It was a blustery day, however, and as soon as I stepped onto the exposed cliff path I found that I was struggling into the teeth of an icy wind. My eyes watered copiously and my face and ears smarted despite the woollen shawl that was wrapped about my head. The track was narrow and uneven, zigzagging between steep patches of gorse and furze dotted with grazing sheep. While making a precipitous descent, I glanced down at the churning grey-green mass of the ocean and felt a momentary giddiness, which made me lose my footing, sending a shower of stones tumbling down the cliff side. I righted myself and crept onwards, keeping my eyes fixed just in front of me. At last the path dipped down into a small hollow, as MacIntyre had told me it would, and there as I ascended the other side was a little circular hut with whitewashed walls and a thatched roof, perched on a jutting outcrop of the cliff.

Upon entering, I discovered MacIntyre standing with his back towards me, gazing out to sea. At the sound of the door closing, he looked round sharply.

"Hello, Miss Trant!" he said, grinning. "It's fearfully windy out here, isn't it?"

I nodded, removed my gloves, dabbed at my eyes, blew my nose and unwound the shawl from my head, making a vain attempt to pin back the disorderly tendrils of my hair.

"Your poor little hands!" exclaimed MacIntyre. "Those gloves haven't done any good at all – they look raw as can be! May I?"

He came forward and clasped one of my boiled-looking hands, chafing it gently until the warmth began to steal back into my fingers, and then took hold of the other one. I hardly knew where to look, yet I did not draw back from him, and when he let go and went to sit on the wooden bench that ran around the wall I felt a sharp stab of disappointment.

"So, to business, Miss Trant," he said with sudden briskness. "You should know that, officially, I am in Hamburg: one of our spies in the region has heard mutterings that an Englishman is being held captive in a village about twenty miles outside the city and the Chief has sent me to investigate the likelihood of its being Hunter, from whom, as you may have gathered, we have heard nothing for some time. However, if you will forgive me for saying so, I believe it to be an error of judgement on Rivers' part; there is far too much going on in Seacombe for me to abandon my post here at present. Indeed, I suspect that the rumour may have been deliberately manufactured by the Scorpions as a decoy to deflect our attention from the conference. Nevertheless, as a precaution, Hampson-Smythe sailed for Germany two days ago and will tele-graph immediately if he discovers anything to substantiate the story."

"Do you suppose the Scorpions know that they're being watched?"

"Who can say? They might not know for sure, but no doubt they suspect it."

"Well, they're certainly being very careful about maintaining their cover. I'm afraid, as yet, I haven't managed to discover anything untoward about their activities in Seacombe at all. However, I did make one rather extraordinary discovery . . ."

As I described the events of the previous evening I became aware that MacIntyre's eyes were focused attentively on my face and, feeling somewhat self-conscious, I moved towards the narrow slot in the wall that would have served as the watchman's window onto the ocean.

At the conclusion of my account, he came up behind me and pointed over my shoulder to a line of jagged rocks, which stuck up amidst the spray like the spikes on a sea-monster's back. "Do you see those rocks, Miss Trant?" he asked. I nodded. "They look treacherous, don't they? Yet it's the ones beneath the surface that are truly deadly. I'm afraid that Miss Bartholomew is just such a rock; one doesn't see her coming until it is too late."

"I'm afraid I don't quite understand what you mean."

"Not the innocent flower, but the serpent under it. A woman who is attractive in such a style – the fragrant English rose, a clergyman's daughter unblemished by any stain upon her dewy innocence and so forth – such a person will always be above suspicion, even in the eyes of a cynical old cove such as myself. No wonder Hunter was duped! And I'm afraid the fact that she is here for the conference suggests that she is more than a mere tool. She must be deeply entangled with the Scorpions, even perhaps a high-ranking member of the organisation."

"You met Miss Bartholomew once, didn't you?" I asked. "Do you think there's any risk that she might recognise you?"

"I very much doubt it – there's my disguise, for one thing, and fortunately the light in that restaurant wasn't awfully good. Nevertheless, I will do my best to avoid her. And you have already stirred her interest, my dear – you must take care not to arouse her suspicion. I advise you to do as I am doing: wait and watch from afar until the moment comes to strike."

"And what ought I to do about the player piano?"

"Most probably it's one of Smythe's red herrings. And yet . . . You say that the melody you played was "Lilly Dale" – why was that, Miss Trant?" MacIntyre's blue eyes widened enquiringly and his long forefinger began to caress his upper lip.

"I wasn't thinking about it really," I said. "I suppose because it was my father's favourite song and I heard him whistle it so often."

"Indeed! Do you recall the list of numbers you gave me, the

ones that you found inside your father's edition of *The Last Chronicle of Barset*?"

"Yes, of course."

"What was the inscription that he wrote on the flyleaf?"

"*To Margaret, in the hope that your fondness for detective stories will one day prove profitable*," I answered, wondering where all this was leading.

MacIntyre moved away from me to stand in the centre of the tower. "Well, the first thing I did on Monday morning was to obtain a copy of the book, though in order to do so I had to catch the train into Exeter; bookshops are few and far between in this benighted region. Fortunately, my time was not wasted; those numbers all refer to chapter headings in the *Last Chronicle*. Have you read it, Miss Trant?"

"No. My father was quite right; detective stories are much more to my taste."

"I'm rather fond of Trollope myself; there's not much poetry in his work, but still, there's a great deal of human interest. However, that's irrelevant to our purposes. All you need to know is that there's a character in the novel called Lily Dale. The numbers that your father wrote down appear to relate to the chapter headings that refer to her. There is such an obvious correspondence between 'Lily Dale' and 'Lillian Lauderdale' that it must have been a deliberate allusion on his part, don't you think? Do you suppose he meant to give you a hint about his involvement in the Arrowsmith affair?"

I turned to stare out at the churning ocean for a few moments before saying, "When I was a child my father would sometimes plan treasure hunts for me. I simply adored them! I think that the numbers and the inscription in that book were intended to be a diversion along similar lines; he must have dreamed it up in the first flush of enthusiasm and then, when things took a turn for the worse, abandoned it." I stood transfixed by the crashing waves, my mind sinking back into the past.

"What are you thinking about, Miss Trant?" asked MacIntyre sitting down on the bench and patting it invitingly. "Please don't be shy of telling me."

"I wanted to say something last week, in the tea shop, but it was very difficult," I said, coming to sit next to him. "I was so ashamed, and then when you told me that you had been working with someone else, it was such a surprise – it drove everything else from my mind."

"Never mind," said MacIntyre, reaching out to give my hand a reassuring squeeze. "The important thing is that you're telling me now."

I took a deep breath, trying to my best to summon my scattered concentration, and then I began.

"About three months before his death, Father went away suddenly on business. He was rather mysterious about it beforehand; he would say only that he was going to stay at the house of a wealthy client. Mother didn't like the idea at all; she said that he ought not to leave us, in case all the tradesmen to whom we owed money decided to call in their accounts before he came back. However, I knew that the real reason was that she could not bear him to be away for so long, only she was too cross to tell him so. Father laughed and told her that we could manage without him for a few weeks; he would settle all the bills upon his return. Then he said, much more seriously, that she must trust him – that this affair would be the making of us.

"He was gone for a little over a month and during that time we did not hear from him at all. When he got home he did not look at all like himself. His eyes were bloodshot and his clothes were grubby and rumpled. When he bent to kiss me he smelt of tobacco smoke and stale whisky. I noticed that he was carrying a bouquet of yellow lilies tied with a red ribbon, which I understood to be a peace offering of some kind. He winked at me when he saw me looking at it and then he trotted upstairs to see Mother.

"When they came down for luncheon, Father had bathed and changed his clothes and Mother was wearing a pearl necklace which I had never seen before. I had expected there to be a furious row, but both were in high spirits and no mention was made of the period that Father had spent away from home either then or afterwards.

"In the weeks that followed, Mother told me that Father was no longer working at Bellows and Tuttle, but so far as I could see he was making no attempt to get another job. He went out in the evening a great deal; once I heard him telling Mother that he had been with Mr Plimpson and that they had been 'talking over the business again'. It surprised me very much that she did not object to his idleness or his going out, but I did not trouble very greatly to wonder why.

"Although Father was nearly always at home for most of the day, I saw very little of him. He stayed in bed late and by the time I got back from school he was usually in his study, where he would remain until it was time to go out. On those occasions when our paths did happen to cross, his demeanour was one of teasing good humour. He would twit me about my fondness for detective stories and dropped all kinds of sly hints about the fascinating secrets I might discover, if only I put my mind to it. One of his favourite tricks at the time was to whistle 'Lilly Dale' with a meaningful look, or he would hint that 'a certain gentleman' would provide us with the answer to all our prayers – by which I supposed he meant the settlement of his debts. Of course, all this drove me into a frenzy of curiosity, as it was designed to do, but he refused point-blank to tell me any more, saying only that patience would have its own reward and that one day I would be proud to have such a clever and enterprising father. I believe he was half mad already; there was an air of wildness about him which I had never seen before – it was almost as if he had been transformed into a different person. He bought himself a new coat because he wanted to look like a prosperous gentleman – he even began to talk a little differently. Then the reality of what he had done must have started to close in on him.

"I don't know what happened to bring about the change, but all of a sudden there were no more jokes about 'our noble benefactor', no more hints about the riches that might be awaiting us round the next bend in the road. He kept more and more to his study; indeed he rarely went out of the house. Mother began to mutter darkly about 'false promises', but he didn't pay any attention; in fact, he scarcely seemed to notice that we were there at all.

"One night at about ten o'clock I was awoken by a loud banging on the door. I heard Father shouting to Mother to go back up to bed; that it was not the bailiffs, but an acquaintance of his who had called round on a matter of business. There was a murmur of voices and then the study door closed and I heard nothing more until, after about ten minutes, Father and the visitor came back out into the hall. I crept onto the landing and peered down through the banisters just in time to see Father wrenching open the front door. To my astonishment, the visitor spat on the floor and thrust his head violently towards my father's face. I can't remember precisely what he said, but I understood that he was threatening to hurt Mother and me if Father refused to comply with his wishes. After he had gone, Father went to sit at the foot of the stairs, breathing heavily. I flew downstairs and flung my arms round him, but he shook me off at once and told me to go back to bed. Then, without looking at me or saying another word, he took down his hat and overcoat from the hallstand and went out into the night. That was the last time I saw him." My voice broke, and I swallowed hard to hold back my tears.

"My dear Miss Trant, you are a very remarkable young woman," said MacIntyre, shifting so that one of his long legs was pressed firmly against my skirts. "Never has the phrase 'still waters run deep' been given a more apt expression than in your person." Timidly, I glanced up and saw that his face was working under the influence of some strong emotion. He remained stock-still for a few moments, as if lost in thought, then rose abruptly.

"At one time there must have been a collection of music rolls for that player piano," he said, pulling on his gloves without taking his eyes off me. "You might try looking for them if you get the chance. If there did happen to be one of 'Lilly Dale', it would be worthy of further investigation."

"There's a part of the attic that's used for storage, I'll try to get up there if I possibly can, though it might be difficult to slip away," I said, astonished that I could sound so calm when my heart was thudding so hard in my breast. "There are more and more guests arriving now that the banquet is only a few days away."

"Will you be waiting at table on Saturday evening?"

"Yes," I answered, blushing furiously, for we were standing so close to one another that when he spoke I could feel his warm breath on my upturned face.

"Be unobtrusive, but listen carefully to everything that is said – on an occasion like that, when the wine is flowing, it will be all too easy for someone to make a slip." He reached down and brushed my cheek with the tips of his fingers. "We must both make the most of the next few days to gather as much evidence as we can before the Scorpions disperse. Perhaps we could meet again on Sunday afternoon?"

"Yes, I might be able to get away for an hour or so before tea," I whispered, seized by a delicious trembling.

"Shall we say two o'clock again?" said MacIntyre, lunging clumsily for the door. "And if you discover anything of note before then, you must send the kitchen boy with a message at once."

I passed out onto the cliff top, feeling as if I had been rudely awoken from a long and blissful dream. We stood awkwardly outside the watch tower, the wind whistling about us. MacIntyre looked as if he were about to speak, hesitated, then placed his hand on my shoulder and gazed solemnly into my face.

"Miss Trant, I have come to . . . that is, would you do me the honour of allowing me to call you by your first name?"

For a moment I could scarcely breathe, and when I spoke my voice was so faint that it was drowned by the howling of the wind. Nevertheless, MacIntyre appeared to have understood me; his face broke into an uneven grin and he stooped to kiss me with a tenderness that made me long to cling to him weeping with joy, though of course I did no such thing.

"Goodbye, Margaret," he said, and then turned and strode off along the track that led down to Seacombe.

I stood watching his retreating figure until he rounded a curve in the path and vanished from sight. It is an image that I have held in my mind ever since.

# Thirty-Seven

From that point onwards, events moved so quickly that when I look back it seems impossible that so much can have happened in so short a time. It was as if the accumulating pressure of circumstances had been building and building like water behind a dam, until it burst forth in a gushing cataract, which swept away everything in its path.

I was completely unprepared for any of it. I had returned to the hotel after my meeting with MacIntyre in a state of dreamy anticipation that made me slow and clumsy in the performance of my domestic chores and inattentive to my work as a spy, despite the awareness, impressed on me by my beloved, that we were running out of time. I retired to bed on Wednesday night having received two scoldings from Cook and one from Mrs Rutherford, but I was still thrilling from the touch of MacIntyre's lips and had no room in my mind for anything else.

Fortunately, on the following morning, a new turn of events shook me out of my reverie and forced me to concentrate my attention once again on the task at hand. I was instructed by Mrs Rutherford to clean the rooms occupied by Mr Charter, who had returned to the hotel at the beginning of the week. He and his secretary, Crawley, had been the first of the "geology" party to arrive, but they had been called away to London at about the time of MacIntyre's arrival in Seacombe and, so far as I knew, Crawley had not yet come back. The Chief had told me that Charter's real name was Augustus Harding and that he had been an important member of the Scorpions during the period when Arrowsmith and Stone were at the helm. After Arrowsmith's execution, Harding had emigrated to Germany and had only recently returned to England.

Janet had advised me that I should take great care not to move the gentleman's papers while I was dusting; he was very short-tempered on account of being an invalid, and during the earlier period of his stay had accused her of tampering with his things and threatened to have her dismissed. Of course, this warning immediately provoked my curiosity and I made up my mind that I would do my best to discover what it was that "Mr Charter" was so eager to hide. I had already seen him on several occasions in the corridors and the dining room, hunched over in his invalid chair as if he lacked the strength to sit up straight. He was a shrivelled relic of a man: pallid, painfully thin and somewhat reptilian in appearance, with heavy-lidded, slow-moving eyes. He always dressed in a threadbare smoking jacket worn over several pullovers and kept a checked blanket wrapped about his legs. Even so, he insisted that the fires in his bedroom and sitting room must be kept constantly blazing – such a cold-blooded creature, it seemed, could only survive in the atmosphere of a hothouse.

As soon as I entered Harding's rooms I was struck not only by the suffocating warmth, but also by the extraordinary neatness of my surroundings. I reflected that it was little wonder that he had been so angry with Janet for disturbing his papers. Every object had been set precisely in its place: the cushions were arranged on the sofa with painstaking regularity, his books had been meticulously ordered according to size and colour, and his pens were lined up neatly on the desk, parallel to a small set of drawers which contained trimly stacked sheaves of documents.

I knew from bitter experience how difficult it could be to locate a particular document in the midst of a disorderly heap; this fastidious tidiness might be turned to my advantage, if only I could work out precisely what it was that I was looking for. There were three drawers and, acting on the assumption that the papers were arranged alphabetically, I pulled out the middle compartment and looked under L for Lauderdale. I found only a rather dull letter from a man called Lake so, straining my ears for the sound of approaching footsteps, I tried A for Arrowsmith and S for Stone and Scorpions, but again to no avail. Then, on a sudden impulse, I rifled through the papers in the bottom drawer until I came to R. With a thrill of excitement, I drew out a large envelope labelled *Richard Arrowsmith* and was on the point of breaking the seal when I was startled by the creaking of wheels in the passage outside. I had just sufficient time to close the drawer and to hide behind one of the long, heavy window curtains before the door opened.

I stood rigidly with my back pressed against the window seat, my heart pounding with such violence that I could scarcely breathe. I was close to the corner of the bay window, and found that I had a somewhat restricted view of the room round the side of the curtain. A short, fleshy-faced man with very white skin and thinning hair appeared in my line of vision, pushing Harding's invalid chair. I could see that he wore a dog collar and an expression of weary forbearance. He positioned the chair next to the sofa and sat down, leaning back with a long sigh.

"Well, Crawley, you'd better tell me what Von Trott had to say for himself," said Harding, arranging the rug more comfortably over his legs.

"Of course. But before I do, I beg you to listen to what I have to say without allowing your judgement to be clouded by past events." Crawley turned his head, displaying the wayward glass eye that MacIntyre had told me about.

"Well, go on."

"It's rather a delicate matter. It concerns Arrowsmith."

I suppressed a sharp intake of breath; perhaps now, at last, I might find out exactly what my father's connection with the infamous Scorpion had been.

"Don't tell me that he's taken it into his head not to attend the banquet on Saturday! Why in the devil's name does he suppose that he can do just as pleases, without a thought for the rest of us?"

At this I felt a jolt of surprise; surely Arrowsmith had been hanged more than a decade ago?

"Oh, no – it's nothing like that. The boat is due to land tomorrow evening and Matthews will be there to meet him with the car."

"Well, what is it then, Crawley, d–n you! Spit it out, man."

The secretary glowered at the old man. "Look here, Harding, it's all very well being so quick-tempered, but you don't give a fellow a chance to speak! Von Trott has informed me of certain developments, which I thought it best to discuss with you in person before Arrowsmith arrives."

"And what are they?"

"I'll come to that in a moment, sir." Harding gave a growl under his breath, but said nothing. Crawley darted him a nervous glance with his good eye before continuing, "I have to tell you that he suggested, not to put too fine a point on it, that someone has been meddling in our affairs."

"Meddling? What do you mean?"

"Von Trott has a theory that there have been so many coincidences and peculiar happenings of late that something must be amiss. I must admit that when he first put the idea to me I was sceptical, but if one thinks about it carefully then it's hard not to see his point."

"I'm not quite sure that I understand what it is you're driving at, Crawley. Von Trott is just the kind of man to get carried away with some nonsensical idea . . ."

"If you'll just allow me, Harding, I'll give you an example, a recent one. How was it that Bureau 8 knew that Stone was to be at the Alhambra that night? The Trant woman can't possibly have communicated with them about her appointment with Miss Hagger; the house couldn't have been watched more closely."

At this unexpected mention of my name I felt a peculiar churning in my stomach, for Crawley's words had impressed upon me more forcibly than ever just how dangerous was the position in which I found myself. I tried to picture the reaction of the two men

334

if they found out that the "Trant woman" was hiding a few feet away behind the curtain, and suppressed a shudder.

Harding shifted irritably in his chair. "As I wrote to you at the time, Hagger must have had a damned loose tongue. I suppose she still hasn't been found?"

"Not yet. We traced her to Dover and after that the trail goes cold. But there is more to the matter than meets the eye, I'm convinced of it. From all that I know of Miss Hagger, I refuse to believe that she would have been easily persuaded to co-operate with Bureau 8. And as Von Trott said, what leverage could they possibly have used? They could never have afforded a bribe to match the sums that we have been paying her. Besides, how did Bureau 8 come to discover that she was working with Stone in the first place?"

"Of course it's impossible to say precisely, but there are all kinds of ways that they could have found out. That isn't enough to convince me that one of our own men betrayed Stone." Harding's gaze strayed to one side. "Look, that cursed fire is nearly out again. Put some more coal on, would you, before I catch my death of cold."

Crawley stood up with a grimace of irritation and moved out of my view. Harding turned to look after him and I heard the crash of coals being tipped into the grate and then the grinding of the poker. Hastily, I took advantage of the din to shift my stance to a more comfortable one, for I had begun to develop a painful crick in my neck.

"That's the last of the coal," the secretary remarked, sitting back down on the sofa.

"Curse that Rutherford woman! I told her to make sure that the coal scuttle was always kept full. The old miser . . ."

"To return to what I was saying," interrupted Crawley, setting his pale lips in a thin line of frustration. "It isn't just Stone – there was Gresham's death too."

"Confound you, we've been over this a dozen times. The most likely explanation is that . . . What was that fellow's name who was injured in the explosion at Victoria?"

"Ravelli, sir."

"Yes, that's right – Ravelli. Well, it seems to me very probable that Ravelli killed Gresham before making his escape from the hospital. It's quite possible that he saw through Gresham's disguise and realised that he was one of us and not a doctor at all. And once it occurred to him that his nemesis had caught up with him, so to speak . . . well, when a man is cornered like that he might do all kinds of things of which he is ordinarily incapable."

"Indeed. But Gresham was a clever man and a very careful one; he would never have allowed himself to be surprised by an oaf like Ravelli. Furthermore, Von Trott believes that even if Ravelli *had* set upon Gresham and run off, we would have succeeded in finding him by now – and I agree with him. Ravelli must have had help, or he could never have concealed his movements so effectively."

"If it wasn't Ravelli who did away with Gresham, then it must have been Bureau 8. And in that instance they would no doubt have taken Ravelli into custody, which would provide a suitable explanation for his disappearance," declared the old man, darting Crawley a look of exasperation from beneath his heavy lids.

"Come along, Harding! You know as well as I do that it would be frankly astonishing if anyone belonging to that gimcrack organisation had managed to assassinate Gresham," the secretary said with a sneer. "To kill a man by stabbing him in the eye with a syringe demands a certain ruthless brutality, which one cannot help but admire, however regrettable the consequences. The agents of Bureau 8 would be quite incapable of such a thing; they'd think it was too unsporting. An unseen hand has been interfering in our business all right, but it was not theirs."

Harding gave an explosive sneeze and blew his nose vigorously before remarking with a disapproving look, "Nevertheless, I fail to understand why all this is so urgent that it should have necessitated your staying on in London when our work here is still incomplete. Nor do I see what any of this tendentious speculation has to do with Arrowsmith."

"Von Trott is convinced that a spy has penetrated our inner circle."

"I rather gathered that from everything you've just told me." Harding gave a cavernous yawn, exposing an expanse of pale gums sown with a few worn, yellow teeth. Then he closed his eyes and allowed his chin to descend onto his chest, as if he had abruptly dropped off to sleep. Crawley said nothing more, but sat watching him with a wary sidelong look.

Meanwhile, my thoughts were racing. The more Crawley had said, the more convinced I had become that the "spy" he was referring to was Hunter. The Chief had threatened to report Hunter to head office as a rogue agent, but that had been only because of Hunter's refusal to leave Germany; clearly he had had no idea of the extent to which the young man had decided to take matters into his own hands. Somehow, Hunter must have engineered the killing of the Scorpions' fake doctor and Stone's arrest – episodes that had been very damaging to the Scorpions. I could not help marvelling at his pluck and ingenuity, but my admiration was somewhat diluted by the awareness that in acting alone and without consultation he had put Bureau 8's operation – and possibly the lives of its other agents – at risk.

After a few moments, Harding opened his eyes and turned his head to regard Crawley, as leisurely as an old tortoise.

"Look, we went through all that not long ago, with Robinson. This is a trying time for our organisation, a period of growth, and it is no wonder that the nerves of our fellow Scorpions are under a considerable strain. At such times people can become suspicious; they begin to see spectres where there are none. We lost a good man when Robinson disappeared like that; I for one never believed that the evidence against him was strong enough to condemn him as a traitor. When I heard that that young hothead Arrowsmith was proposing to use dynamite against him, I was among the first to voice my objections."

"Yes, you've said all this before. But even if that package had been delivered to the professor's house, he wouldn't have been there to receive it. Von Trott has just found out that Robinson went away on the day *before* the explosion, not the day after, as we had thought. It can't have been mere coincidence – someone must have advised him to clear out."

"Hmm, yes, I see. And I expect you're going to tell me that it could not have been Bureau 8."

I pictured to myself Hunter's handsome, boyish face and reflected, not without a little smugness, that *I* had a pretty good idea as to who it had been.

"Well, of course not, sir. Arrowsmith insists that they had no notion of our plans."

"And who is Arrowsmith? A young upstart with no understanding of the world! Why, even Marcus Stone recognised the necessity of leading his everyday life under an assumed name. But Arrowsmith, whose father was more famous than the rest of us put together, refuses to do so out of pure arrogance, though it's not just himself he's putting at risk."

"Well, sir, I would argue that lately he has been obliged to do precisely that. I beg you to listen to what I have to say without allowing your judgement to be skewed by . . ."

"Skewed? D—n your impudence!"

"Please, just listen for a moment and I'll explain. Von Trott believes that at this crucial stage of our movement's development it is essential that we have strong leadership. Of course men such as yourself, from the founding generation, will always hold a special place . . ."

"Don't imagine that you can win me round so easily."

"Sir, the idea of formally recognising Tomas Arrowsmith as our leader has great popular support. He is the natural heir . . ."

"Now, Crawley, listen to me. Richard Arrowsmith was my dear friend, as you know. Before Tomas reappeared so suddenly, I hadn't set eyes on him since he was a boy – and an unpleasant brat he was even then; not at all like his father. He took a dislike to me from the first, and so whenever I had business with Richard I took care to avoid him."

"But as Von Trott says, we cannot allow personal prejudices to enter into this matter. The symbolic value of setting Arrowsmith at

338

the head of our organisation will be tremendous. He will be a uniting force. You cannot deny the threat that the other factions pose to us, even if you reject the possibility that there is a traitor in our midst."

"Tomas was in Canada for more than a decade. I admit that he seems to have studied his father's writings very thoroughly during that time, but his understanding of them remains superficial; he fails to grasp the context in which they were written. Furthermore, he is arrogant, headstrong and disrespectful – not qualities that one would normally associate with effective leadership. He once told me that he considered his father to be a potentially great man, corrupted and brought down by greed. He regards him as a failure. Richard – a failure! To think that that puppy should say such a thing to me – I could have torn his eyes out! Of course it is pure envy and resentment on his part – he knows as well as the rest of us that Richard was a greater man than he will ever be; a hero who sacrificed his life to obtain that woman's inheritance for the Scorpions. That money would have been the making of us if it had not been lost . . ."

"And Tomas Arrowsmith has promised that he will help us find it again and use it to fund the successful completion of the Second Phase."

"That, Crawley, is precisely the kind of thing I mean. Tomas is all bluster and big ideas – he is a populist who targets his words at power-hungry imbeciles with a penchant for violence. He has no real understanding whatsoever of the beautiful intricacy of the philosophy that his father outlined in *A New Dawn*. If Richard had lived, he would have gone on to become one of the great thinkers of our age. To implement the Second Phase so soon would be a travesty of his ideas. The general public is simply not ready for it; the transition of the Scorpions into government must seem inevitable when the time comes."

"But you must acknowledge, mistake as it was, the explosion at the railway station has been the best thing that has happened to the Scorpions in years. Arrowsmith is right – the sensation that it made in the newspapers has shown us the way forward. Surely you're not going to dispute the fact that the most effective means of furthering the objectives of the New Dawn is to create a climate of fear and insecurity amongst the general public?" Crawley's eye glinted with fanaticism in his pallid face.

"You are wilfully misinterpreting the philosophy of the First Phase."

"That is a matter about which I am sure there will be a great deal of further discussion. In my own view, the emphasis that Arrowsmith placed on education as the driving force for the achievement of the First Phase is outmoded and unrealistic; indeed, it is one of the few flaws in his great work. The fact remains, however, that Tomas is to be the guest of honour at our banquet and I'm sure that I speak for many others besides Von Trott and myself when I say that it would be an extremely resonant gesture if you, the most senior surviving member of the old guard, were to be the one to formally invest him as the Scorpions' leader."

"And if I refuse?"

"That would be a great shame, sir, but I'm certain that Von Trott would be more than willing . . ."

Harding gave a heavy sigh and hung his grotesque old head, his whole frame seeming to crumple inwards. "I see; if I refuse to go along with it, I shall finally be consigned to the scrapheap."

"I'm sure Arrowsmith would be honoured if you were to agree," said Crawley, regarding him with an inscrutable expression.

Harding looked up quickly, his wizened features animated by spite. "Oh, do you think so?" he enquired with a parched cackle. "Very well, in that case I'll do as you ask – but you can tell Von Trott that there are those among us who do not share your faith in Tomas Arrowsmith as the long-awaited saviour of our movement."

My position was very cramped, but so far I had managed to ward off an incipient stiffness by shifting my weight very cautiously from foot to foot. Now that the two men had fallen silent I was obliged to forgo even this slight respite, for I knew that the faintest creaking of a floorboard would be enough to betray my presence. After several minutes, during which I remained as rigid as a statue, the pain in my limbs had become excruciating and I was beginning to grow increasingly fearful that I would give myself away through some involuntary muscular spasm. At last, to my immense relief, Harding handed the secretary his empty glass and enquired with a sigh, "Have we made any progress in finding Trant's ledger?"

"No – it's only the daughter who remains to be questioned, but she appears to have disappeared without trace."

"What do you mean?"

"She hasn't been seen at the shop for several days, and when Von Trott enquired at her lodgings the landlady sent him away with a flea in his ear. She seemed remarkably put out – he thought at first that Miss Trant must have absconded without paying her dues – but then she told him that the young lady had laid down two months' rent in advance and gone off without leaving a forwarding address."

"What did I tell you? *Carpe diem*, Crawley, *carpe diem*! We should have secured her for interrogation as soon as we realised her importance and let the consequences be d—d! If only Arrowsmith had had more gumption. He should have stuck to Miss Trant like a limpet . . ." Harding was interrupted by a knock at the door. "Come in!" he barked, and the door opened to admit Mrs Rutherford. With an icy shudder trickling down my spine and Harding's words echoing like a trumpet of doom inside my head, I shrank back as her shrewd eyes darted around the room, passing over Crawley and coming to rest on the old man.

"I'm so sorry to disturb you, Mr Charter. Some of the other gentlemen have gathered in the saloon and I've been sent to ask whether you would care to join them."

Harding gave a groan. "Oh, very well, I suppose I must! Would you oblige me by pushing my chair? My secretary has some business to attend to. Crawley, wire our friend in London immediately and make it clear that these rumours about betrayal must be put to rest. They are bad for morale."

"Very well, Mr Charter," said the secretary, hurrying out.

"Shall I draw the curtains before we go?" asked Mrs Rutherford. It does get dark so early these winter nights."

I pressed myself into the furthest corner of the alcove, but before Mrs Rutherford could carry out her intention Harding wheezed, "I do not wish to be kept sitting here, madam! Send one of the maids to attend to the curtains and take me to join my colleagues at once!"

Mrs Rutherford's face darkened for an instant before, adopting a fixed smile, she took hold of the handles of the invalid chair. "As you wish, sir," she said.

As soon as I was sure that they were gone I slipped out from behind the curtain and left the room, weighed down by a burgeoning conviction that "Smith" and "Arrowsmith" were one and the same. Even setting aside the obvious similarity between the two names, when Harding had criticised Tomas Arrowsmith for failing to stick to me "like a limpet", whom else could he have been referring to but Smith, the man who had clung to me like a shadow for the past few months? Evidently, the Chief's "diversions" had not been as effective as he had anticipated, but of course he had been working on the assumption that "Smith" was a lowly spy, not the son of the Scorpions' founder. The more I reflected, the more convinced I became that I was right. It made perfect sense that the son of the murderer who had once employed my father as an accountant should take it upon himself to spy on Mother and me in the hope that we would lead him to Lillian Lauderdale's missing fortune. I gave a shudder at the thought that, though I might temporarily have succeeded in escaping Arrowsmith's clutches, he would soon be arriving at the hotel. And of course the moment that he set eyes on me my true identity would be exposed.

I locked myself in an empty room and took out the paper and pencil that I always carried with me; a habit I had learnt from MacIntyre. I fought to impose order on my jumbled thoughts, doing my best to outline the most important points from all that I had overheard with as much brevity as I could muster. I concluded with a short explanation of my theory that Hunter had been working independently of Bureau 8 for some time, and a more detailed account of my reasons for believing that the sinister lodger about whom I had been so suspicious was no ordinary Scorpion, but was in fact Richard Arrowsmith's son and the future leader of the movement.

It was not until I had signed my name and folded the note that I remembered the envelope that I had found in Harding's room, which was still in my apron pocket. I broke the seal and took out several letters and a silver locket engraved with a lily.

The letters had been written to Harding by Richard Arrowsmith. They did not contain any startling revelations, but after reading them I felt an aching sense of pity for poor Miss Lauderdale. It was clear that she had been a naïve and over-imaginative young woman, whose fascination with revolutionary ideals had been exploited in order to lure her into marrying a man who had cherished murderous intentions towards her from the very beginning.

I had skimmed through the correspondence once and was about to read over it again when I was interrupted by the sound of Janet's voice. "Louisa! Louisa! Mrs R says you're to come at once! Where are you?" I thrust everything back into the envelope, together with my note to MacIntyre, and hurried downstairs.

I found the kitchen boy, George Donahue, cleaning boots in the cullery. Having made sure that we were not being observed, I gave him the envelope and urged him to take it to MacIntyre without delay. The natural misgivings that I felt about entrusting him with such important documents were somewhat allayed by the steadiness of his gaze and the earnestness with which he assured me, "Don't worry, you can trust me to keep mum. Mr MacIntyre's told me all about it. I won't let one of them crooks get his hands on this – no fear!" And then, jamming his cap onto his tousled head, he sped off.

# Thirty-Eight

On the afternoon of the Scorpions' anniversary banquet Janet and I were polishing the silver in the scullery when Mrs Rutherford sailed in and placed a large box on the table in front of us.

"You may stop doing that for the time being," she snapped. "I want you to decorate the dining room and the saloon and the passageways round about. Make everything as festive you can; the gentlemen want it to look as if Christmas has come early this year and we must ensure that they are not disappointed." She drew her thick brows together and scowled at us as if she already anticipated that our efforts would prove inadequate. I coughed and turned away to hide the smile that sprang to my lips as I envisaged the depth of her horror if she were to find out the truth: that we were putting up these gaily coloured ornaments to brighten the revels of a band of bloodthirsty revolutionaries.

We began with one of the gloomiest corridors. Janet took charge of what she referred to as the "hartistic heffects" and I was allotted the job of looping red, green and gold ribbons along the length of the grimy cornices, which obliged me to take my life in my hands by standing on a rickety wooden stool which Mrs Rutherford had provided for the purpose. No one interrupted us and we worked for some time in an industrious silence, broken only by Janet's occasional consultations about the positioning of a paper rosette or a glass bauble.

Then out of the blue she remarked, "Well, Miss Cat's Got Your Tongue – I can guess why you're so quiet! You're dreaming about your sweetheart, ain't you?"

I started guiltily. "Whatever do you mean?" I said, getting off the stool to pick up a piece of crêpe paper that had drifted to the floor.

"I've got sharp eyes and I notice things others wouldn't, but you needn't worry, for I won't say a word to no one. You'd best be careful, mind – Mrs R don't like us girls to go gadding about with young men."

My mind began to tie itself in knots of anxiety. The only man Janet could possibly have seen me with was MacIntyre. Might she have contrived to follow me to the watch tower? If she had, she was more cunning than I had suspected, for it would have been difficult for her to evade detection. Yet why would she have gone to such lengths to pursue me? The weather had been so stormy that it must surely have taken a stronger motive than curiosity to drive her out along the cliffs. Perhaps someone else had sent her? Could she be in the pay of the Scorpions?

"I can see you think I must've been prying, but you're wrong, I ain't," Janet went on, picking up her skirts and clambering onto a chair in order to lay a sprig of holly on the mantel above the saloon door. "I was cleaning upstairs on Wednesday afternoon – when you was on your half day – and I stopped for a few minutes to catch me breaf. I looked out the winder and saw the pair of you coming up to the house. Your beau was walking behind you, but I could see you'd been together, cos he took off his hat and give you a queer sort of wave – I suppose you know the kind of thing – before he made off down the road."

"I see," I said, relieved that my suspicions appeared to have been unjustified, though it seemed peculiar that if MacIntyre had had something else to say to me he had not caught up with me or at least called out to me before we came within sight of the hotel.

"I'm sorry, I shouldn't have said nothing," she muttered. "It's only that I didn't want you getting into Mrs R's bad books." With a crooked little shrug, she descended from the chair, hobbled over to the box and pulled out a paper chain.

But something was niggling at me; a shadowy presentiment that was beginning to take shape at the edge of my awareness. "Janet, this gentleman, what did he look like?" I asked.

"Oh, ain't you pert? You surely don't expect me to believe you don't know?"

"Oh, go on, Janet, play along," I returned, giving her an arch look. "What did *you* think he looked like?"

To my surprise, she suddenly became serious. "I wasn't going to say nothing and I hope you won't take it amiss, but I should never forgive myself if anything were to happen."

"Why do you say that?"

"I should be careful of that one if I were you – I'd say he ain't the sort of fellow a girl can mess about. Why, he looks as like as two peas to the villain I saw in a play at the Palace last summer."

I felt a queer, cold sensation wrap itself about my heart.

"He's so *big*," she continued, warming to her subject, "and what with that bald head of his . . ."

I stared at her in horror. So Smith had been skulking about in Seacombe without the knowledge of his own cronies! What was worse, he had already found me and now he was toying with me, biding his time until he saw fit to reveal my true identity to the other Scorpions. George Donahue had brought back a few hastily scribbled words of reassurance from MacIntyre with regard to my belief that Smith and Arrowsmith were one and the same, the essence of which was that I must watch and wait, and that for the time being there was no need to do anything more. But I felt sure that even the circumspect MacIntyre would agree that Arrowsmith's appearance here in Seacombe warranted a more decisive course of action.

Janet began to apologise for having offended me, but I was scarcely listening. My first instinct was to flee at once to seek advice from MacIntyre, and I have often wondered since how things might have turned out if I had done so. However, fate thwarted my intention before it could be executed. There was a sound of footstep striding smartly along the corridor and I looked back to see a strapping young man hasten round the corner and then stop dead. I was unabl to see his face clearly in the murky light, but his stance radiated disquiet. After an instant's hesitation he turned to hurry off in the direction from which he had come, only to find that his way was blocked by Mrs Rutherford, who had come trotting up behind him.

"Terribly sorry to keep you waiting, Mr Arrowsmith; I'm afraid one of the maids hung up your key on the wrong nail. Some of them are terribly flighty about such things, I regret to say." She scowled towards Janet and me as if we were the ones that she held responsible. I peered down the corridor, straining my eyes in bewilderment, for even from the little I could see it was immediately evident that the young man whom Mrs Rutherford had addressed as Mr Arrowsmith was not Mr Smith.

"That's quite all right," he replied nervously. "As a matter of fact, I've decided . . ."

"Louisa, come here at once and show the gentleman to his room," Mrs Rutherford ordered.

I handed Janet the piece of crêpe paper I was holding and walked down the passageway with a pounding heart. I raised my eyes timidly to Arrowsmith's face and froze, feeling as if the air had been sucked out of my lungs. For there, frowning at me with a troubled expression, was Bureau 8's rogue agent – Tom Hunter!

# Thirty-Nine

I nodded in answer to Mrs Rutherford's request to show Hunter to his room and scuttled away down the corridor, leaving him to follow if he would. I decided that I ought not to speak before he did, but by the time we reached the second floor he had still not said a word and I began to wonder whether I might have been mistaken about his identity after all. It was not until I turned the key in the lock and stepped aside to allow him to enter his room that he asked, "Do I know you?"

"I'm Miss Trant, Mr Hunter," I whispered. "I'm the secretary at Bureau 8 –you may not recall, but we met just before you . . . before you went out on your last mission. I'm working undercover as a maid. Don't worry, I'm not as green as I was then; I won't do anything to give you away."

He scrutinised my face with fierce intentness and I felt the colour mounting to my cheeks. Then he nodded as if he had ascertained who I was, and flashed me a smile that displayed all his even white teeth.

"Good. Then I think we can trust one another, my dear. I'll find you after dinner and we'll talk properly. *Au revoir!*"

The door slammed shut and I was left bursting to tell him a dozen different things. I raised my hand to knock, but thought better of it. Instead, I hurried down to the kitchen, where Cook was in the midst of a heated argument with the visiting chef, an dispatched George Donahue to MacIntyre's lodgings with a note conveying news of Hunter's arrival.

It turned out that MacIntyre was not at home. George left the letter with the landlady of his lodgings and sped back to the hotel, managing to slip back into the scullery without being missed. I spent the remainder of the afternoon in a state of unbearable apprehension, waiting to hear from MacIntyre, but no word came.

Twenty minutes before the gentlemen were due to dine, Mrs Rutherford sent me up to the dining room to make sure that everything was in order. It was a spacious, high-ceilinged apartment decorated in faded hues of crimson and gold. Janet and I had hung wreaths and paper chains on the walls and set sprigs of holly above the grimy oil paintings, and now that a fire of aromatic fir boughs was blazing in the grate and the great chandelier had been lit, the room looked very much as it must have done during the days of Lillian Lauderdale's residence at Ham Stone House. I walked up and down the length of the three great tables, occasionally straightening an item of cutlery or smoothing down the red cloth, but I was so nervous and excited that I could scarcely concentrate even on so simple a task, and my mind kept drifting back to the encounter that I had had with Hunter earlier that afternoon.

I picked up a table decoration that had been knocked over and reflected yet again how impressive it was that he should have succeeded in pulling off such a fantastic deception. I was full of admiration for his gall in exploiting the fact that none of the Scorpions had seen Tomas Arrowsmith since he was a boy; after all, who could be more trusted by his fellow revolutionaries than Richard Arrowsmith's son? He must have pretended to have infiltrated Bureau 8 and to be reporting back to the Scorpions about our investigation, but naturally he was giving them false information. And of course this new development explained the mystery of Hetty Bartholomew. Hunter had not been the victim of a cruel trick as we had supposed; he must have known all about the creation of his "fiancée's" false identity and pretended to go along with it in order to maintain the illusion that he had so painstakingly built up. I guessed that he must have been absolutely infuriated when he received the Chief's telegram informing him that we had discovered the imposture; it must have been at that point that he had begun to cut his ties with Bureau 8. Whereas formerly I had perceived his decision to act alone as reckless and inconsiderate, I now saw that it had been a wise and necessary one. No wonder he had looked so appalled when he had seen me in the corridor! Of course, I would still have to be careful; the man that Janet had observed following me sounded, from her description, so much like Mr Smith that it seemed very likely that he had come to Seacombe to attend the conference. If he did turn up at the banquet, I decided, I would have to pretend to be taken ill.

I was roused from this train of thought by the dinner gong and hastened down to the kitchen. Cook was in a towering rage and boxed my ears for dilly-dallying, though the first course was not yet ready to be served. The dumb waiter had not been mended and Mrs Rutherford had given Janet and me the task of taking the food up from the kitchen and carrying down the empty plates. When eventually I went back into the dining room bearing a steaming soup tureen, the Scorpions were sitting round the tables drinking champagne and the air resounded with the lively hum of conversation.

With a shock, I saw that every man present was wearing a white arum lily in his buttonhole. Perhaps this macabre allusion to the late Lillian Lauderdale coloured my impressions of the gathering, for it seemed to me that there was something grotesque about every one of the individuals present, young, middle-aged and elderly alike. A man with protuberant yellow teeth guffawed loudly at a remark made by his neighbour, who was bald and perspiring with feverish red cheeks. A youth with the well-proportioned features of a Greek sculpture turned towards me as I began ladling out the soup and his glinting blue eyes made my blood run cold. I prickled all over with the insidious dread one sometimes experiences upon realising that one is trapped inside a nightmare and my hands quivered as I passed the soup bowl to Sarah.

"Is there something the matter?" she whispered.

I shook my head and struggled to pull myself together; the las‹

thing I wanted was to draw attention to myself by becoming hysterical. I scanned the tables for Mr Smith's bulky figure, but to my immense relief there was no sign of him. Hunter was sitting between Harding and Hetty Bartholomew, the only woman present who was not a member of the hotel staff. Theirs was the table at the far end of the room, which Mrs Rutherford had made it her special business to wait upon, and as I hurried to and fro I was aware of Hunter only as a presence at the edge of my vision.

Just as we were bringing in the roast goose, Harding banged his knife on the side of his glass, producing an immediate hush.

"Gentlemen! As the oldest and dearest friend of that most eminent of palaeontologists, Richard Arrowsmith . . ." He paused to look up at Hunter, who gazed imperturbably ahead, and then repeated in a tone of intense malice, "His *dearest* friend, I have been asked to bestow upon young Tomas here the honour of leading our – rather remarkable – geological society." There was a collective intake of breath as he held up what looked like an enormous gold coin before passing it to Hunter. "May you use the power vested in you in the manner that your father would have wished. And now I would like to propose a toast to the man without whom we would not be here, the architect of the grand design that is the *raison d'être* of our noble organisation: to Richard Arrowsmith!"

All round the room chairs were pushed back, glasses were raised and chinked together, and Harding's words were echoed back to him: "Richard Arrowsmith!" Then there arose a murmur that grew louder and louder until it was a resounding chant, accompanied by a stamping of feet: "Arrowsmith! Arrowsmith! Arrowsmith! Arrowsmith!" Hunter raised a hand to request silence and at once the tumult died down.

"I would like to begin by thanking Mr Harding for his *kind* words," he said with a grin, and waited for the laughter to die away before his expression became more serious. "And of course I would like to thank you all for the great honour of being chosen as your leader. I swear that I will do everything in my power to ensure that the aims of this distinguished society of ours are realised. Now do, please, sit down, ladies," he nodded at Miss Bartholomew, "and gentlemen." He waited until all the Scorpions were seated once again before resuming. "I will be brief in what I have to say, for you all have hearty appetites, I'm sure, after spending a few days in this invigorating sea air. If you look about you, you could be excused for thinking that Christmas has come early this year, and indeed, we hope that for us it has. We have come together here for a very special purpose." He paused while significant glances were exchanged and one or two people laughed wryly. "We have all been searching very hard, but though we have discovered a number of interesting geological specimens, together with a large quantity of seashells and several peculiarly shaped pieces of driftwood," again there were guffaws, "we have not yet come upon the rare prize that we came here in search of." Here, I fancied that I saw him glance over towards me before he continued, "Yet, my dear comrades, I am now going to make a prediction: we will be in possession of the elusive gem that you have all been seeking so tirelessly very soon indeed!" There was a loud cheer and Hunter raised his glass. "To success in all our undertakings!"

"To success!" all the Scorpions responded in chorus.

Then Hunter sat down, and as the assembled throng fell upon the tepid fare with the ravenous appetites that he had predicted, I reflected admiringly that if he continued to play his part with such charismatic conviction there was little prospect that his deception would ever come to light.

The rest of the evening passed in a blur of activity. I overheard snatches of conversation in English, Russian, Italian and German, as well as several other tongues that I did not recognise, but it was so noisy and I was so busy that I was unable to concentrate for long enough to distinguish any noteworthy remarks. Towards the beginning there was a great deal of laughing and light-hearted banter, but as the hours passed by and more and more champagne was consumed, the faces of the diners grew increasingly flushed and in several quarters voices began to be raised in anger.

As the clock was striking eleven, the last of the Scorpions drifted raucously towards the saloon and Janet and I began to clear the plates. Despite my weariness, I managed to fill my tray with crockery quite quickly and plodded out of the room while she was still collecting glasses from the top table. As I passed along the corridor on the other side of the saloon someone hissed at me from a doorway and I spun round with a great clattering of porcelain. Hunter stepped forward and took the tray from my hands.

"After you, my dear," he said, nodding his head at the open door.

I entered a dingy little room that I had never seen before. It contained nothing but a few broken pieces of furniture and a crate emblazoned with the words *Epps's Cocoa*.

"I enjoy a nice cup of Epps's just before I go to bed. How about you?" Hunter remarked with a grin as he set down the tray.

Reddening, I gave a polite little laugh. "I'm afraid that someone is certain to miss me if I remain here for too long, Mr Hunter."

"It would be much safer if you avoided using that name – I'm sure you understand why."

The floorboards creaked under Janet's ponderous tread as she made her way down the corridor and he turned his head to listen, then added, "You're right, of course – we mustn't stand talking just now. I'll be waiting for you here at a quarter past one – you should have finished your chores by then, shouldn't you?"

I nodded.

"Go up to bed with the others and then make an excuse to come back downstairs – I dare say they'll all be too tired to concern them-selves much with your movements by then." He handed me the tray and peered out of the door into the passageway. "All clear! I'll be waiting for you here in two hours' time; I look forward to hearing all about the progress of the investigation then. Perhaps, between us, we might even manage to move matters on a little."

# Forty

It took longer than I had anticipated for the kitchen to be restored to order and the other servants to retire to bed, and it was after two o'clock by the time I re-entered the store room. Hunter was sitting on a stool next to the Epps's Cocoa crate, on top of which he had placed an oil lamp. As soon as I came in he leapt to his feet, trembling with agitation.

"Where the devil have you been? I thought you might not come!"

"I'm terribly sorry. Tidying up took much longer than I'd anticipated and I didn't dare stir until the girls I share a room with were asleep."

Hunter took a deep breath and exhaled slowly through his nose. "I'm sorry, Miss . . . Louisa. As you can imagine, my nerves are somewhat on edge – it's a terrible strain having to keep up this charade in front of such a large audience. Please forgive me!" He looked so upset that I could not refrain from smiling.

"That's quite all right – I'm not offended," I assured him. "My horizons have widened considerably in the past few months."

"Well, thank you for being such a brick about it," he said with a smile that made me feel quite weak at the knees. "Now, if you don't mind, perhaps you could tell me what's been happening at HQ while I've been gone. Of course, you understand that I've been obliged to stay out of contact to protect my alias."

354

"Yes. We've all been frightfully worried; the Chief thought you might have been kidnapped by the Scorpions. In fact, Hampson-Smythe is in Germany looking for you even as we speak."

"Really?" He flashed me an inscrutable look. "I thought Smythe had thrown a temper tantrum and stormed out on us."

I proceeded to outline the events that had occurred since the explosion at Victoria, up until my meeting with MacIntyre on the cliffs, and Hunter listened to every word with rapt attention.

"Most interesting!" he said after I had concluded. "It's rather a shame that I have had to be out on a limb for so much of the investigation, but there was nothing else to be done in the circumstances. However, I'm sure you'll agree that *this* – or at least all that it represents – was worth the effort." He put a hand into his pocket, pulled out the large gold disc that Harding had presented to him at the banquet and pressed it into my palm. It was surprisingly heavy for its size and I judged that it must be made of solid gold. The Scorpions' insignia was stamped on the surface that lay uppermost and when I turned it over I saw that the opposite side bore a picture of a lily.

"It was made especially for me – or rather for Arrowsmith," observed Hunter, with a lopsided grin that set my heart fluttering.

I gave the disc back to him and there was a pause during which I waited for him to begin telling me about his own activities during the past weeks, but instead he gave a quizzical frown and burst out, "Louisa, I hope you don't mind my mentioning it, but you have been very modest to omit any mention of your father's involvement in the Lillian Lauderdale affair."

"How did you know?"

He fixed his green eyes upon mine, his lips curling into a smile, and I felt myself pulled into a tide of slow sinking warmth. He really was remarkably handsome!

"Surely you don't imagine that the Scorpions have forgotten the part he played? They want desperately to find the missing ledger; the future success of their organisation depends upon it. And it is therefore naturally imperative that Bureau 8 gains possession of it before they do. Surely your father must have let fall some clue about its whereabouts, however small?"

I perched myself on one of the broken chairs and spilled forth everything I knew, intensely conscious of his attentive, green-eyed gaze. When I came to the part about the player piano he sprang to his feet, exclaiming impulsively, "Come on – let's look at it now!"

"But I've examined it carefully already," I objected. "MacIntyre thinks that the song 'Lilly Dale' might be significant but I haven't had time to hunt for the music rolls, and . . ."

"Ah, I happen to have an inkling as to where we'll find them!" he said with a grin. Then he took up the oil lamp and seized me by the wrist, a stray lock of hair dangling down over his forehead and casting a long shadow across his face. I allowed myself to be dragged from the room without protest; indeed, I found the urgency of his manner rather thrilling.

As we entered the saloon a jade carving of a snarling dragon loomed up at me from the darkness and I emitted a whimper of disquiet. I glanced at Hunter in embarrassment, but to my relief he appeared to be deep in thought and gave no sign that he had heard me. He set the oil lamp on top of the piano before crossing over to a carved mahogany cupboard which stood against the adjacent wall. He seized the handles and tugged at them violently, but the doors remained shut. Without a moment's hesitation he picked up a bronze paperweight cast in the form of a Buddha and smashed the lock with a great splintering of wood. In the instant that he turned towards me, I seemed to glimpse upon his face a snarl of malevolent destructiveness which was so unexpected that it took my breath away. I reminded myself that a man prepared to encounter risks of the magnitude of those that Hunter had taken must of necessity have a dangerous and ruthless side to his character, and reflected, somewhat wryly, that it was extremely fortunate that he was on our side.

He recovered himself almost at once and flashed me a roguish smile, remarking, "You know, one of the Scorpions, an anglicised Hungarian who plays the fiddle, is very interested in tha mechanical piano. This afternoon, I happened to overhear Mrs Rutherford telling him that the music rolls were kept in a cupboard in the saloon to which she had temporarily mislaid the key. I rather suspect that this might be it!" And so saying, he opened the doors with a flourish, only to reveal three empty shelves and a fourth containing a stack of old newspapers.

"D–n!" he spat through gritted teeth. "Where in heaven's name are the confounded things?"

He made no apology for his bad language; indeed, for the present, he scarcely seemed to be aware that I was in the room. He began to pace wildly about, peering high and low, until his eyes came to rest upon a nondescript cabinet which stood in a gloomy recess to one side of the fireplace. He made a hasty and unsuccessful attempt to open it, and then darted across to snatch up the paper-weight again. He brought it down on the lock with a resounding crack, opened the doors and peered inside, then stepped back with a sigh of satisfaction. "Not a terribly convenient system if there's a song that you want to find in a hurry. Could you bring the lamp over here please, Louisa?"

I saw that the cabinet contained scores of cylinders, stacked end on so that it was impossible to tell what music they contained. Hunter proceeded to slide them out one by one, glancing in turn at the labels on which the names of the compositions were recorded. At last, upon pulling out the tenth or eleventh roll, he exclaimed, "Got it!" and brandished it under my nose, so that I was able to read the words *"Lilly Dale" – H. S. Thompson 1852*.

He hastened over to the piano and I followed with the lamp and set it back down on top of the instrument's lid. Its beams cast distorted shadows across the panelled walls, making the row of African masks that hung just above us appear more sinister than ever. Their empty eyeholes leered down balefully as Hunter set about fitting the music roll onto the metal holders that stuck out on either side of the slot at the front of the piano. He held the roll steady with his right hand while he turned it round with his left and then hooked the ring at the end of it onto a spool that fed into

357

the instrument's mechanism. He turned the spool a number of times before sitting down on the piano stool and adjusting several of the levers that were set just below the keyboard. He then placed his feet upon the pedals and began to pump them up and down. Nothing happened. He cursed under his breath and renewed his efforts with greater resolve, but still to no avail.

"Do you know how to play the pianola?" I asked in surprise.

"Yes, I learnt some years ago," he said without looking up. He continued working at the instrument for several minutes and then suddenly let his head fall onto his arms with a discordant crash. "There must be a way!" he muttered despairingly.

"Is it possible to remove the roll? Perhaps it has been fitted incorrectly," I suggested.

Hunter sat up with a jerk and I fancied that I saw a gleam in the dark pools of shadow that were his eyes. "Was your father especially musical?" he enquired.

I shook my head. "Not really, no. He was fond of sentimental songs – that one in particular."

"I believe I've been struck by an inspiration of some kind," said Hunter slowly, "though it hasn't quite dawned on me yet. I fancy that notion of yours about taking out the roll was a good one, though – let's see."

Carefully, he set about unhooking the music roll from the little mechanism that it fed onto. It came out quite easily and he brought it closer to the lamp to examine it. "By gad!" he remarked in a tone of suppressed excitement. Then, with a sudden violent gesture, he began to unravel the roll from the spindle on which it was wound. I watched him in dismay and bewilderment, wondering whether the strain of playing the part of Arrowsmith really was beginning to tell on his nerves. At last, when the whole length of perforated paper spilled out in a long white curl across the carpet, he held the end that was attached to the spindle up to the lamp, frowning in concentration.

After a moment he looked up, his face flushed, and reached out to clasp my hand with fingers that were as hot and dry as if he were in the grip of a fever.

"It's fortunate that I have good eyesight. Did your father always write so small?" he said, indicating a row of minute digits that had been inscribed just below the stitching that attached the paper to the spindle and which, to my weak eyes, were wholly indecipherable.

"Yes, sometimes," I answered, thinking of the doll-sized clues that Father had used to mark out our treasure hunts. "But those figures are far too small for me to read without a magnifying glass. And besides, why on earth would my father take the trouble to do such a thing?"

Hunter let go of my hand. "What's this supposed to be?" he said, pointing to a drawing of a pyramid with a human eye above it which had been scrawled near the top of the roll, in a different ink. He did not trouble to wait for an answer, but took out a pen and notebook from the breast pocket of his jacket and copied the numbers down. Then with great care he proceeded to wind the perforated paper back onto its spindle, talking to me as he did so.

"I suppose you know that your father came to stay at this house after Richard Arrowsmith's wife died, to make sure that her inheritance was put away safely, where it would not be traced by anyone else? Arrowsmith trusted your father and left him alone here while he went back to his son, whom he had left in the care of his servants in London. Your father divided up the capital into much smaller sums and, making use of false papers that he had obtained from his friend Arthur Plimpson, he spent several weeks travelling around depositing the money in different bank accounts. He recorded the details of all the transactions in a ledger, which he then hid. For some reason that remains obscure – though it's my belief that your father was contemplating blackmail – he refused to disclose the whereabouts of the ledger to his employer; indeed, he claimed to have mislaid it altogether. And of course, without the ledger Arrowsmith had no means of gaining access to any of the money, for there was no other record of the accounts.

"Naturally, this is all pure speculation, but I would hazard a guess that your father initially wrote down those co-ordinates as a reminder to himself, to ensure that he did not forget where the

ledger was hidden. After all, the countryside in these parts w
unfamiliar to him and one cliff or stretch of sand must have look
very much like any other. I expect, at first, he intended to tell Richa
Arrowsmith where the clue was concealed, but then, as I sa
something made him take it into his head to keep the location secr
How terribly clever of him to secrete the information that his employ
was so eager to find in the man's own house!"

Hunter put the music roll back into the cabinet and pushed t
battered doors together.

"If those tiny numbers don't refer to the spot where your fathe
ledger is hidden, I shall eat my hat! What's more, I suspect th
once I have had an opportunity to consult a map I will discover th
the hiding place lies somewhere on the shoreline, within two
three miles of this very hotel. Thank you, Miss Trant," he sa
briskly, walking towards the door as if he were eager to be off. "Y
have been most helpful. I could never have got so far without you

"Will you let MacIntyre know about this, or shall I?" I asked, feeli
somewhat disoriented by the sudden alteration in his demeanou

Hunter came to an abrupt halt and stood stock still, his ba
towards me. "MacIntyre? Hmm . . . Yes, why not? After all, one mu
not forget the whirligig of time, and so forth . . ." He spun roun
"Here, I'll write down the co-ordinates for you to send over to hi
in the morning." He took out his pen and notebook, scrawled dov
the figures, ripped out the leaf of paper and handed it to me. Th
he glanced at his pocket watch and seemed to sink into himself, h
lips moving silently, as if he were making a mental calculation
some kind. "I should think the tide will be all the way out in le
than two hours. You had better make sure that he gets this fi
thing or the spot marked X, wherever it is, may well have becor
inaccessible. Now, we must both try to get some rest. Good nig
my dear Miss Trant!" he said, and after a moment's hesitation
bent and pressed his lips to my hand.

He followed me into the passage and strode away without looki
back. I lit my candle and made my way up to the attics, hugging r
shawl tightly around me, my mind circling round and round like

spider steadily constructing her web. I conjured up a vision of my father's thin face, his sensitive lips and the candid hazel eyes into which, in the months leading up to his death, a shadow had gradually stolen. He was a man who thrived on taking risks; that was why his gambling had got him into so much trouble, and he had staked everything on the assumption that Richard Arrowsmith was a fellow who could be trusted. Of course, the offer of generously paid work must have seemed a heaven-sent opportunity to clear himself of his crippling debts. What was more, to a man who had long been resigned to eking out a respectable living as a lawyer's clerk, Arrowsmith and his circle must have embodied the kind of exciting, glamorous existence that he had always envied, but which, hitherto, had appeared to be far beyond his reach.

I wondered how long it had taken for the glamour to pall. Perhaps one day he had sat down in his study and, looking up at the commemorative photograph in which he and Mr Plimpson wore those lilies in their buttonholes like badges of triumph, had been overwhelmed by a sickening realisation of his own guilt. The elaborate puzzle that he had constructed to conceal the ledger's whereabouts, which no doubt had begun as a kind of game, had then become the means by which he sought to right the wrongs that he had committed.

Hunter was mistaken, I reflected indignantly – my father would never have stooped to blackmail. On the contrary, I now felt certain that MacIntyre had been right after all; Father's refusal to return the ledger had been a belated attempt to square his own conscience by preventing Richard Arrowsmith from profiting from his ill-gotten gains. I had never quite managed to bring myself to suppose that Father could have been so utterly heartless as to joke about Miss Lauderdale in the full knowledge that he had benefited from her murder, and I felt tremendous relief at the realisation that in his repeated whistling of "Lilly Dale" he had not been alluding to the heiress at all. No, it had been an expression of defiance; a reference to the clue that he had left on the piano roll without Arrowsmith's knowledge. And perhaps, for a while, he had intended to enlighten me about these obscure hints; to make *me* the chief guardian of the mystery, the heroine who would ensure that good would triumph over evil at the end of the story.

Unfortunately, of course, Father's cunning had proved to be no match for the ruthless determination of the Scorpions. His feelings of remorse and regret must have been compounded by the deepening apprehension that his actions had placed his wife and child in fearful danger. Father had been no coward; I felt certain that he had sacrificed his life in order to save Mother and me from becoming embroiled any further in the tangled predicament that he had created. He must have seen it as the lesser of two evils; the scandal of his suicide would grieve us, of course, but it would protect us from physical harm and from a disgrace that my mother could never have survived.

As I approached my room, I heard footsteps behind me and looked round in fright. A rumpled-looking George Donahue stood blinking sleepily in his pyjamas.

"Oh, it's you," he remarked in a disappointed tone. "I thought it might be one of them wicked fellows come up to cut our throats while we was all a-sleeping in our beds."

"I shouldn't think they'd trouble themselves with the likes of us, George," I assured him. "Now, I've got a most urgent message to be delivered to Mr MacIntyre. Get dressed as quickly as you can – but you must take great care not to wake anyone."

George, suddenly wide awake, disappeared at once, his face aglow at the prospect of this early morning adventure. While he was gone I scribbled down a brief account of the night's happenings on the back of an old laundry list, which I handed to him together with the co-ordinates upon his speedy return.

"Make sure you find me directly when you come back," I finished.

"I will, miss, you can be sure of that," he flung back over his shoulder, darting towards the stairs and out of sight.

I had no idea how late it was, but I thought it would be wise to obtain whatever rest I could before the bell rang at half past five s

I crept towards our room. As I stepped through the door a floor-board creaked and Janet groaned, "Where've you been?"

"I had a stomach ache and went to get some water."

"All right, I believe yer, though thousands wouldn't," she muttered, turning over and immediately beginning to snore.

I lay down, aching with weariness, but my mind was still racing and little pulses of agitated excitement kept shooting through me. Try as I might, I could not sleep, and as the minutes wore on I began to flounder more and more deeply in the grip of some uncanny intuition, a shadow of dread that lurked just below the surface, to which I was unable to put a name. And so I lay, tossing and turning and staring wakefully into the darkness until Mrs Rutherford rang the bell for us to get up.

I was halfway through my breakfast of tea and bread and dripping when George burst through the back door, red-faced and breathing heavily. Cook seized him by the ear and marched him into the scullery, scolding him furiously for wandering off when he ought to have been about his work. As he passed me he gave an exaggerated wink, and at the earliest opportunity I went out after him.

"Mr MacIntyre went off at once when he got your message, miss," he said as soon as I entered the scullery. "He said he was goin' to the place what you writ down and on no account was you to go near Mr Hunter if you saw him and that you must keep yourself safe. He give me a note for you, miss, and this telegram from Mr Hampson-Smythe." He handed me a sealed envelope and the telegram, which was folded neatly several times, and turned back to the dirty dishes. "I'd best get on now, miss, or Cook will skin me alive. I don't suppose you could see your way to smugglin' me in some bread and dripping, or *she* won't give me none, not now she's in one of her takings!"

I managed to evade Cook's watchful eye for long enough to carry out George's request and left him chewing contentedly. Then, wrapping myself in Mother's old cloak, I crept out of the back door.

A thick white mist hung in the air and I could see no more than few feet in front of me. I made my way cautiously to a spot behind large dripping elm which was out of sight of the hotel, though the precaution was scarcely necessary, for there was no possibility of my being detected through the heavy curtain of fog. I unfolded the telegram first. It was encoded, but the translation, written below in MacIntyre's sprawling hand, read: *Hunter and Arrowsmith are one. Proceed with caution. HS.*

I stared at the words in perplexity, scarcely able to take in their meaning. Then the realisation knocked the breath out of me, like a blow to the stomach. Hunter had not been impersonating Tomas Arrowsmith after all; Arrowsmith had disguised himself as a man named Tom Hunter. I had helped to reveal the secret that my father had fought so hard to protect to the son of the very man whose threats had driven him to his death!

Overwhelmed by a sickening sense of shame, I bowed my head and covered my face with my outspread hand. I had admired Hunter's cleverness in disguising himself as Tomas Arrowsmith, yet how much more cunning it was of Arrowsmith to disguise himself as a man disguised as himself!

I looked up, recalling Arrowsmith's peculiar hesitation when I had asked whether I should send a message to MacIntyre. Had he written down false co-ordinates that would send MacIntyre on a wild goose chase along the coast? Or, much worse, remembering how instrumental Bureau 8 – and MacIntyre in particular – had been in bringing his father to justice, he might have scented an opportunity for revenge. Even now, he might be lying in wait for him on some deserted beach, concealed from view by the heavy sea mist.

With trembling hands, I tore open the envelope containing MacIntyre's letter. I was obliged to hold it close to my face in order to read it, for the light was poor, and by the time I had finished the paper was spotted with tears. Struggling to bear up beneath an almost intolerable burden of remorse, I stole inside to fetch my revolver from its hiding place.

# Forty-One

*My dear Margaret,*

*I hope that you will not object to my addressing you in these terms – it is how I think of you, which I do very often, and it would seem strange now to call you anything else.*

*I regret deeply that thus far I have not found an opportunity to communicate fully the great regard and affection – no, dash it all, the love – that I have come to feel for you. Though I am more timid in this than in other things, I am not so much of a coward that I would deliberately have chosen to lay my heart bare in writing rather than face to face, whatever trepidation I might have suffered at the prospect. I am sorry to say, however, that the most recent turn of events has left me with no alternative.*

*You must not blame yourself for trusting Hunter; we have all been blind to the truth. And perhaps, after all, things have turned out for the best; it will be much easier to apprehend him on a deserted beach than in the midst of his cronies in the hotel.*

*There is a great deal more that I long to say to you, but alas I dare not linger to write it. You must remain at the hotel, my dear; do not try to follow me. Hampson-Smythe ought to be back within the day and I have left him instructions to escort you safely to London, if that should become necessary.*

*I have been faced with some impossible decisions during these past weeks, and though I have endeavoured to follow a*

*course of the utmost integrity there are a number of important
facts that I have been obliged to keep to myself. If for any reason
we do not see one another again, I must beg you to believe that,
whatever you may hear to the contrary, I have acted for the best,
and to trust in the sincerity of my feelings for you.*

*Do not forget me, dearest Margaret.*

*M.*

# Forty-Two

MacIntyre's Story

The white fog closed in on all sides, cocooning MacIntyre so that he could hear nothing save for the plashing of the oars and the steady rhythm of his own breathing. The masts of fishing boats at anchor emerged only when he was within a few feet of them and he was obliged to maintain constant vigilance in order to avoid a collision. He laid the oars down at frequent intervals to check the reading on his compass, burnishing it with his sleeve to wipe away the condensation; he would have to take care to land in the right spot or he would waste valuable time. About halfway across the estuary he was gripped by the horrifying fancy that he was not moving at all, but had drowned and been consigned to Purgatory, and would remain suspended in this nothingness for aeons. At last, after what seemed an age, the prow of the boat grated against shingle and, buoyed up by an eager desire to set his feet once again upon dry land, he leapt out to haul it onto the beach.

In the course of weeks of exploration, he had discovered a route from this side of the estuary to the sea, which would be less hazardous than the coastal path and was also at least a mile shorter. He clambered over a stile and started to ascend along a track slick with mud and fallen leaves. Dripping holly branches and the skel-etal boughs of oak and beech arched over his head; above them the sky hung white and heavy.

At the top of a rise, the path opened out and once again he found himself swallowed up in a swirling wall of fog. A dark shape ambled past a few feet away; he felt a tremor of alarm and his hand leapt to the handle of his revolver. Then he heard a gentle lowing and relaxed his grip with a wry smile; he must take care that his nerves didn't get the better of him! He took out his watch, noting that by now the tide would have dropped sufficiently to allow access to the cave on Starehole Head where the ledger had been hidden and reflecting that, most probably, Arrowsmith would already be there. He climbed a gate and squelched across the saturated turf in the direction of the sea and then crossed the narrow road leading to the Ham Stone hotel, which loomed up on his left. For a brief moment he pictured Margaret sleeping inside with her cheek pillowed on her hand, like a girl in a painting that he remembered seeing in a Paris gallery. The thought filled him with renewed determination and he strode past the coastguards' cottages, past Garo Rock with its thatched lookout hut where he and Margaret had last seen one another, and struck out onto the perilous cliff path.

He knew that the sea was on his right; he could hear the crashing of waves on the shore and pictured the jets of foam shooting up above dark crags of rock, which emerged from the water like the humps of sea monsters. Just a few feet away there was a sheer drop; one false step and he would plunge over the brink. A little way ahead, he could just make out the shadowy forms of some sheep, browsing among the gorse and stones on the cliff side, and as he picked his way along the path he found himself wishing fervently that he were as sure-footed as they. With excruciating slowness, he passed one little bay and then a second and arrived at a third, which was sheltered by a jutting finger of headland. He scrambled down over slippery rocks, beginning to regret the weight of the canvas bag full of digging equipment that he carried slung across his chest.

At last his feet slapped down onto wet sand and he consulted his compass. The mist clung to him, wrapping him in the smell of rotted seaweed and sharp salt; he could feel it working its way into his lungs. He wound his muffler more snugly about his throat and then struck out, moving west. He had scarcely taken a dozen strides, however, when a distant whistle drifted towards him through the still, foggy air. He stopped, turning his head to and fro with the exaggerated deliberation of a pantomime, for he was bent on making it clear to anyone who might be watching that he had heard the signal. Then he waited, motionless, really listening now for something more. But there was nothing, and when a gull called from high above, bringing him back once again to an awareness of the seconds ticking past, he took a careful step, peered for a moment into the vaporous whiteness, and then strode on, singing under his breath, "*Oh Lilly, sweet Lilly, Dear Lilly Dale . . .*"

As he ducked into the dark entrance at the foot of the cliff, he gave no indication that he was aware of the figure crouching behind a rock a few feet away. He struck a match and lit the small oil lamp that he had extracted from the leather satchel. Its wavering light revealed narrow walls glinting with damp, stretching into the darkness of the hillside. The floor of the cave was rough and uneven and scattered with jagged fragments of flint, its ceiling so low that he was forced to bend almost double in order to progress any further. On and on he went, his feet squelching with every step. The heavy contents of the leather satchel had begun to exert an unpleasant strain across the back of his neck, yet he maintained a steady stride, mouthing the words of the refrain that still haunted him: "*Oh Lilly, sweet Lilly, Dear Lilly Dale . . .*"

He trudged onwards, into the darkness, haloed by the lamplight that sheened the dripping walls. The wet crunching of his footsteps faded into a gentle splashing and he found himself wading through a shallow ooze of water running from deep within the cave. The passageway began to widen, a draught blew cold on his face and neck and the flame of the lantern wavered precariously. Cursing silently, he reached to shield its open crown with his hand, allowing the final verse of the song to die on his lips.

He saw that he had come to the edge of a cavernous chamber and put down the satchel, then straightened up and shrugged his shoulders to ward off the stiffness that had begun to creep along his spine. He paused for a moment to listen, but could hear nothing save for the sound of his own echoing breaths. At length he spoke with calm deliberation.

"Arrowsmith?"

The syllables resounded about the shadowy space, dying away into a brooding silence. Unperturbed, MacIntyre called out once again, "You won't find the ledger – it's already been removed." There was another pause. "Arrowsmith, old chap, there's absolutely no point in hiding. I'm afraid that I really have got you cornered. There's no escaping it – the only way out of this hole is by means of the tunnel, which I presently occupy."

Arrowsmith, if he was there, did not speak, but there was a loud shiver of stones slipping into water, as if someone had trodden awkwardly and lost his footing.

"It would be far better if you would give yourself up immediately, my dear fellow. Make a peaceful surrender – I shan't hurt you." MacIntyre reached into his breast pocket for his cigarettes.

Whether the man lurking in the darkness had misinterpreted the gesture, or whether all along he had been poised to commit an act of violence against his pursuer, was uncertain. Either way, as MacIntyre's fingers began to close on the battered cigarette case, a gunshot rang out and he crumpled to the floor. A tall silhouette launched itself out of the shadows, leapt across MacIntyre's prostrate body and disappeared at breakneck speed into the tunnel.

With a clamour of pounding footsteps, Arrowsmith hurtled head-long through the darkness, his lungs burning, the blood thumping through his veins. He burst out of the cave mouth and came crashing into the steely embrace of a pair of gigantic arms. A brawny hand seized him by the collar, his head jerked back and he saw a pair of cold grey eyes staring down at him.

The eyes watched, unblinking, as a blade was pushed into his throat; saw the way that his pupils flared in shock before his eyes

370

filmed over. As the knife was pulled out, rasping unpleasantly against the windpipe, blood gushed into his mouth and he fell forward, choking and gurgling, spattering the sand.

The assassin squatted down, wiped his knife clean on Arrowsmith's jacket and then rose back up, returning it to his belt. A muffled cry, like a gull's shriek, reached him through the dense mass of fog and he sighed, stood perfectly still and closed his eyes, waiting.

# Forty-Three

Iran through the mist on that Devon beach to find Mr Smith with his arms folded and Hunter lying dead at his feet. To be confronted with this monstrous tableau when my emotions were already in such a turbulent state was too much to bear. I started to scream and Mr Smith cocked his head to one side a little, as though he considered my reaction to be in some way unexpected. At the sight of his implacable countenance I fell silent, feeling somewhat foolish and also humiliated, as if I had succumbed to a fit of school-girl hysterics. He lowered his eyes towards Hunter's blood-drenched body and informed me in a weary, almost reluctant tone that he was a government agent. The terms of his explanation, though brief, left no room for doubt, and when he proposed that we search for MacIntyre I followed him unhesitantingly into a fissure in the cliff face.

The roof of the cave was so low that in some places Mr Smith was forced to shuffle along on his knees. Even in the more spacious stretches he was obliged to double over and lurched along in front of me clutching his hat in one hand, without speaking or looking back. His lantern made a bobbing circle of light which cast faint gleams over the dripping walls, though most of its radiance was shielded from me by his tremendous bulk. I could scarcely see what was directly in front of me and stumbled several times on the stone ground. It grew wetter and wetter underfoot and at length we were squelching ankle deep through ice-cold water. My nerves were screwed up to an unbearable pitch at the prospect of finding MacIntyre lying wounded, or worse, and the time it took for us to reach the point where the narrow passage opened out into an echoing cavern seemed interminable. Mr Smith straightened up, rubbing his neck with his meaty fist, and contracted his jutting forehead into a frown.

"Well, here's a nice little mystery," he remarked. "There's no way out, save for that tunnel – your friend MacIntyre seems to have vanished into thin air."

We searched high and low, peering into crevices and behind rocks, though in my heart I knew already that we would not find him. At last Smith cried out, "Enough!" Then he turned and began to make his way back down the tunnel, the word echoing behind him. I stood still, gazing into the enshrouding darkness that had swallowed MacIntyre, and called his name. It was taken up and repeated by a host of ghostly voices as I turned and stumbled towards the distant trace of lamplight, tears coursing down my cheeks.

The hours that followed passed in a blur of numbness, exhaustion and disbelief. Mr Smith escorted me back to the hotel and then he disappeared. The place was in a state of upheaval; there were policemen swarming everywhere and white-faced Scorpions were being carted off in prison vans. I saw the servants gathered together in an excited little cluster off to one side and hastened away in the opposite direction, making a loop round the back of the hotel until I came upon the gigantic elm beneath which, in another life, I had read MacIntyre's letter. I sank down into a cleft among its roots, heedless of the mud and the cold sodden grass, thrust my forehead against its slimy bark and wept as I had never wept before.

It was there that Hampson-Smythe found me – limp, emptied out my tears and shivering. He put his coat round my shoulders, crouched down beside me and coaxed me with tremendous patience until at last I allowed him to help me up. I vaguely recall going upstairs to gather my things; after that followed a jumbled passage of time which ended when I awoke, with my head on Hampson-Smythe's shoulder, to find that we were just pulling into Paddington station.

It was late in the evening by the time we arrived at HQ. Hampson-Smythe had tried to persuade me to go back to the boarding house in a cab, but I had resisted him so stubbornly that at last he had been obliged to give in. The shop was dark and the front door was locked, but there was a light burning in the office, for Hampson-Smythe had telegraphed ahead to inform the Chief of our imminent return. He rang the bell and the familiar jangling echoed back to us, like something once heard in a dream.

It was a cold, clear night and the small patch of sky that was visible above the alleyway was strewn with stars. Looking up at it, I was swept back to the moment when MacIntyre and I had stood side by side in the grounds of the Merrivale Sanatorium, gazing at the night sky. I felt a painful tugging at my heart and my eyes filled with tears. No doubt I should have begun weeping in earnest had there not just then come a rattling of bolts from the other side of the shop door. It edged ajar and then flew wide open to reveal the Chief. He flung his arms around me and shook Hampson-Smythe vigorously by the hand several times, before ushering us both inside.

The conversation took place at the deal table in the meeting room over tea and a slightly stale Madeira cake.

"There's been no one else here to help me eat it," the Chief said with an apologetic grimace.

"What about Liebowitz?" asked Hampson-Smythe.

"He hasn't been in the office for several days and I don't suppose he'll be back – but we'll come to that shortly. First you must tell me everything that has been happening in Seacombe."

Hampson-Smythe and I exchanged glances. He gave a sympathetic nod, as if he understood that I did not feel like talking, and then embarked on a rather shame-faced account of the deception that he and MacIntyre had concocted in order to be able to work together in secret. He concluded by begging the Chief's pardon for not having had more faith in him, his fair skin turning puce with embarrassment. The Chief, however, seemed determined not to bear any grudges.

"There there, my boy – let's say no more about it," he declared. "You did what you thought was for the best. And to be perfectly truthful I had my doubts about you too – nothing personal, of course, just the ghastly situation we found ourselves in – and if you're happy to let bygones be bygones, then so am I."

In the end, Hampson-Smythe was not called upon to say very much about events in Seacombe, for it turned out that the Chief had endured a lengthy telephone conversation with head office on the subject earlier that afternoon. Indeed, he appeared to have a more complete overview of everything that had gone on than we had and eventually ended up explaining some of the details to us.

He asked a few questions about the part that MacIntyre had played in the investigation, most of which we were unable to answer for, as Hampson-Smythe explained, "Dear old MacIntyre likes to keep his cards close to his chest." I disclosed that MacIntyre had written me a letter just before going out after Arrowsmith – a letter that, unbeknownst to my companions, was still folded up tightly in the top of my chemise, next to my heart – and that in it he had intimated that there was a strong chance that he would not be coming back. At this the two men looked grave.

"Surely he cannot have believed that he was going to his death?" said Hampson-Smythe, voicing the possibility I most dreaded.

"One never knows with MacIntyre," mused the Chief. "However, I would not surprise me in the least to discover that he had some startling new scheme up his sleeve."

"I simply can't understand why Hunter – or rather, Arrowsmith – should have given him the correct co-ordinates in the first place. Surely it would have suited him better to throw MacIntyre off the scent? Do you have any idea what he might have been up to, Miss Grant?" enquired Hampson-Smythe.

"He did mutter something very queer when I asked him about passing on the co-ordinates to MacIntyre – I think it had to do with 'the whirligig of time'."

"Ah yes, that explains a great deal," said the Chief. "The quotation from Shakespeare – *Twelfth Night*, I believe: 'And thus the whirligig of time brings in his revenges.' The desire to wreak vengeance will drive a man further than any passion I know – and don't forget, MacIntyre was the agent primarily responsible for bringing about Richard Arrowsmith's arrest. I expect Tomas hoped to lure MacIntyre to the cave so that he could kill him in order to avenge his father."

A lump rose into my throat. "When we looked in the cave, Smith said there was no other way out, but MacIntyre was nowhere to be found. It was as if he had vanished from the face of the earth!"

The Chief reached across the table and squeezed my hand. "As I said, my dear, one never knows. MacIntyre is capable of springing all sorts of surprises."

There was a short silence, during which we all sat with sober expressions, wrapped up in our own thoughts. Then the Chief said "I suppose Smith explained the business about Bureau 9?"

"Not really," I replied. "He only told me that he worked for another secret department, and said enough about the investigation to persuade me to believe him, but he didn't reveal very much."

The Chief's face darkened. "I only found out myself when R1 told me over the telephone this afternoon. I don't suppose that either of you will take it any better than I did. I was aware of course that we are not the only secret department in existence, but I had always understood that the other bureaus have their own particular remits, which are quite different from ours. Occasionally, I am sure we must have profited from information that has been thrown up in the course of their investigations, but we have always done so indirectly, through the auspices of head office.

"It turns out that two years ago a new top secret department was created – Bureau 9. Its designated purpose was to 'complement' the work of Bureau 8 – though in my view they seem to have taken upon themselves to oversee and even to manipulate our investigation without our knowledge, and to use us as a screen to hide behind when things become difficult. I can only suppose that this unfortunate development was intended as a response to the fact that the world is changing and new techniques and approaches are being established in the realm of espionage, to which, I am very glad to say, the strengths of our department are not thought to be suited."

"What kinds of things?" Hampson-Smythe demanded.

"I am tempted to say inhuman ruthlessness, brute force and crude manipulation, though I dare say the official line would be rather different. The frustrating thing is that for most of this investigation Bureau 9 has managed to stay one step ahead. All along they've been there, lurking just out of our sight. They were at the hospital and in the music hall and the hotel. They were in tea rooms and trams and trains and alleyways – they even managed to carry you back from Deptford in the dead of night, Miss Trant! Though of course they have made mistakes too – the chief one being their failure to unmask Hunter. And then of course there is the embarrassing fact that the ledger in which Miss Trant's father recorded the whereabouts of Lillian Lauderdale's money appears to have gone missing."

"Missing?" exclaimed Hampson-Smythe with a look of incredulity.

"Yes, quite," said the Chief, raising his eyebrows. "Apparently, Smith recovered the ledger from the cave two days ago, but at some point yesterday it disappeared and no one at head office seems to have any idea how it happened. Fortunately, we now have all the members of the Scorpions' inner circle in our custody, so there's not much of a risk from that point of view. However, it isn't the kind of thing one wants to have floating about in the ether." He frowned and his gaze grew distant, as if his thoughts were drifting off after the vanished ledger.

"You were telling us about Bureau 9, sir," Hampson-Smythe prompted gently.

"Yes, indeed; I'm sorry. Now, where was I? Ah, yes! A few months ago, Liebowitz was recruited as an agent of Bureau 9 . . ."

"Of course!" muttered Hampson-Smythe, glancing at me.

"And Mr Smith, their chief agent, was placed in your boarding house to see that you and your mother were safeguarded from the Scorpions, Miss Trant," the Chief went on, looking very serious.

"But Smith must have known who Aggie Hagger was as soon as he arrived at the house. And yet he did nothing to protect my mother!

He might as well have signed her death warrant when he left them alone together."

"I can quite understand why you would think so my dear, but I don't suppose that even Mr Smith is quite as ruthless as all that. No, I suspect that it was more of a misjudgement on his part; he probably underestimated Miss Hagger and failed to realise that she would be capable of murder. But I agree with you – he should never have taken such a risk; it reveals a distinct carelessness for human life which, I'm sorry to say, seems typical of 9's agents. Smith claims that he hid in some cupboard or other while Miss Hagger was with your mother and heard some sort of scuffle, but by the time he entered the room it was too late to do anything because Hagger had already administered the dose of cyanide; a statement that of course can never be proved to be false, though one might easily doubt its veracity. In any case, once he understood that your mother could not be saved, he used the fact that he had caught Hagger in the act of committing murder to put pressure on her to go along with his plan to trap Stone at the music hall; a typical piece of cynical opportunism on Bureau 9's part, I'm afraid. R12 gave me a detailed account of the whole thing."

I remembered that it was a creak from the cupboard on the landing that had scared Becky away, and tears of anger and frustration stung my eyes. "So Smith won't be punished for what he did?'

The Chief shook his head. "I'm afraid not, my dear. At times this secret world of ours can be a bleak and unjust place."

I nodded, struggling to comprehend the fact that the murder of my mother had received official sanction. The Chief laid his hand over mine and I felt my face working frantically as I fought to regain a degree of self-control.

"Here, Miss Trant – a few sips of this will do you good," said Hampson-Smythe, thrusting an ornate silver hip flask across the table

The Chief withdrew his hand and unscrewed the lid from the flask before holding it out to me. "An excellent suggestion, Smythe, he said with a grin. "And it's rather a splendid flask too, if you don mind my saying."

"Family heirloom," responded Hampson-Smythe, looking pensive.

I sipped the brandy, and as its warmth spread through me I felt my composure start to return. The flask was passed round the table and then the Chief looked from one of us to the other. "You're both tired," he said. "I can finish explaining things tomorrow morning – you ought to go home to bed."

"No!" Hampson-Smythe and I exclaimed in unison, and he added, "Please, sir, I think Miss Trant and I will sleep much better for knowing the full story."

"Indeed we will," I assented heartily.

The Chief smiled at us fondly. "Very well! Where was I? Ah, yes . . . The elusive Professor Robinson was also an agent of Bureau 9; he successfully infiltrated the Scorpions for a while, until they grew suspicious and decided to dispose of him with dynamite – though, as you are aware, he got wind of it in time and managed to disappear. There were others too – I don't know how many. One of them was the agent who sent our friend Smith those seaside postcards while he was visiting various banks in towns on the south coast. Trying to trace Lillian Lauderdale's money, no doubt."

"But why should they want to draw attention to themselves like that?" Hampson-Smythe burst out with a look of scorn. "Fancy sending each other postcards covered in bizarre hieroglyphics, like a pack of silly schoolboys! We would never have dreamt of doing anything so clumsy."

"I don't think it was clumsiness, Smythe – no, from all that I have seen there is a distinct arrogance about these agents, a desire to flaunt their own cleverness. After all, none of us had the faintest idea where those postcards really came from – they merely confused us. And of course Liebowitz was here, ready and waiting to throw us off the scent. In fact, it seems to me that Bureau 9 took a positive pleasure in leaving mysterious calling cards wherever they went, of which the postcards were only one example – you remember the device with the pyramid and the human eye that we thought belonged to the Scorpions? I suppose, to them, it was a kind of game . . ."

"There was a pyramid and an eye on the music roll, just above the co-ordinates of the ledger's location!" I exclaimed. "Hunter didn't know what it was either. I suppose Smith or one of the other agents must have put it there, to show that Bureau 9 had discovered the co-ordinates before anyone else."

"So those cads were shoving their supposed superiority in our faces at every turn – and leading our investigation astray into the bargain!" growled Hampson-Smythe, banging his fist down onto the table.

"Calm down, old chap," said the Chief. "I can understand your being angry – I wasn't any too pleased about it myself – but I'm afraid that losing our tempers won't do us any good. As it happens, I'm pretty certain that Bureau 9 have done everything in their power to make us look foolish and incompetent; no doubt they wanted to ingratiate themselves with head office at our expense. I ventured to suggest as much to R12, but of course he pooh-poohed it at once – said we mustn't try to blame Bureau 9 for our own shortcomings. So I'm afraid, for the time being, it looks as if they've succeeded."

"Are head office intending to get rid of us?" said Hampson-Smythe, with an air of abject gloom.

"Get rid of Bureau 8? Of course not, my dear boy!" spluttered the Chief, looking rather taken aback. "When you've been in this game for as long as I have, you'll understand that one always encounters such temporary setbacks. In this particular investigation, we happen to have been pitted against a crude and bloodthirsty adversary. Ruthlessness and brute force, which seem to be the characteristic elements of Bureau 9's approach, unfortunately turned out to be the most effective strategies for tackling an organisation like the Scorpions. However, in other situations, when one is obliged to deal with foreign governments and the intricacies of diplomacy and so forth, the demands that one faces are quite different. Such circumstances require subtlety and circumspection; qualities that come naturally to us, but which are quite alien to a department like Bureau 9. No, my dears, we three must look to the future, for it will be up to us to ensure that in the next investigation Bureau 8 comes up trumps."

"To Bureau 8!" exclaimed Hampson-Smythe, getting to his feet and brandishing his teacup.

"Bureau 8!" cried the Chief and I, leaping up and raising our cups to meet his.

With a sudden pang I looked from the Chief's rosy face to Hampson-Smythe's pale, bearded one. I pictured MacIntyre's gangly figure; the tenderness that shone in his blue eyes when they rested on me; his roguish smile. Feeling very solemn, I held my teacup aloft once again and made one last toast.

"And to MacIntyre's safe return."

# Lilly Dale

'Twas a calm, still night,
And the moon's pale light
Shone soft o'er the hill and vale;
When friends mute with grief
Stood around the deathbed
Of my poor lost Lilly Dale.

*Chorus*

*Oh! Lilly, sweet Lilly,*
*Dear Lilly Dale,*
*Now the wild rose blossoms*
*O'er her little green grave*
*'Neath the trees in the flow'ry vale.*

Her cheeks that once glowed
With the rose tint of health,
By the hand of disease
Had turned pale,
And the death damp
Was on the pure white brow
Of my poor lost Lilly Dale.

*Chorus*

I go, she said
To the land of rest,
And ere my strength shall fail,
I must tell you where,
Near my own loved home,
You must lay poor Lilly Dale.

*Chorus*

'Neath the chestnut tree,
Where the wild flow'rs grow,
And the stream ripples forth
Thro' the vale,
Where the birds shall warble
Their songs in spring,
There lay poor Lilly Dale.

*Chorus*

H. S. Thompson (1852)

383

# Acknowledgements

Thanks to Oliver for his ingenuity in helping me out of tricky narrative corners and for being such a perceptive and discerning reader – this book could not have existed without him.

Thanks to Daisy and Jack for being so patient.

Thanks to everyone at Birlinn for being so supportive and welcoming; to Alison Rae for guiding me so seamlessly and patiently through the editorial process; to Head Design for their wonderful cover design; to Neville Moir, Anna Marshall, Vikki Reilly and Jamie Harris. And thank you to Nancy Webber for doing such a meticulous and sensitive copy-edit.

Thanks to my agent, David Smith, for all his excellent advice. I will be eternally grateful for his faith in my writing and for his willingness to give me a second chance.

Thanks to the Escalator scheme and everyone at the Writers' Centre in Norwich for giving me the confidence and determination to keep going. Thanks to Midge Gillies for her excellent mentoring and for her expert guidance about music halls. Thanks too to Jim Kelly for his invaluable feedback and suggestions. Thanks to Arts Council England for the generous grant which gave me time to write and enabled me to go on a research trip to Salcombe in Devon.

Thanks to Miranda Doyle for all her kindness and support, for reading *An Unlikely Agent* more than once, and for always giving such good advice.

Thank you to Alice Allen for listening to me talk about this book and for inspiring me to keep writing.

Thanks to Judith Murray for her enthusiasm, for her astute comments and for being so generous with her time when helping me to knock an earlier draft of the novel into shape.

Thank you to Stephen Munday, Peter Law and Jez Frost for their support at various stages of the writing and publication process.

Thanks to Miss Henderson at Brampton Junior School for asking me to dedicate my first novel to her when I was ten years old.

Thanks to Mum and Dad for making me love books from the very beginning and for their unstinting encouragement and support.